A ROYAL SHADE OF BLUE

The Modern Royals Series

AVEN ELLIS

Cover Design by Becky Monson
Formatting by AB Formatting

For Jamie and Paige
Two incredibly strong, fierce, resilient, young women who served
as the
inspiration for Clementine. I love you both.

ACKNOWLEDGMENTS

Thank you to CeCe Carroll, you once again did a brilliant job copy editing this book and for supporting my adventure into a new territory. Thank you for your dedication and guidance in taking my work to the next level.

Thank you to Paula and Joanne for proofreading and polishing my work.

To Alexandra, my British expert and assistant. Thank you for being you on a daily basis and always being my calming center. Huge thank you for fine-tuning Christian and all things British in this work.

To the SJFC-thank you for reading, debating, and supporting every step I take. I love you girls to pieces!

Thank you to my Beta Baes. Thank you for always giving me what I need, and not just with the writing process. Thank you for reassurance, for reading, for being a part of my life every day. None of these books happen without you.

Amanda and Claudia-Your love, friendship and support are always a given. I love you so much!

Alexa Aston, thank you for always providing your thoughts and your feedback. You are the best.

To my Twinnie, Holly Martin- Thank you for always reading my work, offering suggestions, helping me be a better author. But it is your friendship I value about all else. I love you.

Thank you to Jennifer and Mary, who run the Aven Ellis reader group on Facebook (Kate, Skates, and Coffee Cakes.) You both are such amazing women with such a passion for books. I love you ladies so much!

The Aven Ellis ARC Team-thank you for wanting to read my words and review my books. I'm so lucky to have such an amazing group of readers with me, no matter what adventure we take!

A big huge thank you to Amy Barnes for your royal expertise and letting me bounce endless ideas off you. You are the best!

Finally, thank you to all my readers. None of this happens without your support. I'm truly blessed.

PROLOGUE

THE MESSAGE THAT CHANGED EVERYTHING

I pop open my umbrella, trying to shield myself from the unrelenting rain that is cascading down on Palo Alto. I move around to the back of my Ford SUV, which is nearly as old as the sun, and open the hatch to find my dog waiting impatiently.

"Come here, Bear," I say, stifling a yawn as I wait for my Airedale rescue to come to me. I juggle the umbrella, sticking the handle under my arm, and grab Bear's collar. Bear begins to lick my face, and despite the fact that I've just left work, and it's three o'clock in the morning, and I'm standing in the cold rain, I smile. "You're such a good boy. I'm lucky I can take you to work with me, you know that?"

I help Bear down and slam the hatch shut. I re-adjust the umbrella, and I walk through the parking lot, shivering as the rain pelts my face. Northern California is chilly this January night, the temperature below forty now. I see my breath escape in puffs in the damp air, and even though it's late, and I have class at nine tomorrow—er, today, actually—I want a cup of hot chocolate before bed.

I grin despite the weather and the hour. My beverage selection hasn't changed since I was five. You can keep your fancy coffees and exotic teas. I'll take a cup of hot chocolate with whipped cream for the win every time. Besides, when you walk down the street with a cup full of hot chocolate from a coffee shop, nobody is the wiser that it's not some fancy latte.

I take a minute to let Bear do his business before directing him toward my building. I close my umbrella as soon as we're under shelter, and Bear leads me up the stairs, pulling me along because he doesn't like the rain. I glance up at the fourplex where we live, built in the 1940s and not far from the Stanford campus where I'm in my last semester of school. I love living here. I share a two-bedroom corner unit with my best friends at Stanford, Bryn Ryan and Chelsea Beckwith. Since Bryn has a steady boyfriend, she has a room to herself. At least that is what Chelsea and I told her. The fact that she talks in her sleep all night long and never shuts up is the real reason, however.

Sometimes a little white lie is a super handy tool.

I put my key in the lock and turn it gently. I've become a pro at making a quiet entry since I started my internship at the Fashion Mall of San Jose. The upscale shopping center has a curated art collection that rotates museum-level art throughout the mall, giving the public free access to incredible pieces. I assist the art coordinator with the exhibits and community art outreach programs. Even if I have to do sculpture installations in the middle of the night and go to classes half-dead the next day, it's been a great learning experience.

My dream job, however, is working with antiques in either an auction house or a museum. I love the stories objects can tell, and how they can be used to pass down history from generation to generation. It's fascinating to me, and that is the focus I want to pursue after graduation this June.

I open the door and step inside, grabbing a towel out of the basket next to the door. I take a moment to wipe his paws and belly before letting Bear off his leash. As soon as I shut the door behind us, I hear the squeaking of a bed and the sound of it banging against the living room wall.

"OH, GRAHAM! YES!" Bryn screams. "RIGHT THERE! RIGHT THERE!"

Before I'm even out of my coat, I'm fumbling for my phone and earbuds. Please let me get them in before she reaches the height of orgasm.

"GRAHAM! YOU ARE SO G—"

Bryn's cries are cut off by the sounds of Harry Styles singing "Sign of the Times" in my ears. Whew! That was a close call, I think, as I slip out of my trench coat and kick off my wet Converse kicks.

But now I'll never know if Graham is:

- So Good
- So Gorgeous
- So Gigantic
- So ... Godly?

Sometimes it's best for things to remain shrouded in mystery.

I head into the kitchen, grab a hot chocolate cup for the Keurig, and place my favorite mug underneath it—my Disney mug with Princess Ariel on it. My older sister, Paisley, got it for me because she said I reminded her of Ariel, with my long, flaming-red hair and love of the water. Mom missed her opportunity to name me after a Disney princess, choosing Clementine instead. She said the first time she saw my little head with its patch of red hair I reminded her of a sweet orange. Hmm. Maybe it says something that she thought not of princesses but of food when she first laid eyes on me. I probably should be offended, but glancing down at my ripped jeans and favorite charcoal V-neck sweater, I'm definitely closer to a citrus fruit than a princess.

If I were to be a princess, though, I'd be more like Fiona from *Shrek*. I love her. Fiona is spirited. Independent. Strong. She can save herself, which makes her fabulous.

Soon my hot cocoa is ready, and I take it over to the sofa and sink down into the cushions. Harry continues to sing to me as I reach for the remote and flip on the TV.

Another great mystery of the universe that remains unsolved to me is how I can have hundreds of TV channels at my disposal and still find absolutely nothing to watch. I skim over horror movies—no thank you; adult cinema, which I have playing in the room next door if I care to hear a live version; TV shopping; old sitcoms I don't like; and news. Meh.

I stop on some wildlife hunter trying to capture a dangerous rattlesnake and leave it there as background light. It's now ten after three. I'm going to give myself until four to unwind, drink my hot chocolate, and climb into bed. I take a sip of my steaming drink, closing my eyes as the warm liquid sides down my throat, and feeling the much-needed warmth. Ah. Bear jumps up on the sofa and drops his big head into my lap, and all feels right in my world.

I put my thumb on my phone to unlock it and see I have some notifications. Some are for Facebook, and there's a text from Paisley, and a slew of emails from companies that I signed up for to get a discount and now get bombarded daily as a reminder to never again give out my email for ten percent off. I have some Instagram likes and a direct message in my inbox from someone I don't know.

Curiosity gets the better of me, and I decide to read it. The profile pic from the stranger is of a beautiful setter-type dog. Inside is my picture from last month's *The Ritual of Tea* exhibit, when we installed a piece that represented the bamboo tea whisks that are used to make matcha tea. The message reads:

Ms. Jones,

I was scrolling through Instagram recommendations —yes, I realise I don't have a life if this is what I'm doing at night instead of going to a pub quiz, so let's get that out of the way upfront—and came across your account. The idea of tea whisks two stories tall inside of a shopping centre is quite fascinating, more so because I prefer matcha to English Breakfast or Earl Grey. You had me with the tea whisks, and I confess to spending the rest of the night checking out the art installations on your Insta. I don't know why I'm writing to you; you probably think I'm a stalker. Well, I guess if I spend the night going through your Insta account I am, but I assure you it's not in a creepy way but rather in a "this-is-interesting way." Regardless, it looks like you have a job you love, and for that, you are one incredibly lucky woman.

CP

I stare at the message in shock. This is the first one I've ever received about my work. And this CP—whoever he or she is—has a sense of humor. I click on CP's account and read the profile:

Student of History and Politics at the University of Cambridge. Lover of dogs and odd-flavoured M&M's.

Appreciates a good pint with his mates and beating them soundly on pub quiz nights.

Hmm. The account is set to private. He's a male. At least that is what he says. I mean, who knows if any of this is real? CP could be an elderly woman in a retirement home for all I know. But CP does have fifteen followers. Fifteen? Wow. This person is very picky about who they allow to follow them. I elect to allow the message and decide to test this "CP" and message him back:

CP,

Thank you for your kind words. I'm happy to know someone appreciates the work we do to bring art to the public in an easy, free, accessible way. We hope to expose people to art who never might have gone out of their way to look for it. I feel like a kind of commando in that regard.

I crept on your page, but I can't see much since it's private. You say that you study at Cambridge. First, I would like to see proof that this is true. You might be in a retirement village in Boca for all I know, or some woman named Mildred chatting with me and laughing with her friends around the four o'clock early bird dinner. Or you could be a cheating husband from Houston looking for a piece on the side. I need verification that you are indeed a student of history and politics at Cambridge, or the jig is up, CP.

CJ

P.S. What is a pub quiz? You mentioned it in your message, and it's in your profile. Obviously, you have some kind of thing for it.

Then I hit send.

I take another sip of my hot chocolate, getting some whipped cream on my nose. I rub Bear's head affectionately and feel the vibrating on the other side of the wall has stopped. Yay, I won't have to sleep with earplugs in tonight. Victory is mine!

Beep!

I glance down at my phone. CP has sent me another direct message on Instagram.

I set my mug on our circa 1991 end table, swiped from my mom's storage unit, and eagerly open the message.

It's one picture.

A sign above a glass door reads the "Alison Richard Building," and the landscape is dusted with snow. In fact, falling snowflakes dot the picture. There's a hand extending forward, the left hand, holding up a textbook of a political nature. A silver Rolex watch adorns his wrist, peeking out from underneath what looks like a black cashmere overcoat.

I eagerly read his message:

Ms. Jones,

As you can see, I am standing outside of the Alison Richard Building at Cambridge. Google should provide validation that this is not a retirement village. You can also see I'm holding my textbook for part of my year three studies and, according to my watch, it's twenty past eleven my time. Now my hands are about to go numb, as I had to take off my gloves to type this, so my other validation pictures will come after my lecture.

CP

P.S. I will answer the pub quiz question later, if you are inclined to send me a follow request. As you did admit to creeping on my account, you know I have fifteen followers. We'll see if you make that sixteen, if you are curious about a bloke in Cambridge who likes dogs and mysterious pub quizzes.

Ooh!

My heart flutters. CP is sharp. He's British and at Cambridge, and he has to be near my age, right? He loves dogs, and he's not wearing a parka but an overcoat.

With epic watch porn.

It takes me less than one second to make my decision.

I click follow on his profile.

As soon as he accepts my request, I'll be CP's sixteenth follower.

A weird sensation fills me, one I've never felt before.

I think this decision, to follow the mysterious CP, will change my life.

I don't know why, but something in the stars must be aligned for a guy from Cambridge to randomly stumble on my Instagram feed and begin a conversation that already has my heart fluttering.

How it will change things remains unseen.

But I'm curious to see where it goes.

CHAPTER 1

THE GOLDEN PRINCE

I lean back and stretch in my chair in the Bowes Arts and Architecture Library on campus. I'm updating my internship journal and making notes for my research paper due at the end of the semester. This weekend, I got to lead an art experience class at the mall, engaging children to create sculptures out of wooden sticks and glue and using nature as the inspiration for their works.

I can't even begin to describe how rewarding it was to see their faces change from considering the theme I had given them to moving forward with creativity. That's what I love about working with children. Their minds aren't filled with restrictions about what is right or overcome with fear of failure. They just do, with gleeful abandon.

I type into my laptop:

The most important thing about art is following your own passion and inspiration. One little girl built a heart and decorated it with pink glue and lots of glitter. I asked her what her inspiration was for the piece, and she said Valentine's Day, as that was way more inspiring than a leaf. She also added that she hoped she would get a Valentine's Day card from a particular Collin at school, because he was cute and shared his Chips Ahoy cookies with her at lunch. While she flew in the face of the directions, her passion led her to create, and that was what mattered.

I have to say, Collin sounds like a keeper. If I had Chips Ahoy, I'd keep them to myself.

Hmm. I'll make sure I toss some of those in the cart this week when I go shopping.

"Hey," Chelsea says, taking off her coat and draping it over the vacant chair next to me.

"Hey, Chels," I say, watching as she sits down. "How are you?"

"Good," she says, retrieving her iPad from her backpack, along with a textbook, a notebook, a fountain pen, and a stash of tabloid magazines.

I grin as soon as I see them. This is what I love about Chelsea. The woman is majoring in comparative literature; can recite some of the greatest works ever written—in both English and French—and hails from an old-money San Francisco family. But she also gleefully reads every issue of *People* or *US Weekly* she can get her hands on with the same abandon that she reads Shakespeare.

I glance at a glossy tabloid, one of the ones that is fond of writing the most outlandish headlines. The formula seems to be two "appetizer" headlines on the side and a "main course" in the middle of the cover. I check out the appetizers first—come on, isn't that what you do at a meal? —and see the face of a beautiful blonde woman on one side, with a handsome hockey player on the other, and the classy headline of "TOM WHO? Skye Moves on with Hunky Hockey Star!' Next, there's a shocking revelation of a celebrity divorce that is about to happen due to the inability of a cheating actor to keep his tongue out of the nanny's mouth. I recognize the main course immediately, no headline needed for identification.

It's Prince Christian of Wales, looking very serious as he gets out of a car in a crisp, white, dress shirt; a luxurious, navy overcoat; and no tie. His blond, curly locks appear windblown, his blue eyes serious.

I read the screaming headline at the top:

HERMIT PRINCE MAKES RARE PUBLIC APPEARANCE

Prince Xander the Philanderer secretly confides in friends that the Golden Prince is a hoarder recluse in Cambridge. Palace fears he's unstable and buried in empty curry takeaway tubs. Appearance forced for PR sake. Page 15.

I furrow my brow as I study the cover. None of this can be true—although I do hope that Skye from the reality dating show *Is it Love?* is with a sexy European hockey player because Tom, her suitor on the show, was a total assclown.

But I seriously doubt Prince Christian is a hoarder. Or even a hermit. He probably just wants to be left alone, which I can relate to on a minor level. Obviously, the press isn't hiding in the bushes to get a shot of Clementine Jones, art history major at Stanford University, the second I leave the library, but my sister and parents might be.

Especially this week.

"He's gorgeous, isn't he?" Chelsea asks, tapping Prince Christian on the nose and interrupting my thoughts.

"Gorgeous but sad," I say, staring down at the image. "Look at his eyes. You can see it."

"I think you should have been a creative writing major," Chelsea teases. "He's probably bored because he has to go cut some ribbon somewhere. He can only hide at

Cambridge so long before the family forces him out for the occasional appearance to prove he's not a hermit."

At the word Cambridge, I can't help but glance down at my phone. Usually, CP texts me around this time, while he's eating dinner. For convenience, we exchanged numbers soon after we started swapping messages. He won't tell me his full first name. He enjoys letting me guess and insists that kind of reveal has to be earned with time. But I did force him to give up his last name, Chadwick, before giving him my phone number for WhatsApp.

CP.

A tingling sensation sweeps over me as I think about him. Since the message he sent me that January night, we text multiple times a day, every day. We exchange long private messages, too, about our studies; life in Cambridge and Palo Alto; and our favorite TV, books, and food. He's still just as funny and intellectual as he was in that very first message.

I have access to his Instagram account now, too, which is filled with pictures of his beloved dog, Lucy—a red and white Welsh springer spaniel—the English and Scottish countryside, and food he's eating. None of him, though, as he told me he loathes having his picture taken.

He says he is an "ordinary bloke" and he doesn't want to ruin my image of him. He thinks I might change my mind if I saw his face. He obviously hasn't blown up my pictures to see what's flawed with my face, but I don't want to push too hard now.

I wonder if he has an illness or is disfigured in some way, if that's why he's hiding parts of himself. I know it's odd that he can see me when I can't see him, and that red flags should be flying, not only at attention but straight out screaming caution, but I don't care. I get the impression people have disappointed him, and he enjoys having the keyboard as a protective barrier.

I enjoy our conversations so much that I don't mind this veil of secrecy around him. I do know he's a guy, and I do know he's in the UK, and that's enough for me at the moment. I've gone out with guys at Stanford, a few serious, a lot not, and I've never had these kinds of fun, wickedly clever and stimulating conversations in my life.

I'm willing, for now, to just let CP be CP in order to keep talking to him.

My phone begins to vibrate in my hand, and I see MOM flash on my screen.

I sigh. "It's Mom. I'll be right back," I say to Chelsea.

"I'll be reading about the hoarding prince, which we both know is crap because the king would have housekeepers clean up his shit."

I stifle a laugh and answer the phone. "Mom, hold on. I'm walking out of the library."

"Okay, honey."

I wait until I'm outside before speaking. "I'm out now."

"So, you're all ready for Thursday night, right?" Mom asks, a twinge of nervousness in her voice. "Paisley is flying with you, and we'll all go to the appointment together on Friday morning. I made sure there are a couple of flights after yours in case there's any kind of mechanical difficulty, and if you have to charge a full fare on another airline, that's fine."

I feel a headache coming on. I know Mom is worried, but her worrying, and Paisley's worrying, makes everything a thousand times worse.

"I'll be there," I say, drawing a breath of cold air and letting it fill my lungs.

"We don't want to miss this appointment. You know

how hard it is to see Dr. Choi, and you know how important it is for him to go over the results an—"

"Mom," I interrupt, "we've been through this before. We'll deal with the results as we get them."

Mom sniffles. "Of course, of course, you are one hundred percent fine, absolutely you are. It's just another scan."

I can't take this anymore. I can't. I feel as if everything is closing in on me and I can't breathe.

"Mom, we'll see you Thursday night in Phoenix," I say. "I need to study now."

I need to be normal.

"Of course, study. I love you. I promise you everything will be just fine. Don't worry."

We hang up. I move over to the bench outside the beautiful McMurtry Art and Art History Building and drop down onto it, drawing my knees to my chin and tucking my head down on top of them.

Fine. My whole life I've been told I'm going to be "just fine," but how can I be when my family treats me like a fragile baby bird that might never fly, always awaiting news that my broken wings are back and I'll fall with dire consequences? They fret over me, and I know the only reason I was allowed to go to Stanford was because Paisley was nearby in case anything happened. They are forever preoccupied with test results, and it's all my fault. So how can I be *fine*?

Tears fill my eyes, and I determinedly blink them away.

Buzz!

I sniffle and flip over my phone.

It's a text from CP.

I pull down the sleeve of my Stanford hoodie and glamorously use it as a tissue before I open his message.

Tonight's pub quiz question, specifically curated for Clementine by CP:

Work out the name of this dessert from this anagram: Cloacae Heck To

I smile despite my tears. CP always starts chats with a pub quiz question. As he explained to me last month, it's a trivia night held in a pub. If I get the question right, he always says, "That's ace, Clementine."

The Online Slang Dictionary tells me this means "excellent."

Ha. We both speak English, but sometimes I feel like he's speaking a completely different language.

I text him back:

I'm afraid I'm not going to be ace on this one, CP. I can't think when I'm upset.

CP is texting …

Are you OK? Do you want to talk about it?

My fingers linger over the keys for a moment. In my quest to be normal, I haven't told anyone at Stanford about my medical past. I can't handle any more people worrying about me than I already have. But somehow CP and his guarded world seem like an outlet to me. He's someone I can vent to, who can't smother me because he's an ocean away.

This time, the little bird doesn't sit on the branch and wonder if a broken wing will appear. The little bird chooses to fly.

Do you ever wish you could be someone other than who you are? Without the cards life has dealt you? I wish I could fold and start over, with a new card up, asking to be hit with another one. Shit. I'm losing it. I'm talking to you like life is a round of blackjack. I'll message you later

when I'm no longer crazy. Promise I'll have an answer to your pub quiz question then.

I hit send and put the phone to my head. I don't know if he'll give me space after that comment or text me back. And even though I retreated, I hope CP doesn't.

When there's no familiar buzz on my phone after a few minutes, I realize CP is giving me space to get my head right for a normal conversation, and to solve that anagram, because I'm shit at those kinds of word puzzles and he knows it's going to take me awhile.

I stand up and sigh heavily, sadness creeping through me. I need to shake it off and get back to my studies. I have to get to the mall this afternoon, as I'm giving an art tour of this month's exhibition to a senior group and I need to be "on" for it.

I take two steps before my phone rings. No doubt Paisley's turn to talk about my appointment and how everything is going to be "fine."

I'm about to reject the call when a different name catches my eye. My heart stops. I freeze on the sidewalk, causing other students to move around me on the path.

The name of the person flashing on my screen isn't Paisley.

With a shaking hand, I answer it.

"H-Hello?"

"Hello, Clementine," a sexy, deep, English-accented voice says into my ear. "I do understand what you mean about the cards. *Exactly* what you mean. No, we can't change the hand we've been dealt, but we can decide whether to stand or hit, to take the risk. You don't strike me as the standing type. Perhaps we should talk about how you can take the hit. If you'll risk a conversation with me, that is. So, will you? Will you talk to me, Clementine?"

CHAPTER 2

JUST A BLOKE FROM ACROSS THE POND

I hesitate. Would CP really want to hear my story? I don't want him to feel sorry for me. The last thing I need is for one more person in my life to treat me like a fragile Fabergé egg. I've come to value my exchanges with CP because they are thought-provoking and fun.

I don't want my story to change that.

"I-I understand if this is too weird," CP says, his voice breaking through my thoughts. "I can hang up. Right. Well, I'll just go n—"

"No," I say, my instincts taking over, as they have throughout the forging of my friendship with CP. "I want you to promise me something. After I tell you, promise me you won't change toward me. Please promise me that."

"I can't promise that," CP says gravely. "I mean, if you are laundering money or hiding bodies in the cupboards, my opinion of you would change."

I laugh. "Well, duh, of course not. I embezzle not launder, and I keep the bodies under the floorboards."

CP laughs—a rich, throaty chuckle—and I think I just felt the first signs of a swoon coming on.

"Well, that changes everything. Go on."

I walk back toward the bench where I was sitting a few minutes ago and slowly sink down onto it.

"Okay. Nobody outside of my family knows this," I say, my voice growing quiet. "When I was fourteen years old, I started not feeling well. I had headaches, nausea, and vomiting. My vision gave me issues. I was irritable. I was misdiagnosed at first, a doctor said I had a virus. But it turned out that virus was a brain tumor."

CP releases an audible gasp on the other end of the line, and I squeeze my eyes shut.

"God, Clementine," he says, his deep voice resonating with shock. "I'm so sorry."

"Talk about a shit hand of cards, right?" I quip, as I've come to use humor to help deal with my medical past. "It was benign, a stage one. I had brain surgery to remove it, and they were able to get all of it. I didn't need to have radiation or chemotherapy. But it did cause some paralysis of my right eye. If you blow up a picture of me, you can see it. It's not hugely obvious unless you are super observant or studying my face, but part of it droops. Ironically, getting Botox injections helps the appearance, so yes, I'm already getting Botox, and I'm not even twenty-three."

"You and my mother could compare notes. Except her Botox makes it look like she has zero facial expressions. Or that could just be her personality. Ice usually doesn't have much of an expression, unless it begins to melt, but hell would have to freeze over for that to happen with her."

I pause. CP just served up something very personal in response to my sharing, and I make a note to ask him about this at another point in time. I get the impression his mother isn't a warm woman who bakes cookies and asks how your day was.

Or in the case of my mother, "How was your day?" followed by, "Did you have any headaches? Dizziness? Vision okay?" as she runs through a tumor symptom checklist.

"How are you now?" he follows up. "Are you okay?"

"I have to have scans regularly to make sure it hasn't come back," I say. "I have been tumor free in all of them. But I started having headaches again, and I had to have an MRI last week. I'm going to get the results from my doctor in Phoenix on Friday. Hopefully, another tumor hasn't taken up residence in my brain matter."

CP is quiet for a moment. "Clementine, that was a lot for a teenager to go through. It had to be frightening. Now you have to fight the ghost of it as an adult, don't you?"

A lump forms in my throat. "I'm scared," I whisper, my voice thick. "I know it could be back. I know it could be worse. Headaches were my first sign before. It could be bigger, or malignant. I could be told I only have years, if I'm lucky, to live. But I can't share those fears with my family. Ever since I was sick, they have been nothing but fearful for me. The worry might have receded, but it has never left them. I've scarred them. Worse, I'm treated like a fragile bird, who might re-break a wing at any moment, who must be watched and protected above everything else. Sometimes, it's suffocating. Then I feel guilty for thinking that. I just want to be normal, not the girl who had a tumor."

To my surprise, a sob escapes me.

"Clementine, listen to me," CP says, his British voice coming through the line in a commanding tone. "You have every right to feel these things. Every single one of them. In my family, it's always the British mantra 'keep a stiff upper lip.' Well, I say bollocks to that. You can feel anger over what cards you've been dealt. You can feel the frustration of being smothered, the sadness over the part of your childhood that has been taken from you, and the fear any time you get a headache that it means something. You are allowed to be human. At least you are with me."

CP's words wash over me like a powerful wave, knocking the pent-up emotions free and allowing them to crash against the rocks on the shore. I begin crying, and as if he's right here with me, he continues to tell me he's here and he will be as long as I need him to be.

The tears finally subside, and I wipe my face once again with the sleeve of my hoodie. Ick, I can't wait to get this off and throw it into the washer when I get home. But until then, I get to walk around with snotty sleeves. Serves me right for not throwing a pack of portable tissues into my backpack.

"I wish I could see your face," I say aloud, "to thank you for what you've done for me."

CP remains silent.

"I don't care what you look like," I blurt out. "I want to see you."

He exhales softly, so softly I can barely hear it.

"I'm just an ordinary bloke from across the pond," he says simply.

"No. No ordinary bloke would help a stranger like you have," I say, shaking my head. "You're anything but ordinary. At least to me you're not."

Silence fills the line.

"Thank you," he says simply. "Clementine?"

"Yes?"

"I know this sounds mad, but I don't feel like you are a stranger to me."

"I know it sounds crazy, but I agree with you."

We chuckle together.

"You do realize that I need to see you at some point, right?" I say.

Silence once again.

"CP. Unless you are a middle-aged professor playing a charade with me, I expect to see your face. Oh, wait, unless you are hiding a secret identity. Either you're keeping bodies under the floorboards; or you're Prince Christian, hiding in mounds of crap and curry takeout tubs."

I can't help but laugh aloud, as both examples are equally crazy.

"This isn't a game to me," he says, his voice sharp as he cuts through my laughter. "You are very real to me. Do you understand how much I look forward to texting you? To our conversations? It's ridiculous how much I enjoy them, and I've never even met you. I don't want my face to change that, Clementine, not when I'm still discovering who you are."

My heart does a weird flutter, something I've never felt before.

"I feel the same way. I can say things to you that I can't say to anyone else. But if you are worried about what you look like, just remember, I'm the one with the Droopy Dog eye!"

I hear a pen click. "Got it. I'll make a note to compare your eye to Droopy Dog."

I burst out laughing. "Hearing you say 'Droopy Dog' with your posh accent has been the highlight of my day."

He laughs again, that low-throated, sexy chuckle. "You're easy to please."

Definitely swooning now.

"If you think I've forgotten about your face, you're wrong," I remind him.

"Perhaps since you like puzzles—"

"Wait just a minute. I never said I liked puzzles. You just insist on making me do those anagrams, which I completely suck at, for the pub quiz question."

"I've got an idea for my face reveal."

"I feel like I'm talking to the Phantom of the Opera," I wisecrack.

"Shut up."

I laugh. "Okay, go on."

"No, you don't deserve to know after that crack, Ace. I'll text you details later. I do, however, ask for one thing."

He called me Ace.

A huge smile spreads across my face. I like that he's given me a nickname.

"Of course."

"When you figure it out, I want you to call me. No matter what day or time it is. Promise me that."

"I promise."

"Swear to me, Clementine. Swear to me."

"I swear."

"I'm holding you to that."

I know he could be horribly disfigured, but in this moment, I don't care. CP is a special guy. He gave me a lifeline today when my emotions threatened to drown me.

I want to see him.

I also know his face, no matter what he looks like, will never change our friendship.

"I will, CP."

He breathes a sigh of relief. "Thank you."

"You have nothing to worry about."

"I also want you to call me from Phoenix. No matter what time. I know your family is suffocating you, and I promise I'm not adding to that. But I'm here for you, Clementine. I'm going to be here for you every step of the way."

Emotions overwhelm me. CP's goodness is like nothing I've ever known in a man, outside of my father and brother-in-law. I know it's rare to possess this kind of wisdom and maturity at his young age of twenty-three.

"I would like that," I say, my voice thick.

"Well, good. 'No' wasn't going to be an option for you, regardless."

I manage a small laugh. "Listen, you probably need to reheat your dinner by now, which I'm very sorry about, and I have to get back to the library before Chelsea thinks I've run off and abandoned her."

"Please, my dinner was frozen. It's probably not even done in the middle, even though I followed the package directions."

I gasp. "Are you one of those people who read the directions and cook at the instructed power level and rotate at the exact right time?"

"Well, yes."

I groan. "CP, I need to loosen you up. Live on the edge next time. Just nuke it."

"Fine. But I'll be calling you if my dinner turns out burnt."

"Report back later," I say, lightness filling me.

"I shall. Oh, and Clementine?"

"Yes?"

"Look for a puzzle piece later tonight."

CHAPTER 3

PUZZLE PIECES

I throw my dinner into the microwave, smiling as I punch in what seems like a good amount of time to heat a frozen chicken pot pie. CP Chadwick would be appalled at my recklessness.

My mother, however, would be appalled that I'm eating a frozen pot pie and not a meal that is organic, freshly prepared, and full of superfoods to keep tumors at bay.

I glance at my phone, willing it to ding with a notification. I still haven't received my puzzle piece from CP, and I probably won't since it's two o'clock in the morning in the UK. I hope he didn't change his mind. His intense need to keep shrouded makes me think he's terrified of what I'll think when I see his face, or body, or whatever he is so desperate to hide.

I should send him a copy of *Shrek,* my favorite movie of all time. He's kind of like my Shrek—at least he is in my head. Maybe he's not good looking, but his depth, humor, and intelligence all shine through. Of course, with my red hair and light eyes, I can be Princess Fiona, especially if you throw in a bit of Droopy Dog.

The door opens, and Bryn walks in, amazingly without Graham behind her like ninety-eight percent of the time.

"Hey, how are you?" she asks, her brown eyes studying me.

"I'm good," I say. "Where's Graham?"

"He has a study group tonight," she says, taking off her coat and tossing it onto the back of one of our kitchen chairs. She misses, and it slides down to the floor in a heap. She acts like she doesn't see it and goes over to pet Bear, who has come to greet her, on the head. "Aren't you a good boy?"

Bryn has the uncanny ability to not care that she missed hanging up her coat. That coat will stay there until either she needs it or I can't take it anymore and pick it up for her. The second option wins way too often, and I'm already getting twitchy looking at it on the floor, her gorgeous Kate Spade coat no doubt soaking up crumbs and Bear's dog hair like a sponge.

I can't stand it. I pick it up, shaking the coat out and gently draping it over the back of the chair.

Graham better have an excellent job or trust fund lined up, because if they get married, he's going to need a live-in housekeeper.

"What are you making?" Bryn asks, standing upright and wrinkling her nose.

"You'll love it," I tease, going over to the coffee table and swiping the remote to navigate to our saved movies. I'm suddenly in the mood for *Shrek*. Or maybe *Shrek II,* when they go to Hollywood.

"Oh, that means I'll think it's gross," Bryn says, moving

past me and into the kitchen. "It's cheap and has meat chunks, doesn't it?"

I find the movie and hit play. "Why yes, yes it does."

"Ew," she says, retrieving her pre-made Whole Foods meal. Bryn only eats Whole Foods meals, ones she carefully selects from the takeout section. While I have absolutely nothing against Whole Foods or eating well, she is missing out on a key experience of life.

The bliss of frozen pot pies.

And Chips Ahoy.

The microwave beeps, and I grab an oven mitt to retrieve my tray. I take it out and wave it under Bryn's nose. "You know you want some," I tease.

I watch as she practically turns green. "Um, no, I don't. You can keep that nastiness, thank you, while I have salmon."

"Talk about gross. Fish. *Bleurgh,*" I say, sitting down at our kitchen table.

"Fish is good for you," Bryn says, taking off the lid and setting it inside the microwave. Then she furrows her brow. "Is that *Shrek?*"

"*Shrek Two,*" I say, breaking my fork through the top crust of the pie. "Your food doesn't have crust, the greatest thing ever," I declare.

"I swear you are five. Which is why I adore you," she says, smiling affectionately at me.

I feel love in my heart for my friend. Bryn was a surprise discovery for me. We met in FroSoCo, the Freshman Sophomore College residence halls, when we were assigned a room together. I assumed—incorrectly—she was your typical only-child, spoiled, rich girl. When she was moving in, it was one Louis Vuitton garment bag after another. Everything about her seemed classy and perfect, from her long, sleek jet-black hair and flawless makeup to her polished and buffed, expertly manicured nails. I thought I saw her looking at my room décor items with disdain, but now I realize I projected that onto her. She was quizzical, not judgmental.

As soon as her parents left, Bryn turned to me, shot me an amazing smile, and asked if she could do my nails because she loved giving manicures and found it relaxing. I rolled with it, and she immediately quit organizing her lux tins of fancy teas on her shelf, leaving the half-empty box unpacked and tea accessories strewn across the bed, and grabbed her tackle box of manicure supplies.

That's when I knew I would like Bryn. She wasn't perfect; she was messy. As she did my nails, she told me all about her life back in Boston and how her parents were livid she didn't choose Harvard. She talked with excitement about how happy she was to be on her own in Palo Alto, and I related to that need to be out of the view of your parents.

An hour later, after her telling me my cuticles were a hot mess and applying products I've never seen in my life, I was left with beautifully manicured nails, painted in Goldissima by Christian Louboutin—silly me, I thought he only made shoes—and a friend I'll have the rest of my life.

Bryn takes her fish out of the microwave and takes a seat next to me. I practice my willpower not to gag as she eats.

"Where's Chels?" she asks, breaking a piece of salmon off with her fork.

"She's at the library," I say, "with Lars."

"Oh, the Swedish import," Bryn says, grinning.

Lars—I have no clue what his last name is because when he said it all I heard was Charlie Brown teacher-like speak—is from Sweden. They are "just friends," but I think Chelsea would give anything for it to be more. But after three years of knowing each other, she still refuses to say anything about how she feels.

"I wish she'd tell him she liked him," I say, taking another bite of pot pie.

Bryn chews thoughtfully for a moment. "Yes, but that could ruin a friendship if he doesn't see her that way."

"Yes, but wouldn't the risk be worth taking? For a chance at love?"

"But what if it makes everything weird and awkward for them? Is tossing a friendship aside for a chance at romance, one that probably wouldn't work out due to logistics, worth it?"

"Yes," I say.

"No," she counters at the same time.

We both laugh.

Buzz!

My heart flutters as my phone goes off on the countertop in the kitchen. My reaction is dumb because it can't possibly be CP. He's asleep at his house in Cambridge. More than likely it's Paisley with her daily *Have you documented all your headaches today?* text.

Bleurgh.

I get up and pick up my phone. I swipe it, and to my absolute delight, it's a WhatsApp message from CP. I eagerly open it and find a picture of full lips and a chin, with the image put into the shape of a puzzle piece. I read his text attached to it:

Ace, consider this reverse Humpty Dumpty. I'm giving you pieces of a picture of me. Now you see my lips

and my chin. Let's see if you can put me back together again.

P.S. The rhyme is completely unintentional.

I can't lift my eyes from the picture. There's nothing disfigured about his lips and chin—in fact, they're beautiful. His lips are wonderfully full, and the chin is strong and masculine, with no shading of facial hair.

"Why are you smiling like that?"

I blink. "What?"

"You're smiling while you're reading your phone," Bryn says. Then she arches an eyebrow. "Did you get a message from a boy?"

I bite my lip. I haven't shared CP with anyone yet. While our relationship makes sense to me, I know everyone else would freak out that I'm talking to some guy in the UK whose full first name I don't know and whose image, outside of his hand, I have never seen.

"A funny GIF," I lie, as I'm not yet ready to explain.

Much in the same way I don't want to explain my medical past.

I message him back:

Mr. Chadwick, you need to go to bed. While it's only six here, and I'm eating a delicious pot pie, you should be sleeping before you go to class in the morning.

I hesitate before typing more. Should I tell him what I think of his lips? Is this dangerous territory? What if it creeps him out?

But then I remember my thoughts on Chelsea's situation. After years of being protected by my family, encouraged to take every precaution for my health and well-being, I decide the little, caged bird needs to fly a bit more. I finish my thought:

Your lips are beautiful.

Then I hit send.

Within seconds, the "typing" word flashes, and I know he's answering me. I begin pacing in the kitchen, wondering how he's going to respond. Soon, I have my answer:

Beautiful is the word I'd use to describe YOU, Clementine.

Is it weird I feel tingly all over?

Whatever. I don't care. I like it, and I'm going to enjoy it.

CP continues to type. Another message drops in:

Enjoy your pot pie. I, myself, love a steak pie. Have you ever had one? That's what I always order at the pub. As you are a declared carnivore, I'm certain you would like it. More on that later. I should get some sleep. So, goodnight, Ace. Sleep well. Obviously later, as I hope you aren't going to bed before seven o'clock.

I'm still smiling as one more message from CP comes through:

P.S. Upon my exhaustive study of Droopy Dog, I see NO resemblance, unless cuteness counts.

If it wouldn't be so obvious, I swear I'd put my phone to my heart and let out a little squee.

The door opens, and Chelsea slams it shut behind her, practically tearing it off the hinges.

"Chels?" I ask, concerned.

Her eyes are red and rimmed with tears.

"L-Lars," she says, choking on the words. "H-he asked out another Swedish girl!"

She promptly bursts into tears.

"Oh, Chels," Bryn says, leaping up from her chair.

Before Chelsea can say another word, we have her enveloped in a three-way hug. She clings to us and cries.

Then, as if she realizes something, she breaks free of the embrace and shakes her head.

"This is stupid," she blurts out. "I mean, Clem, you have your results on Friday. That is what's important; this is dumb!"

I stare at her. How does she know about my test results?

"Chels!" Bryn gasps.

Chelsea's hand flies to her mouth. "Shit! Oh, shit."

"Wait. You know I'm going to a doctor on Friday?" I ask, my heart pounding in my ears.

She shifts her gaze to Bryn, who looks at me with fear in her eyes.

"C," she says, using her nickname for me, "don't be mad. Your parents told me when we were in the dorm."

I'm shaking, stunned by the admission. "You ... know? For years, you've known?"

She exchanges another glance with Chelsea. "Yes. Your parents wanted us to know symptoms in case something started happening. They begged me not to tell you so you wouldn't be upset."

"Well, I am!" I roar, my temper going off. "How dare they! I'm not a child. I'm freaking twenty-two years old. I have my own medical rights now, and I don't want people looking at me like I might grow a tumor and drop dead!"

"No, we don't, and we never have," Chelsea implores through her tears. "All of this was done out of great love for you."

I clench my jaw. "Everything is done out of love for me, but it's killing me."

The room falls silent, except for *Shrek* blaring in the background. Bear comes up and sits next to me as if he knows I need him.

"Did you tell them about my headaches?" I ask.

"I did," Chelsea says, taking responsibility. "I'm worried about you."

"So that is why Mom kept bugging me about how I felt until I told her."

Bryn nods.

"We love you. You're family. This was all done because we want you to be healthy and happy," Chelsea says.

"I know, I know, but this still hurts," I say. "I need time to process. Come on, Bear."

I take Bear with me down the hall to the room I share with Chelsea and flop on my bed, hot tears stinging my eyes as he jumps up and we both squeeze onto the small bed.

They knew this whole time, I think, hurt filling me. *How could they not tell me?*

The tears begin to fall. I hate deceptions. Probably because my parents sugarcoated my diagnosis all those years ago, leaving me confused and afraid of what was going on inside my body. I had a right to know the truth, and it was denied to me because they didn't trust me to handle it. Not until I had to have surgery did I get an abridged version, leaving me terrified when I searched everything on Google.

Despite my anger, I know they did all of this out of love. But that doesn't make it right.

I was given a second puzzle piece tonight with Chelsea's admission, but only one piece was needed to solve this one. Bear begins licking my tears, and I entwine my fingers in his curly fur.

I wish I could talk to CP.

The thought is so normal and so natural it should frighten me, but it doesn't. I know he would have some wise words to make me feel better, and then he'd find a way to make me laugh. I close my eyes, hearing his rich voice, the deep chuckle he has, and remember the full lips I saw in the picture he sent.

Unlike the puzzle I put together tonight, I have a good feeling about the one I'm starting to put together of CP.

All I hope is that he sends me another piece sooner rather than later.

CHAPTER 4

AN OMISSION FOR THE GREATER GOOD

I can't sleep.

I glance at the clock, which blinks back at me that it's three fifteen in the morning. I want to roll over, but since Bear is taking up that side of the bed, I stay in place and stare at the glowing numbers on my clock that are taunting me that I have to get up in a few hours.

Not helping matters is my headache, which I'm sure if I mention in the morning, my friends would contact my parents the second I walk out the door to go to class.

I'm at war with myself over my discovery last night. I know they were doing it as a favor to my concerned parents, and over time, it became something they did out of love for me. But, dammit, when do *I* get to decide what is best for me? My health is my business. I don't want them to feel sorry for me, or be afraid that any time I feel like crap I have a tumor. Or cancer, or a month to live.

I'm tired of everyone worrying about me. I'm tired of everyone trying to protect me from things we have no control over.

Will I always be the wounded bird who needs to be protected and sheltered?

A heaviness settles over my heart. I wish I had the courage to say this, but my illness has inflicted enough pain on my family. I feel immense guilt at the idea of adding more pain on top of it.

I reach for my phone and pull up CP on WhatsApp. I know he's about to go into a lecture, but even though I know he won't respond for a while, I find comfort in sending him a message.

I pull the blanket over my head, although Chelsea can sleep through anything, and begin typing to CP:

More crap from me. You're going to be sorry you ever messaged me because, unluckily for you, I find I can talk so easily to you. I can't sleep. I found out tonight that my friends have known about my tumor for years and never told me. How? My parents asked them to keep an eye on me and to contact them if I started to present any symptoms. I'm hurt. I'm mad. I feel betrayed, even though I know all parties were acting out of concern for me. Shit, I'm reading back what I wrote, and I sound ungrateful. I'm not. I just hate feeling like no one trusts me to take care of myself, to decide things on my own. I hate feeling like I'm being watched. All I want right now is to go to the mall and work the art exhibits and be normal, instead of the girl who might have a tumor.

P.S. I could really use another puzzle piece right now.

I hit send and put the phone down at my side. I exhale, feeling a bit better for getting that off my chest to someone who won't judge me for it, someone who truly listens to me and I know will be there for me.

It's strange to have these feelings for someone I've never truly seen, or met, or even know the full name of. If Bryn or

Chelsea were talking to a guy like this, I would be warning them that it is nuts.

Maybe that's why I've kept CP to myself. I don't want to hear all the reasons why this is not normal and how I should be careful.

That, or they would chart it as me presenting the symptom of "irrational behavior" and text my mom.

Ha-ha. Tumor humor.

I think of CP again, the picture of his lips and chin, the sound of his voice.

All I know is that when I talk to him, the world makes sense.

It feels right.

With that thought in my head, I find myself relaxing enough to drift off to sleep.

"It's time to take off your mask," I whisper to CP as we dance.

I'm singing. We're on the stage of a *Phantom of the Opera* production, and CP is wearing a mask so I can only see part of his face.

"I don't know if I can," he sings back to me in a rich baritone, twirling me around.

"Why aren't we singing songs from the musical?" I ask, pausing before I whirl back in toward him.

My neon green dress is huge, like something from the eighties, with ridiculous poufy sleeves. I don't know why I'm in neon green; it's a hideous color on me.

CP draws me to him, and what I can see of his face is perfect.

"Please reveal yourself," I plead. "I've revealed so much to you, more than anyone else."

"After we sing."

"Sing what? We have multiple options here."

He whirls away from me, but his cape gets wind under it and whips around and smacks me in the face.

Why is his cape wet?

And why does it feel like a tongue?

Why doesn't CP smell like some luxury cologne instead of like a dog that needs to go to the groomer?

I open my eyes. I'm not with a masked CP, but with Bear, who is licking my face as a precursor to my alarm going off.

Oh.

Well, that's a bit disappointing. Even though the whole *Phantom of the Opera* thing was odd, CP was a good dancer. He was kind of sexy as the man in black.

However, now he won't see me in a horrible neon green dress, so that's good.

"You need to go to the groomer," I whisper to Bear while affectionately rubbing his head.

I reach for my phone and see CP has returned my message:

I know it feels like you were betrayed, but sometimes a lie of omission is done for the greater good. In this case, to take care of you. I can't argue with that one because, well, it's YOU.

I smile as I message him back:

I know you're right. I'm calmer now. Besides, Bryn barely knew me at the time. What was she going to say? "Screw you, hire someone to monitor her blood pressure, pulse, and chart her reaction to Chips Ahoy because I'm not a nurse!" And then flip them off?

I see CP is typing me back. His reply drops in:

You just made me choke on my water. What are Chips Ahoy? Is that a version of french fries at sea?

Now I burst out laughing. I type a response:

OMG no. They are chocolate chip cookies. My favorite are the s'mores-flavored ones.

Now the conversation is going back and forth:

Isn't a s'more some other American thing?

I text my reply:

Yes. It's combining two desserts in one. Rather handy. So, you were in my dream last night. Very odd. You were the Phantom of the Opera, with the mask and everything. Except you didn't kidnap me and hold me against my will in your lair. Because, you know, that would have been creepy.

To my surprise, CP bypasses texting and calls me. My heart does a happy little dance, and I answer it, as Chelsea has already gotten up and is out of her bed.

"Hello?"

"Clementine. Do you actually think I'm disfigured?" CP asks, his deep voice full of surprise. "Like the Phantom?"

"Well, maybe," I admit. "I mean, why else would you hide your face?"

"I promise you I'm not."

"Your looks don't matter to me, CP."

"No, I'm not hideous," he says. He pauses. "I promise you; I'm just a bloke."

I furrow my brow. "If you're just a bloke, why not show me your bloke-like face?"

CP is silent for a moment. "I will. I had to be sure about you first. And now I've made all these puzzle pieces, so it would be a pity not to use them."

"Sure of what?" I ask, backtracking to that comment.

"You'll understand when you put together the puzzle."

I groan aloud. "You're maddening."

"Part of the charm."

"Ordinary blokes wouldn't put a girl through this."

"Then consider it a bonus: an ordinary-looking bloke with an exceptional personality."

I start laughing. "You're weird, in the best way possible."

"Hmm. I think that is a compliment."

"Absolutely it is," I say, sitting up. "What are you doing now?"

"Playing a round of study-avoidance by watching *The Chase* online. It's a quiz show, and it's brilliant."

"Your guilty pleasure TV is a quiz show*?* This is as bad as your microwaving."

CP laughs, and a happy tingle flows through me from the sound of his deep, reverberating chuckle.

"All right, since I'm so boring with the quiz show, what should I be watching whilst I burn my dinner with the wrong time and power level?"

I laugh. "Hold on, I'll need to research what is available in the UK. I'll message you a more suitable mental cleanser."

"Mental cleanser? You aren't CIA, are you? Trying to reprogram my brain to reveal the secrets of the UK?"

"Yes. I am. And I'll do it through trashy reality show programming."

He laughs again.

I glance at the clock, regretting that I have to get off the phone.

"CP, I have to get ready for class," I say, hearing the regret resonate in my voice. "But I want to thank you for something."

"What?"

"You didn't bring up the test. You didn't say everything will be fine. You treated me like everything was normal. I feel like you understand."

"I do, Clementine," he says softly.

There's a little silence between us, and I get the feeling he doesn't want to get off the phone, either.

He clears his throat. "Well, right. You'd better get on with it."

"Okay. I'll message you later."

"I'm looking forward to it, Ace."

Then he hangs up.

A happy sigh escapes my lips. Now I'm more curious about him than ever, knowing that he's not disfigured.

I think on this as I throw on some clothing so I can take Bear out before I get ready. This time, I don a gray Stanford hoodie and ripped jeans. After I shove my feet into my slip-on Converse, I'm ready. I open the door and see Chelsea is already gone. Bryn's door is shut, so she must still be sleeping. I'll talk to both of them tonight and apologize for my overreaction.

I hook the leash to Bear's collar and head outside. The air is cool, and the sun is shining brightly. It's going to be another beautiful day in Palo Alto.

I yawn as Bear heads out to take care of his business. I am staring blankly at the green grass when my phone goes off.

I flip it over and glance down at the screen. CP has messaged me again, this time, another piece of the puzzle.

It's his nose, his absolutely perfect nose.

I can put the two pieces together in my head, his full lips and perfect nose, and he's already looking rather handsome, much to my delight.

Then he sends me the day's pub quiz question, another flipping anagram. I study the words, my brain trying to sort them out to make sense:

Ye Gout I

Why is it I can remember all the details of the Edgar Degas painting *The Dance Class,* but I can't unscramble these words? My brain can be such a freakishly weird place.

Bear finishes, and we head back up the stairs as my brain continues working on the puzzle. Suddenly, as if everything fell into place, I see it:

I get you

Butterflies take off in force.

I have no idea what's going to happen between us. He's at Cambridge. I'm in Palo Alto. Common sense says nothing.

But my heart says *something.*

And for the first time in my life, I choose to listen to my heart.

CHAPTER 5

VALLEY OF THE SUN

I draw a breath of air as I sit in the sterile waiting room of Dr. Choi's neurosurgery office. Cheesy, soft pop songs fill the air, which has a temperature of "this close to freezing." I think I might see an air puff as I exhale. Then I'll fall asleep due to hypothermia.

"You okay?" Paisley asks, leaning across my mom, who is doing a needlepoint of Tom Hiddleston's face. Mom says one of us can have the Tom throw pillow when she's done. Paisley, the ever-generous soul, has decided I can have it.

"I don't know. That breath could have been one of my last," I snip.

Paisley's brown eyes widen. I know I've hurt her with that, and worse, I almost don't care.

Almost.

"I'm sorry," I say, picking up my phone and messaging CP. "I'm anxious, that's all."

"It will be fine," Mom says, her fingers moving the needle up and down. "Just fine."

Anger surges through me from her words. How does

she know that? Does she have ESP? If so, then why are we waiting in this room with magazines from six months ago and chairs that have the comfort of sitting on cold concrete slabs?

"Everyone, relax," Dad says, flicking a page in *Woman's Day*, one of the few available choices for him to read. "We'll know how to tackle everything very soon."

I wish CP could be here. He would make me laugh. He'd let me talk about how I am processing everything and tell me a steak pie and stupid anagram would be waiting when I was done.

I glance at my family. How can the people I've grown up with not know what I need, but a man in the UK who I have been talking to for two months does?

It's now four o'clock his time, and CP has been texting me all morning. I decide to try and take the edge off by continuing our conversation:

Waiting now. Mom is doing a Tom Hiddleston needlepoint cushion cover to settle her nerves, Dad is reading a women's magazine, and Paisley is watching every breath I take. Good times. You should totally be jealous you aren't here to sit next to me in a very orange, uncomfortable plastic chair.

CP is typing …

Why on earth is your mom needlepointing (is that a word?) Tom Hiddleston's face? Was Benedict Cumberbatch not available?

I grin. *This* is what I mean. CP knows what I need, without me even telling him. I text back:

Well, the Golden Prince was on back order, so she had to settle for Hiddles.

I hit send.

CP is typing …

Do tell. Does the Golden Prince pattern include piles of rubbish and curry takeaway tubs? You know what the tabloids say about him.

I burst out laughing.

I feel everyone in my family stare at me, as if there is no reason in the world I should be laughing right now.

"Sorry," I say, going back to my typing:

Please. No. I don't believe that for one second. Besides, the prince has PEOPLE. He would never live in a hot mess. They would be in there with shovels and dumpsters before letting him live like a hoarder. Have you ever seen the show called *Hoarders*? Sad and fascinating at the same time. If I stumble on it while flipping channels, I stop and watch. Very motivating for cleaning the apartment, I must say.

CP is typing …

Ha, you might be surprised. You never know how people live behind closed doors. I don't have time for *Hoarders*; I'm too busy watching your prescribed viewing of *The Real Housewives of Cheshire*.

Right on cue, the door to the waiting room opens. A nurse is holding a chart in her hands, and my stomach fills with dread. It's the moment you want, and don't want, at the same time. You want to get it over with, but you might also receive news that is shattering.

"Clementine Jones?" she asks.

I stand up, and so does my family. We all follow her back to Dr. Choi's office. Nerves come up full force. Nobody in my family is talking. I take the chair across from his desk, and my dad sits next to me. Mom and Paisley take the two chairs against the back wall.

I study all of Dr. Choi's diplomas on the walls, knowing I'm in good hands with one of the best neurosurgeons in the

United States. Even if they find something, I know he'll have a plan to treat me. We'll discuss the options: surgery, chemo, radiation. I go through everything like a checklist for my survival.

I swallow hard. Dr. Choi's treatment will possibly give me more time to live if the results are bad.

I blink back tears. *Please, God, I feel as if I'm finally starting to live now. I'm finishing Stanford. I want to pursue a career with antiques. I've met CP, and I'd love the opportunity to meet him in person someday. Please let me be okay,* I pray. *I'll find ways to do good with my life, to serve others, if I'm given another chance.*

I know I'm bargaining. I know God is listening.

In this moment, I turn it all over to Him.

There's a brisk knock on the door, and then it clicks open.

I want to throw up.

"Hello," Dr. Choi says, smiling at all of us. "I see the whole crew is here today. Nice to see you all again."

I nod. Dr. Choi is a slender man in his fifties, and he has been my neurosurgeon since I was fourteen. He's grown older, and I've grown up, in our years together.

He shakes all our hands and takes a seat behind his desk, placing his laptop in front of him.

"Clementine," he says, addressing me directly, "I've had a chance to review your scans, along with your blood work."

I bite my lip, nodding. Praying. Preparing.

He smiles gently at me. "Your scans are negative. Your blood cells look fantastic. Clementine, you look absolutely fine."

I hear my mom gasp, and Paisley lets out a cry. Dad exhales.

"I-I'm okay?" I ask, getting choked up.

"Whatever is causing your headaches, it's not a tumor."

I choke back tears. *Thank you, God. Thank you. I promise I'll keep my word to You.*

I don't trust myself to speak, so I nod.

"But what could be causing her headaches?" my dad asks.

"It could be any number of things," Dr. Choi says. "Vision. Stress. Inflammation. Tension. An allergic reaction. It's a long list, but we can el—"

"Wait," I interrupt, something clicking into place for me. "Could an essential oil cause me to have headaches?"

Dr. Choi nods. "Absolutely."

I exhale loudly. "I'm an idiot," I say.

Dad glances at me. "Why do you say that?"

"Chelsea put in a new essential oil diffuser in our room. She fills it with lavender. I started getting headaches around the same time, but I always thought lavender was good for headaches, so I didn't connect it."

"Let's discontinue that and see if your headaches improve," Dr. Choi says, typing some notes into his laptop. "It's possible you might have an allergy to lavender."

The feeling of relief is overwhelming. I want to cry. Laugh manically. Jump for joy. While I'm not a doctor, I'm pretty damn sure it's the lavender that's causing my headaches.

We say goodbye to Dr. Choi, and I feel nothing but gratitude for my clean bill of health. As soon as we're out of the office, Paisley throws her arms around me.

"I love you," she says, her voice thick. "My prayers have been answered."

My heart swells with love for my sister. "I love you, too."

Mom reaches for both of us, and I hear her stifle a sob. "I'm so grateful. So, so grateful."

Mom releases us and nods as if she's trying to regain her composure. We walk toward the exit of the medical plaza, the doors automatically opening for us.

"But I always knew you'd be fine," Mom says, her eyes sparkling as we walk out into the bright Arizona sunshine. "I knew it!"

My dad affectionately loops his arm about my shoulders. "Love you, kiddo."

"I love you, too," I say.

"We need to celebrate," Paisley adds, brushing back a strand of her long, dark hair from her face. "Lunch before we fly back later this afternoon, Clem?"

I smile. "I want Pizzeria Bianco," I say, referring to the famous Phoenix pizza place.

"Done," Dad says. "We have plenty of time to get that before you girls need to head back to the airport."

"Let's go home. I'll put on some coffee," Mom says. "And hot chocolate."

I grin. "Perfect."

Before we get in the car, I stare out at the Phoenix landscape, the rugged mountains behind the city and the palms dotting the area around the medical building we've just left.

"Hold on, I want to take a picture," I say, moving underneath one of the palm trees and angling my phone so I'm looking up through the palm leaves and to the blue sky above. I snap it, and then I hurry to catch up with my family, who are getting into the car. I take my seat next to Paisley in the back of the Lexus, and I see CP has messaged me while I was with Dr. Choi:

I know you are going in soon. I'm with you. Imagine

me holding your hand. I'm with you, facing this with you, whatever this is. I'm also asking for every favour in the universe for you to get a good result.

Tears sting my eyes. I'm touched by his words. He's sincere and genuine in what he says, and I feel blessed CP has found his way into my life. I attach the picture of the palm tree and message him back:

Beautiful day in the Valley of the Sun. A day made even more beautiful because I don't have a tumor but rather an allergy to lavender oil. I'll never let poor Chels with her essential oil diffuser live this one down, ha-ha.

While I see he is typing a reply, I send a quick group text to Chelsea and Bryn telling them I am, without a doubt, one hundred percent fine, and we'll celebrate when I get home tonight. By the time I'm finished, CP has sent me a new message:

BRILLIANT, ABSOLUTELY BRILLIANT, ACE! Thank God. THANK GOD. I just exhaled for the first time today. We'll figure out a time to celebrate at the same time.

I smile to myself as I type:

I don't think I could have gotten through this without you. I'm grateful you are in my life. Headed back home now, then going to have the best pizza in the world for lunch. I have a flight at five tonight to San Jose. Send more puzzle pieces while I'm at the airport. I will have a lot of time to kill.

CP is typing …

Maybe it's time to complete the puzzle.

My heart leaps inside my chest. Is CP ready to show himself to me? I reply:

You know I would love nothing more than to see your face. You can trust me, CP. You know that.

CP is typing …

I know I can. Just … just promise me you will call me from the airport after you get it. I need you to promise me that, Clementine. I need to explain some things. Once you get the puzzle completed, you might not understand.

I furrow my brow. What is he so afraid of? CP has told me he's not disfigured, that he's not Shrek. Okay, so he didn't say that, but he said he's an average guy, so I can safely say he's not Shrek.

I promise I will call you. I can't wait to see you.

I don't know how else I can reassure him, but I know every word I'm saying to him is true. I'm falling for this man I've never seen, and to anyone else, this would be an absurd lack of caution on my part.

Or sheer stupidity.

But all I know is when I talk to CP, everything makes sense. For the first time in my life, my attraction has grown from CP's thoughts, his words, and his cleverness.

My heart is falling for his mind, his heart, and his soul.

No picture required.

I don't need to see him to *know* him. I know what drives him crazy, like how he can't deal with indecisive people or extreme plastic packaging that no human can open without a saw. I know he's a horrible dancer and loves taking long walks in the countryside with Lucy. I know we share the same sense of humor.

I know he loves M&M's and is jealous of all the flavors we have in America, and his favorite Christmas treat is a Christmas pudding. I know he's passionate about Arsenal football and playing polo. I had to tease him about the polo thing. It made him sound oh-so-posh, and he told me he's only posh if he's in an all-white uniform.

CP even told me he's expected to go into the family

business upon graduation. I remember he got sidetracked after that comment, so I don't know what the family business is, but he didn't seem passionate about having to work for them.

And I'm able to talk to CP about all of my idiosyncrasies, like my love of *Shrek* movies and how I hate mean-spirited people. He knows I worry I'll never find a job with antiques. He knows I don't like crispy taco shells because I got a fragment of one stuck in between my teeth and it hurt and I can't get past it, even though it happened when I was six. He knows I hate eating fish and love anything with marshmallows. I've told him about my parents, how my dad is a chief financial officer for a company in Phoenix and my mom is a preschool teacher, and I told him of my childhood adventures with Paisley growing up in Phoenix. I also informed him it's a myth that Phoenix is full of only old people, thank you very much.

CP knows my most guarded secret, too. Well, besides the tumor one. Okay, my second most-guarded secret.

I don't like the Harry Potter books.

Luckily, he forgave me for that one.

But that is what makes us different: the way we can talk about everything and anything for hours, unfiltered, one hundred percent real.

I've never had these kinds of conversations with any other guy.

The thing is, after having them with CP, I don't want to have them with anyone else.

I put my phone down and gaze at the desert landscape that is rolling by out the window as we head back to my parents' place in Scottsdale. I take in the stucco and mountains and cactus, loving everything that makes up the landscape of the Southwest. Normally, I cherish my visits home, not only to see my mom and dad, but to bask in the desert that I've always known and loved.

Today, however, is different.

I can't wait to get to the airport.

Because when I'm there, CP is going to send me the pieces to complete the puzzle.

I draw an excited breath of air. The fact that CP is willing to reveal his true self to me marks a significant step for both of us.

One that will change everything.

CHAPTER 6
THE COMPLETE PICTURE

"Okay, out with it. Who is the boy?"

I blink. Paisley and I are sitting in Sky Harbor International Airport, waiting for our flight back to San Jose.

I try to ignore the flush climbing up my neck and take a swig out of my water bottle instead.

"What boy?"

"Exactly! What boy?" Paisley asks.

"Why on earth do you think there's a boy involved?"

Paisley lets out an exasperated groan. "You keep checking your phone every five seconds."

"Oh my God, so if I'm looking at my phone, it means I'm waiting for some *guy* to text me?"

Okay, she totally doesn't have to know she's bang on with that comment.

"Clem. You are my sister. You've been weird this whole time, since we left for Phoenix yesterday. You read your phone and laugh and smile before manically texting back. But the telltale sign is the blush you get when you're doing it. You're smitten with somebody, and I can't believe you haven't told me!"

"I haven't told anybody!" I blurt out.

Crap.

Paisley's eyes pop wide open. "There is a guy!"

How do I begin to explain so Paisley doesn't freak out and think some serial killer is going to come after me? How do I tell her I haven't met CP in person, yet I'm falling for him, without sounding crazy?

I bite my lower lip. Paisley—rightfully so—will think I'm acting rashly. How can I know someone without having met him, let alone have such strong feelings? She'll say it's infatuation, that I have no clue who I'm really dealing with and I should grow up and quit acting like a teenage girl with a crush.

Except I have communicated with him—via text, WhatsApp, private messages, or long emails—every day, for nearly two months. I've also talked to him on the phone. I talk to CP more than I talk to Paisley.

"It's, um, complicated," I say.

"Shit, he's not married, is he?"

"No!"

Paisley exhales. "Is he older? If he's as old as Dad, I'll be kind of creeped out. I mean, if you love him and everything, I'll accept it, but I'm just being honest here."

"Oh my God, stop it."

"A professor?"

"If you've seen my professors, you know that is a big fat no."

"Then tell me!"

My phone buzzes in my hand.

I gasp aloud when I look down. It's a notification from CP.

I'm about to see him for the first time.

"Excuse me," I say, getting up as excitement shoots down my spine.

"What? Where are you going?"

"I need to take this, but I promise, Paisley, I'll tell you everything soon."

I stand up, and Paisley scowls at me.

"By soon you better mean you'll tell me everything by the time the flight attendants come out with drinks and peanuts!"

I ignore her and walk down a few gates, to one where the board shows a flight to Chicago has just departed, leaving it deserted. I sink down in one of the faux leather chairs and steel myself. This is the moment I've been waiting for: to see if his picture matches the one I've been painting in my head.

I swipe open my message. CP has attached a picture of his eyes, which are a piercing shade of blue.

I study the picture, and a memory begins to surge to the surface. I furrow my brow as I study the eyes. They are sad. I can see that.

Wait.

I've seen these eyes before. I start sorting through my memories, much like Sherlock Holmes does on the BBC version of the show, things coming in and out. I keep flipping through them until I get the one I want.

My mind goes back to the day in the library when Chelsea had her tabloids out.

These eyes belong to the Golden Prince.

I drop my phone, sending it crashing to the floor.

This whole thing is nothing more than a freaking charade. I have no idea who I'm talking to. None.

Everything has been a lie. When it came time to show his face, he sent me a photo of Prince Christian.

CP.

Christian.

I'm going to throw up.

I slide down to the floor, grabbing my phone. I sit against the chair, using it for support, and I Google Prince Christian with a shaking hand. His serious face appears on the screen, and I scroll through his Wiki profile, which gives his name as Prince Christian Phillip, House of Chadwick.

I begin violently shaking. CP Chadwick? He lied about his whole identity to fool me? To take advantage of me? Or to get me to fall for him and then reveal he's a married man? A psycho? To try and eventually steal money from me?

I try to breathe, but I feel like I can't.

CP is typing …

Please call me, Clementine. I need to explain.

Call me.

I find my breath as anger rips through every inch of me. Seeing this person—whoever he is—type me a message has lit the firecracker in me.

And now this fraud is about to get the explosion.

I pull up his number in my contacts and tap the dial icon.

"Clementine," his familiar voice answers on the first ring. "Clement—"

"You lying bastard!" I yell at him, causing some people walking by in the terminal to stop and stare at me, but I don't give a shit. "Prince Christian? You stole his identity to try and deceive me?"

"What?" CP says, shock resonating in his deep voice. "Is that what you think?"

"I'm such an idiot. I hate myself right now. I hope you're happy that you've completely ripped me apart with this. I belie—"

"Clementine, listen to me. I *am* Prince Christian; I can prove it. We can FaceTime right—"

I laugh manically, as I'm moving into hysteria now, and he stops speaking mid-sentence. "Stop it. Just stop. You probably think I'm a stupid American, but I'm not anymore. How could you? To think I've told you things I've never told anyone! ANYONE! You must have been laughing your ass off, whoever the hell you are!"

"I am telling you the truth. Please. You need to listen to me," the stranger says firmly.

"Don't you ever tell me to listen to you again," I roar back. "CP Chadwick. Very clever."

"I *am* Christian Phillip. Our house is the House of Chadwick. I'm not lying."

"Oh, shut up!" I yell. "Everything coming out of your mouth is some sick fabrication."

"Explain to me why I would spend hours talking to you if this was all a fabrication? I meant every word I said to you. Every. Single. One."

"How should I know how your sick mind works? I bet you really loved the tumor bit. That must have added some dramatic flair."

"Don't," he says, his voice deepening with anger, "make light of that. Ever."

"Don't you tell me what to say or do," I fight back. "In fact, I don't want you to talk to me ever again."

"Clementine, don't say that."

"The game is over; don't you see that? Your fun is up, whoever you are."

"You promised me you would listen to me," he pleads. "I know you're shocked. I know it's unsettling."

"You," I say with a shaking voice, "don't know anything."

"Clementine, I car—"

"You do not. Don't say you care; don't you dare."

He falls silent for a moment. "I was falling for you."

His words slice through my heart, ripping it in half. The hysteria evaporates in that instant, and a crushing, horrific pain replaces it.

"I'm done with this. I hope you've enjoyed being a life ruiner. Don't text me. Don't call me. You do not exist—"

I choke on the last word as I realize I will never talk to him again.

"I was falling for you, too," I say, my voice thick with unshed tears. "You just broke me."

Then I hang up.

I'm sobbing as I block his number from my phone. I block his email address and his account on WhatsApp.

The worst, however, is when I get to Instagram, where it all began with what I thought was a genuine message about the work I was doing with art.

My finger hovers over the key to block him, wishing I could, even if only for a second, believe that he was Prince Christian instead of a lie.

But I can't.

The complete picture gave me the truth.

I hit the button to block him.

CP never existed.

With that thought, I bury my face in my hands and weep as if I'll never stop.

CHAPTER 7

ELEVEN HOURS

I blankly stare at the laptop parked on my knees. I'm binge-watching all the episodes of *Is it Love?,* where last season's lead tells multiple girls lies about how special they are and how much he loves them, only to take it all back.

All lies, I think, blinking back tears.

I'm on the third episode, and girls are crying right and left as he's telling them none of them have the potential to be love. Each season, Bryn and Chelsea and I sit around on Tuesday nights, sipping wine and eating pizza and rolling our eyes at these women crying over men they don't know.

Little did I know I'd understand this all too well. At least they met Tom. I don't even know who I was falling for.

The semi-permanent lump in my throat grows. I'm going to bawl again. I've done nothing but since I removed *him* from my life. I can't bring myself to say his name because I know that isn't even real. I told Paisley the horrible story in fits of sobs that were so bad a gate agent brought me tissues and a bottle of water.

One of the things I love about my sister is that in a time of crisis, she doesn't ask a million questions or judge. In fact, she took me straight back to her apartment in San Francisco, said I was spending the night, and opened a bottle of rosé, and after we downed that; we opened another one. Her husband, Evan, offered to track *him* down and punch *him* in the face, which made me cry again because they love me so much.

Either that, or me drinking a bottle of rosé by myself was making me a wee bit more emotional than usual.

Evan brought me back to Palo Alto this afternoon, worse for wear with a swollen face and a headache from getting drunk on wine. I schlepped myself upstairs to an empty apartment. Chelsea was out shopping with her mom today and planned to spend the night at her family home. Bryn stays at Graham's on Saturdays. Neither one of them know, although I know they were sad I didn't come home Friday night so we could celebrate my good diagnosis together.

Now it's me and Bear.

I try to swallow the tears away. I've got to stop crying for a man I never really knew.

"I wanted so badly to believe you were real," I whisper to myself.

A single tear runs down my face, past the side of my nose, and splashes onto the keyboard, followed by another.

I grab another tissue from Chelsea's box and dab at my eyes, hoping to keep the flood at bay.

Don't cry, I will myself. *You've got to stop crying.*

Suddenly, there's a knock at the door. Bear leaps up, barking as he races to the living room. I don't move. Whoever it is, they can go away.

The knocking doesn't cease—rather, it gets louder and more determined—and Bear keeps barking.

Shit. I'm going to have to deal with this so the neighbors don't complain about the noise.

I toss my rumpled tissue on the bed and get up by sheer force of will, as my body is exhausted beyond belief.

"Quiet," I say, and Bear immediately ceases barking.

The pounding on the door begins again.

I go to the peephole and press my eye against it, curious as to who is knocking so relentlessly.

As soon as I see who is standing on the other side, I step back in shock.

No. No. It can't be. I'm going crazy. I'm losing all my shit. It ... can't be.

It can't.

I take a second look as he knocks again, shaking as I do.

Oh, my God.

I throw open the door and gasp, my hands flying to my mouth. My knees actually give out, and I'm about to drop to the floor when strong hands reach out and grab me, catching me from falling.

I stare up at the man who is holding me, my heart pounding. I can't breathe. I can't think. I can't do anything except stare at him in disbelief.

Because the man holding me up is Prince Christian of Wales, third in line to the throne of the United Kingdom. Two men are with him, ones I assume to be his security detail, but they step back as CP holds me.

"I've got you," he says, in that deep British voice I know by heart. "I won't let you fall."

It's CP's voice.

"You ... y-you're ... " I can't get the words out. I'm

shaking so hard CP has to put both hands on my arms to try and steady me, and I tremble violently in his grasp.

Bear begins to circle in excitement, barking as he does, but I ignore him.

"Yes, I'm a prince," he says softly, his piercing blue eyes full of sadness. He stares down at me, as he's incredibly tall, at least six foot three, and I stare up at him in shock. The beautiful golden curls, the full lips, the long eyelashes. His gaze is moving over my face as if he's trying to imprint every feature of mine in his memory.

"I haven't slept since our phone call," he says, his voice thick.

I don't say anything. I can't speak. I can't believe he's here, that CP has come all the way to Palo Alto to stand before me.

He was telling the truth, I think, reeling. *CP is a prince.*

"I have flown eleven hours to come here, to tell you I am CP," he continues. "I never meant to hurt you. God, that is the last thing I would ever do. But for the first time in my life, I felt normal. I wasn't a prince. I was CP to you, and that was all I needed to be."

"You're a prince," I finally manage to get out. "My God, this changes everything."

He winces as I say the word "prince."

"I know it does," CP says, his voice full of regret. "But I want you to know you were the one real thing in my life, the one person who liked me for *me.* I never lied to you. I used my initials, my house name, but I never lied. I didn't reveal everything, but every word from my lips to you was the truth."

To my surprise, he releases my arms. "Actually, there is one thing I lied about. I'm not falling for you. I already love you," he says quietly, his eyes filling with tears.

CP turns and goes to the door, putting his hand on the knob to leave.

"You're a prince; do you realize what this means?" I cry out, stopping him.

He turns around and gazes at me, his eyes rimmed with red. "Yes. It changes everything."

"No, it means you're real. You're CP, and you're *real,*" I say, my voice cracking. "You exist. What we had—our world, us, it's real."

His eyes take on a questioning look. "You mean … you … "

"I love you," I blurt out. "Yes, you dropping this prince thing is kind of a bombshell, I'll give you that, but compared to you not being real? I don't care. I feel as though I have you back." Tears begin falling freely. "Don't you see? I don't see a prince standing before me. I see CP. The man I fell for, without ever seeing your face. You're the man I love. You. As CP."

A gasp escapes his lips. My chest is rising and falling rapidly, and my heart is about to explode.

CP pulls me into his arms, his mouth moving against mine in a desperate kiss. The second his warm mouth parts mine, every part of me comes alive, acutely, wonderfully, richly *alive.* His tongue is rapidly taking everything I can give. God, he can kiss. I've never been kissed with such passion in my life. CP's kiss is hot and seeking, and I respond by rapidly matching his kisses, causing a groan to escape from his full lips. The second I hear that desire, heat flashes through me.

I feel his stubble burn against my face and his large hands spanning my back, then into my hair. I slide my hands up to his face, his beautiful, perfect face, and I rake my fingers through his gorgeous curls. I inhale the scent of his skin, which smells crisp and clean, like he just took a shower. I lose myself in his arms, his scent, his kiss, knowing what is happening in this moment is different than anything I've ever known before.

CP tears his mouth away from mine, putting his hands on my face and sensually caressing it as he gazes down at me.

"Why did you stop, CP?" I ask breathlessly.

"Christian. You may call me Christian now. My life, with being a royal, is complicated, Clementine," he says, breathing hard. "Nothing with me is normal. I want to take you to bed and make love to you for the rest of the night, but you have to know this means something to me, if we do this. You aren't a fling to me. You're everything. But no matter how badly I want you, and God, I do, I can't let passion take you to a place you might regret being."

Tears of love for CP—err, Christian—fall from my eyes. I reach up and touch his face, lightly sweeping my fingertips across his cheek, committing the feel of his skin to my memory.

"I've dealt with a brain tumor," I say, my eyes never leaving his. "Handling your life might be hard, a challenge, but I know what I'm getting into, and I'm not scared."

"You don't know though," he whispers painfully, pressing his head to mine. "You say you do, but you don't."

"Then you'll teach me," I say simply. "We'll face it together."

I lift his head and take a step back so I can look into his eyes. "I love you. You are Christian to me, not Your Royal Highness, not a prince. You're my Christian, and right now, I want to make love to you. Love me, Christian. Love me as Clementine."

The mood in his eyes shifts from concern to desire. With

one swift move, he lifts me up, and I wrap my legs around him. He kisses me hard on the mouth, and I kiss him back furiously.

"Where's the bedroom?" Christian murmurs against my mouth.

"Second door on the left. Bed is on the right side of the wall."

Christian resumes kissing me, his tongue dancing against mine. I can't explain how natural this feels, as if I was meant to kiss this man, as if his body was made to fit with mine.

We reach my room, and Christian pauses to shut the door with one hand behind him. He lays me down on the bed, and we begin to discard our clothing. I pull off the navy quarter-zip he has on and reach for his T-shirt. He kneels for a moment, ripping it off and throwing it aside.

I bite my lip as I study him, his skin ivory and muscular, his abdominals and pecs sculpted magnificently, with that sexy V that tapers down to his waist. Christian lowers himself toward me, his tongue tracing my lips as his fingertips reach for the waistband of my yoga pants.

I gasp as he drops his fingertips down lower, reaching the edge of my panties, his touch teasing me with what is to come.

I run my hands up his forearms, over the sexy veins running through his pale skin, and pure need to entwine my body with his runs through me.

Christian kisses me, his hands continuing to play with the lace on my underwear, and I shudder from his touch.

"You're so beautiful," he whispers against my lips.

I kiss him back, gently and sweetly, as our bodies wrap around each other. I hook one leg across his lower back, and Christian moves his fingertips lower, down the inside of my thigh, teasing me, blissfully torturing me, and letting me know tonight isn't going to be rushed.

I reach for the bottom of my T-shirt, tugging it up. Christian stops to help me and I push myself up so I can take it off. I toss it on the floor next to the bed, and I see Christian draw a sharp intake of breath as I'm now baring my breasts to him.

He flashes me a wicked grin. "No bra."

"No," I say, grinning mischievously at him.

Christian draws me to his body, and as we sit up, I wrap myself around him again. God, this feels instinctively right. I know I am meant to love this man. My breasts are pressed against his chest, his huge hands spanning my back, making me feel warm and protected.

His eyes lock on mine. "I love you," he whispers.

To my surprise, he brushes his lips ever-so-sweetly over my right eye.

Where I have paralysis.

"I love every single magnificent part of you," he murmurs against my skin.

I fight back tears. That kiss, that pausing to take that moment to address my flaw, tells me everything I'll ever need to know about Christian and what we have.

This is love.

As he begins to kiss my neck, my collarbones, and my breasts, I arch back into his hands, closing my eyes and letting the happy tears fall.

I dip my head into his hair, his wonderful, golden locks, and take a deep breath, breathing in the intimate scent of his hair, his cologne, and feeling the heat from his body.

"I love you," I whisper, "I love you, Christian Chadwick."

I feel his whole body harden against mine when I say

his name. He lays me back on the bed, closing his mouth over mine, and as our bodies move together, I give everything I am to the man I love.

CHAPTER 8

RED WINE AND FIRE PITS

"I feel like I was made to be here," I murmur, gently pressing my lips to Christian's warm chest. He has me cradled in the crook of his arm, holding me tight, after we made love for a second time.

The first time was hot and desperate, the actions of two people who thought they'd never see each other again. It was full of raw need to explore this passion, to discover each other, to express our emotions and physical desires.

That was the first time.

The second time was all about love. Christian was gentle. It was slow and beautiful and filled with the sweetest kisses I have experienced. I felt adored by this man, cherished, as if I were the most beautiful woman he had ever seen or touched.

Now I'm in his arms, listening to his heart beat, feeling the warmth of his skin against mine. I have never felt more content than I do at this moment.

"You're a perfect fit," Christian comments as he plays with my hair. "I might have to keep you here forever."

I laugh softly, and he does, too.

I roll over so I'm propped up on his chest. I take a moment to stare at him, this beautiful man that I love.

Christian cocks an eyebrow at me. "What?"

"Your eyes," I say, studying them carefully. "You're happy."

A slow smile tugs at the corner of his full lips. "I am."

"I can tell. Your eyes shine when you are happy."

"You make me happy," he says. "I've never felt more alive than I do right now. I'm not a prince. I'm Christian. Your Christian."

As if to punctuate the point, he brushes his lips to mine.

"You didn't even have to play the prince card to get me," I say, grinning at him.

He laughs, that beautiful, deep, throaty laugh that I love to hear.

"I knew that wouldn't mean anything to you. Though I was fully prepared to play the art card to win your heart. I would have tempted you with seeing a van Dyck painting in Windsor Castle."

I burst out laughing.

"I'm in love with a man who actually *has* the keys to the castle."

"One of the perks of the title."

"I can't imagine what your life is like," I say softly. "Born into such history and tradition; your place in the world was pre-defined before you arrived in it."

I see the lightness fade from his eyes.

"I don't want to sound ungrateful," Christian says as if he's trying to carefully choose his words, "as I was born to great privilege. Nothing, however, comes without a price. I'm lucky to never have to worry about finances or how to pay for an education at a prestigious university. I'm lucky to have these amazing historical palaces to call home and to have the ability to travel the world. I can serve the people, both in the military and through the work of the monarchy, which is an honor. But my role in life was decided for me before I could speak. I can't go off and be a surgeon or a private investigator or follow a career dream outside of the few choices I have, because I'm a prince. The ability to pursue a career of my choosing is not in my hands. It's never been mine."

I stay silent as I have a feeling some long-repressed emotions are about to come tumbling out. I link my fingers through his, holding his hand just as he did long-distance for me when I was awaiting my test results. I let Christian know, without a word, that I'm walking with him right now in whatever he is about to say.

"As a public figure, I understand that people will be interested in what I do, the things I say, and where I go. But it's extreme. Ever since I was a little boy, I've had photographers snapping away at me. I remember the first day of nursery school, holding my father's hand, with nothing but cameras going off. I was more scared of that than leaving Father for class."

I notice he says nothing about Queen Antonia and make a note to come back to that topic later.

"Everything I do is discussed, speculated on, written about," Christian says. "The press has been decent about leaving me alone while at Cambridge, but then there's everyone else. I'm stared at when I walk to class, stared at in class. When I go to a pub, people want to be near me not because I'm funny or smart or interesting, but because of the title. They want to know a prince. Girls want to date a prince. Very few can see me. If they do, they must go along with all the crap that comes with me, like my protection officers. When I lived in the hall, my protection officers lived in the next room. Now that I'm in a house, they have a room. They are downstairs in your car park now."

I sit straight up. "You mean your protection officers have been waiting for us to finish having sex?" I blurt out, more than slightly embarrassed by that thought.

Christian's face lights up. "They'll give me a high-five for getting a beautiful red-headed American to take me on."

I groan, and he laughs.

"So … when you decided to fly over here, they came with you?"

He exhales. "Yes. I'm never without them, essentially."

I can't imagine. There are men sitting in the parking lot of my building, waiting for Christian to leave, and that is what they do for a living.

Stay alert to protect the prince.

"If I met a girl I wanted to go out with, they would drive her to one place, like a restaurant, have her walk through it, get in another car, and only then be taken to see me. All so she wouldn't be in the spotlight. Not many will put up with that."

I squeeze his hand again, and he squeezes it back.

"The press is going to come after me once I graduate in June," Christian continues. "They've already started, as you know, with the curry and hoarder bit."

"That was the dumbest thing ever," I say, rolling my eyes. "That and the Xander the Philanderer title."

"Well, my part was fabricated, but Xander *is* a philanderer," he says, his eyes sparkling.

I burst out laughing, which I punctuate with a hiccup, making a ridiculous loud sound, which makes him really laugh, a true, deep-from-within-his-soul laugh.

"Do you hiccup laugh?"

"I do," I say. Then I arch an eyebrow at him. "Are you willing to take that on?"

"I don't know. I don't think hiccup laughing is allowed in the House of Chadwick."

I think on this for a moment.

They probably have strict protocol.

Like no hiccup laughs or eating Chips Ahoys in the royal bed.

"Kidding," he says. "As long as you don't do it in a walkabout."

"Oh, that's when you shake hands and chat with people waiting to see you at an appearance."

Christian grins. "Ah, very good."

"I've watched my fair share of prince movies on TV, thank you very much."

"Oh God, those are the worst. If you based my life off those, I'd be running around all the time with a sash on and I would have met you after you came to work in the palace as a tutor for my deceased brother's children or something."

Now I'm dying laughing. "You've totally watched some."

"Indeed," he admits, then he continues. "The press has been curious about me because, unlike Xander, I don't do anything. When Xander is on his leave from the army, he loves the posh nightclubs in London. He likes beautiful girls. Xander has a tight-knit group about him, like I do, so you don't see stories leaked to the press, but they always know where to go to get a picture of him leaving a club with a beautiful society girl. But me? I prefer an American girl," he adds, shooting me a sly look.

I blush.

"I also prefer a pub, where you can talk. I don't like the nightclub scene at all."

"Duh, that's because you can't dance. Who wants that reported to the media?" I tease.

He flashes me a huge smile. "Do you know what I love about you, Ace?"

My heart becomes a puddle when I see the look of love on his face.

"You give me shit."

"I wouldn't be much of a girlfriend if I didn't." I stop. "Wait, am I your girlfriend?"

Christian squeezes my hand. "Yes. I don't waste time. Meet girl for first time in person, make love to her twice, declare relationship."

We both laugh, but then I turn serious.

"Yet with us it feels right," I say.

"It does," he says softly. "But you do need to understand what you are getting into. Once we go public—which I don't want to do right away—the media will be relentless. Wherever you are living, they'll lie in wait for you. Photographers will chase you, and it can be dangerous. You will be adored one minute and kicked about the next, with horrible, nasty things said about you. And that's just the public and the media. My family is a whole other level of insanity you will have to cope with. That is why I spend so much time in private or in places where nobody can find me. The media thinks I'm a recluse, but I don't want to share everything with the world, especially you. I want this time to be ours, and I'll fiercely protect it for us. You have my word."

I'm touched by his words. I'm about to speak when he continues.

"Clementine, I should shove you away out of love and not bring you into this world. You don't deserve what your life will be with me."

I gently take his hand and place it over my heart. "Do you feel that?" I ask softly.

"Yes."

"You have made it come alive," I say. "I love you. Your life comes with you, and I'm aware of that. But I know you will help me navigate it. I'm not saying it won't be hard, and some days I will certainly hate it, but I will never hate the choice I made to be with you."

I notice his eyes have grown watery. "I don't deserve you."

"You do."

He sits up, keeping his hand over my heart, and places a loving kiss on my lips.

"Now I need the primer on your family. Not the Wiki page version," I tease. "I need to know the inside stories."

"Let's save that for after dinner," Christian says. "In fact, we should be going."

"What? You just said you don't want to be public, so where are we going?"

Christian runs his hand over my hair, sending shivers of delight down my spine.

"I have a suite at the Ritz-Carlton Half Moon Bay," he says, referring to the luxury resort on the Pacific Ocean. "Let me show you."

He reaches down for his jeans on the floor, retrieves his phone, and then swipes open the resort's web page.

"I have this room," he says, showing me the suite. "Don't worry, my protection officers have the suite next door, so they won't be waiting in the car," he quips.

"Shut up," I say, leaning in to study the picture on the Ritz-Carlton website. "Oh! It has a fire pit!" I say excitedly.

"My own private fire pit," Christian says. "I booked for one night, as I was sure you would toss me out the second you could, but I think I need to extend this stay a few days."

"What about Cambridge?" I ask, concerned.

"I'm feeling rather ill. Might have to miss classes on Monday and Tuesday. How are you feeling, Clementine? Feverish?"

Why yes, I am, I think, wanting nothing more than to hide away in this suite with Christian.

"Yes. Dehydrated, too. And chilled."

"Hmm. Sounds like wine and a roaring fire are just what you need."

"I might be able to keep a little food down," I say, taking his phone from him and tapping on all the luxurious things offered at the hotel.

"Room service. So, we don't spread our disease to others. We're being thoughtful in that regard."

"Yes," I say. "Oh! They allow dogs! We can bring Bear," I say. "I'm sorry, but I can't leave him alone here. I'll pay the fee if he can come with us."

"Um, I think—and I'm going out on a limb here—I can cover the fee for Bear," Christian teases. "I love that you are a dog person. We're absolutely bringing Bear."

As if he has been following along to our conversation, Bear lifts his head and barks from his dog bed on the floor, then comes up and drops his head on Christian's thigh.

"That's right; you are spending the weekend at the Ritz. Don't tell Lucy. She'll be incredibly upset she didn't get to come," he teases, referring to his own dog as he affectionately rubs Bear's head.

"How will you explain this bill to the palace people?" I ask, not knowing what they are called or if they review his bills.

Now he snorts. "Please, it will still be cheaper than

Xander's nightclub tabs; they have no leg to stand on. Even more so because I'm not stumbling out drunk in Palo Alto."

"I'm glad you aren't like Xander."

"What, you don't fancy being the queen one day? You realize you are settling with the spare, you know."

Whoa.

I realize with Christian, *whoa* moments are going to be frequent, where I'm reminded that while he's Christian to me, he is His Royal Highness, Prince Christian, son of King Arthur of the United Kingdom, and brother to Prince Alexander of Wales, the future king.

"No, I don't 'fancy' that, as you say, but I also don't fancy a man who runs around with a lot of women, getting trashed at trendy nightclubs. I do, however, fancy a sexy blond man with gorgeous curls and an affinity for creating anagrams. A man who has a gorgeous, cut body from playing soccer and polo, who is clever and brilliant, and who flew eleven hours, and across an ocean, to see me. Now those things, Christian, are turn-ons. I might have to jump you as soon as we get to our room. I get hot just thinking about you taking a pub quiz."

He roars with laughter, and I smile, loving that I make him happy and carefree.

"It's football, not soccer; British lesson number one complete," he teases.

"Oh, we'll debate that later," I say. Then something hits me. "Hey, how did you find me, by the way? Did you have your people do it?"

He snorts. "Um, no, I used Google, not MI5. You need to button up your privacy, by the way. It was very easy to find your address."

"Well, that's a little disturbing, but I'm glad Google

worked for you," I quip as I continue to peruse the resort webpage.

I spy something that makes me giddy.

"Christian!" I gasp, turning the phone toward him. "They have s'mores kits for the fire pits! We can have s'mores after dinner!"

Christian furrows his brow. "I've never had a s'more."

"What?" I shriek, which makes Bear bark. "How is that possible?"

"I don't know. Chef never whipped those up at Kensington Palace while I was growing up. I'll have a word with him the next time I'm home."

Whoa count: Two.

"I'll be your s'mores concierge tonight," I say.

"I think you'll be my concierge for many things," he says, dipping his head and kissing me.

As I kiss him back, I know we are beginning a crazy adventure together. He's a prince who lives in England. I'm a girl about to graduate from Stanford. Logistics alone says there will be a long road ahead. Where will I work? What will Christian do when he graduates? Will he go into the military like a lot of royals do? Where will we live? And how many years will we be apart?

I break the kiss and look into his beautiful eyes. I realize it will be hard, but I have faith we both want the same thing: to be together.

Somehow, we'll figure it out.

Starting with wine, s'mores, and a roaring fire on a private patio tonight.

CHAPTER 9

CHECKING THE DIARIES

"Christian?"

"Hmmm?" Christian asks, affectionately nuzzling me.

For a moment, I'm distracted by the feel of his breath against my neck. I'm sitting on his lap in an Adirondack chair in front of the fire pit. Christian has wrapped me in a thick, cozy blanket, and we're sipping wine and watching the waves roll in from the Pacific Ocean on our private terrace at the resort.

"Is this real?" I ask quietly. "Because it feels like a dream. If it is a dream, I'm afraid I'm going to wake up and you'll be gone."

Christian slides his hand up underneath my hair, to the back of my head, cradling it lovingly in his palm. He draws my head toward his, easing my lips open in a gentle kiss. I taste lush cabernet wine on his tongue and inhale his crisp, clean cologne that is mingling with the salty ocean breezes and smoke from the roaring fire.

The moment is wonderfully, breathtakingly magical.

And absolutely perfect.

"It's real," he whispers against my mouth.

I lose myself in his kiss, in this romantic moment I know I'll never forget. Then I break the kiss and stare deeply into his eyes.

"How is this going to work?"

"I thought we'd finish off this bottle of wine first before joining Bear inside," Christian says, nodding his head in the direction of the suite door behind us. "I thought he might want to enjoy his room service delicacy alone, much like I'm enjoying my time alone with my own delicacy right here," he teases.

I reach over and flick him on the forehead, and that rich laugh escapes his throat.

"You know that's not what I mean."

Christian links his free hand with mine, dragging his thumb back and forth across the top of my hand.

"We'll consult our diaries and block out time to see each other. I refuse to let the continental United States and an ocean keep us apart. It's a miracle I found you, and now that I've been with you, I'm not settling for long separations."

"Wait, diaries?" I ask quizzically.

"Well, yes. Schedules."

"Oh! You mean a planner," I say.

"We also call them diaries."

"Here, that would be a personal account of your day. Like today mine would say, 'Dear Diary. Today was a great day. I found out that CP is real. His name is Christian, and not only did I kiss him passionately upon meeting him, but I told him I love him and had the hottest, most emotionally intense sex I've ever had.'"

Even in the darkness, I can see he's blushing.

"You realize, Ace, we're going to have to re-write our history for how we met for everyone else."

I decide to tease him. "You mean our real story wouldn't play well with our parents?"

He begins to laugh. A happy shiver shoots down my spine from that rich, deep sound.

"I can't imagine telling Her Majesty this one. Mum, I met a gorgeous American on Instagram. I fell in love with her without meeting her first. Then we had this huge misunderstanding, a horrible row, and I had to fly off to America to prove I was real. As soon as I saw her, as soon as I looked into her green-gray eyes, I told her I loved her. Then I took her to bed, made mad, passionate love to her multiple times, and now she's my girlfriend."

Now I'm dying. "When you say it like that, Christian, you make it sound freakishly crazy."

"It is crazy," Christian says, smiling at me. "Mum would lose her head if she ever knew this story."

"I can't imagine what my overprotective parents would say." I imagine them freaking out about, oh, sleeping with a man most would consider a stranger within minutes of meeting him. "Or even my friends. This isn't a normal way to start a relationship."

"I know. Yet I have no doubts. Absolutely none."

Warmth surges through me. "Neither do I. It's insane how we connected in our messages and email conversations."

"I always felt guilty because I could at least see your pictures," Christian says. "I knew how beautiful you were before we started talking. I could picture your face when we chatted on messenger, and I fell a bit more with each conversation. But you—you fell for me without seeing me."

"I did. I fell in love with your mind and this," I say,

putting my hand over his chest. "I fell in love with your heart."

Christian kisses me again, a kiss telling me how much he loves me.

"Okay. Our story. Let's write it, love."

Love. I think my heart just did a cartwheel with that one.

"Okay. We met in an online art community," I say.

"Not far from the truth."

"We communicated every day," I continue, "to the sleep detriment of both of us."

"Also true."

"We had deep intellectual conversations and connected over our concerns for the world and finding our place in it."

"Nice. I see you edited out our life-changing discussion on sugar cookies: overrated or not."

"I still haven't forgiven you for saying they are overrated," I say, giving him the evil eye. "They are the greatest cookies ever. Not only are they delicious, but they can be amazing works of art. Decadent, delectable, sugared, glorious art."

"If that's true, then why do you keep talking about Chips Ahoy?"

"Because you have to get the perfect sugar cookie from a great bakery or it's crap. Didn't you read that whole conversation we had?"

"Sorry. That might have been the one where I fell asleep and you continued the conversation you were having via WhatsApp so I'd find it when I woke up. Which I found immensely charming, even if you forgot to message me the critical bakery part of the story."

"I'm going to look for that message to prove you wrong. I absolutely told you that, and you must have skipped over my brilliant descriptions of the glory of sugar cookies."

"No, I've read every word you've ever sent to me, so you're wrong," Christian says, a smile tugging at the corner of that mouth of his in a playful, sexy way that makes me want to kiss him.

But we have to finish our storyline first.

"Okay, I am not wrong, you are, but that's for later. You're losing focus. We're supposed to be writing our meet-cute."

"Meet what?" Christian asks, a confused expression on his face.

"You know, in those cheesy TV romance movies. The hero and heroine have to meet in a cute way to set up the love story."

"Oh. In other words, the impossibly unrealistic way of meeting like in those ghastly royal movies."

"Hmm. Like the prince who conceals his identity from the unsuspecting American heroine?"

Christian laughs and reaches for his wine glass. "Oh, touché, Ace. Touché."

"Anyway," I say, smiling as he takes another sip of wine, "we connected so well we decided to meet, and you came to America to see me. We spent a weekend talking and getting to know each other, and it was the best weekend ever. Then we decided I should come to Cambridge to see you and continue our dialogue to see where it goes."

"I see we are omitting the made wild, multiple orgasm-inducing, passionate love part and the 'you are the sexiest woman I've ever been with' part from our story."

Now I'm the one who is blushing.

"Stop. But, yes, we talked and talked and were a very good boy and girl. We didn't even do this," I say, sliding my hands to his face and opening his lips with mine, giving him a slow, deep kiss and teasing him with my tongue. I break it and stare into his eyes. "It was all very proper and chaste, our time in the Bay Area. You might get to kiss me when I come to Cambridge, *if* I let you hold my hand, that is."

I see desire flickering in his blue eyes. "So, I have to court you."

"Yes," I say, flashing him a wicked grin.

"Then we should plan when you are coming over."

Reality hits me. "Christian, I don't know if I can afford a ticket to London. My internship doesn't pay that much, and while my parents are paying for school and rent, I don't have that kind of money in my bank account."

"I'll buy your tickets; I already intended to do that."

"What? The House of Chadwick wouldn't want British taxpayers footing my airfare!"

"No, from my personal account," Christian explains. "My maternal grandfather was a very, very wealthy man who left his only grandchildren—me, Xander, and James, my younger brother—very large trust funds. I have an annual allowance from that, and this is money I choose to spend on you. I'll buy your tickets."

"I'll pay you back," I promise. "As soon as I graduate and find some kind of job, I'll start paying you back."

Christian falls silent for a moment.

"What?" I ask.

"I love you for treating me like a normal guy," he says. "But this is a gift for both of us, one I not only can afford but one I want to give. To make this work, we have to commit to traveling to see each other on a regular basis. I know it will be hard with school, but when can you come to Cambridge?"

"This might be too soon," I say slowly, "but I have a week off for spring break in two weeks."

Christian's face lights up. "Brilliant. You can come spend it with me."

Excitement sweeps through me. "I'm really going to the UK, to see you," I repeat, needing to hear the words aloud to believe this is my life.

"Yes. We'll still keep it secret, but you can stay with me and my roommates."

I grin, as I've already heard all about them. There's Stephen from County Wicklow, Ireland—the heir to a brewing empire—and Charlie, his best friend from his days at Eton College.

"You're sure they won't mind?" I ask.

"No, they'll be thrilled I've brought a girl round at last," Christian says, flashing me a mischievous smile. "Then they'll wonder how the hell a strange bloke like me got a girl like you."

"I can't wait to see your world," I say. "Will you take me to a pub quiz?"

A gust comes in from the ocean, blowing my hair across my face, and Christian gently brushes it back for me.

"Yes. I might even throw in a steak pie. In exchange for a chaste kiss, of course."

A squeal of excitement escapes me. "I'm so excited!"

"For the kiss or the pie?"

"Duh, for the pie," I say, teasing him. "Because I want more than chaste kisses from you."

Christian gazes at me as he tucks a lock of hair behind my ear. "Clementine, remember this won't be a normal visit with a boyfriend," he says, turning serious for a moment. "I can't hold your hand in public. My protection officers will follow us wherever we go. They have a room in the house."

"They live with you," I say, realizing Christian meant it when he said he's never alone.

"Yes. So there's that bit," he says slowly. "Then there's the public. People will take pictures and stare at us, wondering if you are the one who got the 'Golden Prince' to leave his house. Girls will try to approach me, talk or flirt with me, whether you are next to me or not. They make the most of a rare public opportunity."

I hear anguish lacing his voice. He can never go out to a bar and have a drink and have it be as simple as that.

Just a normal bloke, I think, remembering his words to me, *is something Christian can never be.*

But you can with me, I vow. *I will do my best to give you that, the normalcy you crave, like you gave it to me when you found out about my medical tests.*

"I know why you chose to close yourself off from the world," I say quietly. "It's safer that way for you."

"After university, I'm supposed to enter the military, but Father said that was another way for me to hide and he's forbidding it."

He's opened the door for me to ask about his family life. What goes on beyond the beautiful palace walls the rest of the world sees.

"How do you feel about that?"

Christian shifts his gaze to the fire, and I watch as the shadows from the flames dance across his handsome face.

"All royals tend to serve in the military, so I understand it's another pre-determined part of my life that I have to accept."

"Do you want to be in the military?"

"Honestly? It appealed to me," Christian says. "I'd be a service member with a purpose. I want to serve the country that has given me so much. In the military, I'd be another man, no special treatment given to me because I'm a prince. I'd be protected from the press and the public, and I wanted that. It was more time to be normal, at least as normal as life can be for me. My parents, however, think I've made myself too isolated."

"Have you?" I ask gently, running my hand through his golden curls.

"I have had eyes on me since the moment Mum and Dad walked out of the hospital with me cradled in Mum's arms. I find it suffocating to be watched all the time," Christian says, the words coming out in a rush. "I feel like I'm being celebrated for no reason. What have I done? If I go out in London, I'm photographed the whole time, even if I'm in a store like Waitrose buying a bag of crisps. My security detail is following me, people are snapping me with mobile phones, and I swear to God, I just want to be alone to buy the damn crisps."

I continue to stroke his hair, aware the dam is about to burst.

"I don't know what my purpose is," Christian says, his eyes fixated on the flames dancing in front of us. "When I'm in school, I have a purpose. If I go to the army, I'm given a new purpose. But I don't know how to find my life in the monarchy. Do I show up where Mum's secretary tells me to go? What does that do? Shouldn't I do something that has meaning to me? If I'm going to use my name, shouldn't it be for something I'm passionate about, rather than what the king and queen think I should do? I'm a prince, but I have to be *more* than that to be deserving of the life I've been born into. The people expect more, and so do I. I just don't know what more is."

Once I figure it out, will I do it justice like my father does with his work?" he continues, the words continuing to tumble out in a rush. "Can I ever do anything without being judged and watched and written about, if what I'm doing is right or important enough? No, I can't, and when I think about all this being the rest of my life, I suffocate inside. That's when I want to stay inside my house watching quiz shows and dreaming of going to an army base where nobody can bother me. And now that option has been taken away, and it's one more thing I have no choice in, one more reminder that I'm not normal. I'll never be normal, and I don't know how to cope with all of this."

He falls silent and exhales sharply. I lean my head down onto his shoulder, not saying a word, but watching the roaring fire and listening to the surf crash against the shore. I wince as I feel Christian's heart pounding inside his chest, and I know he has carried this burden alone. I know, by the way the words came bursting out, his friends don't know this. I don't even think Xander knows this. Christian tried to be the mature, dutiful son and shove this all down, finding it easier to stay out of the eyes of the world than to bear the consequences of being judged by everyone around him.

I give him a moment to recover, and then I speak from my heart, probably in a way nobody has ever spoken to him before.

"I think," I say softly, "you will find your purpose. You will find something that is meaningful and yours. Not Queen Antonia's programs, not King Arthur's, but something that touches your heart where you can make a difference. Something you'll fight for. You'll challenge people and create something that belongs to you. But you can't find it in your house or by staying away from people. You have to be in the world to find out what it needs.

"You are a prince, but a student prince," I say, continuing. "You haven't been a true working royal, and if you go straight into the military, you delay that. Maybe

King Arthur is trying to let you explore what your future could be so you can find it, Christian. Maybe he wants you to be exposed to all kinds of people and experiences to help you find yourself on that level before going into the military."

Christian remains silent.

"I promise I'll help you find it," I whisper to him.

He slides his fingertips to my chin, tilting my face up toward him. His eyes are now filled with gratitude.

"Thank you," he whispers to me. "For being here. For being you."

He lowers his mouth to mine, kissing me lovingly, slowly moving his warm lips against mine, his tongue gently exploring my mouth, and love for Christian fills every inch of me.

Christian breaks the kiss and brushes his lips against my forehead, and a blissful sigh escapes my lips.

"Father might be as noble as you say," he says, as I tuck my head back down on his chest. "But if Mum is driving this, she wants to use her *Golden Prince* to deflect from the bad press Xander is getting. I think she might have leaked that recluse story to the press to get Father to press me into royal service faster. She says it's to save me from myself. At least that is the story she's spinning."

I sit straight up. "What?" I ask, appalled. "Your mother would do that to you? She actually leaks lies to the media to get you to do what she wants?"

Christian sighs. "I told you my family was a whole other layer to deal with, including my manipulating mother."

My God, it is a TV movie, I think, shocked.

Every time I've seen Queen Antonia on TV or in a glossy celebrity magazine, she is smiling. Always perfect, with her jet-black hair done in an elegant chignon at the nape of her neck, and always dressed in an impeccable suit. She is always bending down and accepting flowers from her adoring well-wishers, looking genuinely happy to be with people.

Unless she is not what she seems.

Whoa Count: Three.

"Are you still in?" Christian asks quietly, interrupting my thoughts.

"What?"

"I've only given you the tip of the iceberg with my family tonight. We're talking a *Titanic*-sized iceberg. It's straight ahead of you, Clementine. Except unlike the *Titanic,* you can avoid this one. I'm giving you fair warning."

"Queen Antonia is not scarier than a brain tumor. I'm solid."

"I love you," Christian says.

"I love you, too."

Christian yawns, and I can see not sleeping has finally caught up with him.

"You need to go to bed," I say.

"Only if you come with me."

"I will, but we have one order of business first."

Christian cocks an eyebrow. "What's that?"

"We have to make a s'more!"

He begins laughing. "Yes, that was the allure of this place. Not the view, not the luxury suite, but the fact that you can make a s'more."

I get off his lap and reach for the s'more kit we ordered. "You will understand once you eat one."

"I can't wait to be enlightened," Christian says dryly.

"Oh, you will," I say, opening the box. "These are fabulous marshmallows; look how big and thick they are!"

Christian stands up as I put the marshmallow on the end of a roasting stick.

"Here," I say, handing the stick to him. "Get that nice and lightly browned, not charred. Charred is gross. Your job is to get a perfectly toasted marshmallow."

"What if I mess this up?"

"Then I veer the *Titanic* away from the iceberg."

Christian begins laughing, and oh, how I love being the one who can add lightness to his life.

"Yes. You don't fear my crazy family, but you do fear I won't be able to toast a marshmallow to your liking."

"Christian. Life is all about priorities."

I take a graham cracker, place a square of chocolate on it, and wait for Christian to finish roasting the marshmallow.

He takes it off the fire and examines it, and I realize when he's thinking about something he gets a cute little crease across the bridge of his nose.

Oh, how I love these little moments of discovery with him. And now that we'll be able to FaceTime, I can continue to see these things in him.

My heart catches when I realize he will go home Monday night. Now that he's here, I can't imagine him leaving me.

"How is this, Ace?"

I shove that thought away. We still have Sunday and Monday together, and I want to savor every minute with him.

"I'm so glad we don't have to break up," I tease. "It's perfect."

I take the marshmallow and put it on top of the chocolate, then add the top graham cracker and give it a slight squish.

"You get the first bite," I say, holding the s'more up to his mouth.

He takes a bite and chews thoughtfully for a moment.

"It's sweet," he mumbles with his mouth full.

"I know, isn't it so good?"

Christian swallows. "No. It's too sweet."

"What?" I cry, pretending to be aghast. I turn and take a bite of the s'more and groan the second I get that magical combination of sticky toasted marshmallow, melting chocolate, and graham cracker. "Mmm. So. Good!"

I can feel marshmallow on my lower lip, and I'm about to lick it off when Christian's mouth is on mine, his tongue lightly trailing the smudge of marshmallow.

Oh, my.

"I think I'm coming around on the s'more," Christian murmurs sexily against my lips.

I drop the s'more.

Christian scoops me up in his arms.

"Let's go to bed," he whispers, kissing my temple.

I smile as I lock my arms around the back of his neck. While I know he'll be crashing any minute now, I'll be up for hours, touching Christian every few minutes to make sure he's real. This is my life, and this spectacular man is my boyfriend.

If I am dreaming, I definitely don't want to wake up.

CHAPTER 10

I LIKE LONG, ROMANTIC WALKS BY THE SHORE ...

"I can't believe it's already Monday," I say, a lump forming in my throat. "You'll be leaving in hours."

Christian and I are walking along the Pacific Coast, our last walk before he heads to the airport. Bear is scampering ahead, happily running along the edge of the ocean, letting the cold water splash him. The overcast sky reflects the feeling in my heart. The clouds have covered my happiness and won't go away until I land in the UK in a few weeks.

Walking behind us are Oliver and Peter, two of his protection officers, dressed casually in half-zips and baseball caps, blending in with everyone around us. Christian has drawn a few stares from people on our beach walks in a "he looks familiar" kind of way.

Otherwise, our weekend together has gone under the radar. He told his friends he was going away for the weekend but left it at that. Christian told his parents yesterday that he had gone off the grid for a few days and would be back on Tuesday. From the side of the conversation I heard, it didn't go over very well when he said he was in Northern California.

I told everyone I had checked into a hotel while giving the lavender oil a chance to leave the apartment so I could be headache-free. Paisley asked why I didn't stay with her, but I said I wanted a weekend with the remote and room service and needed lots of rest time. Of course, they couldn't argue with that logic. For once, nobody knows what I'm doing. I should feel guilty about lying, but I don't. My parents and Paisley are overly cautious with me, always checking where I am and what I'm doing. It's exhausting living in that cage.

With Christian, I feel free. There's a new normal with him, one where he doesn't see the girl who had the tumor.

Christian only sees the woman he loves.

We spent our time together enjoying long walks by the ocean, taking in the sunset from our patio while trying the local wines, ordering room service, binge-watching stupid reality TV shows, and making love.

I've never been happier.

"I don't want to go," Christian says. "But we both have to get back to our lives."

I nod as another big wave comes crashing ashore. "I know. It's just so hard," I say, my voice shaking.

"Hey," Christian says, stopping to gaze down at me, his piercing blue eyes blazing with conviction, "we are going to make this work. We are going to see each other and see where this goes. I know one thing for sure, Clementine. I'm in this. I'm not going to go home and let this die out. If that means waiting for weeks before I can see you, touch you, kiss you, then so be it. I will do it because I want to be with you."

"I love you," I say as a gust of air rolls off the ocean and blows my hair dramatically across my face. I reach up and push it back.

"I wish I could do that for you," he says, his expression full of longing.

"You can do it in private," I say.

"We could go back to the room and do all kinds of things in private," Christian teases.

"You just want me for sex."

"Who do you think I am, Xander?"

I begin to laugh. While my heart is still sad, I know Christian is nothing like Xander. He is as invested in this as I am, committed to me, to starting a relationship, and to seeing what this could become between us.

"Come on, let's sit," Christian says, moving up from the shoreline before taking a seat. I call Bear, and he happily comes running back to me as I drop down on the cold sand next to Christian.

We're both silent as we look out over the gloomy horizon.

"Clementine?"

I turn to find he's already staring at me.

"These past few days with you have been the happiest I can remember," he says quietly. "You make me laugh. You make me feel loved. For the first time in my life, I feel normal. You are the only person who has ever made me feel that way."

Tears fill my eyes. "I feel all those same things about you. I'm not the girl who had a tumor. I'm not fragile in your eyes."

"No, I've never seen you that way. You're Clementine to me. The beautiful girl with flaming red hair who wants to work with antiques because they have stories. You talk to me about normal things, even if it's that nonsense about sugar cookies being the greatest cookie of all time. You're the girl who has horrible taste in TV and can't do anagrams—"

I burst out laughing. "I love that my top qualities include my argumentative spunk regarding sugar cookies and that I'm shit at figuring out your anagrams."

A sexy chuckle escapes his throat. "I love those things about you."

"Good. I'll make sure in our next FaceTime that I go over the merits of royal icing with you. Ha-ha! *Royal* icing, should be right in your wheelhouse."

Christian groans. "Next you'll tell me your favorite color is royal blue."

"Hmm, I think I could fancy a royal shade of blue," I tease, putting on an accent for him.

"If you start using all British terms or a fake accent I'll break up with you," Christian says, his eyes sparkling at me. "Nothing is worse than an American trying to act British. Besides, part of your charm is the fact that you are an American with a wonderful accent and odd terms for things."

"I could see that as part of your online dating profile," I say. "Young, quiz-loving man seeks American who is crap at puzzles, loves reality TV, and enjoys long, romantic walks by the shore."

"You forgot insanely sexy."

"Oh, yes, insanely sexy would definitely be a part of it. Now, what would mine say?"

"Vivacious redhead seeks recluse hoarder who loves curry takeaway."

I roar with laughter, so much so that Bear barks and

moves over to Christian, who begins rubbing his head affectionately.

"Confession," I say. "This might change everything."

Christian's mouth turns up in that sexy smile that makes my heart skip a beat.

"Go on."

"I hate the smell of the spices used in curry," I admit.

"What?"

"I can't stand it."

"How is that possible? Curry is brilliant."

"No, curry is nasty."

"You're right. This does change everything."

"As in?" I ask, arching an eyebrow at him.

"I'll obviously have to find another American who is curry-compatible."

I give him the stink eye, and he laughs loudly.

Christian clears his throat. "We need to talk about what we do in the next few weeks, until you come to Cambridge."

"Okay."

"Who do you think should know about us?" Christian asks. "We need to be careful. People can promise not to say anything, but they can't always resist the urge to tell."

"This is a difficult secret to keep. I want to tell Chels and Bryn, but they'll freak out over the prince thing."

"I know," he says, nodding.

"Your friends will have to know since I'll be staying with them."

"Yes."

"Maybe we leave it at that for now," I say. "What about Xander and James?"

"They can keep secrets, so they can know," Christian

says. "What about Paisley and Evan? Can they keep this from your parents? Can Paisley be an ally for us?

"An ally? What, are we invading a country?"

"Your new nickname is going to be Sassy Pants."

I giggle, and he laughs.

"But do you think Paisley could help me win your parents over when the time comes? When I meet them, I mean?" Christian asks.

My heart skips at how he sees the future that I do, that yes, we're going to make a go of this, and that will include meeting my family someday if things go in the direction we hope they do.

Then I see the anxiousness in his eyes. Christian truly has no idea what a good man he is, that once he lets people in, it's impossible not to like him.

Because people don't give him the chance to be normal.

"I don't think you'll need help, once we revive Mom with smelling salts, that is. But trust me, once the shock wears off, they will love you. And yes, I will tell Paisley and Evan. Paisley is protective, but I think she would like the idea of knowing I am going to see you and not going alone to London. So that will be our circle of trust for now."

"How are you going to explain this sudden trip to the UK to your parents?"

I smile. "I cooked up a devious plot while you caught up on your sleep," I say proudly. "To celebrate my good brain health, I'm taking a trip to London and Cambridge to take a stately home tour and study antiques. I'll get Paisley to back me up; they trust her with being the wiser, older sister."

He nods. "All right."

I frown for a moment. "They will flip out that I'm going

alone. But I think they would flip out more knowing I was going to see my boyfriend who they have never heard of."

"If they knew I was a prince, they'd fear for the vortex you were about to be sucked into," he says, his voice tinged with regret. "If I were them, I'd fight to keep you away from the House of Chadwick with everything I had."

I see the sadness has returned to his eyes.

"Well, that's too damn bad. I'm choosing to get sucked into this vortex, so stop with this talk right now."

He blinks in surprise. "What?"

"I'm exactly where I choose to be. I'm not a delicate flower who will lose all her petals if things get a bit rough. Or really rough. I want to see you, and that makes everything worth it."

"I would kiss you right now if I could."

I smile at him. "I know."

Christian pushes the sleeve back on his sweater and checks his watch, flashing me a bit of seductive watch porn as he does. There is something delicious about a man with a fantastic watch.

"We've got to head back. I need to pack and get to the airport."

The lump returns to my throat. "I don't want to say goodbye."

"We won't."

"What?"

"I refuse to say that word to you."

My heart fills with love for him.

"So what will we say instead?"

Christian stands up, and I do the same, brushing the sand from my clothing as Bear barks and dashes around us.

"I think 'see you soon' is much better. And we'll do that

here so you can go home and we don't have a dramatic airport exchange that might attract attention."

"See you soon," I repeat. "I like that much better."

As we head back to the resort, I already feel better knowing this isn't goodbye.

And I'll be counting the days until I head to Cambridge in a few weeks.

CHAPTER 11

A LITTLE TRIP TO LOOK AT ART

"Would you uncork that chardonnay for me, please?" Paisley asks, not lifting her eyes from her food-splattered cookbook.

I open her kitchen utensils drawer, which is a hot, jumbled mess. It's Friday night, and I'm joining her and Evan for crab pasta, sourdough bread, garden salad, and conversation.

And I'll be dropping the Prince Christian bomb on them tonight during said conversation, too.

Christian has been gone for four days. I miss him like crazy. When we parted in Half Moon Bay, he took a part of me back with him. The overwhelming sadness I felt when we said "see you soon" ripped my heart in half. I dried my tears on my sweatshirt—I seriously need pocket tissues—and vowed no more tears. I'll see him in a few weeks, and my heart will be whole again.

I've already downloaded a Cambridge app on my phone, planning the activities I'm going to do while he's in lectures. There are amazing museums and gorgeous stately homes the likes of which I've never been in, with incredible art and antique collections. I'll spend the rest of my time with him, cooking dinner in his house, getting to know his inner circle of friends, and going to a pub for steak pie and a quiz. Then we'll fall into bed at the end of the night and lose ourselves in each other's arms ...

I'm still finding it hard to believe this is my life and that my love is at Cambridge and wants me to come be a part of his world.

Keeping him a secret is harder than I thought it would be. Now that I'm in love, I want to shout it from the rooftops. I'm so happy, so full of appreciation for this new adventure, I want to tell everyone about the amazing man who has entered my life.

But I can't.

It's been killing me to keep him a secret. I want to share my joy with Bryn and Chelsea, but I know that's asking them to keep an impossible secret. I can't put that on them, at least not yet. But finally, finally, I get to talk about him tonight.

"Clem, wine?" Paisley reminds me.

I grin. Patience was never Paisley's strong suit.

"How do you find anything in here?" I ask, as I can barely open the drawer, it's so crammed full of crap.

"Well, it might seem unorganized to you, but I know where everything is," she declares, a defiant tone entering her voice.

Sure. I bet if I asked her right this second the location of the corkscrew she'd have no clue, but I decide not to poke the bear. After all, she's a great cook. I love her Dungeness crab pasta. I don't need to distract her when she's making it.

I bend down to peer into the drawer. I spy it at the back, but I can't slide the drawer all the way out because the corkscrew is jammed up at the top, keeping the drawer from opening.

"Paisley, this is a stupid mess," I say, trying to wedge it free without scraping my hand. "I'm organizing this for you."

"You will do no such thing," Paisley declares, chopping some herbs on the cutting board.

I free the corkscrew at last, and the drawer pops open.

"Yes. I see you have this completely under control," I quip.

"Shut up."

I chuckle and uncork the bottle of chardonnay for her.

"I think I'm ready for a glass now, too," I say.

I move to the cabinet where she keeps her glasses and select one. I know her home in the Russian Hill neighborhood as well as she does, and I adore the old apartment building, with its breathtaking views of the bay and the cypress trees nestled around it. I love the details of her apartment, like the crown moldings and stunning bay windows, as well as the renovations, like her super-modern kitchen.

I pour some wine for both of us and set the bottle next to her.

"Thank you," she says. Paisley finishes chopping and sets the knife aside. She clears her throat. "Um, so, did you ever hear from CP again? I've wanted to ask you, but I didn't want to upset you. For your sake, though? I hope that asshole fell off the face of the earth."

Door. Open.

"I did hear from him," I say, an anxiousness beginning to swirl in my stomach. Good lord, my story is crazy to me, so how on earth do I expect Paisley to understand?

Paisley picks up the bottle of wine. "I hope you told him

he's a jerk for what he did to you and blocked his creepy ass."

She adds a splash of chardonnay to her copper pan, expertly tossing it about off the flame, and I draw a breath of air for courage.

"No, I didn't. In fact, we're talking. Things wer—"

The pan lands down on the burner with a crash, and I stop mid-sentence, jumping back from the loud noise.

"What?" she shrieks, her brown eyes wide in horror. "Clementine! He's a psycho. Oh, my God, what if he finds you and stalks you? He could kidnap you! Murder you! No, this is bad-bad-bad and you nee—"

"I can assure you, Prince Christian of Wales is not about to murder me."

Paisley's mouth falls open. "You believe this guy is Prince Christian?"

"I know he is. I know this is crazy, Paisley, but that is who CP really is. When I started talking with Christian, I only knew him as CP. It was to protect himself. He's used to people only liking him for being a prince, and he wanted a true friendship with me—"

Before I can say another word, Paisley puts her hands on my shoulders, turns me around, and guides me to the living room.

"Paisley, what are you doing?"

She sits me on the sofa, and then she drops in front of me, and I see tears in her eyes.

"You're going to be okay. We'll get a different doctor to see you."

"What?"

"You aren't well, Clem," she says, her voice breaking. "But I promise we'll get you better."

"You think I'm crazy?"

"No, of course, I don't, but you've been under a lot of stress, and you're vulnerable to believing these kinds of thin—"

"I am not," I say, growing irritated. "I'm not crazy or vulnerable. He came here. This past weekend, when I said I was at a hotel, I was at the Ritz, with Christian."

The key turns in the lock, signaling that Evan is home, but Paisley keeps going.

"Oh, my God!" Paisley goes stark white. "You were sleeping with some stranger pretending to be Prince Christian!"

"No, I was sleeping *with* Prince Christian!" I shout right as Evan walks through the door.

Nobody says a word.

"I need to call Mom and Dad. You're not well."

"I can prove to you it was him!" I cry, leaping up off the couch to get my phone. "CP is Prince Christian."

"Wait, are you talking about *the* Prince Christian, as in the hoarder?" Evan asks, trying to make sense of the shitshow he's stepped into.

"Evan, we need to get her to the hospital," Paisley says, choking up. "She's not well. She thinks she's dating Prince Christian, and she's sleeping with some creepy guy pretending to be him! Dr. Choi obviously missed something!"

"Would you listen to yourself? That is absurd!"

"You're the one sleeping with a stranger who just showed up on your doorstep pretending to be Prince Christian! He's a-a *doppelgänger*! You are having sex with a man you don't know, one who is a creepy doppelgänger, and you're lucky you didn't end up dead and dumped in the bay!"

"Stop," I say, retrieving my phone.

"I think we all need to take a breath here," Evan says.

"I'm calling Dr. Choi. We need help," Paisley says as she reaches for her phone.

"Here!" I yell as I run up to her. "This is me, with Christian."

I shove my phone in her face, and Paisley takes a step back, staring at the picture of me and Christian that I took.

"Sweetheart," she says gently, "it's going to be okay. I promise you it is."

"Are you looking? That's *Christian.*"

"I don't want you to be frightened," Paisley says gently, placing her hands on my shoulders, "but I know you photoshopped his head in there. It's okay. Your brain chemistry isn't right, but we'll get this all sorted out. I promise you that. I love you. We'll fix this."

Oh, my God.

She thinks I photoshopped him.

"But that's Christian," I say. "That's *him.*"

Evan takes the phone from Paisley. "Honey, that doesn't look photoshopped. But I'm sure it's a lookalike, Clem."

Shit.

Then I remember something about Christian.

"Zoom in on the photo," I say. "If you zoom in on his hand, his left hand, there's a scar across the back of it. He cut it as a child. It required stitches, and the scar never faded. If you blow up pictures of Prince Christian's hand, you'll see the same scar. I'm not that good at photoshop to be able to crop in a hand seamlessly."

Evan enlarges the picture. Paisley gasps as soon as he does.

"You … you aren't making this up?"

"No. I will FaceTime us together when the time zones are decent, but I'm dating Prince Christian."

Nobody says anything.

Suddenly, I smell something burning. Oh, crap, the pasta sauce!

"Paisley, your sauce is burning," I say.

"I don't care, you ... you're ... with a prince?" she sputters.

I decide I'm the only one not in shell-shock, so I take it upon myself to hurry to the kitchen and pull the pan off the burner.

"A prince?" Paisley repeats as if her brain can't compute this.

"This is crazy," Evan says.

I wave a towel over the charred sauce so the fire alarm doesn't go off, and then I run it under some cold water. I wait as the pan makes a loud sizzling noise. Once it's silent, I answer Paisley's question.

"Yes," I say. "I'm seeing a prince."

"How? How did this happen?" Paisley asks, confusion in her voice. "I don't see how this is possible."

"It's because I'm charming on Instagram," I say helpfully.

"You met a prince. On Instagram," Paisley says. "This is insane!"

"Why don't we get a pizza, and I'll explain everything."

I order us a pizza and sit down with them in their living room, telling them my story of how I met Christian. I explain how we connected instantly and talked all the time and how I fell for him without even seeing him because we get each other in ways nobody else does. I talk about how he was there for me when I was waiting for the test results and how he flew eleven hours with his protection officers to prove to me who he was, figuring I'd want nothing to do with him afterward.

"This is surreal," Evan says. "I can't get my head around this."

"This happens in royal romance novels and TV movies," Paisley says. "And now you are stepping into the fairy tale."

"It's not the fairy tale I want," I say. "It's Christian. I don't think of him as a prince because, to be honest, that makes everything harder. Much, much harder. But for now, we want to keep this quiet as we see where this can go, without the media finding out."

"When you talk about him, you're different," Paisley says. "Your eyes sparkle. You smile. I've never seen you talk about anyone like this before. What's even better? You had this look at the airport when you didn't know who he was. This is real."

"It is," I say. "What we have is special. It's like what you and Evan have."

Evan laughs. "Yeah, except my parents live in Napa. His parents live at Buckingham Palace."

"You know what she means," Paisley says, smiling at him. Then she turns back to me. "I'm glad you told me."

"Christian and I agreed only a few people can know. We can't risk someone getting excited and sharing our story with someone else. You know how that goes."

Paisley nods. "Your secret is safe with us."

I exhale, knowing that is true.

"I can't tell Mom and Dad right now. Think of how much you guys freaked out."

Paisley chews her lower lip. "You're right. Mom wouldn't believe it, and once she did, she would worry. She can't know until you're ready and you two are super serious about moving forward."

"I haven't even told Bryn and Chelsea. You two are the only ones who know."

"Okay," Evan says.

I draw a breath of air. "I'm going to fly over and see him for spring break," I say.

Paisley grabs my hand. "Ahh! This is so exciting! You're going to England!"

I realize Paisley isn't worried about me taking this trip. It's like her seeing my excitement over being with Christian has put my health scare in the backseat for a moment, which has never happened before.

Excitement surges through me as I squeeze her hand back. "I know! I'm going to see Christian and Cambridge and soak up a new country and art and I can't wait. But I need your help."

"Anything," Paisley says, nodding.

"Mom and Dad are not going to be on board with me going out of the country by myself, not knowing I'm going to be with Christian. They are way too protective, even though with Christian I'll have access to his doctors if anything should happen, which are obviously some of the best in the world."

Of course, I know I'm normal and won't need them unless I fall and break a leg or something, but I have to assure over-protective Paisley I'll be in good hands.

"Right," Evan agrees.

"We'll have personal protection officers surrounding us wherever we go. His house has a bomb-proof door, bullet-proof windows, and a high-tech laser security system. There will be nobody safer than me when I'm with Christian."

Both of them look startled by those details, but I continue.

"I'm going to be very, very safe, but of course, Mom and Dad won't know that. What I plan to tell them is that to celebrate my good, tumor-free health, on a whim, I'm off to explore stately homes and buildings near Cambridge. I'll stay in a flat through a certified exchange program and take tours, and I'll promise to make them all aware of my medical history, which, I might add, hasn't changed since I was in high school."

"Ha-ha, exchange program," Paisley says, shooting me a wicked grin. "I bet Prince Christian offers some interesting options for paying for your bed for the night."

I blush, but secretly I'm thrilled. If Paisley is teasing me about sex, she's come around.

Now that I have my team behind me, I'll tell Mom and Dad I'm off to discover art in England.

And reunite with the man I love, I think happily.

CHAPTER 12

LONDON CALLING

I exit customs at Heathrow and stop in my tracks, feeling like I need to pinch myself. Or slap my face. Yes, I need a slap, something strong to make sure this is real, and that I'm actually here, having stepped off a British Airways flight from San Jose into this busy airport on a Saturday afternoon.

I am in London.

And I'm minutes away from being with Christian.

Ahh!

I drag my wheeled bag behind me, butterflies swarming in my stomach. Christian's best friend, Stephen, and his girlfriend, Emma, are going to pick me up outside of customs. Christian is waiting in his car to avoid the media. This way it will appear I am here to see them and not Christian.

I've talked to Stephen on FaceTime, so I know what he looks like, and I stop and scan the hoards of people waiting outside the exit area of customs.

Then I spot him.

It's not hard because he's holding up a sign that Christian made; I can tell by the handwriting. It says:

WELCOME TO THE UK ACE

I grin the second I see it. A beautiful dark-haired girl, who I presume is Emma, is standing next to Stephen. I head toward them, pulling my bag behind me, and stop when I'm in front of them.

"Hello, I would be Ace," I say, smiling.

"So, you are real," Stephen says, his words coming across with a strong Irish accent that sounds like music to my ears. "We accused CP of making you up. You know, paying an actress to play an American on FaceTime as a prank. He was uninterested in girls prior to you," he says, flashing me a charming smile.

CP is what Christian goes by to his friends, to help conceal his identity, and now I understand how he let me into his world right away by telling me to call him this when we first started chatting.

Stephen extends his hand to me, and I shake it.

"No, I'm very much real. I'm Clementine. It's nice to meet you."

"Pleasure," Stephen says, his green eyes dancing at me. "This is Emma."

"Lovely to meet you," she says, her brown eyes shining warmly as she extends her hand to me. While there is no doubt Stephen's accent is Irish, there is also no doubt that Emma's is pure English.

I take a moment to study her. Emma is a true English rose, with a creamy, pale complexion that is nothing short of perfect. Her long, dark hair cascades past her shoulders and her eyes are bright.

"It's nice to meet you," I say, shaking her hand.

"Did you have a good trip?" she asks.

"Let me take that," Stephen says, retrieving my suitcase.

"Oh, thank you," I say. I turn to Emma as we walk through the busy terminal. "It was long. I tried to sleep, but I was too excited."

She nods. "I can imagine. CP says this is your first trip to England."

"This is my first time crossing the Atlantic. My passport had two stamps prior to this trip: Canada and Mexico."

"Oh, CP will have you filling that up in a hurry," Stephen says as we head toward the exit. "Except his favorite place is somewhere you've been. He loves the ruggedness of Canada."

I smile, as I already know this. Christian loves nothing more than going remote in Banff and Lake Louise and is already dying to go back next winter.

We head outside; the sky is overcast and drizzle is falling.

"Welcome to London," Emma says. "I hope you packed an umbrella."

She retrieves one out of a Louis Vuitton tote and pops it open, directing it half over me.

"Thank you," I say, shivering from the damp air that is surrounding me.

"You're welcome."

Emma and Stephen continue general chit-chat as we walk, and I do my best to concentrate, but with each step I take, I'm looking for Christian. My heart is beating against my ribs. Excitement is driving my rapid pulse. With each second that goes by, I grow more eager.

"It's the black Audi at the end of this row with the Range Rover parked behind it," Stephen says, lowering his voice. "His team is in that car. CP will be driving us, though."

I spot his car and force myself not to run to it.

I start to shake, but this time it's not from the dreary London air.

I quicken my pace.

I reach his car, the Audi with the blackened windows, hurry to the passenger side, and throw open the door, but not before realizing I'm on the wrong side of the car.

"Ah!" I scream in fright, shocked to find myself in Christian's face when I was prepared to jump into the seat.

He roars with laughter and catches my wrist before I fall backward.

"Hello, love," he says, smiling broadly at me. "Are you that eager to see me, or did you forget we drive on the other side of the vehicle?"

"Both!" I cry happily. "Oh, Christian! I'm so happy to be here. I've missed you so much!"

I drink him in, from the curly locks to the wonderfully full lips and the blue eyes that are gazing at me with adoration through his fringe of long lashes.

His thumb circles around the inside of my wrist, sending delicious shivers down my spine as his calloused skin brushes sexily against mine.

"You have no idea how much I've missed you," he says, his deep voice low.

Our eyes lock for a moment. It's as if we've never parted, exactly how I knew it would be between us.

"Go on around and get in," he murmurs, "so I can kiss you properly before Stephen and Emma get in the car."

I hurry around to the correct side—the one with the passenger seat—and climb in, slamming the door shut behind me.

I turn to face him, and the second I do, his hands are on my face, his fingertips delicately sliding over my cheekbones, my nose, my chin, up to my hair. Christian leans forward and presses his forehead to mine, and I close my eyes and breathe in the familiar clean scent of his cologne, the scent I have missed so much.

"I love you," he whispers, lowering his lips to mine.

We kiss, slowly and sweetly. I lift my hands to his clean-shaven face, tracing my fingertips over his skin, savoring the warmth of his lips, the caress of his touch, everything that makes up the man I love.

He breaks the kiss as we hear Stephen and Emma approach the car.

"I love you more," I whisper back to him.

His eyes light up the second I utter those words to him. "Not possible."

Emma gets into the seat behind Christian. "Christian, if you can pop open the boot, Stephen will put Clementine's luggage in."

"Yes, of course," Christian says, hitting the button to release the trunk.

I hear Stephen place my bag inside. He slams the trunk shut and slides into the seat behind me.

"Thank you, Stephen," I say.

"You're welcome," Stephen responds.

"Ready to go?" Christian asks as I fasten my seatbelt.

"I am," I say. "I can't wait to see Cambridge."

"Don't let the drive there put you off," Stephen says. "It's rather underwhelming."

"Oh?" I ask. "No rolling English farms? Villages? Castles?"

Emma laughs. "It's a motorway drive. Very bland."

"Oh," I say, rather disappointed to hear this. "So, no charming buildings that have been around since the 1200s standing on the side of the road?"

"No, but I can show you a fantastic petrol station circa 2006," Christian quips.

"In an hour, she can see Knebworth House," Stephen says. "That's old."

"I don't think you can see it from the motorway," Emma says, her voice taking on a thinking tone as we exit Heathrow.

"Yes, you can," Stephen insists.

"No, I don't think so," she says.

"You can see the Adventure Playground, I think," Christian says. "However, that wasn't built in the 1200s, Clementine, so you are going to be sadly disappointed unless Stephen is correct."

"Which I am," Stephen insists.

"No, you're not," Emma counters. "All you can see will be trees, I'm sure of it."

"I see this is up for debate. It also sounds like a brilliant pub quiz question," I say, smiling at Christian while he drives.

We fall into an easy conversation, and I can see why Christian likes Stephen. Stephen is very much like him, as in you would never know he was the future heir to an Irish brewing empire. He's friendly and down to earth. Emma is lovely, and I keep wondering if she has a lady title in front of her name, one of those long English names, like Lady Emma Smythe Potter Cox-Wenworth. Between the Louis Vuitton tote and matching umbrella and the Burberry rain coat and Wellingtons she has on today, I picture her to be the type to sip champagne and watch Stephen play polo before zipping off to Harrods for a consult with her on-call personal shopper.

"So, you met Christian online?" Emma asks, breaking through my thoughts.

I know his inner circle knows the real story, like Paisley, so I answer honestly.

"Yes," I say. "We are an Instagram relationship. I had no idea who he was."

I can see Christian smiling out of the corner of my eye, which makes my heart flutter.

"I can relate to that meeting."

"Oh? How did you two meet?" I ask, turning around so I can look at them both in the backseat.

I'm already willing to bet that it was at Cambridge at some posh mixer. In fact, I'd bet my meager bank account on it.

Stephen laughs. "She told me my family's beer was shit."

"What?" I ask, laughing.

A pretty rose color tints Emma's cheeks. "I work as a server at a pub near Cambridge University. I attend Anglia Ruskin University, and I'm working my way through uni. I was this one's server that fateful night. I had no idea who he was, other than he was a Cambridge guy who hung out with the prince."

It's all I can do not to let my mouth flop open in shock. She's obviously not a lady, nor wealthy.

She's like me, I think, feeling more comfortable by the second.

"I asked her what she thought of my family's beer, if it was a good pint," Stephen says, his green eyes sparkling. "And Emma said, 'Oh, I don't like that one at all, very overrated,' and steered me to Guinness, the competition. I knew immediately I would fall in love with her."

Emma smiles. "It's true. I still don't like their beer."

"I asked her out, and she said no," Stephen says.

"You did?" I ask.

"I did. I told him I wasn't a casual pick-up in a pub. He had to prove to me he wasn't looking for that."

"I came back every night for two weeks until she gave me her mobile number."

"It became our pub," Christian interjects, "as I had to live there until Emma gave him her number."

"We've been together ever since," Stephen says.

"I love this story," I say, as Emma reminds me a lot of myself. She's a woman not impressed with titles or money, but the man on the inside, and she fell for this man not caring that he came from one of the wealthiest families in Ireland.

"Is this the same pub where I'll get my steak pie?" I ask.

"Yes."

"You should come for Sunday roast tomorrow. I'm working." She flashes me a smile. "I might even throw in an extra Yorkshire pudding."

Ah, the Sunday roast. Christian explained this to me, that it's a huge deal to eat on Sunday. The Sunday roast involves roasted meats and vegetables and gravy, a British tradition, and Christian loves it.

"I've never had a Yorkshire pudding," I say.

"What?" Emma asks. "How is that possible?"

"I've never had Sunday roast either."

"This is why I had to bring her to England," Christian says. "Her food experience in America is seriously lacking."

"Oh, is that so?" I say, bending over and grabbing my backpack. "If America is seriously lacking, then why do I have White Chocolate Cheesecake M&M's in my bag?"

"Get out," Emma says. "There is such a thing?"

I wave my M&M's triumphantly in the air.

"You mean we've been in the car this whole time and

you've been holding out on me?" Christian exclaims. "What are you waiting for? Open those up!"

"You were too busy talking about the Knebhouse, which nobody can decide if it can indeed be seen from the freeway or not."

Christian bursts out laughing. "*Knebhouse?* It's Knebworth House."

"Whatever. You were so excited about Adventure Playground that you didn't think to ask me how many bags of M&M's I brought for you. In fact, maybe we need to stop at Adventure Playground first before opening the candy." I get out my phone and type it into Google. "Shut up. Christian, you didn't tell me there is a Dinosaur Trail at Knebworth House! They have seventy-two life-sized dinosaurs and pre-historic creatures there; we absolutely need to do this!"

"So, we're going to walk in the rain on the Dinosaur Trail before heading to Cambridge?" Christian asks. "What, are you going to get an exchange going to bring the dinosaurs to the mall for an art exhibit?"

"Oh, good idea, but no. This is just for us. We need to do the Dinosaur Trail," I say.

"You want your first memory of England to be a Dinosaur Trail," Christian repeats.

"Yes."

He grins and glances in the rear-view mirror. "Slight detour before home?"

"I can call some media outlets. We can have the Golden Prince snapped in public studying a brontosaurus," Stephen teases.

"Odds are we'll end up on social media if we do it," Christian muses.

I hear the hesitation in his voice.

My goal is to shove him out of his comfort zone.

I want him to feel normal.

"So?" I challenge.

"So?"

"So what? You're out walking a trail and looking at fake dinosaurs with friends. Let people post their pics. It's not like the paparazzi is going to spring out from behind a T-rex and begin snapping away. Although that would be entertaining. I'll feed you exotic imported M&M's afterward if you do it," I say flirtatiously.

"You do know how to drive a man mad, Ace."

I burst out laughing, then punctuate it with a loud hiccup, which makes Christian roar with laughter.

"All right. We'll do it."

I am smiling from ear-to-ear as I gaze out the window. *Mission accomplished,* I think happily.

With the Dinosaur Trail being the first of my many adventures in England.

CHAPTER 13

I'LL TAKE THE WOOLLY MAMMOTH FOR THE WIN, PLEASE

"Isn't this fantastic?" I say as we walk along the wooded Dinosaur Trail, which is not crowded due to the light rain that is falling from the gray sky. "It's beautiful here, absolutely majestic," I say, words falling out of me at a rapid clip I can't control. "I can't get over the scent of the English grass and rain, the flowers in bloom, this magical rolling countryside on a real historical estate. It's like a movie. I can't believe I'm here with you."

Christian smiles as we head along the trail. Before he got out of the car, he covered his blond locks with a red Arsenal baseball cap to help conceal his identity. He's gallantly holding an umbrella over me as we walk, and Stephen and Emma are next to us. His lucky protection officers, Oliver and Peter, are strolling behind us, no doubt thinking I'm adding a whole new layer of work to their days.

"Films are shot here, you know. But not the American-falls-in-love-with-a-prince-she-met-on-Instagram story," he teases. "That one hasn't been written yet."

"That house," I say, "is magnificent. Those spires and turrets and gargoyles; the history is screaming from that home. Oh, I'd love to see the inside of it someday."

"You're into estates?" Emma asks as we come across a T-rex.

"Oh, yes, I love antiques. I'd love to curate antiques in a museum or work for an auction house someday. When CP here is busy with classes, I plan to go on some tours."

"She's not here for me," Christian says, his blue eyes dancing. "Clementine is here for the stately homes."

"That is not true," I say, smiling at him. "But it is an incredible bonus for me as an antique lover to see homes filled with amazing pieces while I wait for you to be done with your lectures."

Christian stops on the path to study the T-rex. "This was my favorite dinosaur as a child," he says, smiling at the memory. "Father would buy me books on dinosaurs, and I knew them all, every fact and physical detail. I had figurines, too, which I kept organized in cases in alphabetical order."

I smile, as I expect nothing less from my rules-and-organization-loving boyfriend.

"Tell me something about the T-rex," I say.

"What?" Christian asks, laughing.

"Come on, I know that little boy who loves dinosaurs is still in there. Share him with me."

Something shifts in his brilliant blue eyes. I realize it's surprise.

"While I want to know about the prince who grew up in the palace," I say, lowering my voice so only he can hear me over the light drizzle of rain coming down on his umbrella, "I want to know the little boy who loved dinosaurs more. Because that is your heart, not your station in life."

He stares down at me, his telling eyes growing emotional now. "Just when I think you can never amaze me more, you do."

"I know. Now amaze me with your mad dinosaur knowledge."

He chuckles. "Okay," he says, staring straight ahead at the fierce replica with wicked-looking teeth. "The name is Tyrannosaurus rex. The first part of the name is Greek, meaning tyrant lizard. Rex is king in Latin."

"Tyrant lizard king," I say aloud. "Sounds about right."

"Indeed. It had the strongest bite of any animal ever. The teeth were replaceable," Christian says, getting into his element, "and the jaws are massive, up to one-and-a-half meters long."

I need to study UK conversions as I don't know what that translates to, but I can see they are indeed massive, and eyeballing it, I'm guessing four feet.

Which is crazy to think about.

"They always scared me in the *Jurassic Park* movies," I say.

"The arms are one meter long and have two fingers," Christian says, pointing to them. "Obviously, too short to bring food to its mouth."

Christian juggles the umbrella under his arm and does the T-rex baby arms for me. "See? Impossible to get food up to the mouth with arms like this."

I burst out laughing, as he looks wonderfully ridiculous.

"I need a picture of you doing T-rex arms in front of the T-rex," I say, retrieving my cell.

"What? Oh, no, I'm not doing that."

"Why not?"

"Why so?"

"Great argument, CP," Stephen quips. "Come on, she

comes all the way to England, and you won't give the poor girl T-rex arms?"

"We can all do it," Emma says, getting into it. "Stephen and I will go first, won't we?"

I can't believe I've met people within the past hour who will roll along with my suggested shenanigans.

I love them.

They move in front of us and pose in front of the replica.

I begin to laugh as they are getting into it and pretending to fight each other with little T-rex arms.

"Why did you pick the dinosaur with the baby arms as your favorite, CP?" Emma teases as she continues to battle Stephen.

"I like the frightening teeth and big head. It was a trade-off for the little arms."

"Good thing those aren't your requirements for girls," Stephen teases. "Scary teeth, huge head, little arms—because sadly, Clementine doesn't tick those boxes."

"Oh, shut up," Christian says, laughing. "Besides, she's Princess Fiona from *Shrek*."

"She becomes an ogress at night? Now that's better than anything you've got, and infinitely more interesting than a palace," Stephen teases.

I'm dying.

"Idiot," Christian says, grinning.

"It's the red hair," Stephen says knowingly. "It's a little obvious."

"You're a right genius, my love," Emma says dryly.

"Okay, none of this is getting CP here out of doing T-rex arms," I say, getting back to the task at hand. "First, you do the arms by yourself."

Christian closes the umbrella and leans it against the

rail. He moves in front of the T-rex and does it, and to my delight—my absolute, heart-warming *delight*—he begins laughing as he mimics the movement.

"I dare you to roar," I encourage.

"I will not, because the roar you hear in the movies is incorrect according to science," Christian declares.

"Yes, and it would be a travesty if you did an incorrect T-rex roar right now."

"Indeed, it would."

"Like not microwaving your frozen meal at fifty percent power."

"That is weird, isn't it?" Stephen asks. "I noticed that about CP, too. Who actually uses the auto defrost setting?"

"Right?" I say, nodding at Stephen. "I'm going to make CP here throw something in the microwave and nuke it without using settings this week, to see if he gets hives."

"Why is using the microwave properly such a source of debate?" Christian asks as he stands in the drizzle.

"Come on, let's get a pic of you two doing a T-rex battle," Emma says. "I can take one with your mobile if you like."

"Okay, thank you," I say, handing her my phone.

I move next to Christian and put on my fierce face. I pull up my hands and turn to him, assuming a fighting stance.

"Dare you to roar," Christian says, drawing his arms in and looking utterly ridiculous.

"Do you? Do you really?" I ask, lifting an eyebrow.

"No."

We both burst out laughing.

"Come on, fight," Emma encourages.

We begin stupid fighting, our arms tucked in, and I'm laughing so hard I'm crying.

"I could take you out," Christian declares, "if only my arm were longer!"

He waves his short hand a few inches from his chest, and I die all over again.

"I can't breathe," I cry happily.

My heart swells when I see Christian has tears of laughter in his eyes, too.

We stop our dramatics, and after I've wiped the mascara that is no doubt running down my face, I retrieve my phone from Emma.

"Hold on, one selfie in front of your favorite dinosaur," I insist.

Christian complies, and we move in front of the replica so it's looming over us.

"Say your favorite cheese on the count of three," I say trying to angle the camera.

"Let me do that; I do have longer arms now," Christian teases.

I laugh and hand him my phone, which he positions to get the best shot of us.

"One, two, three, double Gloucester," Christian says.

"Pepper jack," I say at the same time.

"Pepper jack, huh?" Christian asks as he hands me back my phone.

"What can I say? I like things spicy."

"And CP ticks that box for you?" Stephen teases.

"You can sod off," Christian jokes back.

"I've never had double Gloucester," I say, feeling hunger set in.

Christian retrieves the umbrella and, even though we're already wet, opens it back over me as we move down the trail again. His protection officers flank us as we walk.

"I have some back at the house," Christian says. "It's buttery and mellow."

"See? This is what happens when you get involved too soon," Stephen says as he and Emma fall in with us as we head down the trail. "You don't know if you are cheese compatible."

I glance at him, and Stephen winks at me.

Two mothers in chic casual wear come around the corner, both pushing strollers and chatting while their toddlers shove tiny crackers into their mouths with chubby fists. They are engrossed in conversation until one of them looks up and stares straight at Christian. She stops walking and her jaw drops open.

"My God, it's Prince Christian," she says aloud, as if he's not walking right in front of her.

She turns to her friend. "Look, it's Prince Christian. What is he doing here?"

"You're right. I thought he only did forced royal appearances!"

The other woman picks up her phone and begins taking pictures of us as we move past them.

A strange feeling washes over me. They are gawking and talking about him and recording him with their cell phones like he's not a human, but an animal in an exhibit.

I knew this would happen.

But I had no idea how it would actually feel.

My stomach begins to hurt. His whole life, since he was born, has been people staring at him, talking about him, criticizing him, or loving him without knowing him.

Among the people watching his every move are those who wonder if the monarchy still has a purpose, therefore creating more anxiety in Christian about trying to find not only his own goals in life but ones the public will approve of and embrace. His choices are not only about him but for the future of the monarchy as well.

I swallow hard, feeling the weight he carries on my shoulders, too.

I vow, from now on, Christian is not going to carry this weight alone.

Christian keeps his gaze straight ahead, his happy expression shifting to a mask of neutrality.

As we move past them, and eventually out of earshot, Christian turns to me.

"Are you okay?" he asks. "I know that had to be weird for you."

I'm touched that his first thought was for me.

"Please. Weird is having your family discuss your X-ray with your doctor in front of you like you aren't there. But they're my family. This is different."

"Oh, that was nothing. I'm used to that. However, you aren't, and that will always be a part of being with me that I can never change. Once we go public, you will never have anonymity back, Clementine."

I hear hesitation in Christian's voice, as if I might start building doubts about this life now that I'm seeing it first hand.

"Moms pushing strollers don't bother me."

"Pushchairs," Christian says.

"What?"

"We call those pushchairs."

"I think I need a translation dictionary," I joke. "And I don't fear losing my anonymity when the time comes. Your Princess Fiona will find a way to handle it."

Christian's eyes shine warmly at me. "You're right. I trust you."

We continue our walk, encountering more people as we

do, with some yelling out greetings to "Your Royal Highness" and inquiring if he was enjoying himself, which Christian answered with a smile on his face.

Finally, we reach the spot on the trail that I've been waiting for: the woolly mammoths.

"Here we go," I say, moving out from under the umbrella and going over to the railing in front of three large woolly mammoth replicas. "You can keep your tiny arms; I'll take the woolly mammoth for the win, please."

I snap a few pictures with my phone. Then I turn to get a selfie of me in front of them.

"The tusks are cool," I say as I smile for the camera. "Okay, come here, CP. Get in the shot."

Christian once again sets aside his umbrella and moves next to me, taking my camera from my hand. "On three. No cheese needed."

I laugh, and he counts us down to take the picture.

"Thank you," I say as he hands my phone back to me.

"Why do you like the woolly mammoth?" Christian asks as we study them for a moment.

"I love the long fur," I say. "And the cool tusks. Amaze me some more, CP. What can you tell me about them?"

"They only had four teeth."

I wrinkle my nose. "Seriously?"

"Seriously. Two upper and two lower."

"That is crazy!"

"I know."

We start walking again, and Christian continues to share his scientific knowledge with me, from how they had smaller ears to minimize frostbite to how scientists use the rings on the tusks to determine a mammoth's age.

As we finish our walk and head out to go home, I realize that Christian's love of dinosaurs and science could be something he taps into for his future. He could support programs to prevent animal extinction, connect with children on the importance of animal conservation, or use his position to raise money for scientific research into these animals of our past and to protect the ones we have on earth now. I can't wait to talk to him about this later, when we're alone.

I turn and look over my shoulder at the magnificent estate we are leaving behind. I've barely scratched the surface of England, but I'm already smitten with the lush countryside and the one stately home I've had the pleasure of seeing.

I should be dead tired, but energy zips through me at a rapid rate, because the next stop is Cambridge.

Christian's home.

And I can't wait to see what adventures await me there.

CHAPTER 14

IT'S LIKE WALKING THROUGH THE PAGES OF A WONDERFULLY OLD, GLORIOUS HISTORY BOOK

"You have to stop the car," I say urgently. "I need to get out. I need to walk these streets right this second!"

I'm serious about my request. As I stare at the city unfolding before me, rich with amazing architecture and narrow streets made of cobblestones, I need to feel it. I need to breathe the damp English air, dodge the bicyclists, and absorb the city of Cambridge with all my senses.

It's the most beautiful place I have ever been.

I crane my neck to look up at the historic church towers, and I can practically hear the bells ringing as I do. And the colleges! Oh, the wonderful collection of thirty-one colleges that make up Cambridge, all uniquely majestic and rich with the echoes of the past. The gray sky, swirled with white clouds, provides a stunning backdrop for the most breathtaking architecture I've laid eyes on.

The art history student in me has sprung to life in a way I've never known. I'm desperate to walk the streets and study everything, taking in the magical experiences of a world I've only known through the internet but is now wonderfully real for me.

"Stephen, Emma, are you up for another walk?" Christian asks, glancing in the rear-view mirror.

"I think we'll head on back. I've got some studying to do," Emma says.

"Drop us at the train station, and we'll grab a taxi," Stephen says.

"No, we can drop you home first," Christian says, shaking his head.

"Don't torture Fiona. She wants to get out of the car now. I thought she might be planning her escape from you, rethinking that whole weird microwave habit of yours, but after hearing that plea, I think your American guest genuinely wants to see Cambridge."

I smile. I love the way Stephen treats Christian like an ordinary bloke, just like I do.

"You're an idiot," Emma says, teasing Stephen.

"But I'm *your* idiot," Stephen reminds her.

"I might need an idiot upgrade. My next idiot will like Guinness."

"Ooh," Christian and I say at the same time.

"Your next idiot wouldn't know to get you vanilla fudge from the Fudge Kitchen," Stephen says.

"You're right, my Irish One. You're a keeper," Emma says.

"Wait, fudge what?" I ask, turning around in my seat.

"Christian, have you not told her about the fudge shop?" Emma asks, her eyes sparkling. "It's one of my favorite places in Cambridge!"

"What has he held out on me?" I ask.

"Oh my, he has kept you in the dark on one of the most glorious places in the city. It's a fudge shop with incredible flavors of fudge, the best you've ever had, and they give generous samples so you can make an informed decision about what to get."

"Oh, I forgot. You'll love this place because they have drinking fudge," Christian says.

"What?" I gasp. "Drinking fudge?"

"Yeah," Christian says as he drives. "You can have it hot or cold, or in a milkshake, and it comes in different flavors. It's something you'd love, Ace. They sell it in packets for you to take home."

"Do you even know me? How could you keep drinking fudge a secret? This is all kinds of sideways, Your Royal Highness. I might need to find a new British boyfriend," I declare. I swipe open my phone. "If it's still open, you are taking me there as soon as we drop Stephen and Emma off."

"She only pulls the 'Your Royal Highness' bit when she's annoyed with me," Christian explains with a grin on his face. "Otherwise, she gives me no proper greeting."

"Which is why I like her already," Stephen says good-naturedly.

"What about your need to walk the streets and embrace the culture?" Christian teases.

"I can embrace it better with fudge in one hand."

He laughs, that wonderful throaty chuckle, and warmth fills me the second I hear that lovely sound.

The sound of a happy and relaxed Christian.

"It's across from the King's College gatehouse," Christian says.

My ears perk up. "Your college," I say aloud. I've studied pictures of it and marveled at the beautiful neo-Gothic gatehouse and the utterly breathtaking King's

College Chapel next to it. Thanks to Google Maps, I feel like I've practically walked beside them.

Soon, we're at the train station. We drop off Stephen and Emma, and they say they'll see us back at the house later. Christian takes a moment and picks up his cell.

"I'm going to let Oliver know we're going into town to walk around a bit," he says.

"They must hate me already," I say, shaking my head. "They've had to do the Dinosaur Trail, and now they're going to have to be tourists in the drizzle."

Christian texts a message into his phone and then puts it down. "Trust me, this is more interesting to them than following me on my morning walk with Lucy, or waiting for me to get out of the library. I think they'd rather be assigned to Xander. He's more fun. When Xander is on leave, his officers are going non-stop."

"You're fun; you just keep it here," I say, lightly tapping his heart. "You show that side to me. You had fun being stupid today and indulging my whim. Now you'll have fun tasting fudge with me and showing me Cambridge. The important thing is that you are true to yourself. Have the fun you want to have. That is what makes human beings great. We're individuals. Being a prince doesn't change that, Christian."

Adoration for me shines in his eyes. "You make me braver."

"Same," I say. I flash him a grin. "Now, are you brave enough to take me to the Fudge Kitchen? I might embarrass you with all the fudge I'm going to stuff in my face. It's not going to be pretty."

"You stuffing your face with all the fudge will be sexy."

I burst out laughing as he begins to drive. "You mean messy."

"Oh, I meant sexy. You attack things you love with abandon. That's a turn-on."

"I do, which means I'll be attacking you later."

"Don't tempt me to turn this car around and take you home this second, Princess Fiona," Christian says.

"While I want nothing more than to have crazy hot sex with you," I say slowly, "I think if I don't walk around Cambridge, I'll die. The art history lover in me is dying to absorb a sliver of it right this second, and the idea of not doing it makes me twitchy."

"Twitchy?"

"Twitchy."

"Well, I can't have you twitchy, so let's go," Christian says.

As he drives, I remain silent, taking in the city like a visual feast for my eyes. I can't get enough of the distinct types of architecture, the quaint shops, the pubs and churches.

Christian eventually turns into a parking garage, and his protection officers follow suit. We park, wait for them to park, and when they are out, Christian opens his door. I follow.

"I'm sorry," I say directly to his protection officers, "but I couldn't bear staying in the car another moment, not when this magical city is in front of me. Your choice of fudge is on me when we get to the Fudge Kitchen, as appreciation for your patience."

They both looked shocked at my offer, but Christian doesn't.

"She's nice, this one," Christian says, inclining his baseball-cap-clad head toward me.

"Oh, Ms. Jones, that's not necessary," Oliver says, shaking his head in a firm no.

"Do you not like fudge?" I ask.

"Well, I do, but—"

"No buts. Let's get out of the parking garage and into Cambridge," I say excitedly. I instinctively reach for Christian's hand, but he quickly moves it away.

"I'm sorry. You know I want to," Christian says, his bright blue eyes pleading with me to understand.

"No, it was an instinct. I'm sorry," I say, shaking my head. "I know you, er, your, um, family, let's say, doesn't show public affection, so even when we do eventually come out, I don't expect it."

Christian furrows his brow. "We don't show affection?"

"Um, unless it's a certain older brother with a hot blonde at a nightclub kissing, not that I've seen pictures of anything. I assumed it was an understood thing."

Christian begins to walk, and I fall into step with him. Oliver and Peter, of course, are close behind.

"I never thought of it, because my parents don't get along. It makes sense that they don't touch each other during the show."

"The show?" I ask as we make our way toward the street.

"You know, when we do our jobs," Christian says, adjusting the brim on his baseball cap so it covers more of his eyes. "Neither did Grandfather and Grandmother. But that doesn't mean I'm going to follow that."

I shoot him a look. "You won't?"

"No. I want to be affectionate with you in public, and you can be sure when the time comes, I will be."

There's a strength in his voice, a conviction, that this man is going to fight the traditions of the monarchy that he doesn't agree with when it comes to us.

Oh, how I love him.

"Cambridge," I gasp as I get a glimpse of the outdoors.

"Um, yes, it still is," Christian quips.

A squeal escapes me. "I can't wait!"

I hurry ahead, and Christian does a little jog to keep up with me. I practically burst from the garage and out onto the street, pausing to take in my surroundings, not having a clue where I am but loving it all the same.

"Head left," Christian directs.

We head up a narrow street, and when we get to the corner, I see it's marked Wheeler Street. There are cobblestone streets and restaurants, and oh, it's magically old and wonderful. I should be freaking exhausted, not only from the flight but also the time change and the walk at Knebworth, but I'm bursting with energy.

"This is the Corn Exchange," I say.

"Have you been studying?" Christian asks.

I nod. "Yes! It's a concert venue."

"Your pub quiz question: When did it open?"

Dammit.

"A long time ago," I say.

Christian laughs. "1875, and I'll take that point, thank you."

"Oh, you will not," I say as we walk along. "You can't get a point for answering your own question."

People with umbrellas jostle around us, and the sidewalk is a sea of patterns and stripes and bright colors as people try to shield themselves from the rain.

I notice a few people look at Christian, but he said Cambridge has been good about respecting his privacy. I know he's still off-limits to the media for the next few months, but that doesn't mean he's off-limits from regular people throwing a picture of him on Instagram.

"CP," I say, "what if someone posts a picture of us from today on social media?"

"You're a friend from America," he says, and from the immediacy of his answer, I know he's thought about this. "I'm showing you around. That's it."

"You make it sound so simple."

"It is, when it comes to you and me."

Swoon.

We continue down Wheeler Street, and I must fight the urge to whip out my cell and take pictures of everything I'm seeing. I know I'll have plenty of time to do that when I explore on my own, and that's the only thing restraining me.

Wheeler Street becomes Bene't Street, and as we walk further along I see the St. Bene't's Church. It's the oldest building in Cambridge.

"Look at that," I say in wonder. "That bell tower is from the Anglo-Saxon period, the eleventh century. It's incredible!"

"You know what's at the intersection of Bene't Street and Trumpington Street, right ahead?"

"I do," I say proudly. "The Corpus Clock."

"Well done, Ace," Christian says, smiling.

We reach the Corpus Clock, which is street level outside the Taylor Library of the Corpus Christi College. There are people standing on the corner staring and taking pictures, and we stop for a moment to look at it, too. It's round and gold-plated, with a huge cricket-type sculpture on top. This is a clock with no hands. Time is revealed through slits with a blue light as the mean-looking cricket thing moves back and forth.

"The grasshopper creeps me out," I say to Christian as we watch it move.

"He's eating up time; he's supposed to be scary."

Time.

My chest draws tight as I realize the precious time I have with Christian this week is going to go by way too quickly.

I feel Christian studying me.

"I know, I don't want to think about time either," he says, reading my mind once again. "Come on, King's Parade is right here. So is your Fudge Kitchen."

"Oh, I can't wa—"

I turn away from the clock, but as soon as I do, I stop speaking.

Because as I gaze down King's Parade, I see King's College. The neo-Gothic style of the King's College Gatehouse is set behind a beautiful green lawn beside the breathtaking King's College Chapel, a glorious representation of perpendicular Gothic architecture, with the most incredible medieval stained-glass windows and turrets reaching into the cloudy, gray sky above.

As I stare at the magnificent buildings before me, I'm overcome by the history and the gift Christian has given me by bringing me to Cambridge, a trip I never would have made on my own at this point in my life.

"Fiona?" Christian asks.

I blink the tears away as I gaze up at him.

"This is the most beautiful sight I have ever seen," I say, my voice growing unexpectedly emotional as I turn my attention back to the chapel. "That chapel was begun in 1446."

"I know."

I turn back to Christian, and a tear escapes my eye, which I quickly brush away.

"What's wrong?" he asks, his eyes wide in concerned surprise.

"Do you realize what you've given me with this trip?" I ask. "It's like walking through the pages of a wonderfully old, glorious history book, one I would linger over while studying the old homes and the photos of the interiors. Now I'm here. I'm in this magical city, with all these incredible places rich with art, and I get to explore them. It's a dream to me, an incredible, wonderful dream. I'm standing here because of you, and it's the greatest gift, to see all this history in person. It's a fairy tale, one I only want to share with you."

Christian stares down at me, his eyes searching mine.

"I never appreciated where I lived as much as I do in this moment, seeing Cambridge through your eyes," he says softly. "That is a gift you've given me in return."

I smile at him. "Thank you."

"Thank me after you've had some fudge," he says as we head down the street toward the Fudge Kitchen, past tiny shops housed in quaint buildings.

And with happiness filling my heart, I let Christian lead the way to the next experience we are going to share together.

CHAPTER 15

GAME CHANGING MOMENTS

"I will never want another kind of fudge ever again," I say, sighing happily as Christian drives us back to his place. "That was a complete game changer."

It was lush. Creamy. Sublime. I tried dark chocolate with sea salt, traditional toffee, and Belgian chocolate swirl. I bought slices of all of them and insisted that Oliver and Peter share them with me. I've decided I don't care how much it costs. I'm going to have some shipped back to Palo Alto.

To Christian's shock, not only did I refuse to let him buy my order, but I treated him, too. I told him it was so I had full rights to his stash of flapjack fudge if I wanted some, but he knew I simply wanted to get him something for a change.

"Wait until you try the drinking fudge tonight," he says. "Another game changer, as you would say."

As he drives into a residential area, I feel the excitement of the day catching up to me. I rest my head against the seat, and a contented sigh escapes my lips.

"Are you tired?" Christian asks.

"Happy," I answer.

"You're happy here?"

I turn my head so I'm facing him instead of looking at the lush greenery rolling by my passenger window.

"I can be happy wherever I am as long as it's with you."

He smiles as he drives. "I hope you fall even more in love with England during your stay."

I find myself holding my breath for a moment. I know why this is important. Because if we are ever going to truly find out what we are together, I'm going to have to move to England. I'll need to leave my family, my friends, and my entire life behind to see if Christian and I have the potential to build one together.

"I'm sorry," Christian says, interrupting my thoughts. "I shouldn't put that pressure on you. We'll take this one step at a time."

"It's not pressure. It might seem crazy to talk about the future, but it's right for us. That's all that matters, Christian."

He turns down another winding road, filled with lots of leafy green trees and hyacinth blooming in front of fences.

"I feel the same way," he says gently. "I don't care what other people say or think. All that matters is that you are happy."

"I do have a request, though."

"Anything."

"I have to have Sunday roast before I give my assessment of England."

He chuckles, and a tingle floats through me at the sound.

"You will have your Sunday roast tomorrow, love," Christian promises. He slows his car and turns into a gated driveway. A tall fence surrounds it, one covered with mature trees, shrubbery, and beautiful purple crocus flowers intermingling with bright yellow daffodils.

Christian clicks a remote on his visor, and the gates swing open. I find myself staring at an old, brick two-story home with strong Georgian period details. Christian parks the car, and I eagerly get out, wanting to see the place Christian calls home.

"The original house was built in the Middle Ages," Christian says as he moves to the trunk to collect my luggage.

"This is incredible," I say, staring at it.

"You haven't even seen the best part," Christian says, pulling out my bag and slamming the hatch shut. "I'll give you a tour of the house, and then I'll show you."

While Oliver and Peter get out of their car, I follow Christian down a sidewalk. There's a lush and bright green lawn that, if it weren't raining, would be perfect for a picnic. Huge trees tower over it, providing shade, and there are shrubs and more spring flowers in bloom.

An idea hits me. I have on my itinerary this week to explore the outdoor market in Cambridge, which has everything from bread and cheese to vintage fabrics and old albums. I'll get lunch for us one day. Christian can bring his reading, and we'll have a romantic picnic here in this private oasis.

"This is the rear entrance," Christian says, interrupting my thoughts.

I turn around and see Christian heading up the steps to a door. He takes a moment to remove his wallet, which he holds up to a sensor. He glances at me and lifts an eyebrow. "All to protect the prince who only leaves home to go to lectures. Or to run off after a princess from a faraway land called Stanford and claim her upon first kiss, you know."

Then he flashes me a grin.

Oh, he's so adorable I want to kiss him right this second.

Instead, I hear the door click, and I follow him inside.

My eyes dart around the space, trying to take everything in. While I see cool period details, like high ceilings and beams and sash windows, as well as a beautiful fireplace, the décor is hideous.

There's a bright red, floral-patterned rug covering the floor. Its pink and blue flowers are so loud they hurt my eyes. The drapes covering the windows are also red. The furniture is no better. Oversized, round, wood tables sit at each end of the sofa—oh, God, that sofa. It's in a pale-blue upholstery to match the flowers in the awful carpet.

I wrinkle my nose reflexively. Gosh, it's musty in here. Like an old library. Which is great, if we were in an old library. *Seriously, can these guys not smell this?*

"This is a home that came with the furniture, and Charlie's dad said we were on our own for that. So, um, yes, it's hideous because we couldn't be faffed to invest in new stuff. Well, that's not entirely accurate. We did for the media room because that's the most important room in the house. Oh, we also bought a table from IKEA for the kitchen as the other one was practically from the Middle Ages. We feared if we put more than one plate on it, it would collapse in a heap."

The light bulb goes off. Christian might be a prince. He might have a ton of money. But true to his word, he's still an ordinary bloke going to university, one who will invest in a TV but not a sofa.

My heart warms. This fact makes me fall in love with

him even more.

I slide my hands up his quarter-zip sweater, and I playfully tug on the zipper. "If you tell me you assembled it without directions, I'll take you right now on this living room floor, because that is one very sexy skill," I say.

"Well, now I see why you're so smitten with her, Christian," a male voice from behind says.

I whirl around, my face flaming in embarrassment. A young man with curly, ginger hair is grinning broadly at me.

"Charlie," he says, walking up and extending his hand to me. "You must be the famous Clementine."

"Famous for saying completely inappropriate things," I say, trying to recover as I shake his hand.

"Pleasure to finally meet you," Charlie says.

I smile and shake his hand. "Likewise."

"How was your trip?" he asks, his green-gray eyes shining in sincerity.

"Very good," I say.

Oliver and Peter step inside but immediately go down another hallway and disappear.

I can't describe how weird it is to have protection officers always around, but I know I'll eventually get used to them disappearing and re-appearing whenever I'm out with Christian.

"She made us stop at Knebworth House on the way here," Christian says, affectionately looping his arm around my shoulders and interrupting my thoughts.

"Oh, do you like stately homes?" Charlie asks.

"I love them, but I didn't make Christian take me on a tour. I made him walk the Dinosaur Trail."

Charlie's eyes widen. "She got you on the Dinosaur Trail?"

"Yeah, we went with Stephen and Emma. It was rather fun."

"Dear God, he's going to marry you," Charlie says, grinning. "You're the only one who can make him do things outside of a royal diary or lectures."

I glance up at Christian, who begins to blush.

"Shut up! Don't scare her off," Christian says.

"She doesn't look scared to me," Charlie says. "I approve."

The door opens again, and this time, I see Stephen and Emma come in with Lucy, who is on a leash.

"Hold on, we've got to clean your paws," Emma says. "It's muddy today."

Lucy spots me with Christian, and she immediately starts swishing her tail and barking in excitement.

"Christian, she's beautiful!" I cry as the dog lover in me comes out.

"Here, I'll get it," Christian says, moving over to Lucy and taking a towel that is by the door. "Come here, girl."

My heart melts as I watch him gently wipe Lucy's paws, talking to her as he does.

"How did you find the Fudge Kitchen?" Stephen asks.

"Did you try the double trouble?" Charlie interjects. "That's my favorite."

"I saved that one for my next visit. Tomorrow," I joke.

"There you go," Christian says, setting the towel aside and taking Lucy off her leash.

She makes a beeline for me, and I drop down and let her sniff my hand first. She wags her tail furiously, and I start stroking her silky red coat.

"Hello, Lucy," I say as she licks my face. "You're a beautiful girl. I'm glad to finally meet you."

I feel Christian's eyes on me, and I steal a glance at him.

He's watching me, his blue eyes shining with affection.

I have a feeling he might have fallen a little bit more in love with me, too.

"Come on, I have something to show you," Christian says.

I rise and smile at Charlie. "Pleasure meeting you."

"You too," he says, nodding. "Here, CP, let me take her bag up to your room for you."

"Oh, you don't have to do that," I say, putting out my hand.

"It's not a problem," Charlie says.

"Thank you," Christian says.

"I'll expect a pint on quiz night," Charlie says.

Charlie disappears with my bag, and Christian leads me through the rest of the house, which is also filled with wonderful windows, horrible furniture, and musty scents. I'm going to get plug-in essential oil diffusers for this house when I'm out. No lavender, of course.

I follow Christian to the front of the house, and through the window, I see another amazing lawn. Behind it is a river with large trees dotting its banks. I gaze out in wonder.

"You have your own private bank," I say.

"That's the River Cam," Christian says, sliding his arm around my waist and drawing my back into his chest. "We can enjoy it together."

I melt into him, happy to finally be alone.

"I'd love that," I murmur as he nuzzles my neck. "I love you."

"I love you, too," he says.

He places a sweet kiss on the side of my neck. "Are you tired, sweetheart?"

I close my eyes, shivering from the feeling of his soft lips against my skin. "Mmm. I might need to go to bed."

"Yeah?"

"Mmm-hmm," I say. "I might need to get comfortable and change out of these clothes."

Christian's lips find my collarbone. "I could assist you with that task."

Then he kisses me there.

Oh, yes. We need to go to bed.

I swivel around in his arms so I'm facing him. I slide my hands up to his face, feeling a hint of stubble slide underneath my fingertips. Christian lowers his head toward mine. I close my eyes, waiting for his mouth to capture mine, when a sharp ringtone from his cell pierces the air.

He jumps back. "Shit."

"What?" I ask as he fumbles to pull his phone from his pocket.

"That's Her Majesty's notification tone," Christian says. "I need to check it, I'm so sorry."

I bite my lip. His mother sounds more like an overwhelming boss who expects her employees to always be on-call than his mom.

Christian swipes open his phone, taps something, and the color drains from his face.

"Christian?" I ask, putting my hand on his arm. "Are you okay?"

"Dammit!' he roars, stepping back from me. "Dammit, dammit, dammit! The moment I decide to throw caution to the wind and act normal, it's blown up in my bloody face!"

Alarm races through me as I see the panicked look on his face.

"I should have known, I should have *known,*" he says, staring down at his phone.

"Talk to me," I plead.

"She knows," he says simply.

My heart stops. "She … knows?"

He hands me his phone. Attached is a photo of us from that rag *Dishing Weekly's* website, taking a selfie in front of the woolly mammoths. There is another where Christian is looking adoringly at me, and there's no mistaking what he feels for me. They obviously saw the photo on a social media channel and bought it from the person who took it. The caption reads:

The Golden Prince's Secret Love—Who is She?

My hand begins to violently shake. While I am okay with being exposed, Christian is far from ready for this.

I glance down at the text message from his mom, which is brittle and cold:

I expected this from Alexander, or even James because he's younger, but not you. You were the one I counted on to be discreet and show decorum. Now you're taking selfies, Christian? Frolicking in public? This is NOT how we behave. I'm disappointed in you. We will issue a statement saying we do not comment on your private life and we still expect the terms of the media agreement to stay in place while you finish at Cambridge. But you very well may have destroyed that with your incredible lapse of judgment.

I know this girl, who I doubt is nothing more than a plaything, probably does not have a title, so don't get too serious about her. I don't even want to know her name.

Tears flood my eyes.

Christian was right.

His mother is awful.

Despite my pleas that I could handle her, I wasn't prepared for her to hate me so soon.

The game has completely changed now.

And it's all my fault.

CHAPTER 16

THE ROYAL WAY

I can't bear the look of devastation on Christian's face. He's rooted to the floor, staring down at his mother's venomous message, his expression equal parts anger and shame.

My heart wrenches inside my chest. All he wanted was to protect me, to protect what we had. But in my quest to make him feel normal, I got him to let his guard down. We knew people were taking pictures, but I assumed they were innocent. I had no idea he'd get in trouble for a selfie.

I also didn't realize that we were truly wearing our hearts on our sleeves when we were together.

"I did this to you," I say, my voice breaking. I begin to pace, to hold back my real urge.

To flee.

Before I somehow make things a million times worse in Christian's already restricted, complicated life.

"Clementine, don't say that. Don't ever say that," Christian says firmly.

I wrap my arms around myself as a cold feeling runs

through me. "You wouldn't be in this horrible position if it weren't for me and my stupid ideas."

"This is not your fault," Christian says, grabbing me and holding me in place. "My mum has a narrow, suffocating idea of what the royal way should be. It's not modern. More to the point, it's not right. Yes, we have to have some air of mystery about us—that is what makes the monarchy unique—but I think showing people we are real is equally important. Maybe you and I will be the ones to change it."

I grasp the power of his words, and fear runs down my spine.

"No," I say, shaking my head. "No, you can't. Christian, I know your relationship with your mother is complicat—"

"You don't," Christian says, releasing me. "Do you want to know what my mother is really like? Without the immaculate dresses and expensive handbags and signature chignon? Behind that practiced smile? My mother is cold. She loves her title above everything else. She loves the monarchy above everything else. Mum had Alexander to secure her place. She had me to produce the required spare. And James was the baby to prove the tabloids wrong. They were speculating they would be the first royal divorce, and then she was pregnant with James."

I gasp at this admission. "James was planned to distract the press?"

"The press had picked up on their limited number of joint public appearances, and how miserable Father looked in them. Rumors made their way into the tabloids, until Mum turned up pregnant with James," Christian explains. "When James was three, I learned the truth. One night, Nanny brought us down to say goodnight and accidentally walked into a huge fight. She herded us away from the door, but I heard Mother yelling. She revealed the truth about James to Father. She said she got pregnant to put the rumors that the marriage was a sham to rest and that's the only reason she slept with him again. Father felt duped because he actually thought it was a baby to put them back on track. Both are horrible reasons to bring a child into the world."

Oh, my God. This family is truly wheels off. I can't imagine growing up like this, with parents at each other's throats all the time and using babies as pawns.

"You never should have heard that," I say, my heart aching for him.

"Our nanny was bright. She knew we heard, so she told Father. He came to talk to us the next morning. He told us no matter what the reasons were, James was meant to be here, to complete our family, and that he loved all of us very much," Christian says, pausing to look at me.

His eyes have now shifted to immense sadness, and all I want to do is take it away. But I don't make a move to touch him, as I can read his energy. He needs to pace. When he moves, he opens up, and I think after living his whole life repressing everything, this is what he needs most of all.

Christian begins pacing again, moving faster this time, and I feel a lump swelling in my throat as I watch him.

"James doesn't know that story," Christian says softly. "Obviously, they stayed married, not because of James but out of an ancient duty to the crown. It's not modern to stay in a dysfunctional marriage, but it will never change. They're always fighting. The rows they've had are like something off that bloody housewife show you make me watch. Father is always yelling that she is a horrible human being with no heart, while she screams back that she is the one holding up the monarchy and keeping it steeped in tradition and honor, which is a joke. If people could see her throwing glasses at the wall, they'd think we were all nuts and not worthy of the trappings of this life."

Christian turns away from me, stopping to draw a breath. I'm reeling from what I'm hearing coming out of his mouth. I always assumed his sadness was from the pressures of the monarchy and of having his life predetermined and judged.

But it's much worse.

Christian has grown up in a dysfunctional home, with parents who have never given him a good example of what a marriage should be. It's a house mired in lies and secrets, and the pressure of performing the role of the happy, loving royal family whenever they are in the spotlight.

I now understand why Xander is noncommittal. I'm sure he sees no value in love. Christian, on the other hand, has locked himself away from the world. I am amazed he has found the courage to not only love but to receive my love in return.

When I realize what Christian is gambling on with me, not just love but falling for an American with no standing in society, and how he is willing to try and move the monarchy forward because of it, it makes me realize what a tremendous man he is. He's brave. He's strong.

He's willing to risk a journey to hell and back for a chance to love me.

Christian's phone rings again, and I wince when it does.

"It's Father," he says without a glance as the ringtone fills the air. "I need to take this."

"I'll go outside," I say.

"No, you can stay," Christian says as the phone continues to ring.

"No, you need privacy," I say, moving to the door leading outside.

"Clementine, don't. Hold on," Christian pleads.

Christian answers his cell. "Father, can you please hold on for a moment?"

He puts down the phone and stares at me. "You can hear anything I say, you know that."

"I do, but you need the freedom to answer honestly, without worrying about me," I say. "Take the call."

Then I step outside and close the door behind me, heading out into the damp air.

I move across the green grass, mud collecting on my Converse shoes, and I don't stop until I reach the edge of the River Cam. The tears I have been holding back fall freely now. I can't imagine having a mother who prefers receiving flowers from adoring fans more than love from her sons. I can't begin to understand how painful that must be for him.

I drop down on to the wet grass, and my butt squishes into the mud. Okay, not the best idea, but I don't care. I draw my knees up to my chest, the tiredness of the flight and time change hitting me, but not nearly as hard as those pictures.

His mother will never accept me.

This is hard in any relationship, but the fact that she is the queen magnifies everything by millions.

I blink back tears. She will fight this relationship. Queen Antonia will make my life hell, I can feel it.

But what about King Arthur?

Christian has said nothing but loving things about his dad. He has shared fond memories of him playing with them, taking him to his first day of nursery school, teaching him how to play polo. And the story, just now, of how his father reassured him and Xander that all three boys were loved by him was touching.

I close my eyes. What am I thinking? He married Antonia. And he has stayed in a loveless marriage. King Arthur is all about title and duty, too. I will never be a suitable match in his eyes for Christian.

The Golden Prince will need someone with "Lady" in front of her name.

I open my eyes, and the River Cam blurs in front of me. Am I crazy for thinking this far into the future when I haven't even been here twenty-four hours?

But I already know what I want.

I want to move to London after I graduate and be with Christian.

I know it with certainty. I love him. I want to be with him in the country that is his home. I want to explore a life that will be challenging and hard but could also be amazing, with opportunities for us to serve the people not only in the United Kingdom but around the world.

Bryn and Chelsea would think I've lost my mind.

Mom and Dad would be on the next flight over to drag me back to the States and to see Dr. Choi again.

Paisley would understand.

She said she knew by the end of the first date that Evan was the one she would marry. I thought she was crazy and told her so.

She is so going to remind me of this when I tell her.

SHIT.

Pure panic fills me. I'd been so wrapped up in Christian that I didn't think about my mom or Chelsea or anyone I know seeing those pictures on *Dishing Weekly's* website. Oh my God, they are going to freak out and wonder why I've been leading a secret life. I've probably been ID'd and my name is out there and I've royally screwed this up with my stupid idea to act normal.

Ha, royally. Under any other circumstance, I'd laugh at that choice of word.

I don't want to see my phone. I wanted to come here and see Cambridge and spend time with Christian, and now all we'll be doing is freaking damage control. My friends and family will be hurt, and I can't say I will blame them.

I drop my head to my knees, a sick feeling swirling in my stomach.

I hear the back door open, and I turn and lift my tear-stained face to see Christian walking across the emerald green lawn. I rise, and as I do, I pull up patches of wet grass on my ass. I begin to fling the mud patches off, getting mud all over my hands.

"Stop it," Christian calls out.

My hand freezes on my butt. "What?"

He comes closer, and I see the tension is gone from his face. In fact, his blue eyes are sparkling at me.

"You're making it worse, Ace," Christian says, a smile tugging at the corner of his mouth. "But I do have to say, you wear mud on that sexy bum of yours incredibly well."

"I'm good at making a mess of things, apparently. I wouldn't blame you if you sent me on the next flight back to San Jose."

"You make things real, and sometimes that's messy," Christian says, brushing away my tears with his fingertips. "But if you think for a second I'd choose my previous life—a life without you—over this one, you're wrong."

I see the anger has dissipated since speaking with his father. In its place is a calmness.

"What did your dad say?" I ask.

"He asked me questions about you," Christian explains, tucking a lock of my hair behind my ear. "I told him to watch *Shrek*, and that you are Fiona two point oh."

I blush furiously. "You did not."

"I did."

"Does he hate me?"

"For being like Fiona? No, he has to watch the film first before making that assessment."

My heart lifts. Something good happened in that conversation.

"So, he's not mad that I'm an American with no status?" I ask, needing to hear Christian confirm this.

"Oh God, no," Christian says. "In fact, he seems rather chuffed you had me out looking at dinosaurs. He felt his years of listening to me go on and on about the Camarasaurus and Therizinosaurus were worthwhile now. He's not upset; in fact, he's curious."

"Curious?" I repeat. "About me?"

"Yes, about you. So much so we have a change of plans for tomorrow."

I can't breathe. "What kind of plans?" I manage to ask.

"We're not having Sunday lunch at the pub," Christian says slowly.

Nervousness fills me. "We're ... not?"

"No. My father has requested that we meet him for lunch. At Sandringham."

CHAPTER 17

IT'S SIMPLY A SUNDAY LUNCH

"What?" I gasp, alarm filling me. "No. No, no, no. I can't go to Sandringham!"

Sandringham is the private country home of the king. It's the place where the royal family gathers for Christmas and the entire family makes the iconic walk to church on Christmas morning. Normally, I'd be all over seeing this magnificent home, but I always dreamed it would be as a tourist taking a paid tour.

Not to sit down to have a private lunch with the King of England.

"Why? It's simply a Sunday lunch," Christian says, his blue eyes searching mine in confusion.

"It's not just lunch," I cry, panicked. "It's lunch with the king."

"Um, you do remember the whole conversation about me being a prince? The king kind of comes along with that bit."

I shake my head. "I'm not ready for this, Christian. You only get one chance to make a good impression. One. I noticed you have a different way of holding your silverware, and I don't know how to curtsy, and I need to have my A-gam—"

Christian's mouth meets mine, silencing me with a kiss. His mouth is warm and soft, his lips gently caressing mine. I melt into him, momentarily distracted by the fact that his arms are now around me, holding me tight as his tongue eagerly tangles with mine. I taste chocolate on his lips and smell the clean scent of his skin, and oh, how I missed this. Kissing him. Feeling his body against mine, losing myself in his strong arms.

He breaks the kiss and gazes down at me. "Tomorrow," he says, brushing a damp lock of hair off my cheek, "you are not having lunch with the king but with *my father*, all right? He's not going to care how you hold your cutlery when eating your fish."

"There's fish?" I ask, my alarm growing to a harrowing level. "I thought it was going to be beef or chicken!"

Oh, no. This is bad. I'll turn green if I have to choke down fish. I'll have to force myself to eat fish on a nervous stomach in front of the king, and what if I gag at the table? Oh God, I should book the next available flight back to San Jose immediately.

"I'm teasing," Christian says, stroking my face in his hand. "No fish, I promise."

"Don't tease me, Christian," I plead. "I am not ready for this."

The lightness falls from his face, and I know my words have hurt him.

"You know that's not what I mean," I say, wrapping my hands around his.

"It's getting real now for you, isn't it? Perhaps it was

easier to forget this was my life when we were long-distance. The game has changed now."

He stares deeply into my eyes, questioning me. As if I'm going to bolt because the magnitude of his life has hit me square in the face.

"I might not feel ready to meet your father, but that doesn't mean I'm not going to do it," I say firmly. "I have no doubts about how I feel for you. I know what life I'll be walking into if we continue down this road. I thought I'd have more time to prepare, that's all. I've never done a curtsy in my life, and I don't want your father to think I'm some Neanderthal with no proper manners. I want him to like me."

Even more so since I know your mother is going to hate me to the moon and back, I think miserably.

"Show me your curtsy," Christian says.

I cringe.

"Come on, give it a go," he encourages.

"Okay."

I move one leg behind me and bend my knees.

I glance up at him for approval, and I see that sexy smile twitching at the corner of his mouth.

"Can I get up now?" I ask.

He begins laughing. "No, His Royal Highness expects you to hold it for thirty point two seconds before you rise."

"*What?*" I ask, beginning to laugh. "You're lying!"

"Careful, you don't want to lose your balance and land on that lovely bum of yours. Or lose track of your count, because King Arthur will be most appalled if you only hold it for thirty point one seconds. Oh, and no wobbling. You need to work on that, Fiona, my love. And yes, I'm lying."

I start giggling and lose my balance and plop! I fall back onto the wet grass, my ass sticking firmly in the mud.

I look up at him and burst out laughing. Then I hiccup, which makes Christian roar with laughter.

"Looks like we have work to do," Christian teases.

He's grinning as he extends his hand to help me up. Instead of rising, I give his hand a tug and he tumbles forward, landing in the mud next to me, and I shriek with laughter as Christian is now covered in wet grass and mud like I am.

"That's for the thirty point two second lie," I say.

"You just took down the spare. Where are those protection officers of mine when I need them? I should sack them for not keeping a better watch on the redheaded American."

He's grinning at me, and my heart leaps with joy.

"Oh, I'll do more than take you down, Your Royal Highness," I tease.

Christian reaches for me, and I try to roll away. He catches me and moves on top of me, pinning me to the wet grass with his body weight.

"You already have taken me down, Clementine," he whispers before kissing me.

Our bodies entwine, and I feel so alive in this moment. I feel the dampness of the earth and the scent of Christian's cologne and wet grass mingling together as we kiss. We're muddy and flecked with grass and neither one of us cares.

All that matters is being together. I don't care what hurdles I must face to be with this man. I will find a way to clear them.

Starting tomorrow with King Arthur.

I'm inside Sandringham.

I'm a jumble of emotions as I cross the carpeted floor of the great hall, my head hardly grasping that this is reality.

I've been in the UK a mere twenty-four hours, and my world has turned upside down. The *Dishing Weekly* photo has been seen not only by Chelsea but by other friends and acquaintances, and now the tabloid has been calling my mom. The palace released a statement confirming that one Clementine Jones was indeed a friend of His Royal Highness the Prince of Wales, and the palace hoped that our privacy would be respected during the remainder of my visit.

I had a brief phone call with my mother. I told her, yes, I'm friends with Prince Christian and I would call her later and explain everything, but no, I was not acting in a reckless manner and I didn't have headaches. For good measure, I advised I did not need a psychologist or Dr. Choi and if they did fly over here to get me, which she insisted she would do, I'd refuse to go. Paisley said she'd talk to her and try to get her to calm down once the shock wore off. I texted Bryn and Chelsea, saying I would tell them everything when I got home.

All of this will have to wait because trying to make the best impression possible for King Arthur needs my complete focus right now.

I drink in the amazing room, the antique lover in me in awe of what I'm seeing. I'm in one of the most iconic homes in the world, one steeped in rich history. I'm surrounded by magnificent paintings of royal family figures, stunning tapestries, wood paneling, and beautiful lamps. The period tables and sofas signal the furnishings haven't changed much from the Edwardian era. Kings and queens have entertained guests in this very room. I want to know the stories behind everything here. I want to explore every room. I want to see the white drawing room, the ballroom, and the library. This is a living art history book, and I have the opportunity to see it through Christian's eyes, from his family's perspective.

But I'm not here to indulge my love of antiques or revel in the fact that I am breathing historic air.

I'm here to impress the father of the man I love.

I try to tamp down the nausea that is rising in my throat. Christian comes over to me and puts his hands around mine.

"He's going to love you," he says softly, his eyes shining brightly at me.

I exhale. "Okay."

"It's going to be fine," Christian says reassuringly. "You're smart, charming, and funny. Real. He will wonder how I got so lucky as to find you and that you agreed to go out with me."

"Right," I say, shaking my head.

"I am."

I remove my hands from his and anxiously adjust the tie around my green wrap dress, grateful that I did pack a few "date night" dresses for this trip. It has long sleeves and a modern, geometric print, and the green makes my eyes pop. I glance down at the dress, wondering if it should be a bit longer. Is it too short for a royal lunch? It hits just at the knee.

"You look beautiful," Christian murmurs, once again reading my mind.

"It's not too short?" I ask, concerned.

"You don't need to change the way you dress," Christian says, his voice firm. "You stay who you are. I never want you to change for the family."

"Well, I don't think you'd want me showing up in my

Stanford hoodie and ripped jeans, would you?" I cock an eyebrow as I adjust his tie, and damn, my man looks brilliant in a slim-fitting Burberry suit. "Considering you put on a suit."

He reaches for my hand again. "I love the way you dress. It's part of who you are. I don't want to lose that part of you for them."

"You won't. But I still wish this dress was longer."

"Hmm. I disagree. I wish it was shorter."

"Christian!" I chide, but I can't hide the smile that spreads across my face. "Be quiet."

He gazes down at me. "Don't worry. We've got this."

We.

Once again, we're a team. I'm not here alone trying to impress his father. Christian is going to support me every step of the way.

Christian's gaze shifts to something over my shoulder, and he straightens.

My heart leaps out of my chest. I know it's the king without turning around.

"Father," Christian says, his face lighting up in a smile.

I turn around, and I'm struck by how handsome King Arthur is in person. He's tall, at least six foot three, and dressed in an immaculate charcoal suit. His thick, blond locks are swept back from his face, with a bit of product controlling the same golden curls that Christian has. His piercing blue eyes regard me with interest as he moves closer.

My palms begin to sweat as he nears us.

"Christian, I'm delighted to see you under these circumstances," King Arthur says, his voice deep.

To my surprise, they hug. I've never seen shows of

affection from King Arthur in the few bits I've seen of him on TV, but there is genuine warmth between father and son.

"Father, this is Clementine Jones," Christian says.

I quickly curtsy and rise, feeling relief that I can check that off my list.

"It is a pleasure, Your Royal Highness," I say.

Christian informed me that I could call him "sir" after I addressed him as Your Royal Highness for the first time.

"Clementine, I have to say this is a surprise," King Arthur says, extending his hand to me. I shake it with a firm grip. "It is a pleasure to meet you."

"Likewise, sir," I say, my voice taking on a nervous shake.

As soon as Christian hears it, he wraps his hand around mine. King Arthur's gaze shifts toward our locked hands, and a smile appears on his face.

"I think you have some stories to tell me," King Arthur says. "Let's have a drink first, and then we'll have lunch."

Christian leads me to an antique loveseat, where he sits next to me, our legs touching. He places our entwined hands on his leg. I slant my legs to the right, keeping them pressed together at an angle. I've seen Queen Antonia do this in pictures; it must be the official royal way of preventing anyone from seeing up your skirt. I hope I have this right. I would die if King Arthur thought I was an uncouth Neanderthal.

King Arthur takes a seat on another sofa facing us.

As if waiting in the shadows, a well-dressed young man appears in a sharp navy uniform, asking the king what he would like to drink. He requests a glass of cabernet, and Christian and I follow suit with the same.

King Arthur shifts his gaze toward me, his expression

warm. "Christian tells me you two met online. Very modern," he says, his eyes twinkling at me.

I give the king a nervous smile. "Yes," I say, my voice still reflecting that stupid shake. "He found my internship as an art installer interesting. I'm an art history major, and I'm due to graduate in June. And I have to say this home is better than any textbook I've ever read."

"She's with me for the art," Christian deadpans. "For most girls, it would be the whole prince thing, but for Clementine? It's access to antiques."

"Now that makes more sense," King Arthur says, winking at me.

I know we haven't spoken for more than ten minutes, but I already like King Arthur.

"What do you hope to do with your art history degree, Clementine?" King Arthur asks.

"I hope to work with antiques," I say. "I'd love to work for a museum or auction house. I love antiques because they tell stories. Whether it's something personal, such as a treasured set of dishes passed down through a family, or something from generations long ago, such as formal asparagus tongs, they show how society was and how we've evolved to where we are now."

King Arthur doesn't say anything, and oh, crap, have I lost him with my ramblings?

Oy, I talked about asparagus tongs with the King of the United Kingdom.

The young man quietly returns, serving the king his glass of wine, then Christian, and finally me.

"Thank you," I murmur, taking a sip and hoping to calm my nerves.

"See? How could I resist her?" Christian says. He removes his hand from mine and, in a move that surprises me, he strokes my hair. "She knows what asparagus tongs are. Where do you find a knowledge base like that?"

"I find cutlery fascinating. I know it's weird," I say, glancing at the king to gauge his response to my babbling.

"You appreciate the history of things, which is important," King Arthur says, his eyes locked on mine. "I know you'll enjoy seeing the art around the estate after lunch."

"I'm very much looking forward to that, sir," I say.

"We'll be sure to start with the cutlery," King Arthur teases, taking a sip of his wine.

Normally, I'd ask King Arthur a question about himself, but I don't even know if I'm allowed to speak to him first. And what would I even say? So, how is it being a king? Any fun appointments coming up?

Crap.

Then I remember Christian telling me to be myself and treat him as his father, not the king.

"I'm looking forward to Sunday roast," I blurt out. "I've never had a Yorkshire pudding before."

King Arthur furrows his brow. Okay. Zipping from asparagus tongs to Yorkshire pudding is not appropriate discussion.

Maybe I should stop speaking.

That's probably the way to go.

"Never had a Yorkshire pudding?" King Arthur says. "It's a good thing Christian has taken action to rectify this situation. Nobody should go without the joy of a Yorkshire pudding."

He smiles at me, and I find myself relaxing a bit.

King Arthur rises, and Christian follows suit, so I do as well.

"Let us move to the dining room," King Arthur says. "I

look forward to getting to know you over Sunday roast, Clementine. I'd like to hear not only your story, but your story with my son."

I swallow hard. While King Arthur has been kind and charming so far, I know the conversation is going to move past cutlery and Yorkshire pudding now.

I only hope I can pass whatever test he lays out for me with flying colors.

Because I know my future with Christian will depend on it.

CHAPTER 18

PEAS AND TAPESTRIES

I stop walking the second we enter the dining room. I gasp aloud in awe, and my hand flies to my mouth.

I'm not staring at the immaculately set table with stunning silver candelabras and exquisite china, or the collection of breathtaking antique clocks on the pale-green built-in wall display. I'm struck by the gorgeous tapestries hanging on the walls.

"These tapestries," I say breathlessly, "all modeled by the works of Goya. I can't believe I'm seeing them in person. They are exquisite."

King Arthur smiles. "Not that I need to tell you, because you probably know the history, but they were a gift from Alfonso the Twelfth of Spain in 1876."

I nod, still finding it hard to believe that Christian has grown up surrounded by masterpieces of art, by artists such as van Dyck, Da Vinci, Rubens, and Rembrandt. Seeing these tapestries makes it real.

"Incredible," I say, awed.

"If you are this excited by the tapestries, wait until you see the china services in the collection," King Arthur says.

I can't help but smile. "Well, being that my mom collects needlepoint patterns and my father collects running shoes, I will most likely need smelling salts if I see the china service of King George the Fourth, because I'll be passed out from excitement and shock!"

Christian laughs and King Arthur seems amused by my candor as we take our seats. Household staff appears once again, pouring water and refilling our wine glasses, all in a coordinated effort.

It's like being on Downton Abbey, I think as I stare at the menu card in front of me, listing the elements of today's lunch. Except this isn't an old TV show I've binge-watched.

It's Christian's life.

Soon, plates are set in front of us, and I stare down at a plate of fine china filled with a generous slice of juicy, medium-rare roast beef, Yorkshire pudding, fresh spring peas, and crisp, golden roasted potatoes—all cut to precisely the same size.

Another elegantly-dressed staff member comes around with gravy service, and I am rewarded with a sauce that glides like velvet over my meat and Yorkshire pudding. Before I can murmur a thank you, he discreetly slips away. Instead, I turn my attention to King Arthur.

"Sir, thank you so much for inviting me here today," I say, smiling at him. "I'm happy to make your acquaintance, and I am honored to be here for lunch."

Christian shoots me a look, which confuses me. I can't quite detect what I'm seeing in his blue eyes. Concern? Annoyance? What?

But more than what, *why?* I had practiced what to say on the way over here, and that sounded like a perfectly appropriate thing to say to a king. I rack my brain, trying to figure out what I could have possibly said that was wrong or insulting.

"You can talk to Father like you talk to me, Clementine," Christian says, picking up his knife and fork.

Anger prickles me. I do not like Christian telling me how I can—or cannot—speak to his father. I've never seen this side of him, and while I'm irritated, I know there's something driving this, because this is not the man I know.

King Arthur's brow creases. "Of course she can, but I don't see how thanking me is inappropriate."

"It's not, but I don't want her to think she has to speak so formally to you. Or to any of us, for that matter."

I study Christian, vowing I'll find out later what this is really about. For now, he's not getting away with talking about me like I'm not here. I don't care if the king is sitting directly across from us or not.

"I'm quite capable of speaking for myself, Christian," I say evenly as I cut my meat. "My parents taught me manners and conversation starters. I might not hold my cutlery the same as you, but that has no bearing on how I choose to thank your father for generously hosting this lunch."

I pause and take a bite of my roast beef, which, oooooh, is the most succulent piece of beef I've ever had in my life, and chew thoughtfully while I try to figure out what Christian's deal is.

"I'm sorry. I was out of line," Christian demurs. "I don't want you to feel like you need to treat us differently."

He puts his knife down and places his hand on my knee, and when I gaze up at him, I see sincerity is back in his eyes.

Then I get it.

I'm the one person, outside of his very small inner circle, who has treated him like Christian. He doesn't want me to change to fit into his family, and my speaking more formally, in his mind, was like the first domino to fall, when nothing could be further from the truth.

I smile at him. "You're lucky. Because of this incredible roast beef, I shall forget that comment," I say, teasing him. "And for good measure, I promise you I'm still your Fiona even when you are being ridiculous."

King Arthur observes us with interest.

"When I watch you two," King Arthur says, pausing to take a sip of his wine, "I feel as if I'm watching two people who have known each other much longer than you have. How is that possible?"

"We spent hours talking before we met," Christian says, staring at me with love in his eyes. "We got to know each other very well."

"I assume you were the reason for Christian's sudden urge to go find himself in the United States?" King Arthur teases.

I blush. "Yes."

"Meeting her in person just made our bond stronger," Christian says, ignoring his food as he talks. "It was as if we had been dating the whole time and meeting in person made it official."

I nod. "Despite the time difference, lectures, and my internship, we made the time to talk."

"We made each other a priority," Christian explains. "But I knew from her first message that Clementine was special. She was funny. I loved that."

"I like that about you, too," I say, my heart growing warm. "You were sharp. Clever. I couldn't wait to talk to you again."

"Same," Christian says, gently squeezing my knee underneath the table.

"We talked about everything," I continue, eager to share our story with King Arthur. "From the state of the world to our dreams to our favorite TV shows and what we liked to eat."

"Don't ever serve her fish," Christian says. "Clementine has a mortal fear of it."

"Ha, at least I like cilantro."

"It's coriander, and it's disgusting. It tastes like soap."

"Did you eat soap to make that comparison accurately?"

"I'm ignoring you."

"Ha, you'd like to try," I say, "but you can't."

"No, I can't," Christian says, smiling lovingly at me.

I feel King Arthur's gaze from across the table. I look at him, and with a jolt, I realize his blue eyes, identical to Christian's, also reflect his emotions.

I see sadness in them as he studies us, which makes my heart break for him.

He must feel me staring at him, because he picks up his cutlery and busies himself with the task of eating.

Christian fills the void, asking his father about his upcoming trip to Denmark, and I listen quietly as I hear the various events on the king's schedule, including dinners with the queen, prince, and prime minister; visits to various charities and meetings; and trips to local museums in Copenhagen.

I see how the king's eyes change as he talks about this visit. They light up when he talks about meeting the people of Copenhagen and explains how he always loves the exchanges that come when he interacts with people on the street.

He's like Christian, I think. He enjoys people who engage

him with what they do in their day-to-day lives. King Arthur likes learning about what they do and likes drilling down on it, asking questions and seeing how other people live.

He enjoys hearing about people who live differently than he does, who have normal lives as opposed to those chosen by birth.

"Let me guess, Her Majesty's diary is full that week?" Christian asks as he finishes his meal.

I nearly choke on my Yorkshire pudding. This is the first time all afternoon Queen Antonia has been brought up.

King Arthur blots his lips on a napkin and lays his knife and fork across his plate to signal he's finished. The household staff springs into action like ninjas on a mission, and as I'm about to take a bite of roasted potatoes, my plate is taken from me.

"I-I'm not finished," I say.

The room is silent.

The man with my plate appears perplexed by my comment.

Christian clears his throat. "When the king is finished, we are all finished with the meal."

Oh, crap.

My face burns in humiliation. I had no idea that was a rule. I thought I was doing well with the curtsy and keeping my knees locked into that most uncomfortable position at that practically protractor-measured angle.

"Miss Jones may finish in her own time," King Arthur insists.

The man with my plate immediately sets it back in front of me, and now I'm really embarrassed.

"No, it's fine. I'm so sorry. I eat very slowly. Ask Christian. It took me forever to eat two pieces of fudge. I'll drive him batty in the future because I'm such a deliberate eater. So you can take it away. I'm fine."

I stop to take a breath, and Christian and King Arthur are both smiling at me.

"You know, that rule is woefully outdated," King Arthur declares. "Handy for a state dinner when you want to get things moving, but since Queen Antonia isn't here to remind me we don't deviate from the house rules, I'm fine with it. It has to be annoying to have your plate removed mid-bite."

"I'm enjoying my meal so much," I say. "I'm not a woman who picks at her food. I want to eat everything, and I'm already wondering what the menu card means when it says assorted desserts. I'll probably want to try all of them, and now I'm rambling, so I'm going to eat now."

I quickly spear a roasted potato and eat to shut myself up. King Arthur laughs at my admission—a true, deep laugh—and Christian and I join him.

"I see why my son is smitten with you," King Arthur says, smiling at me.

I keep my gaze down as I eat, my face growing hot from his kind words. I swallow and force myself to meet his gaze.

"Thank you, sir," I say.

He clears his throat and shifts his attention back to Christian. "In regard to your question, Christian, your mother does have a full diary next week with her patron charities and will not accompany me on this trip."

"Let me guess. She's busy caring for her subjects and couldn't come to meet Clementine today?"

I freeze mid-bite. I know she wants nothing to do with me, and there's no doubt in my mind she is probably mortified the king is sitting here in my presence, let alone letting me keep eating my meal after he's finished.

"No, I didn't invite your mother," King Arthur says slowly. "I wanted to meet Clementine and see how you were without the dramatics that come with Her Majesty."

Whoa. I blink in surprise, and from the way Christian's back went straight, I think he's surprised, too.

"She will be furious," Christian says. "Of course, she would have refused the invitation, but she would have demanded you come nowhere near us. I told you what she said about Clementine in that text message."

"I don't care," King Arthur says. "You are *my* son. I want you to be happy, and I wanted to meet the woman who got you out of your flat and into the open with a smile on your face." He turns toward me. "I'm glad I'm having lunch with her today. In fact, once Clementine is finished with her meal, I'd like to show her the private gardens before dessert—if you don't mind me borrowing her for a little walk."

I nearly choke on my food. The king wants to walk with me alone?

"Are you all right with that?" Christian asks.

I put my cutlery on my plate to signal I'm finished. The same man who took my plate before quickly reappears and clears it before I can blink.

I know this is an important invitation, even if it terrifies me.

The King of the United Kingdom is going to make sure I'm here for his son and his son alone. I can feel it with everything I am.

And whatever his test is, I intend to pass it.

"A walk before dessert would be lovely," I say.

I'm nervous as I stroll with King Arthur through the most beautiful garden I have ever seen. Spring bulbs are blooming everywhere, and the grass is rich and green. Normally, I would savor this walk, stopping to take a video and pictures, but not today. This isn't a walk to enjoy the English countryside.

I know this is a make or break moment. If the king doesn't approve of me, it will make Christian's life harder.

But no matter what he thinks, or if he tries to dissuade me from continuing a relationship with Christian, King Arthur will find I'm just as formidable as Queen Antonia when it comes to my love for Christian.

"These gardens are beautiful, sir," I say as we begin our stroll.

"Please, you can call me Arthur," he says. "At least when it's just us."

I smile. "Okay, Arthur," I repeat.

"Sandringham is my joy," King Arthur explains as we walk. "I'm happiest out here in the country."

I nod. "I know Christian loves his country walks with Lucy. We plan to go on one tomorrow, as a matter of fact."

"My son has changed because of you," King Arthur says. "Those pictures yesterday—"

"Those were all my fault," I interrupt. "I talked him into taking them. I only wanted him to have some fun, and I swear I'll take my lead from him in the future and be very, very care—"

King Arthur stops and puts his hand on my arm. "No. Don't stop being you. Don't you see you are breaking him free from his fears?"

I'm shocked by his words. I keep quiet and let him continue.

"Christian knows what his duty will be," King Arthur

says. He begins to walk again, and I fall into step next to him. "But he hasn't found his own direction yet. He has successfully hidden away at Cambridge. I know he hates the constraints placed upon him. I understand that better than anyone, as I grew up groomed to become a king. Alexander has it worse, but he's gone the opposite direction. He sees this as his chance to have fun and push the envelope before people expect him to be serious. Alexander doesn't care if people like him for his title, whereas Christian has a mortal fear of people using him to get close to the monarchy."

King Arthur is pouring out his heart to me. I know he trusts me, and I decide to do the same.

"I fell for Christian before I knew he was a prince," I say as we walk. "He introduced himself as CP Chadwick. I'm not a follower of the royal family, so I had no idea what that stood for. I know our relationship won't be easy because of who he is, but I know what I feel for him. I will do anything to be with your son, Arthur. He's everything I've ever dreamed of. Christian is strong, intelligent, and compassionate, and he treats me like a normal girl."

"What do you mean by that?" King Arthur asks.

I draw a breath of air. "May I tell you something in confidence?"

"Of course."

"When I was a teen, I had a brain tumor," I say slowly. "It was benign, but I had to have it removed. The surgery left a little paralysis on the right side of my face. I still have to have periodic scans to make sure everything is fine, and so far, everything has been. But because of it, my parents have been ultra-protective."

"I'm sorry, Clementine. That's frightening as an adult. I

can't imagine what you went through as a teenager, or what your parents went through when they were told."

"I feel guilty," I say. "Because my tumor changed them. It was a terrifying time for all of us. But ever since then, I ceased to be Clementine. I'm now the child who had a tumor. Fear drives them to treat me as if I'm fragile. Christian knows all of this, and I had a scare this winter. Christian was the only one who allowed me to speak freely about my feelings. He never wavered in how he treated me. He never saw me as fragile. Christian was strong for me, and I knew he would walk with me on whatever road I needed to take. I also knew I would still be *Clementine* to him."

I look at him, and I see recognition dawn in his eyes.

"With each other, we are normal," I say softly. "I'm not the girl who had a tumor. He's not a prince. We love each other for who we are when the labels are stripped away. The one gift I want to give Christian is the ability to be himself, to find a way to embrace his duty as the amazing man he is and let people into his world."

King Arthur's eyes hold steady on me.

"Christian has kept a high wall around himself, and I don't blame him," King Arthur says, shifting his gaze straight ahead. "His family life hasn't been what I wanted for him, and it guts me that I am part of the reason he is the way he is. I know you know what I mean."

I swallow hard, emotions swelling in me as I think of how Christian grew up.

"This is why I wouldn't let him run into the military," King Arthur says. "It was another wall to hide behind. I want him to take a year and figure himself out. If he's called to serve after that time, I will stand behind him. But now you've entered his life, and the walls are already lowering. I know you love my son for who he is. I hear it in your voice. I see it in your eyes when you look at him."

"I do, Arthur," I say, my voice growing thick. "I know the road for us won't be easy, but when you love someone like I love Christian, you get through it."

"You'd have to give up a lot to be with my son," King Arthur says seriously.

"I'd have to move here," I say as we walk. "I'd have to start over with a new life, one with intrusions from the press and rigorous protocol, like learning to eat faster," I tease.

King Arthur laughs. "There are absurd rules, but some perks as well, like getting a tea tray with exactly what you want on it, delivered to you daily."

"What if I don't drink tea?"

King Arthur stops walking. "What blasphemy is this?"

"I hate it."

"You two better end things now, before the British press finds out."

We both laugh.

"In all seriousness," I continue as we move down the garden path, "I would give all that up for a life with Christian. I'd find a way to share my love of antiques and history as part of my royal duties, if we progress to that point in the future. I'd support Christian in pursuing his dreams, too. There will be awful days, but every couple has them, royal or not. At the end of the day, if I can hold his hand and rest my head on his shoulder, then that is all that matters."

I feel King Arthur staring at me. I lift my gaze to meet his, and he stops walking again.

"You are everything to my son," King Arthur says. "You are his one. No matter what happens ahead, what arguments or bad days you have, I want you to remember that. I see what you have, and you both have my full support."

Tears of gratitude fill my eyes. "Thank you."

King Arthur takes my hand in his and squeezes it affectionately. "The Dowager Queen and Queen Antonia are not going to be so accepting of you. But after talking to you, I know you are strong, a fighter. You love Christian as the man he is. You are formidable in your own right, remember that."

"I will," I promise.

"All right. Let's head back home. I think it's time I return you to my son."

We turn around on the path and head back the way we came, but everything is different now. There's a warning in Arthur's words of what lies ahead, but I know King Arthur will be on our side. The road ahead is going to be hard, with roadblocks and challenges I can't yet imagine. But no matter what they are, Christian is worth it. We'll navigate them as a team.

First, however, I need to do one thing.

I need to address Christian's overreaction to the way I spoke at the dinner table. I need to reassure him I'm not changing to fit into the system but adapting when I need to. It doesn't mean I'm becoming a different person.

And that conversation needs to happen right now.

CHAPTER 19

A PRIVATE WALTZ

King Arthur leads me to the entrance of the grand ballroom. One of his aides, butlers, valets—I still have no idea who all these different people are—but someone on his staff told us Christian was waiting there.

"I think our walk is done," he says, smiling as he stops in front of the closed doors. "I have no doubt my son is eager to see you."

"I enjoyed getting to know you, Arthur," I say, smiling up at him. "Thank you for spending that time with me."

"It was my pleasure," he says. "Enjoy the rest of your stay in Cambridge. I have a feeling I'll be seeing you in London soon."

My heart races from his words as he walks away. Christian and I haven't spoken that far ahead, but I can see that as my future, too.

I push that thought aside and open the doors to the ballroom. I gasp as I enter the majestic room. I've stepped back in time, with a glorious red, patterned antique rug over the hardwood floor, chandeliers hanging from the ceiling, and weapons and armor displayed on the walls.

Christian is leaning against a piano, his suit jacket off, watching me as I step across the floor.

"This is spectacular," I say, staring up at the ornate ceiling as I move across the room.

"I had to show you this ballroom; I knew you'd love it," Christian says.

"I do."

"The weapons on the walls might distract a bit from the romance, however," Christian teases.

I stop in front of him, and he draws me into his arms.

"How was your walk with Father?" he asks, fiddling with a strand of my hair.

"Your father—Arthur—is lovely," I say, sliding my hands around his back, feeling the luxurious fabric from his dress shirt against my fingertips, followed by the warmth radiating from his skin. "I did address him as that, Christian."

He flinches from my words, and I know he knows where I'm going.

"I'm sorry I was such an arse at lunch," Christian says, continuing to stroke my hair. "I heard this strange formal speak coming out of your mouth, and it flipped a switch in me. I love you as you are, and I don't want you to change for the family business."

I take one of my hands and place it over his heart. "There will be moments when I feel I need to act to suit the occasion, but that doesn't mean I'm changing. Please remember that."

"I've had people come into my life and change because of who we are and what we are supposed to be," Christian says. "I don't want to lose you to them, Clementine. The monarchy changes people, and I can't bear the thought of it changing anything about you. I know it sounds crazy, but that's how I feel."

I see fear in his eyes. I don't know who he is talking about, but my gut tells me this has happened to him before. Maybe a former love changed once she was in the presence of the family business, as Christian likes to call the monarchy. Or friends began wanting access to this side of his life once he let them in the golden door.

"I promise you," I say, "I'm never going to change. Might I be more formal in front of your parents? Of course. But I'm still going to come to you at the end of the night and borrow one of your Arsenal T-shirts to sleep in and leave the cap off the toothpaste, whether that's in your room in Cambridge or at Kensington Palace. I'll still sing songs from the *Shrek* soundtrack when I'm driving. And I'll never like tea."

"If you ever say you like tea, I'll know it's over," Christian says, a smile tugging at the corner of his mouth.

"You'll never hear it," I promise.

"I still can't believe this room," I say, looking around the empty ballroom. "I can only imagine the parties the king and queen would have had in this room. The waltzing in gorgeous gowns ..."

My voice trails off as I picture a room filled with royals and elites and the whirling of women in beautiful gowns and men in tuxes.

"Have you ever waltzed?"

I snap out of my mental movie and turn back to Christian. "Noooo."

"Not just no, but noooo?" Christian says, his eyes dancing at me.

"I have no idea how to do a proper dance."

"It's easy. You start with a box step."

"I was always at the pool as a little girl, not dance class. I have two annoying left feet."

Christian leads me out to the center of the ballroom floor. "I can teach you. Mother made all of us learn so we could be proper princes at business events where dancing is involved."

I place my hand on his shoulder, my palm resting against his crisp dress shirt. I feel his sculpted muscle underneath it, followed by the warmth radiating from his skin. Christian takes my other hand with his, holding it gently.

Oh, swoon.

"We'll do the waltz box step," Christian says. "All you are doing is making a box. It's a three count; very easy, Ace."

I feel butterflies form in my stomach as Christian begins to count me through the step. "Back with your right. Side with your left ..."

I hesitantly step backward and listen to Christian's rich British voice guide me through it.

"Now close with the right. Now forward with the left."

Before I know it, we're doing the box step in the grand ballroom.

"I'm waltzing!" I cry excitedly as we begin to pick up the pace.

"Your first waltz," Christian says, smiling down at me.

"I'm glad it was with you," I say, my heart full of joy.

"I've never danced with a woman I love before," Christian murmurs, his expression going soft. "Now I know what I've been missing. *You.*"

The moment is pure magic. Dancing in Christian's arms in a royal ballroom, I see nothing but love in his eyes as he leads me in the box step, and I know this is a moment I'll always treasure. Just me and Christian.

My first waltz with the man I love.

Life couldn't be any more perfect than this.

"I cannot believe you," my mother sobs into the phone as Christian drives us back to Cambridge. "You've run off to England with a *prince?* What is happening here? This sounds like a Hallmark movie! Except I don't have a script in front of me assuring me he's a sweet prince. He's a hoarder. That is a mental illness, Clementine. You can't fall in love with him and think you can clean his apartment and make him all better. Oh God, what are you doing?"

I squeeze my eyes shut. I feel a stress headache coming on. My lovely waltz has been followed up with a hysterical phone call from my mother, who left me a ton of voicemails and texts begging me to call her ASAP while I was at Sandringham.

It's only nine o'clock in the morning in Phoenix.

"Mom, you need to listen to me. I did not run off to England to heal a prince with a hoarding problem."

Christian snorts, and I can't help but smile when I see the amused look on his gorgeous face.

"Paisley said you met him online. How? How does one meet a prince online?"

"By talking about art," I say. "Mom, I didn't know Christian was a prince when I met him. We became friends. I talked to him more than I have any other guy I've ever dated before I met him."

"This is crazy. I forbid you to run off to England for a

prince. Do you follow the stories of royals in *Dishing Weekly?* You are going to get your heart broken!"

"Mom. If I were dating Xander, then yes, my heart would be broken. But that's not the prince I'm dating. I'm dating the hoarder with curry tubs, remember?"

I glance at Christian, who shoots me a side-eyed look. I must turn away before I burst out laughing.

"How can you date someone you don't know?"

"How do you know I don't know him?" I ask, prickling with annoyance. "I know Christian better than my last three boyfriends combined. This isn't some game to us, Mom."

"Just because you have become enchanted with a prince —dear God, I can't believe I just uttered those words— doesn't mean he is with you. Are you telling me you're going to uproot your life for him and give up everything and move to England on the minuscule chance this might work out?"

"You don't know what we have."

"How would I? You've kept him a secret!"

"For this very reason. I knew you'd get upset and freak out and tell me I'm wrong to follow my heart. All you want to do is protect me. I need to *live*."

"Now you're being melodramatic."

"No, you're just not used to me doing something you don't approve of. But you know me; I wouldn't do all this if Christian wasn't exceptional."

"Clementine, you aren't being rational. He's a prince. Don't you think that is clouding your judgment?"

"No."

"How can it not? Doesn't every girl dream of finding a prince? And you got one."

"Wrong. I found a *man* who is perfect for me, in every

sense of the word, and once you get to know him, you'll feel that way, too."

"How can you possibly know that? You met him online. And then you flew off to Europe under the pretense of soaking in estate culture because you didn't want to tell your parents. That's not exactly a ringing endorsement. You've never been so reckless in your entire life, and quite honestly, I'm alarmed. I think you need a psychologist."

"I do not need a psychologist!" I yell angrily. "This is why I said I was going to look at estates. You would never think I was mature enough to make my own decisions. Quit treating me like a bird that needs its wings clipped. I'm not a bird in a cage; I'm your daughter. Don't you trust me?"

"Not when you are acting so out of character, I don't!" Mom cries, her voice cracking. Then I hear Dad take the phone from her.

"Sweetheart, we aren't mad," Dad says, trying to reframe the conversation. "But you aren't acting in your best interests. You are being far too reckless with your emotions. I'm sure some of this is driven by all the stress of the scare a—"

"Okay, stop. Stop it. This has nothing to do with me having scans this winter. This is me making my own decisions. For once in my life, I'm not letting you protect me. Why can't you trust me?"

"Trust you? When you lie to us and run off across the pond to some man we've never heard of? You even roped Paisley into covering for you, which we are none too pleased about."

"You leave Paisley out of this."

"Enough. We are flying over there to get you," Dad says sternly. "We'll discuss this back at home."

"You will do no such thing. If you come over here," I

say, my voice shaking, "I will not go with you. I will talk to you when I get back to San Jose, but this conversation ends right now. I love you, but you need to love me enough to let me be an adult."

"If you gave us reason to believe that, we would," Dad says angrily. "But right now, you're acting more like a love-sick teenager than an adult. One who is defying logic and running off to play romantic games with a prince? This is not the daughter I raised."

His words feel like a slap across the face. This is the first time I have ever defied them. Disappointed them.

Hurt them.

The parents who went through hell and back with my health are now suffering because of my actions, and part of me wants to make it right.

But then I look at Christian, and I know what I need to do.

"I'll call you on Saturday," I say to my dad, my voice thick. "I love you both."

Then I hang up the phone.

Silence hangs between me and Christian, and I blink back tears. The English countryside blurs in my eyes as we drive back to Cambridge.

"Are you okay?" Christian asks softly.

I sniffle. "I've hurt them."

"I'm sorry I put you in this position."

I turn to face him. "No, I put myself here, and I don't regret it, not for a split-second. For the first time in my life, I'm doing what I want. And what I want is to be here, with you."

"Would it help if I called them when we got back?" Christian asks. "FaceTime with them? Show them a video of the house so they know I'm not stashing curry takeaway tubs and buried in rubbish?"

I manage to laugh. God, I love how he knows what I need.

"Maybe tomorrow. They need to calm down. So do I."

"Whatever you need me to do, I'll do it. I guarantee you I could get Father to talk to them if that would help."

I'm trying to imagine my mother taking a phone call from the King of England, and I start laughing.

"What?"

"My mother would die if Arthur called her," I say, smiling at Christian. "I can't imagine her sitting in her big comfy chair doing that Tom Hiddleston needlepoint while the king calls her up to assure her the Golden Prince is a doting boyfriend. Surreal."

"Tom Hiddleston on a needlepoint pattern is still odd."

I snort. "No, odd is your face on a needlepoint pattern."

"I don't want to know if that exists."

"It does."

Christian begins to turn red in embarrassment, and oh, how I love this man and his modest nature.

"Let's put all this aside," I say. "We had such a wonderful day, our first waltz, and I want to enjoy the rest of the evening with you."

"I love you," Christian says softly.

"I love you, too," I say.

I resolve to deal with my parents when I get home. Christian and I deserve this time to be a normal couple in love, without my parents interfering. I don't know what the future will hold for us, but if things go the way my heart tells me they will, Christian will ask me to move to London after I graduate from Stanford.

And I already know my answer will be yes.

CHAPTER 20

WHERE DO WE GO FROM HERE?

The week has gone by far too quickly.

Sadness washes over me as I unload the things I bought this morning from the Cambridge Market for our picnic lunch. My throat swells as I think of having to say goodbye to him tomorrow. I don't want to go back to California. My heart physically aches as the thought of boarding the plane fills my head.

The only way I can leave him, I think, *is knowing I'll be coming back in June.*

Not only to Christian, but to this amazing country I've fallen in love with this past week.

While Christian was in class, I explored England and became enraptured with the place he calls home. It's incredibly rich in tradition and history, and my art-and antique-loving soul immediately felt at home here.

Emma was kind enough to take me to two magnificent estate homes. I saw stunning silks from the eighteenth century in bedrooms with elaborate, carved canopy beds. There were gilded sofas and an exquisite silver cistern to chill wine. It made me want to work at one of these historic estates, curating collections to share with the world.

Christian promised me I'd have access to much more in his family's various homes.

Places like Buckingham Palace.

Absolutely unreal. Even though I was in Sandringham and experienced royal life first-hand, it's hard to believe that when Christian goes home on breaks, he goes to Buckingham Palace to drop his duffle bag and have a home-cooked meal, prepared by an esteemed chef and a whole kitchen staff, of course.

I shake my head and add a wedge of Christian's favorite cheese to the picnic basket while continuing to reflect on the past week. I went into Cambridge on my own and toured the King's College Chapel, one of the most breathtaking buildings I have ever been inside, with its majestic stained glass and incredible fan-vaulted ceiling. I explored the shops and the outdoor market and marveled at so many things during this life-changing visit.

Christian spent time with me whenever possible. He took me on a tour of King's College, and then to my delight, we spent an early evening punting on the River Cam, which was incredibly fun. The punt is a small, flat-bottomed boat, and Christian is quite good at it, as he expertly used the pole to guide the punt down the river. We went along the Backs—which is the back of the colleges of Cambridge—and under bridges at dusk. He told me stories about Cambridge, and pointed out his favorite buildings, and I loved seeing his world through his eyes. We took long walks with Lucy along the Backs, too, and I can still smell the scent of the fresh grass and clean air of the countryside from those outings.

We cooked dinner at home, sharing the work from

grocery shopping to cleaning the kitchen afterwards. Christian made his specialty—spag bol, which is spaghetti with Bolognese sauce—and said the palace chef taught him how to make the perfect sauce.

It was in those moments—cooking a meal, loading the dishwasher, watching TV together—that I knew this is what our life would be like. Behind closed doors, sharing bottles of wine with our friends, playing board games with Stephen and Emma, reading books side by side on the sofa—this is us.

Love replaces the anguished feeling in my heart. I remember seeing him look at me with affection as I sampled his sauce. The way he looped his fingers through my hair as we watched TV. The way he smiled as he listened to me recount my day exploring England. How he brought me a cup of hot chocolate every morning before he darted off to class, parking it on the nightstand next to me and waking me by dropping a kiss on my forehead.

I hear a car pull up in the drive, and I know it's Christian. He's off the rest of the day now, and we're going to make the most of our last day together. Lucy runs to the door, as eager for Christian to be home as I am. I hear the door beep, meaning the security card has been used, and then I hear Christian talking to Lucy.

"Here's my girl," I hear him say to Lucy, and I smile as I picture him bending down and petting her affectionately. "Let's go find Clementine."

"In the kitchen," I answer.

Christian strolls in with a flat white box in his arms. "Hello, Fiona, how was your morning?"

Emotions overwhelm me the second I see him because I realize this is the last lunch I'm going to have with him for a long time. Tears fill my eyes, and I quickly turn back to messing with the picnic basket so he can't see I'm about to cry.

I clear my throat. "I hope you're hungry. I bought half the market today for our picnic."

"I have something in this box for our picnic, too," Christian says, moving next to me. "You didn't cheat and buy dessert, did you? Because I told you I was going to handle that one."

I shake my head. "No, I didn't."

He leans down closer to me, and I inhale the scent of his clean cologne as he noses around in the basket.

"Champagne ... strawberries ... ah! Brilliant," Christian says, picking up the double Gloucester.

"Your cheese, sir," I tease.

He grins. "What else do we have?"

"Grapes, scones, jam, clotted cream," I say, rattling off the contents. "And mini quiches."

"You do English very well," Christian says, his eyes dancing.

"I think I do, too," I say.

He drops a sweet kiss on my lips. "Let me get a blanket, and we'll go sit in the garden." He trots up the stairs, with Lucy eagerly dashing behind him.

As I watch him disappear, despair fills me. What if he thinks it's too soon for me to move to London? What if he wants to do long-distance even longer? How can I do this, when all I want to do is be with him? What if this conversation doesn't go as I hope? I've been positive, but what if this is all me?

What if I'm ready to leap, but Christian is not?

I turn back to the basket, irritated with myself for being insecure. I need to believe in what we have. In Christian.

In us.

"Got it," Christian says, trotting back down the stairs. "You can carry the bakery box, but no peeking."

"I promise I won't even try to steal a peek," I say.

He lifts the basket off the counter, and we head out the back door, to the private garden filled with blooms of purple and yellow and white. Trees tower overhead, with sun shining through the leaves, and best of all, we have it all to ourselves.

We stop in the middle of the lawn, and Christian spreads out a thick blanket for us to sit on. He takes my hand and helps me down before he sits on the blanket next to me.

"Champagne first," Christian says, reaching for the bottle.

I take out two plastic cups, and he uncorks the bottle, the pop sending Lucy into a barking tizzy on the grass.

"Lucy, stop. I'm trying to woo the girl," Christian teases.

"Woo me?" I ask, laughing. "I think you already have me."

Christian doesn't say anything. In fact, he almost looks nervous.

Now I'm confused.

I hold my cup out, and Christian fills it with the bubbly. Then he pours a cup for himself and sets the bottle back into the basket.

"To you," he says, staring deeply into my eyes. "I'm so glad you're here."

My heart holds still. "To us," I correct.

We tap our cups together, and I take a sip, but I notice Christian does not.

"Christian? What's wrong?"

He stares straight ahead for what seems like a long time. I grow jittery as I wait for him to speak.

"I have to talk to you about something."

I suck in air. This is the moment.

The future is now.

"Okay," I say, my voice barely a whisper.

"I have no right to ask you what I'm going to ask," he says. He puts his cup down and takes my cup and places it on the grass. Then he laces his fingers through mine, holding my hand tightly in his. "We have to talk about where we go from here."

I can't breathe.

"I don't want you to leave," Christian says, his voice thick with emotion. "Now that I know what it's like to be with you every day, I know I can't be without you."

Tears of joy fill my eyes. "I feel the same way. I have to be with you, Christian."

He clears his throat. "To be with me, you have to give up a lot. I can't leave the country. You would have to leave your home, your family, your friends, the United States, to live in a fishbowl over here to be with me."

"What are you asking me?" I whisper.

"Clementine, I'm asking you to consider moving to London, in June."

I begin to shake. "You want me to move to London?"

"I know it's soon. I know you might want to wait. We can't live together, lord knows the monarchy hasn't evolved that much, but—"

"Yes," I interrupt.

Christian stops speaking. "What?"

"I have wanted you to ask me to come here," I say. "I don't know how it would work. I know there are visas involved, and London is expensive, and I'll need a job, and I have to figure out how to get Bear over here, but yes. I want to be with you. I have fallen in love with England, and

I know I'll love London. But most of all, I love you. The sooner we're together, the better."

"What if I told you I had some of this sorted?"

I furrow my brow. "How?"

"Father called me after our visit to Sandringham. He asked what I planned to do, and I said I wanted you to come to London. He had already thought ahead and put a call into an old friend who owns a historic estate in London. Lord and Lady Cheltham have agreed to sponsor you for a work visa, and you will be able to give tours in their estate, if you want the job. You don't have to take it, you know. Father knows you hope to work in antiques and thought this would be a great place for you to start."

My heart is racing. "Arthur did that for me?"

Christian nods. "He adores you, Clementine. Father knows you're genuine. He also knows you love me, and he said he believes in us after seeing what we have. Hopefully, someday, your parents will feel the same way."

I bite my lip. I know he's right. If Mom and Dad could spend time with Christian, they would know he's the right man for me.

The only man for me.

"This job," I say slowly, "would be an incredible opportunity. I can't imagine a better way to start my post-college life than working at a stately home in London."

I pause for a moment.

"What?" Christian asks.

"This is going to be my life," I whisper, dazed. "I'm going to work in a beautiful home surrounded by antiques in London. This is crazy!"

"Crazy awesome?" Christian supplies helpfully.

"Yes!" I cry. "And I'll be with you!"

I grab his gorgeous face and give him a kiss. Christian laughs against my mouth, and I laugh, too.

"So I take it I can have Felicity—Lady Cheltham—contact you for a phone interview?" he asks.

"Yes," I say, nodding enthusiastically. Then I frown. "London is expensive. I'll have to start looking now for an affordable place to live."

"I will help you find something, and I can help you pay. Your parents need to be assured you will be comfortable and safe."

I cock an eyebrow at him. "You will not be helping me with rent. You are dating an independent American, Your Royal Highness."

He cocks an eyebrow back at me. "I call it an investment in our future."

"No."

"We'll argue about this later."

I smile. "That I will agree to."

A silence falls between us as everything sinks in.

I'm going to have a whole new life come June.

In London. With my prince.

I can't help but smile. My life *is* sounding like one of those royal TV movies now.

"So, this is really going to happen?" I ask.

"Yes. We'll be together, if that is what you truly want."

"It's *all* I've wanted."

Christian frames my face in his hands and kisses me, slowly and sweetly.

He breaks away and slides one hand underneath my hair. "Let's have dessert first, to celebrate our future."

Our future.

Those words make butterflies dance in my stomach.

Christian reaches around and hands me the white pastry box. "Open it."

I lift the lid, and a gasp escapes my lips as I find a box filled with exquisite sugar cookies in the shape of the icons of London: the London Bridge, Big Ben, a red double-decker bus, a red phone booth, the Union Jack, and one heart in the center, that is cut in half but fits perfectly together.

"Christian," I whisper, touched by his gift to me.

"I know how much you love an artful sugar cookie," he says, picking up one half of the heart. "And I also know my heart will only be whole again when you are back in London."

He puts his half of the heart back in the box next to mine, making it whole again.

Tears fall from my eyes. I know Christian thinks I'm giving up a lot to be with him, but what he doesn't understand is the love he is giving me is everything I have ever dreamed of.

With Christian, this caged bird has found her wings.

And I'm flying.

"I love you," I say, my voice thick with tears. "You are the best thing that has ever come into my life."

"I love you more," Christian says, his eyes shining with emotion for me. "And I can't wait to be in the same city as you."

I lean forward and kiss him. Christian takes the box of cookies and sets it aside, and then he lowers me back onto the blanket, kissing me under the warm sun. I lose myself in his arms, feeling his tongue explore my mouth and his hand slide up underneath my shirt, stroking my waist. I move my hand up to his neck, touching the golden curls at the nape and relishing the feel of his hands on my body. His mouth, warm and soft, seeks mine, his body pinning me to the blanket and making me feel desired. All I want is to spend the afternoon here in our private garden, kissing and touching and knowing in a few months, our future will truly begin.

And just like the English sun shining down on us today, it feels very bright indeed.

CHAPTER 21

GRADUATION DAY

I draw a breath of air as I put my black graduation cap carefully on my head. I stare at my reflection in the mirror, and a mix of emotions swirls through me.

Today, I'm graduating from Stanford.

I turn and glance around the bedroom I share with Chelsea. It's filled with boxes, as we move out of the apartment tomorrow. So many memories were made here: late-night conversations with Chelsea, snickers over hearing Bryn and Graham's sexual ecstasy next door, and exhausting study sessions.

I look at the boxes and, with sadness, realize this is the last time we'll all be together for a long time. Bryn is moving in with Graham to an apartment in San Francisco. Chelsea is moving to New York to attend NYU and work on her master's.

And I'm moving to London to start my life with Christian.

I have been counting down the days until I leave for London. I interviewed for my estate tour job, and Lady

Cheltham said my resume—err, CV as they call it over there—was impressive and Arthur didn't do me justice. She asked me to help find antiques for new rooms they want to add to the tour. I've studied the house, and it's beyond anything I could have dreamed of. Built in 1779, it's a neoclassical gem inside the city. Lord and Lady Cheltham still reside there, but they open certain rooms of the home to share their love of history and art with the public. Lady Cheltham is as passionate about antiques as I am, with her love being for needlework and porcelain. I can't wait to start learning from her.

The day I returned from my visit to Cambridge, I started preparations to go to London. Lord and Lady Cheltham sponsored me for a work visa. Apartment prices in London nearly made me cry, but then I stumbled on a program that matches young people with elderly people looking to rent out rooms. I immediately knew this was the answer. I could live somewhere nice and have company, too. It would be good to have someone to share conversations and meals with outside of my life with Christian.

I was matched with Jillian, a widowed woman who owns a charming Victorian garden flat in Kensington. It even has a private terrace! Jillian has been welcoming over the phone, telling me all about her neighborhood and what I can expect. I told her I was dating Prince Christian and had Christian send over a letter on official Kensington Palace stationery to confirm I wasn't a lunatic. I asked her if she understood this might make her life more complicated, as in photographers being outside and waiting to ambush me, and by association, her. Jillian laughed when I expressed my concern. She quipped that it will liven things up on her quiet, tree-lined street. I can already tell I'm going to adore her. Jillian's even excited Bear will be coming with me. His vaccinations are up to date, his paperwork is certified, and he is ready for his flight to London tomorrow.

Soon, we'll be with Christian.

I smile as happiness replaces my sadness, winning the emotional war within me. While I'm nervous and sad to leave my family and friends and the United States behind, I feel as if I'm going where I'm meant to be. I was destined to have this adventure of a lifetime in the United Kingdom.

With the man I love.

I hear the door open and find Bryn standing in the doorway, also dressed in her cap and gown. The second she sees me, she bursts into tears.

"How can we say goodbye?" Bryn sobs.

"We don't," I say, moving over to her and hugging her tightly, my eyes swimming with tears. "We say 'see you soon.'"

"I can't believe you're going to London. To be with a prince."

I step back from her. "You are required to message me every day."

"You can count on it. And Graham and I are coming to London in August. We want the insider tour of Buckingham Palace."

I snort. "If Queen Antonia ever lets me inside, I'll be sure to give you one."

"She can't avoid you forever."

"Shall we bet on that?" I say, cocking my eyebrow.

"I don't care who she is," Chelsea says, stepping into the bedroom and drawing us both in for a hug. "Christian loves you, and that love is greater than any crap Her Majesty can throw at you."

"You're right. And you are totally going to find love in New York," I say, smiling at her.

Chelsea rolls her eyes. "We'll see. I'm not too worried about that. But if we stay around here and hug anymore, we'll be late for the Wacky Walk!"

I grin. The Wacky Walk is a Stanford tradition, where students dress crazy and enter the stadium in mass for the commencement ceremony. After the commencement, we all head to smaller ceremonies conducted by our schools to receive diplomas.

"Costumes on, ladies?" Chelsea prods.

I laugh as she hands us oversized neon-pink sunglasses with big flamingoes on the sides. We put them on and look at each other, laughing. Then Chelsea hands us each bright pink signs. Mine says "Birds of a Feather," Chelsea's says "Graduate," and Bryn's says, "Stanford Together!"

And, with that, we exit our apartment together.

For the last time.

❦

"One more of you and Paisley!" Mom cries happily as she holds her camera up.

I smile for a picture outside of the McMurtry Building, holding my diploma in my hand.

I'm a graduate.

It's still sinking in. I've graduated, and this is my last day on this campus. I'm thrilled. Sad. Ready to leave. Terrified to leave. Filled with so many memories, but ready to make new ones.

With Christian.

"Okay, got it!" Mom says.

We walk toward her, and I see tears in her eyes as she studies me.

"I can't believe you have graduated," she says, touching my face. "My baby is leaving Stanford."

I will her not to burst into tears.

"I am," I say, smiling. "And I wouldn't be here without you and Dad. Thank you for giving me Stanford," I say, speaking from my heart. "I didn't earn this degree without your support and belief in me."

"You can stop thanking us," Mom says, reaching for another tissue from her purse and dabbing her eyes. "We know you're grateful, sweetheart."

"You know you don't have to go to England tomorrow," Dad says, his blue-green eyes appraising me. "You can relax and clear your head post-college. Take some time to think before making any rash decisions."

Paisley is typing on her phone and doesn't bother looking up as she says, "Hello, she's been with Christian since January for all intents and purposes, so she's not staying here. I wouldn't either if Evan was in London and I had a kick-ass awesome job lined up."

I love my sister.

While she and Evan are pro-Clementine and Christian, my parents were not won over on FaceTime. They insisted they were concerned about the stressful toll it would take on me and feared for my health. Christian said he understood their concerns but knew as long as he could help me transition, I would not only handle it but do it successfully. It was hard for them to argue when I pointed out that I had the king's personal medical team at my disposal, per Arthur's instructions.

"I'm moving to London, and I'm not changing my mind. I have a job. I'm going to live in Kensington. I'm doing what lots of women only dream of doing upon graduation. I'm going to live and work in London, and that's final."

A commotion erupts behind us.

I turn around, and a squad of men and women in suits and earpieces move through the crowd. Cell phones begin popping up, and voices begin to murmur.

"What's going on?" I hear someone say.

"Who is that? Someone famous?" another man asks.

I feel my heartbeat pick up.

"I-I'll be back," I say, leaving my family for a moment.

I move closer to the security team, then I freeze in place.

It's Christian.

He's dressed in a light-gray suit and has dark aviator sunglasses on, but there's no mistaking the Golden Prince with his famous blond curls.

"Christian!" I yell out, not caring who hears.

He turns in my direction, and a huge smile lights up his face.

Christian, surrounded by agents, moves to greet me. The comments from the crowd fade away, so does the idea that we're being filmed. I don't care.

"Oh, my God!" I cry, throwing my arms around him. "I can't believe you're here!"

Christian slides his hands up to my face, obviously not caring about being in public.

"Happy graduation day, Ace," he says, smiling brightly at me.

Happy tears fill my eyes. "I can't believe this is real. You came to my graduation! Wait, don't you have Royal Ascot on Tuesday?" I ask, shocked. Royal Ascot is the social event of the summer, when the royal family heads out to Windsor Castle and attends horse races. Chelsea lives for the fashions of the week, and we'd always check out the princes in their morning suits and top hats.

A surreal moment passes over me.

I studied pictures of Christian riding in a carriage to Ascot last year, when he was nothing more to me than a handsome famous person in a glossy tabloid magazine.

And now he's the man I love. Standing before me on my graduation day at Stanford.

"I had a more pressing engagement written in my diary for Tuesday," Christian murmurs, moving his fingers to my hair. "I'm here to take you home, Clementine, to England."

I beam at him before wrinkling my brow. "But Ascot," I say.

"I told Father and Mother I would attend the rest of the week, starting Wednesday."

I cringe. "Is your mother furious?"

Christian flashes me a wicked grin. "Perhaps a smidge."

"Christian, you didn't have to put yourself in that position," I say, hating that he did this for me.

"You," he says firmly, "are my priority. Also, I was thinking, you know, since I'm not going to hide in the cupboard anymore, you should come to Ascot on Ladies' Day."

What?

My mouth pops open. Me. At Ascot. As Christian's girlfriend.

I'm so shocked and excited by the prospect, I can't formulate a response.

"If that's too much pressure, I understand," Christian says, retreating from his invitation. "I know the media will be intense if you are in the royal box, and you might want to ease into life in a regular manner, not at the social event of the summer."

"Don't you dare take back this invitation!" I say gleefully. "I can't wait to go with you!"

A smile lights up his gorgeous face.

"You will stay overnight at Windsor in your own guest room. I'll try to visit, but I very well might find grandmother sitting outside my door with a golf club to bash me on the head if I try to slip out to your room."

I laugh at the image of the Dowager Queen, in one of her signature belted jackets with a brooch pinned on it, snarling at Christian as he dares to open his door.

"You're a prince; I'm sure it's in your DNA to scale a wall or something, right?" I tease.

He chuckles, that wonderful throaty laugh I find so sexy, and I feel butterflies in my stomach.

I'm going to be a guest at Windsor Castle.

"Christian! What am I going to wear? I don't have anything for an event like this. I need a hat. How do I get a fancy hat last minute?"

"Darling, I will pay for everything you need," Christian says as my panic takes over. "Just plan on going shopping while I'm at Ascot on Wednesday. You'll need multiple outfits, as we change several times a day, but I'll give you all those details later. For now, please put Ascot aside. I want to celebrate this day with you. You graduated from a top university, and that will not go unnoticed."

I'm beaming and shaking with excitement.

"You know you'll have to go to dinner with my family tonight," I say, straightening his navy silk tie.

"Paisley already adjusted the reservation for one more," Christian says, his full lips curving up into a smile. "She also made sure there is a table for my security team next to us."

"Paisley was in on this?" I ask.

"She thought it was brilliant," Christian says, grinning broadly at me. "How do you think I found you in this crowd, Fiona?"

I turn around, and Paisley and Evan wave at us. Paisley has truly come around to seeing me as an adult now, and I think Christian has been a huge part of that.

"Um," Christian says, "your parents are the ones over there glaring at me, yes?"

I sigh. My dad is indeed glaring at Christian, while my mom stares at him like he's a hologram.

I sigh and face Christian. "Yes. But you know you aren't going to win them over on the first visit, or maybe even the tenth. You're taking their little bird away. Worse, you are encouraging her to fly rather than stay in her cage."

"I suppose it's fair," Christian says. "You have to deal with Her Majesty. You still get the bad end of the deal, I'm afraid."

"No. I get you, and that's all that matters."

"Clementine?"

"Yes?"

"I'd rather like to kiss you now."

I smirk at him. "I thought your family doesn't believe in showing affection in public."

"They don't. But I told you before, I'm not going to live that way."

"So, you want to kiss me in public?" I ask, elated.

"I do. But only if you are okay with us being recorded and photographed. I understand if you'd rather not start today, Clementine."

"I feel like it's the perfect day. We're graduating to the real world, and I'm overjoyed that you want to show the world what we have."

"I do."

"Then kiss me already," I tease.

"There's no going back now," Christian says as his hands glide through my hair.

"Good, because I don't want to."

Christian lowers his mouth to mine, claiming it in a sweet kiss. This will be all over social media today, the papers tomorrow, and I don't care.

To my heart's delight, the prince who used to hide from the world doesn't care, either.

Not only have I turned a page with Stanford, but I'm turning a huge one with Christian in this very public display of affection. What we have known in our hearts is official to the world now. We'll punctuate the moment with my appearance in the royal box at Ascot next week.

We are a couple.

Tomorrow, we'll write the first chapter in our story.

Together.

CHAPTER 22

GIN AND TONICS

"You need to pinch me right now!" I cry excitedly to Christian. "London is amazing. Ah-ma-zing! And this is my city now. I can't believe I live here!"

"Careful, Ace, you might get whiplash with all your head turning," Christian says, smiling.

We might be dead tired from our flight from San Jose—Bear is snoring in the back seat—but I can't get enough of it. I'm soaking in every historic site, telling Christian everywhere I need to go in a non-stop rambling list. I must get in a red phone booth and take a double-decker bus and shop at the Harrods food court. I want to see the Tower of London—ha, funny to think that is part of Christian's family line—and see a show at the theatre. The London Eye is a must, and so is the Victoria and Albert Museum—and it blows my mind that this is another part of Christian's family tree.

"Oh! I recognize this from Google Maps," I say as Christian turns down a street in the Kensington neighborhood. "We're near my flat!"

Christian's smile broadens. "Your flat. God, I love how that sounds."

"Me, too."

I'm so happy, even seeing our kiss splashed across social media didn't bother me. The headlines probably made Queen Antonia go into a rage: *The Hermit Prince in Love! An American Lands the Heart of the Golden Prince! Clemmie Snags a Prince! Love Graduates! The Prince Finds His Princess?* We laughed at them, but I did tell Christian if he dared to call me "Clemmie," we'd have serious words.

I recognize the white-stucco Victorian building on the corner of the tree-lined street, and my history-loving heart swoons at the sight. It has glorious bay windows, and you step down stairs and through a black iron gate to enter the unit.

My new home.

"Oh, that's my flat," I gasp as Christian parks the Range Rover and waits for his security detail to follow suit. "My home. I'm home."

"You are home," Christian repeats, smiling at me.

He leans in and gives me a sweet kiss on the lips.

"Do you want me to walk Bear first?" I say, thinking aloud. "So you can stay in the car as long as possible? And not attract attention?"

"The press will be all over this place in days," Christian says, his eyes darkening. "As soon as they start following you, I'll have Father issue a warning."

"What? No," I say, shaking my head. "I don't want you to do that."

"For God's sake, Clementine, they will be relentless. We went public at Stanford, so we're fair game now. You are the game, my love. They will pursue you and hound you like prey. I won't let them do it."

"I don't want to start off on that foot with the media," I say, shaking my head. "I want to prove I can handle them."

"To whom?" Christian says. "Who do you have to prove anything to, Clementine?"

To your mother, I think. *To my parents. I want to show them I'm not weak and that I can handle this life without the Golden Prince running to my rescue the first day I'm in the United Kingdom.*

"I'm asking you not to," I say, avoiding his question. "Please."

Christian rubs his hand over his jaw.

"Okay," he relents. "But I don't like this."

I lean over and kiss his cheek. "Thank you. You *are* a prince, you know that?"

"Ha-ha, I'm way too tired to give you crap for that one."

"Let me get Bear out. Then we can meet Jillian together."

"No, I'll come with you. We aren't going to hide, right?"

I'm so proud of his courage I could burst. "No, we're not."

We step out of the car, as do Oliver and James, who always seem to be the agents on duty when we travel. Bear starts barking excitedly, and Christian hooks up his leash.

"Come on, big Bear. Welcome to the city," Christian says, getting him out of the back.

I smile as Bear jumps down and begins sniffing the sidewalk. Christian walks him a bit down the block, and I look around my new street in complete awe.

My life really is a royal romance TV movie.

Except it's real.

Christian returns and says, "Here, if you take Bear, I'll get your suitcase."

"You just want to grab that bag of Caramel M&M's before you head back to the palace," I tease.

"Of course I do. Those are fantastic," Christian quips.

I wait with Bear while Christian retrieves my suitcase and duffel bag. That's all I brought. I can't believe I'm starting my new life with nothing more than two bags in hand.

Christian slams the back door, and Oliver walks ahead while James follows us from behind. I open the black iron gate, and Bear eagerly leads me down the stairs to the cutest little terrace with modern, outdoor wicker seating in black with charcoal cushions and blooming purple clematis flowers climbing up the walls.

"It's so chic," I say in surprise.

"Yeah," Christian says, taking a second to study it. "Definitely not the Dowager Queen chintz."

I snicker at that. Then I lower my head toward Christian so I can whisper, "I have to admit, in my head, Jillian will have chintz inside with lots of house plants and lace."

"What will she be wearing?"

I think for a moment. "A long tunic and pants in the same color?" I say, thinking of what my grandma Allison wears.

"I say," Christian says, lowering his voice conspiratorially, "she'll be wearing florals and a big cardigan."

"Winner buys dinner this Friday night?" I suggest.

"You're on."

I head toward Jillian's shiny black door. I rap against it, and Bear starts barking. I shush him, as I don't want Jillian to be overwhelmed by him before she opens the door.

"Coming!" an English-accented voice calls out.

The door unlocks, and I anxiously wait to see Jillian for the first time. As the door swings open, my jaw hits the ground. I don't need to look at Christian to know his has done the same.

"Clementine, it's lovely to have you here," she says, smiling brightly at me. "Welcome to London—and your new home."

I can't formulate a response.

Jillian isn't in a tunic. Or pantsuit.

Jillian, with her above the shoulders, tousled platinum hair, is wearing full makeup and is immaculately dressed in an oversized, crisp, white, dress shirt; designer skinny jeans; and the most amazing pair of open-toed, black, studded high heels. A huge, multi-colored statement necklace adorns her neck, one filled with crystals and amazing colors of red, amber, green and black, and a smile lights up her stunning face.

She's gorgeous.

And the chicest woman I have ever seen.

"I'm sorry for how I'm dressed," I blurt out, realizing I'm standing before this stylish woman in jeans that should have been retired two years ago and are fraying at the ends and ripped at the knees—and not by design. And to compliment the jeans that need to be recycled? I'm wearing a white T-shirt with a black, pilled, duster sweater thrown over the top. My hair is in a messy knot, and my sunglasses are parked on the top of my head.

I need to learn from Jillian, quickly, because this would not make a good photo for Queen Antonia to see in the press. Oh, crap, a headline flashes through my head:

Hot Mess Clemmie Unsuitable for Buckingham Palace, Queen Antonia declares National Emergency and begs Hoarder Prince to find a Suitable Girlfriend

I make a note to beg Jillian to be my Yoda of fashion.

Jillian furrows her brow. "I beg your pardon?"

Her comment snaps me out of my thoughts.

"I'm sorry. I'm Clementine, and it's good to meet you," I say, recovering. "This is Christian," I say, introducing him as a normal human instead of a prince.

"Your Royal Highness," Jillian says. "It's an honor to meet you."

I notice Jillian follows protocol and doesn't extend her hand first for a handshake, as Christian had instructed me to do with King Arthur. She glances briefly at Oliver and James, who begin their retreat and do their disappearing act.

"The pleasure is mine," Christian says, smiling warmly at her as he extends his hand for her to shake.

Bear begins barking, and Jillian's face lights up.

"And you must be Bear," she says, her green eyes sparkling. "This house will be a proper home now with an Airedale in it." Jillian extends her hand for Bear to sniff, and after he does, she affectionately rubs his head.

"I'll make sure I keep him clean," I say, hoping immaculate Jillian won't have second thoughts about the hot mess American with the big dog being in her home.

Jillian lifts a perfectly arched eyebrow at me. "There's no such thing as living a good life without having a fair bit of dirt in it."

Wow. I need to get that saying embroidered on a pillow.

"Please, come in," Jillian says, stepping aside.

If my eyes weren't already bulging out of my head, they are the second I step inside the flat onto the gray hardwood floors.

There's no chintz, or an abundance of houseplants, or

doilies, or any of the other stereotypical images I had in my head when I thought of Jillian's flat.

It's completely modern.

To my left, there's a small galley kitchen with black cabinets and granite countertops. It's obvious Jillian has done recent updates as everything is sparkling new. All the appliances are stainless steel.

"Obviously, this is the kitchen," Jillian says. She takes a few steps to the right into a large common room. "This is the living room. I do apologize, as I don't keep a TV in here, but I do have one in your bedroom for you."

I keep Bear close to me on his leash as I stare in awe at the stunning room. The color palette is a dove gray with cream and pops of burgundy. The fabrics are sumptuous and inviting. Silk pillows, all perfectly plumped, fill the back of a gray velvet sofa. Two chairs in cream are directly across from it, and a burgundy, fabric ottoman serves as the coffee table, with interior design books stacked on top. A round dining table is in front of two french doors which lead to the terrace, with four upholstered, dove-gray chairs around it.

There's a gorgeous mosaic art piece that takes up the space where a flat-screened TV would be, and there's a low, black table underneath it, with a tray with a bottle of gin and a vintage ice bucket.

"You have Georgian gin glasses," I say aloud, marveling at the wonderful sight. "Those are circa 1770!"

"You do know your antiques," Jillian says, her eyes dancing at me.

"Antique bar wear, dishes, cutlery—it's kind of my thing."

"Oh, yes, I love accenting with period pieces here and there," Jillian says. "I have some exquisite china I can show you later. But first, I must confess something that, as an American with ideas of how we Brits should be, might disappoint you."

"What is that?" I ask.

"I do not believe in afternoon tea, or any tea, for that matter. I believe in an afternoon gin and tonic."

Christian grins. "I'd say that is a definite improvement over a cup of tea."

"We are going to get along just fine, Jillian, because I don't care for tea."

"Perfect. Once you get settled and get some rest, we'll celebrate your arrival with gin and tonics. I have a lovely Scottish gin I'll introduce you to. Now, let me show you to your room."

Christian and I follow Jillian down the hall. She points out a bathroom to the right and my room on the left. Jillian opens the door, and while the room is tiny, it's appointed as luxuriously as the rest of the flat. There's a built-in wardrobe for my things. The queen-sized bed has a tufted, upholstered headboard in dove gray. The bedding fabric is exquisite, white with gray piping, and a thick, cashmere gray blanket is draped across the end of the bed. There's a round, black nightstand next to the bed with a modern-crystal lamp, a few books, and an interesting silver grasshopper figure on top.

"The grasshopper is for good luck," Jillian explains. "I keep one in my room, too."

"I love it," I say, smiling.

"Well, I know you have a bag to unpack, and you must be absolutely exhausted," Jillian says, resting her hand on the doorknob. "I'll leave you alone for a while, but once you've had some sleep, we can continue to get to know each other. Oh, and before I forget, your key."

Jillian hands me my key to the flat and smiles. "Once again, welcome to your new home."

Then she turns and leaves the room, shutting the door behind her.

Christian and I look at each other.

"She's not what I expected, and I mean that in the best way possible," I say as I slip the key into my jeans pocket. "She is cool. And I love that Jillian doesn't seem to care that you're a prince. She didn't go all wide-eyed and fawn upon meeting you."

"I know, I rather liked that."

"I know you did."

"But you lucked out. Not only does she seem fantastic, but this place is incredible," Christian says, his voice reflecting the same shock that I have. "I could live in a home like this. It's ace."

"With enough antique accents, I could, too," I say.

"That goes without saying. I know you need your antiques, Fiona," he says, grinning.

I let Bear off his leash, not like there's much room for him to go anywhere, and since the bed takes up most of the room, he flops down on the spot. I kick off my tennis shoes and drape my old cardigan across the end of the bed.

"He has the right idea," Christian says, taking off his baseball hat and tossing it on the nightstand, where it catches on the grasshopper's antennas. "Oh, handy hat holder for me there," he quips.

"Are you planning to hang your hat here often, Your Royal Highness?" I ask suggestively.

Christian wraps me in his sculpted arms. "Yes," he says, dropping his mouth on mine.

As I kiss him back, I feel so full of optimism for our future. London is the beginning of our fairy tale. Not one about the American girl who falls for a prince, but one of two young people in love. We're starting new chapters in our lives, but we're starting them together. There will be dirt, as Jillian says, but there will be light and laughter and love, too.

This love, I think as we fall back onto my bed, *will see us through whatever the future holds.*

"We need to be quiet," I whisper. "I mean, we just got here."

"I can be very, very quiet," Christian assures me with a wicked grin. He slides his hand underneath my T-shirt, cupping my breast in his hand as his tongue explores my mouth. I instantly grow hot, as it's been too long since our bodies have been entwined, too long since his mouth has claimed mine, too long since we have made love.

"I love you," I whisper against his full lips as I reach for his belt buckle.

"I love you more," Christian whispers back, taking my lower lip between his teeth and sexily tugging on it.

"Oh," I gasp, arching my back as I fumble with his belt.

"I want you so much," he murmurs into my neck. "I've missed you, all of you. I've missed the softness of your skin, the scent of your perfume."

Christian finds that sweet spot between my neck and shoulder and places his mouth there.

"Christian," I whisper as I unbutton his jeans, my fingertips trailing along the band of his boxer-briefs. He groans against me, his mouth seeking mine again, this time with a hot and urgent kiss.

He pushes up my shirt, and I sit up to remove it. Christian tugs off his shirt and tosses it aside. I slowly unhook my bra, and the second it's off, Christian pins me back to the mattress, his hand finding mine, linking our fingers together as he kisses me passionately.

"I've missed you. God, you have no idea," he murmurs, his voice deep with desire. "Your body was meant for mine. I want you. I can't wait."

"Now, Christian," I beg urgently against his lips. "Get the condom. I need to love you."

Christian complies with my request as I lose myself in him.

Joy surges through me as I know this is our life now. I'll never have to be without his love, his presence, his touch again.

This man is my world.

And I know the fairy tale is real.

CHAPTER 23

A FABULOUS HAT

I feel the sun on my face and lazily open one eye. How is it still daylight? I saw Christian out early last night. Did I only sleep for an hour or so? I roll over and reach for my phone, which I have charging on the nightstand, next to the lucky grasshopper. I unlock it and gasp when I see its eight thirty in the morning.

Crap, I slept that long? I knew I was exhausted, but I've slept for more than thirteen hours! I immediately wonder why Bear hasn't woken me, and then I see the door is open a crack. I roll out of bed and open the door, hoping Bear hasn't peed on Jillian's floor—or worse.

I stop as soon as I hit the hallway.

I smell bacon.

Glorious, sizzling-in-the-pan, bacon.

My stomach grumbles. I remind myself that it's Jillian's bacon, not mine, and I'll have to go grab a coffee and a danish, which is disappointing after inhaling that magical scent.

I'm adding bacon to my shopping list.

Along with a day dress, a dress for Ascot, heels, a purse, and a fabulous hat. Oh, and an evening gown for dinner tonight.

Easy.

I walk down the hall, and as I look into the kitchen, I see a sight that warms my heart. Jillian is cooking at her range, turning the bacon, while Bear lays at her feet, happily munching on what looks like a dog biscuit.

I take a moment to study Jillian, who is chic even when preparing breakfast. She is wearing another pair of dark skinny jeans; an orange, three-quarter-sleeved, fitted button-down; and a fabulous pair of strappy, orange heels.

She makes bacon in high heels.

At seventy.

Jillian is so going to be my Yoda.

She turns over her shoulder and smiles at me. "I took Bear out for you. I heard him at your door."

"Thank you so much," I say. "I honestly didn't intend to sleep this long. I wanted to have gin and tonics with you last night."

"Well, you can have breakfast with me now if you like," Jillian says, taking some slices of bread and popping them into the toaster.

Bear comes over to greet me, and I see he indeed does have a dog treat.

"I ran out and got some treats for him," Jillian says, moving to the fridge and opening the door. "Would you like some coffee? Orange juice?"

"Juice would be lovely, and I can get it," I say. "Please don't wait on me."

"Nonsense. I haven't had the pleasure of cooking breakfast for anyone since George passed. Let me revel in it."

She retrieves a small glass from her cabinet and pours me some juice. I remember in our phone conversation that Jillian lost George two years ago after a lengthy battle with Alzheimer's. Jillian cared for him until the very end, right here in this flat. They had been married for fifty-one years.

I can't imagine how you recover after losing someone you had shared a life with for that long.

"Here you go," Jillian says, handing me the glass. "Would you like eggs? A bacon butty?"

I grin. "I have no idea what a bacon butty is."

Jillian cocks an eyebrow. "I need to discuss this with Christian. He's never introduced you to this? What about brown sauce?"

"No, and no," I say. "Obviously he's lacking. I might have to revoke his boyfriend card if he's been keeping the good stuff to himself."

Jillian laughs. "A bacon butty is a sandwich. HP Sauce has a wonderful sweet and smoky flavor that is divine with salty bacon."

"That sounds ridiculously good," I say as I inhale the scent of bacon wafting through her kitchen. "I would love one. And some eggs."

"Scrambled?"

"Perfect," I say. "Excuse me for a moment. I'm going to feed Bear. I packed some food in my bag."

"I hope it's okay, but the poor thing was hungry this morning, so I fed him some eggs and cheese."

"Oh, my gosh, thank you for taking care of him. I should have set my alarm last night. I only intended to take a nap, not crash for fourteen hours."

"I don't blame you; travel from the opposite side of the United States is always tiring. Now, please, go have a seat. Let me fuss over you this morning. I love feeling useful."

Her words reveal a lot to me. Jillian and George had no children, and taking care of George when he was ill must have been incredibly hard. Then having that world suddenly gone must have left her at a loss.

My guess is that when George died, Jillian felt her purpose did, too, in a way.

I move to the small dining table, and Bear follows, barking at the french doors that lead to the terrace.

"May I let him hang out on your terrace?" I ask.

Jillian stops cooking and gives me a stern look. "Darling, this is your terrace now, too, and Bear is free to roam where he likes."

I smile. This reminds me of the first time I met Bryn in the dorm and how we connected within the first few hours of living together.

I already know I'm going to become close to Jillian.

I let Bear out and then head back down the hall to go to the restroom, brush my teeth, and retrieve my phone.

As soon as I come back in the room, I find breakfast waiting for me on an exquisite platinum-rimmed plate beside a linen napkin with a silver grasshopper napkin ring around it.

"More luck?" I ask, sliding off the ring as Jillian sits down across from me.

"George loved grasshoppers," Jillian explains, pausing as she picks up her fine china coffee cup. "I like having them around the house in little ways to remind me of him. As if I could forget him."

I swallow hard. I can feel the ache in her words.

"Can I just say how lovely it is to have you here? And Bear?" Jillian says, shifting the topic. "It's nice to hear other people besides myself prattling about."

I pause as I pick up my bacon butter thing or whatever she called it. "You don't hear everything, right?"

Jillian takes a sip of her coffee. "Hmm, like what? Headboard banging perhaps?"

I blush furiously. I put my sandwich down. I'm about to offer a string of apologies when Jillian begins to laugh.

"Please, if I had a young man like Christian, I'd be getting a go at that as much as possible."

I can't help it. The cool, sophisticated Jillian saying "getting a go at that" makes me burst out laughing, and she does, too.

"I'm so sorry. I told him to be quiet. We missed each other so much and well ..."

"Life has dirt and, with good luck, noisy sex," Jillian declares, taking a bite of her toast, which is smeared with jam. She swallows and studies me. "I also own earbuds and a wonderful collection of classical music on Spotify."

"Oh, my God, my roommate Bryn was loud," I say. "I used my earbuds all the time."

We both laugh.

"The prince loves you," Jillian says, shifting topics. "I can see it in the way he looks at you."

A happy feeling surges through me. "I love him just as much, Jillian. Christian is like no other, and that has nothing to do with him being a prince."

"Tell me about him," Jillian encourages. "How did you meet? Oh, and if you need me to sign confidentiality papers first, I can."

I furrow my brow. It hits me that certain people I meet will try to take advantage of my personal stories with Christian now that our relationship is out. I will have to be careful.

But I don't have any fears with Jillian.

"No, I trust you," I say. "I don't think you'll be running off to *Dishing Weekly* to spill my sex secrets with the Golden Prince."

"Heavens, no, that's a rag. I'd hold out for a higher-end entertainment magazine," Jillian quips.

I laugh and pick up my sandwich and take a bite. Oh, my. First of all, this English bacon is completely different than American bacon. It's thicker and meatier. I taste the fresh, toasted bread; the lush butter; and this amazing brown sauce that pulls it all together.

"Oh, my God," I murmur with my mouth half-full.

"You approve?"

"This is fantastic!" I rave. "How has this been missing from my life? I could eat this every day!"

"I'll up the bacon quantity on the shopping list," Jillian teases.

"I've got to get on Christian about hiding this luxury from me. That hoarder."

"Oh, yes, those stories," Jillian says, rolling her eyes. "I never once thought he was a hoarder."

I pick up my phone and snicker. "Truth? He has very few things. He likes things orderly and neat. *Dishing Weekly* would be disappointed to find out he's not buried in trash and takeout tubs and that Queen Antonia didn't need to hire a hazmat team to shovel him out."

I take a picture of my sandwich to text to Christian.

"Have you met the queen?"

I glance up from my typing. "No. I've met King Arthur, though, and he's a wonderful man, astute and kind."

Jillian nods. "I can see that about King Arthur. He seems genuine in his desire to use the monarchy to help people. It seems he would like to modernize things but is being held back by … others in the palace."

Hmm. She takes another bite of her toast, and I know by "others" she is intimating Queen Antonia and the Dowager Queen.

I go back to my text and send the photo to Christian:

We are going to have a row, as you would say. How could you have kept this bacon sandwich out of my life?

Then I hit send.

Within seconds he replies:

Good morning, my love. I wasn't aware you fancied bacon butties, or I would have made them every morning for you when you were here.

I smile and text back:

I forgive you. Are you getting ready for Ascot?

I put the phone back down. "Christian is at Windsor today. He's going to Ascot."

"Ascot is fantastic," Jillian says. "So much amazing and hideous style all in one place. I adore it!"

"Christian asked me to go to Ladies' Day," I say, taking another bite of my sandwich.

Jillian's eyes light up. "Ooh, you'll be in the royal box! What are you going to wear?"

I'm still chewing when my phone buzzes. I glance down, and Christian has attached a snap of him looking oh-so-dashing in his morning suit with Xander, James, and three young women I recognize as his princess cousins: Liz, Bella, and Victoria, all in dresses with fantastic hats. He has scribbled on the photo for me:

You'll be part of our squad tomorrow, Fiona.

I put the phone down as the pressure of the moment hits me.

"Clementine? What's wrong?"

I glance up at her and push my plate away as anxiety takes over.

"The royal box at Ascot, where everyone will be watching me, comparing me to the princesses and Queen Antonia. I've never dressed for an occasion like this. I need a day dress and an evening gown, and if I mess up, the world will hear about the *Messy American with Shit Taste* who uglied up the royal scene."

Jillian places down her cup. "You will do no such thing."

"But what if I do? What if I get some saleswoman who gives me awful advice and I believe her? What if I look ridiculous? All these royal ladies probably have stylists and —crap, oh, crap. If I mess this up, it will make Queen Antonia dislike me more than she already does."

I cringe. Shit. I totally shouldn't have said anything negative about Queen Antonia.

Jillian doesn't flinch from my verbal breakdown.

"First of all," Jillian says slowly, "have you seen what Queen Antonia wears? She's worn the same sheath dress for the past thirty years. She's fantastically dull. Second, you have a chance to make an impact here, Clementine. You'll wear something fresh and floral and quintessentially UK but with a modern spin. You'll wear a British designer to give a nod to your new country. And you'll wear color, unlike the neutrals Antonia favors, because you are not Antonia two point oh. You are Clementine Jones, the American girlfriend of the Prince of Wales. We will find a dress befitting of not only Ascot but your unique spirit, too."

I hold my breath.

"We? You'll help me?" I ask, praying that Jillian will indeed be my fashion Yoda.

"I used to be an interior designer," she says. "I love art and fashion, and even though I'm ancient, I still keep up with what is going on in the fashion world. In fact, there's a boutique I love because they have a section of up-and-coming British designers. I know we will find the perfect dress there, along with shoes and an utterly brilliant hat."

Relief sweeps through me. "You're my fairy godmother. Thank you. Thank you. I don't know how I'll ever repay you for your kindness."

"You don't know it, but you already have," she says softly. I'm about to ask what she means when she clears her throat. "Now go on and finish that butty. We have a lot of shopping to do today."

I'm in a remake of *My Fair Lady*.

Not the whole correcting Eliza's speech part, but the transforming for Ascot bit.

After breakfast, Jillian dashed us off in her Jaguar to a boutique housed inside an old Georgian townhome. Christian alerted palace staff to expect a call from the boutique and to pay the bill from his account. Once we discreetly had the boutique manager take my passport and call Windsor Palace, we became a blur of activity. Jillian and a saleswoman named Bridget began grabbing dresses and holding them against me, discussing the strap width—one-inch minimum, no spaghetti straps in the Royal Enclosure—and length, which must be at or below the knee. The dress couldn't be off the shoulder, strapless, or halter neck, and the midriff must be covered.

Yet, the dress was still supposed to be fresh, fun, English-designed, and keep me "me."

Oh, and that was just for the Ascot portion of the day.

I study the stunning dresses hanging around the

dressing room in awe. There are florals, stripes, ruffles, and long and mid-length hemlines. I pop open the door and look to Jillian, who is sitting on a luxurious velvet sofa, flicking through the latest copy of British *Vogue*. She glances up at me.

"Which one should I start with?" I ask.

Jillian appears thoughtful for a moment.

"The pink one."

"Okay," I say, nodding.

I slip back inside and shut the door. I kick off my Converse shoes, change out of my jeans, and tug my gray T-shirt over my head. Crap. I need better running around clothes for when the photogs start trailing me. I can't be seen like this; that is for sure.

I reach for the padded, silk hanger of a pale-pink, sleeveless dress that hits right below the knee. It is a fabulous silk satin with a beautiful floral pattern reminiscent of a rose garden. A grosgrain, red ribbon belt adorns the waist, and there is a slight V in the neckline and gathering at the bust.

As soon as my fingertips touch the silk, I know it's the finest fabric I have ever felt in my life. I look at the label: *Emilia Wentworth-Hay*. She was someone Bridget said was an up-andcoming designer in Britain, so Jillian made sure to grab one of her dresses.

I step into the fine fabric, careful not to step on it. I pull the dress up, loving the feel of the silk against my skin. I get the zip halfway up the back and pause to look in the full-length mirror. My eyes widen as I see myself.

I've never looked prettier.

Beads, strewn across the bodice, add sparkle. The waist is cinched with the ribbon and flares out in the skirt. It's graceful and elegant but colorful, like me.

And perfect for Ascot.

I open the door, and Jillian beams the second she sees me. She rises and puts her steepled fingertips to her lips as she studies the dress.

"Perfection," she says, moving around me. Jillian yanks the zipper up, and I walk toward the three-way mirror at the end of the hall.

"Is it wrong to fall in love with the first dress I try on?" I ask, doing a twirl in front of the mirror.

"Not when it's right," Jillian says. "I want you to try on the others to make sure, but I think this is your dress."

I turn around to Jillian and grin. "I love that it has color."

Bridget steps into the dressing area, carrying two flutes of champagne on a silver tray, and gasps when she sees me.

"You are ready for Ascot!" she declares brightly.

"I love it," I admit.

"I have some complimentary champagne for you," she says, placing the glasses on a small table next to the sofa Jillian was sitting on.

"Thank you."

"Bridget, can you bring some hats and shoes that would coordinate with this dress?" Jillian asks. "I'm thinking big on the hats. As far as shoes, no nudes. We absolutely want color."

"Yes, of course, Ms. Park, I'll have some options for you straight away. What size shoe do you wear, Ms. Jones?"

"Six and a half."

Bridget's face looks like she's doing a math equation before she says, "I believe that is a size four UK, but I'll double check."

Wow. I had no idea shoe sizes weren't universal.

I have so much to learn.

Jillian begins fussing with the skirt and moves in front of me. "You are going to get a lot of attention tomorrow, Clementine. Are you ready for it?"

I bite my lip. "You know what? It feels like skiing a challenging new run for the first time. You get more and more excited as you ride the lift up, but then you look down and get a little nervous when you see how tricky the course is to navigate, but you still want to do it all the same."

Jillian puts her hands on my shoulders, squeezing them as she stares back at me. "You've got a wonderful head on your shoulders for someone so young. You're not naïve. You know you are going to get knocked about by the public and the press. They'll love you one day, and rip you apart the next. But you will get up, put your chin up, and get on with it because love like this is worth everything."

Tears fill my eyes. I know Jillian had this kind of love with George without her saying it.

"Enough," Jillian says, clearing her throat. "We have more dresses to try on."

"Wait!" Bridget calls out, rushing in with a hatbox. "I have a brilliant hat in here you need to try on while you have that dress on, Ms. Jones."

I wait as Bridget lifts the top off the box and moves tissue aside. Then she carefully lifts a large, wide-brimmed straw hat in pale pink with matching pink veiling and huge, pink flowers around the side.

"This meets Ascot requirements," Bridget says knowingly.

She places the hat upon my head, situating it just right.

"Beautiful," she murmurs in approval.

I stare back at myself. Never have I felt more like a lady than I do in this moment. The hat—when set against my red hair—is striking. Combined with the dress, I look tailor-made for Ascot.

Jillian meets my gaze in the mirror and smiles.

"I do believe," she says, "you are ready for Ascot."

Butterflies take off in my stomach. I know tomorrow will be thrilling, and terrifying. Queen Antonia and the press are looming over me, yet I return to the reason why I'm going, why I'm putting myself through this.

Christian.

And now it is time to find the next dress, for tonight, that will mark my entrance into Christian's royal world.

And with Jillian's help, I know it will be perfect.

CHAPTER 24
THE GREEN DRAWING ROOM

As Windsor Castle—majestically situated on a ridge with the Royal Standard flying from the round tower—appears in the distance, nausea attacks my stomach, fighting for space with the butterflies that are already residing there.

After spending the day shopping, having alterations quickly made on my gown for this evening, then having Jillian sweep my hair into a fabulous chignon, I found myself packing a new bag for my stay at Windsor Castle as a guest of King Arthur himself.

I'll be one of only twenty-four people invited for Ladies' Day at Ascot tomorrow. *Twenty-four.*

I'm one of twenty-four people who will get to experience the pomp and circumstance of royalty. I'll be dressing in a gown for a black-tie dinner this evening in the luxurious state dining room. I'll have a day dress for breakfast tomorrow, and then I'll be running back to my room to change for lunch, switching into my Ascot outfit.

Then I'll watch the race in the royal box, which will include my first royal tea.

This is enough to freak anyone out, but I have an added layer to my circumstance.

I'm meeting my boyfriend's family for the first time.

Which includes oh, only a future king, princes, princesses, as well as the dowager queen.

And Queen Antonia.

I'm going to throw up.

"You've gone awfully quiet, Ace," Christian says as he drives us closer.

"I'm nervous," I admit. "I want to make a good impression, and I feel like I don't know what I'm doing. I need weeks to prepare for this, not half a day. What was it you were telling me again? That if King Arthur is speaking to someone on his right, we all speak to the person on our right? Then if he turns to speak to the person on the left, we all turn left, even if we're in the middle of a conversation?"

He places his hand on my knee as if he's trying to stop my brain.

"Sweetheart, nobody expects you to know all the protocol tonight," Christian says.

I frown as the castle looms ahead.

"They don't," he repeats, trying to reassure me. "You know I'm here to help, and my cousins are excited to meet you. They'll be fantastic in helping you if you need anything."

That reassures me a bit. I'm excited to meet Liz, Bella, and Victoria. They are close in age to Christian and his brothers, with Princess Elizabeth being twenty-three and the same age as Christian; Princess Isabella being twenty-two; and Princess Victoria being the youngest—and known across social media as the most fashionable young royal—at twenty.

"So will your chambermaid," Christian says, interrupting my thoughts. "She is on hand to answer any etiquette questions you might have."

"My *what?*"

"You'll have your own chambermaid to unpack your clothes," Christian says, unfazed.

"Wait, I don't want anyone unpacking my clothes," I cry, appalled at the idea of a maid having to do that for me. "I'm perfectly capable of doing that myself."

"But it's her job, Clementine."

"I don't want her going through my underwear. I mean, I have skimpy thongs in there, Christian. What if she laughs at my crazy patterns?"

Oh, why, why, why did I decide to throw in the one with lipstick prints all over it as a joke for Christian?

"You don't mind when I go through your knickers," Christian says wickedly.

"Well, that's you. Also, it's enjoyable when you go through my knickers, as you say."

Christian laughs loudly. "I do love you, Fiona."

"I guess it's not a big deal," I say, as I'm sure these maids have seen more eyebrow-raising things than a lipstick print thong. I mentally think of what else I've packed. Thanks to Jillian's help, my clothing and accessories are all elegant and ladylike. Then I have my hairdryer, my universal adaptor plug, and makeup.

Okay, the crisis level is a minimum, unless the chambermaid is on the take for Queen Antonia and reports back that my taste in undergarments is disastrous. But I'll have to take my chances on that one.

I stare up at Windsor Castle, another living history

book I'll have the privilege of spending time in, this one nearly a thousand years old—as well as the oldest occupied castle in the world.

As soon as we park, we're greeted by palace staff, and Christian is whisked through an entrance. My mind blurs as a woman hands me information regarding my stay and gives me directions to my room. Christian stiffens at my side, and I have a feeling something is wrong.

"Your chambermaid will be Hannah," she says, inclining her head toward a woman next to her, "and she is here to help you with anything you might need, Ms. Jones."

"Your Royal Highness," Hannah says, doing a small curtsy to Christian. Then she turns to me. "Welcome to Windsor Castle, Ms. Jones. I'll escort you to your apartment now."

"No, I'll handle that, Hannah. Thank you. You can follow shortly to help Clementine with her bags."

"Of course, sir," she says, nodding.

Christian wraps his hand around mine, and as he leads me along, I can tell from his stride he's annoyed.

"What's wrong?" I whisper.

Christian stops and turns to me. "She put you in the farthest room from the royal apartments. I guarantee you she did it not only to keep you away from me but to try and trip you up to make sure you are late to events. It's rubbish, Clementine, absolute rubbish, and I'm pissed about it."

I have zero doubts *she* is Queen Antonia.

I shrug. "So?"

"So? Do you realize how far you'll have to run between meals and events? To change your clothes? If you're late, it's a huge deal."

"I'm fast. I can make sure I'm ready early so, even if I get lost, I'll be on time."

Shit. I didn't think about it until I said it, but getting lost here is going to be easy, with all these halls and rooms; after all, the place is a freaking castle.

I'll leave one hour before every event starts, I vow.

"Do you know what my biggest fear is?" Christian asks.

My heart hurts when I see sadness in his eyes.

"What?" I ask, squeezing his hand in mine.

"That you'll grow to hate all of this: my mum, these rules, the press. You're handling it now like the ace you are, but someday, you'll despise me for all of this. You'll want your normal back. I won't be worth it. I wouldn't blame you for leaving when that day comes."

"Stop right there. You're forgetting something. I've never had normal. I've had kids who teased me for having a tumor. I've had parents who thought if I winced it meant I was getting sick again. I wasn't allowed to live with abandon. I was always under rules of protection. This is more freeing, even with all these rules, than the worry my parents put over my head. You have as much reason to throw your hands up and walk away, with my parents who want me on the West Coast, in a life without these pressures. You could easily find someone whose parents would be thrilled you wanted to be with their daughter. You could have a woman who knows this culture, who is a lady, who your mother would embrace, but you chose the harder road. You chose me."

Christian exhales. "I absolutely did."

"Then stop wasting my time and see me to my room," I say, smiling happily at him.

Windsor Castle is ah-ma-zing.

I gaze out the window of my guest room. It's like staying at a posh hotel. There's even a schedule of events and a map—a map!–on the nightstand next to the bed with King Arthur's royal crest on it.

Hannah expertly unpacked all my things, from placing my lipstick thong in a drawer and hanging my clothing in the closet to laying out my hairbrushes on the vanity in the restroom, while talking to me about what to expect tonight. She was quite lovely, and I found her knowledge calming.

I turn around and move about the casual, English country-style room, navigating around the four-poster bed with simple white bed linens, while waiting for Christian to come get me. Before tonight's black-tie dinner in the stateroom, which includes being presented to King Arthur and Queen Antonia, I'll meet Xander and James, and his cousins. I'm both nervous and excited because I want them to like me.

Ding!

I pick up my phone and see that Paisley is texting me. I sent her a selfie in my evening gown, a stunning, floor-length royal-blue crepe gown with a cape overlay. I paired it with silver drop earrings and black, closed-toe pumps—per Jillian's suggestion, as Her Majesty prefers closed-toed shoes—and ugh, sheer, shimmery pantyhose.

Pantyhose.

I've never worn a pair in my life, and my legs feel sweaty and itchy.

Jillian said she didn't know why her majesty was inclined to keep pantyhose on her requirement list, as bare legs are nicer, but she suggested I do it to make the best first impression possible.

Ugh.

I read Paisley's message:

This is surreal, Clem! You are going to have dinner with the KING AND QUEEN while I stroll down the hallway for another cup of shit office coffee.

I text back:

I still don't have my head around the fact that this is my life. Now pray for me. I don't know what I am doing, and I'm sure I'll have all kinds of etiquette breaches tonight.

Paisley is typing ...

If you're going to break them, go down in flames, I say. Dare you to dance on the state dining room table. Double bonus if you can get Xander the Philanderer to join you, which I bet he would. That would really make HER MAJESTY go sideways!

I burst out laughing. Since I started seeing Christian, it's as if my sister has accepted I am not only okay but living my best life, and it has brought us closer in the process. And I know she and Evan are doing everything they can to bring—well, more like drag—my parents over to see it, too.

There's a rap on my door, and nerves take over.

It's time to go.

I open the door, and my eyes widen when I see Christian. He's ravishing in a black tux with his golden curls swept back with a bit of product. The cuffs of his crisp, white, dress shirt peek out from his tuxedo jacket, as does a glint of his Rolex watch.

My man is sexy as hell.

"You," Christian says, his voice husky, "are breathtaking."

"You approve, Your Royal Highness?" I tease as I step aside to let him in and retrieve my clutch.

"You're stunning tonight," Christian says, moving behind me and drawing me to his chest. He slides one hand around my stomach, pinning me to him, and then he kisses the side of my neck. I feel heat flicker within me the second his breath is against my skin.

"Christian," I murmur, closing my eyes as his mouth moves up my neck. I slide my hand up behind his neck, finding his curls, and closing my fingers around them.

"We could skip dinner," he teases.

"Oh, don't tempt me," I say. "You are so sexy in this tux. I think I'll have you for dessert tonight."

He chuckles, and a tingle shoots down my spine from the sound. "That's a cheesy thing for you to say, Ace."

"It might be a cheesy line, but you won't deny me, will you?"

"No."

We both laugh.

"Come on, let's go," Christian says and offers me his arm.

Swoon.

I wrap my hand around his arm, and Christian escorts me on what seems like a good half-mile walk back toward the royal apartments.

"See? I wasn't kidding when I said you were banished," Christian says.

I snicker. "I'm not the only guest who has the same accommodations," I remind him.

"I still don't like it."

"I do believe we've become quite adept at navigating distances," I say. "Compared to the distance from Cambridge to Palo Alto, what's the length of a castle?"

Christian laughs. "True. Mum will have to work much harder on her scheming."

I snort. "Christian, you make her sound like one of the villains on a *Real Housewives* show."

"There's no sound about it, not when it comes to her image, or mine. I suppose that's part of being a mother, right? Worrying about your son?"

I realize Christian is trying to rationalize her behavior, as if his mother is somehow acting out of concern for him, rather than herself. I understand. Even if you have a hint of the truth about your family in front of you, you still want to believe the glimmer of good.

I decide to give him that hope.

"Of course. Mothers can be overprotective. I should know, right?"

"Right," Christian concedes, and we fall into silence as we walk.

As we head down the long corridor, we're passed by various people employed by the royal household, all dressed in stylish uniforms according to their positions. I still have no idea what ninety-nine percent of them do, except for Hannah, my chambermaid.

A silence falls over me as I take in the architecture, the paintings, the meshing of the previous monarchs who placed their own style upon the castle. I long to explore it with Christian, to have him show me it through his eyes, with his stories. What was it like to him as a child? It must be strange to think you have blood ties to monarchs who lived here, loved here, and died here.

"Can we come back here on our own?" I ask.

"Of course. Why?" Christian asks. "Do you fancy a trip through the china corridor and the china museum?"

"It would be best to drop me off there with a tour guide who I can pepper with endless questions about Minton bone china dessert plates." I grin. "Though, while I'm dying to see that, I also want your history with Windsor. What memories do you have? What secret places have stories? What experiences make it yours and yours alone?"

Christian stops and turns to face me as a couple, dressed to the nines, enters a nearby room filled with gilded, green sofas and ornate, cut-glass chandeliers.

He smiles at me and says, "I would love to share my history with you, but tonight, Ace, this is where I have to leave you," Christian gazes down at me. "Only for a bit, but I have to enter with the family. It's part of the business. Go have a drink, meet some people, and I'll be in soon," Christian says, releasing my arm.

Then, to my surprise, he leans over and plants a sweet kiss on my cheek, a show of affection I wasn't expecting in front of these exclusive guests, which makes me treasure it even more.

I turn and face the room, which contains the elite of the elite in the world. I know who is in this room: lords and ladies and blue blood friends of the king and queen.

And me.

The weirdest feeling washes over me. I'm not like any of them. While my parents provided me with a very comfortable life, it's nothing like the lives these people have led. I don't know what to talk about, and I don't know all the rules. If this pantyhose didn't feel like it would rip in half, my brain would tell me to run from this situation. Because once I step into the Green Drawing Room, I can never go back to who I was.

I'll make mistakes, I'm sure of it. But I also know I'm a good person, with Christian's best interests at heart. I will navigate this for him, and somehow, I'll grow from it, too.

My nerves shift to resolve, and I square my shoulders as I stare down at the richly patterned carpet. Then I place one foot inside the room, followed by the other.

I'm here, I think looking around the room in awe, taking in the deep-green fabrics, Chippendale mirror, and ornate pieces from a time long ago.

I have taken a big step, not just for me, but for Christian, too.

I know the next one is coming soon, possibly the most important one of the journey so far.

I'll be introduced to Queen Antonia.

It won't be easy to win her over. I honestly don't know how to begin, other than by adhering to her dress code and wearing stupid pantyhose.

I might never be her choice for Christian, which I can live with.

Because Christian is all that matters.

With that thought in my head, I accept a glass of champagne off a silver tray and take a sip, wondering what the evening will bring.

CHAPTER 25

FIVE WINE GLASSES

"Clementine?"

With surprise, I turn around and immediately recognize the woman speaking to me. It's Felicity Cheltham, the Countess of Westwick—and my new boss.

"Lady Cheltham," I say, pleasantly surprised to meet her here. "I'm honored to meet you in person at last."

I shift my champagne glass and extend my hand to her.

Wait. I know I can't do that when meeting royalty, but where does a lady fall? Did I commit my first breech of etiquette?

"Please, call me Felicity," she says warmly, shaking my hand.

Whew. I must be okay on the handshake.

"King Arthur told us you would be here tonight, and I was eagerly awaiting your arrival so I would have someone I could walk around and discuss the splendor of Sèvres porcelain with."

I smile. "You have found the right person."

"I assume you have introduced yourself to our newest

tour guide?" a tall man in his early fifties says, smiling at me as he moves next to Felicity. I recognize him as John Cheltham, the eighth Earl of Westwick. He extends his hand to me. "Welcome to England."

I shake his hand. "Thank you, Lord Cheltham."

"John," he says easily. "Are you ready to start on Monday? I know Felicity is eager to have you on site."

"You have no idea how excited I am. I might have stalked the estate website."

"Ah, so that must be why page visits from the United States have skyrocketed," he says, his deep brown eyes shining at me.

I blush. "Apparently so."

I hear more voices, and we all turn toward the door.

I freeze.

The royal family is entering.

The first royal I see is the Dowager Queen, in an emerald-green, long, satin skirt and belted satin jacket, with an emerald and diamond brooch on her lapel. She is smiling as she takes in the room. Princess Elizabeth is by her side. Elizabeth—known socially as Liz—is stunning in a pearl satin gown with her long, curly blonde hair tumbling past her shoulders. I can't help but see the connection between her and Christian as they share the same hair color.

Next, Isabella and Victoria walk in side-by-side. Isabella is equally beautiful, with her hair a dirtier blonde and worn half up, half down. Her gown is black and sleeveless, but with an elegant ruffled neckline. Victoria is dressed in a fantastic, pale-green, sequined jumpsuit. A jumpsuit! She shimmers like a mermaid when she walks, and her long, blonde hair is swept back in a messy bun with some loose strands sweeping near her cheeks.

I can only imagine how this look is going to go down with Her Majesty.

Behind them is Prince Henry, King Arthur's brother and the Duke of York, who looks strikingly like him, with the same blond hair and blue eyes that Christian and all the princesses inherited. His wife, Arabella, the Duchess of York, is a beautiful brunette, dressed in a burgundy V-neck gown with butterfly sleeves, wearing a necklace that looks like it is from the family vault.

Following them is Prince James, who has thick, dark-brown hair and the same brown eyes as Queen Antonia. My heart jumps when I see Christian behind him. His eyes search for mine in the room, and as soon as he sees me, a smile lights up his face.

When I see that look in his eyes, I know, without a doubt, I can handle all of this.

Prince Alexander is behind him, and I can see why girls are obsessed. Yes, he's going to be a king someday, that certainly plays into it, but he's striking with his jet-black hair, blue eyes, and tall, athletic frame. He's not as gorgeous as Christian to me, of course, but I see why he is a magazine cover favorite.

Lastly are the king and queen. King Arthur's eyes dart about the room, and I wonder if he's going through his mental list of who he must greet tonight and what conversations need to be had.

I swallow hard as I see Queen Antonia for the first time. I'm brave. I know I can do this. But the second I see her, I feel cold inside. I hear all of Christian's painful childhood memories in my head, and I am reminded of the disconnect he felt from her and the horrible secret he and Xander have had to keep about James.

She is dressed in a long column dress in ivory that has a

boat neck top and three-quarter length sleeves. Queen Antonia's hair is in her signature chignon, tight and perfectly pulled back, not a single strand of her black hair daring to fall out of place. Her glittering ruby and diamond necklace sparkles from across the room, and a matching pair of earrings does the same.

A smile remains on her face, never moving, never breaking, as she regally scans the room, inclining her head at the appropriate guests. But as soon as her mahogany brown eyes spot me, she freezes. The corners of her mouth turn down for a brief second, ever so brief, before her smile is right back in place and her eyes move past me.

As if I don't exist.

I take another sip of my drink, wishing I could have a shot of something harder instead.

Because I'm going to need it.

"Ms. Jones?"

I turn and find a woman at my side.

"I'm to bring you to meet His Majesty now," she says. "May I suggest you put down your drink first?"

"Oh, of course," I say, and right as I'm about to look for somewhere to put it, a man in a uniform appears with a tray.

Damn. The royal staff is on it.

"Thank you," I murmur. I turn to John and Felicity. "Please excuse me while I greet King Arthur and Queen Antonia. I look forward to visiting with you more this evening, and tomorrow at Ascot."

"I'm looking forward to it already," Felicity says warmly.

I follow the woman, who leads me over to a small group of people. It's obvious we are all here to greet King Arthur and Queen Antonia. I spy Christian off to the left, with Liz and Xander, and his eyes are glued on me.

The eyes I know so well, the window into his heart, are filled with anxiety.

Not for how I'm going to act, but how his mother will.

I turn back around to the couple in front of me, who are greeting King Arthur and Queen Antonia. They move on to talk to the Dowager Queen, and now it's my turn.

King Arthur breaks into a smile the second he sees me, while Queen Antonia remains locked in place, her eyes cutting through me.

I dip into a curtsy, which isn't easy because my pantyhose feel tight.

"Your Royal Highness," I say to him. "Thank you for your gracious invitation to attend Ascot as your guest."

He clasps my hand warmly in his, and Queen Antonia's eyebrows raise a shocking millimeter before she pulls them back under control again.

"I'm delighted we finally have you back on our soil," King Arthur says. "As is Christian."

A blush fills my cheeks. "I'm so happy to be in the same city; you have no idea."

I shift my gaze to Queen Antonia, and my palms begin to sweat. Oh, crap, I'm sweating everywhere, and my legs feel practically swampy. I try to ignore the sensation as I dip into my curtsy and rise. "Your Royal Highness, it's a pleasure to meet you."

Queen Antonia's eyes quickly move over me. She doesn't extend her hand to me as she did with the previous couple she greeted.

"I see you're wearing royal blue tonight," she says coolly, her arched eyebrows barely moving up.

Was I not supposed to wear blue? Is there some rule against that? Why is she staring at me like this?

My cheeks grow warm. "I love royal blue."

"Oh, yes, I bet a royal shade of blue is rather appealing to you, isn't it, Ms. Jones?" Queen Antonia says.

"Antonia," King Arthur warns through a smile as he prepares to receive another guest. "Not now. Or ever."

Now my face is burning. That was a passive-aggressive way of implying I'm chasing after her son for his title and trappings.

Like she did with Arthur.

Well, she might be Her Majesty, but she's not getting away with this crap.

"Christian loves when I wear blue," I say, beaming at her. "It's his favorite color on me."

Her nostrils flare ever-so-slightly.

"Do enjoy your time here," she says icily, "for however long you manage to stay."

A chill sweeps through me as I move past them. In those two sentences, my first official introduction to her, she put me on notice.

She will lay every trap she can to make sure I don't last.

"You must be Christian's friend."

I snap from my thoughts to find the Dowager Queen staring at me. Unlike Queen Antonia, she makes no effort to disguise the sour expression on her face. Her lips are drawn tight and her eyes are narrowed, as if she just bit into a lemon.

"Yes, your Royal Highness," I say, dipping into my third curtsy of the night. I rise, thankful my dress and pantyhose haven't ripped yet.

Of course, my legs are so sweaty the pantyhose is cemented in place, probably saving me from that disaster.

"Christian says he met you online," she says, her expression one of disdain. "I think that is a dreadful way to interact with the world. In my day, you met people in person, with a proper introduction."

How do I even respond to that? How?

"I'm glad we didn't have a proper introduction," Christian says, moving next to me and saving me from having to come up with an appropriate response. "Or Clementine never would have given me the time of day."

"Tsk, I doubt that," the Dowager Queen says. "Excuse me."

As she walks away, Christian links his fingers through mine. I gaze up at him. He swallows hard, and I put my hand on his shoulder. Thanks to my heels, I can get close enough to his ear to whisper, "Tough crowd in this room, but I'm sure my ability to sing the *Shrek* soundtrack in order will completely win them over. That or my stash of caramel M&M's. I had you and your roommates eating out of my hand for those."

I step back from him and see my prince is smiling now.

"I adore you," he says.

"I know you do."

Christian puts his head next to mine so he can whisper back, "I'm sorry. Please remember that. I'm always going to be sorry for this."

I resolve to tell him later to never say that to me again. No family is perfect, no matter what gilded rooms they live in, and he has nothing to apologize for.

"Come on," Christian says. "I want to introduce you to everyone."

I'm still nervous, but for a different reason. With the queen and dowager queen, I was afraid because I knew they had already formed an opinion of me, and not a good one. However, it's a different story with Christian's brothers and cousins. These are the people who understand the world he has to live in better than anyone else. I want them to accept me because their opinions matter to Christian. I want them to like me, and I want to like them in return.

The modern royals, as I think of them, are all gathered by the fireplace, drinks in hand. As soon as we join the circle, they stop talking, and my nerves go crazy.

"I'd like to introduce you all to Clementine Jones," Christian says, putting his hand on the small of my back. "Clementine, this is Xander."

Xander's blue eyes are riveted on my face, studying me carefully as if he is trying to solve a puzzle.

I furrow my brow back. "What?" I ask instinctively.

Now his eyes widen in surprise. "What?" Xander repeats. "What do you mean, what?"

I freeze. Crap, what am I doing? He's not some guy. Xander is the future king! I'm not supposed to speak to him first; I'm supposed to curtsy!

I snap into action, going into a curtsy, and quickly rising.

"I'm so sorry, Your Royal Highness," I say to Xander.

"I want that to be your last curtsy to me unless we're at some formal ceremony," Xander says, his face lighting up in a brilliant smile. "Please call me Xander, always."

"We don't do the curtsy thing within the squad," Liz says, her eyes dancing at me.

"Squad?" I say, confused.

"We consider ourselves a squad, all of us," Liz continues. "The next generation of the monarchy."

"We don't dip and bow to each other," Christian explains, rubbing his hand up and down on my back.

"Otherwise, it would take all day just to enter a room,"

Xander quips, pausing to take a sip of his cocktail. "Although it wouldn't for me, since I don't need to bow to any of you lot." Then he winks at me. "Perk of the whole next-in-line bit."

I smile. I'm already warming to him.

"Now what was your 'what' about?" Xander asks.

"You were staring at me with a confused look on your face," I say. "Was it my droop?"Now Xander is furrowing his brow. "What? No, I was wondering how on earth my recluse brother found an amazing woman like you. Of course, it was from his laptop. We all know he doesn't go out to nightclubs unless we drag him and tie him to a table."

I laugh. "Oh. I thought you had noticed my facial paralysis. It's a side effect from my brain surgery."

Xander's eyes widen. Obviously, Christian hasn't mentioned my medical history to them, which touches my heart. When he said he kept it between us, he truly meant it.

"Benign tumor, no big deal, but this was the result," I say, wanting to put everyone at ease. "Right here," I say, pointing to the area on the right side of my face which has the slight droop.

"Bloody hell, you've been through the wringer, haven't you?" Xander asks.

"You would never know it," Christian says, smiling down at me.

"I never would have noticed it," Xander says.

"Botox evens it out," I say.

"She has that in common with Mum," Christian declares.

The girls and Xander laugh, but I notice James doesn't.

I remember what Christian told me about James, how he is always trying to please their mother.

I decide to deflect the conversation away from Antonia.

"You must be James," I say. "Is it all right if I extend my hand first to you?"

James grins. While I see he has Queen Antonia's mahogany brown eyes, his smile is absolutely King Arthur's. "Yes. Lovely to meet you, Clementine," he says as he shakes my hand.

"I'm Isabella," the girl in the black gown introduces herself, extending her hand to me. "It's a pleasure to meet you. Christian has told us so much about you."

"Thank God you're finally here, so Curry Takeaway will finally stop moaning about missing you over his tea and toast every morning. It's enough to drive me back to the army ahead of the end of my leave," Xander says.

I burst out laughing. "What did you call him?"

A wicked smile lights up Xander's face, and I glance up at Christian, who begins to blush.

"You didn't tell her about your nickname?"

"I know CP is one," I say, cocking an eyebrow.

"That's boring. Curry Takeaway is much more him," Xander says, lifting his glass to Christian.

"Wait, back to the important bit," I say. "Did you miss me over tea and toast? How quaintly British of you."

"We do love our tea and toast," Victoria says, extending her hand to me. "Hello, I'm Victoria. How do you take your tea? We need to know this."

Christian grins, as he knows the truth.

No white lying on this important question.

"I'm not a tea drinker."

Xander cocks an eyebrow. "And your work visa was still approved?"

I grin. "Shockingly, yes. I was still allowed in."

"Are you a coffee person?" Isabella asks. "I'm obsessed with coffee."

"Wait until you have the iced coffee tomorrow in the royal box; it's my favorite thing about Ascot next to the hats," Victoria declares.

"I'm not much of a coffee drinker, either," I admit.

"If you say cocktails, I'm stealing you from Curry Takeaway," Xander jokes.

Another member of the household staff begins ushering us to the dining room. I feel like I've been invited to a fraternity formal at Stanford. I have that excited energy about being with my date. I'm meeting his friends, and the first introductions have gone well, and now we'll see how the rest of the evening plays out.

As we head toward the State Dining Room, my arm wrapped around Christian's while we walk, new worries take root in me. I know what knives and forks to use, but I still don't use them in the way Christian does. I'll make a joke about it if anyone stares at me, I decide.

If I think of jokes for every possible pitfall, I'll be set.

And have enough material to host my own comedy special on HBO.

"You're doing brilliantly, Ace," Christian leans over and whispers in my ear. "I'm proud to have you on my arm tonight."

I practically radiate joy from his words. I won't be perfect.

But Christian doesn't expect me to be.

I just have to be my normal self.

We enter the State Dining Room of the castle, and my jaw drops as I take in the opulent surroundings. It's another room where time has stood still, done in rich reds and gilt. The long rosewood table is surrounded by crimson-striped gilt chairs, each perfectly placed apart from each other. Candelabras illuminate the place settings, and fresh spring flowers are artfully interspersed between them. Massive red drapes frame the windows, and a huge portrait of Queen Victoria is hanging over the fireplace. Two rosewood side tables flank the fireplace, and I know those pieces are from the early 1800s.

Guests begin moving toward their seats, and I realize this isn't going to be like my family graduation dinner, where I was able to sit next to Christian and hold his hand under the table while my disbelieving parents peppered him with questions.

I'm going to be on my own for dinner.

"Let's see where you will be dining tonight, Ace," he says.

I'm guessing Queen Antonia has made sure I'm at the farthest end of the table.

With Christian placed next to her at the other end.

Sure enough, we keep walking down the long table.

And walking.

And walking.

And at the very last seat, I see my name on a place card. I feel Christian once again stiffen beside me. He's pissed.

"I suppose you are at the other end?" I say.

"This will be addressed later," he says firmly.

"I'll be fine."

Christian pulls out my chair for me, and as I sit down, I feel a pop and hear a loud ripping sound across my crotch.

Oh shit, my pantyhose have ripped!

"What was that?" Christian asks.

"My stomach," I blurt out.

"What?" he asks again, chuckling. "I've never heard your stomach sound like that."

"I'm really hungry," I lie, praying I'm not turning beet red.

Okay. I have a long dress. Even if it creates a hideous run, nobody can see it.

"By the sounds of that, I think your stomach split in half."

"Go sit down," I say, shooing him off.

Christian grins and heads off to the other end of the earth to eat. A couple across from me sits down, friends of Queen Antonia's. I glance at the place card to my right: *Princess Victoria of York*. Oh, perfect, Victoria is someone I can talk to.

I see there is a menu card placed in front of me, and I eagerly pick it up to read.

Except I can't because it's all in French.

I study it, picking out two items I recognize: salade and fruits de desserts.

Fabulous. Mystery dining.

I notice there are five wines listed. There are also five wine glasses at my place setting.

Holy shit, I have to drink five wines? Is it rude if I don't drink them all? I'll be shit-faced if I do. Hell, even taking sips of all these different wines could get me buzzed.

Victoria walks toward me in that fabulous sequined jumpsuit, and a staff person immediately appears and pulls out her chair.

Seriously, are they hiding behind the drapes? Do they have earpieces telling them when to leap into action?

"Thank you," she says, sinking down in her seat. Then she turns to me, her blue eyes twinkling, and lowers her head toward mine so she can speak in my ear. "I'm always banished to the end of the table. But with you here, it won't be dull this evening."

Then she sits, back upright, picks up her elaborately folded napkin, and flicks it open, placing it in her lap.

I smile.

Being at the end of the table might not be so bad. Without fear, I look forward to five wines, a mystery menu, and getting to know Princess Victoria.

And reuniting with Christian as soon as this dinner is over.

Servers begin pouring champagne, and as I watch the bubbles appear in my glass, I can't help but think this evening will end in celebration after all.

CHAPTER 26

PLACE YOUR BETS

I'm buzzed.

I'm still managing to walk upright with Christian, so I'm not drunk. But my brain is a tad fuzzy, and I would absolutely get lost trying to find my own way back to my room. I'd probably end up trapped in the Queen's Guard Chamber or something.

I snort. I bet Queen Antonia would love that.

"What's so funny?" Christian asks as we walk what seems like our forty-fifth mile.

"Your mother was probably hoping I'd get lost coming back, and she'd have her men in black lock me up in one of these rooms for the rest of my life, or until you lost interest, whichever would come first. No. Not men in black, that's a movie. Men in suits. Not the server men in suits, those are more like weird uniforms from the eighteenth century, but her henchmen. Yes. They would lock me up. But at least I like antiques, so I wouldn't be bored being locked up, except I'd get hungry, and I'd miss you so much. I love you. I'd want to have sex with you, and that I can't do by myself.

Well, if I had a phone, we could have phone sex, but that's not the same as sexy sex you know?"

Oh, crap, I'm *really* buzzed.

Christian chuckles, and oh, damn, he's hot when he gives me that deep, reverberating laugh.

"Your laugh is sexy," I continue, unable to find my internal off button.

"You're sexy when you're drunk," Christian says.

"Not drink. Drunk. Not drunk. Tipsy, yes. I'm aware I'm rambling, but I can't stop. I love you," I say, feeling exceptionally lovey toward him in my state.

"I think this is the first time I've seen you drunk. You're irresistible when you drunk ramble."

"I promise I said nothing bad at the table," I blurt out.

I lengthen my stride, and rip! I feel the pantyhose tearing down the side of my leg.

"Fiona. That is not your stomach. What is going on?"

"Pantyhose! I hate them," I blurt out. "They are tearing, and they have been since before that awful fish thing was served for the first course."

"If you hate them, why are you wearing them?"

"I read that's a rule. Your mother wants ladies in pantyhose," I say.

Christian moves around and brings me to a stop. Even in my buzzed state, I can see he's not happy.

"Wait. You put on tights to follow monarchy rules?" Christian asks, his brow furrowed.

I gulp. Shit.

"I wanted to give the best first impression."

He turns and looks at the wall. Some household staff members walk by, and he remains silent until they pass us in the never-ending corridor. Then he turns back to me, a worried expression on his face.

"Please don't do that," Christian says. "I don't want you to feel like you have to be one of us."

"What's that supposed to mean? If we get married someday, which I plan on, I will be one of you, and I will have to follow the rules."

"No!" Christian snaps, with an intensity that takes me by surprise. "You will dress how you see fit. I don't want you to lose yourself to *them.* I won't let this happen."

"Christian. They're pantyhose. Don't get your knickers in a twist about it."

Oh, from the anger that flashes across his face I know that was not the right thing to say.

"You admitted you hate them," he says, his voice low. "So, what's next? Going to start wearing Mum's style of dress? Put your hair in a twist every day? Then start pretending and leave who you are behind? Then we will go off the bloody rails, and I won't lose you to them. I won't."

Pretending? Lose me to them? My brain can't connect the dots in this state, but he is definitely overreacting. I thought we put this issue to bed, so why is he bringing it back up?

"You know what, Christian? I don't know what is going on in your head, and I'm not in the state to be able to figure it out, because I'm operating on a varied assortment of wine, but I can assure you I'm a full-grown adult who can make her own fashion decisions, and if pantyhose are part of the scene, I can tolerate them for a few hours without becoming Queen Antonia two point oh. Now if you'll excuse me, I'm going to take the oh-so-altering garment off, and when you can talk to me without being pissed, we'll talk."

Then I begin to walk down the hall, leaving him

standing there. I can feel the air swoosh up from my dress to my ripped open crotch as I take big steps to move away.

Shit. I have no idea how to get to my room by myself.

Why can't royal household members appear when I truly need them?

"Clementine, wait," Christian says, catching up to me. He puts his hand on my arm and draws me to a stop. "I'm sorry."

"What was that really about, Christian?" I ask.

Christian rakes a hand through his hair and exhales. "My past."

The sadness returns to his eyes, and I'd do anything to take it away. I want to talk to him about this, but tonight is not the night. I know it needs to take place when he's calm and not reacting to a trigger.

I'd also like to be able to respond without tripping over my words and rambling.

"Please forgive me."

"I was never mad," I say honestly. "Confused, but not mad. Besides, I could never stay mad at you for long."

"Promise?" Christian asks.

"Only if you promise the same for me."

Christian smiles at me. "I can promise that forever."

"Then so can I."

We continue our never-ending walk, and finally, *finally,* we arrive back at my room. I retrieve my key, and Christian unlocks the door. The second I get inside, I kick off my heels. The light flickers on, and as I'm about to go into the bathroom to rip the stupid pantyhose off, I spy a large, flat box on the center of my bed.

"What's that?" I ask, nearly tripping over my shoes as I move forward.

"Open it."

I sink down on the bed and lift the lid on the box. To my surprise, I find a huge, heart-shaped sugar cookie with these words written on it:

Masterly We Oh Hi

An anagram.

I begin to laugh. "I can't figure these out without having sampled five different wines."

Christian sits down beside me. He takes his index finger and traces the shape of a heart with it on my chest.

"My heart is whole," he says softly, "now that you are beside me again."

Christian blurs through the tears in my eyes. "You are worth every fish appetizer I'll ever have to eat," I say.

He chuckles, that wonderful throaty chuckle that makes me want to rip his clothes off and have my way with him.

"I do love how romantic you are," he says dryly. "Thank you for thinking I'm worth eating salmon mousse for."

I begin unbuttoning his luxurious dress shirt, letting my fingers trail slowly down his skin as I do. His mouth finds mine. I kiss him deeply, my tongue tangling with his, and he lowers me back on the bed, his lips moving rapidly against mine.

I instinctively draw one leg up, and Christian pushes up my dress, his hand skimming over my calf and up to my thigh, toward my panties. His fingers stop at the gaping hole in my pantyhose.

Christian pushes himself up and bursts out laughing. "Good God, Ace, that hole is the size of Liverpool!"

I begin laughing so hard tears spring to my eyes, and he falls down beside me, collapsing in his own fit of laughter. Once we compose ourselves, I turn to face him.

"I love you," I say, reaching up and playing with his hair.

"I love you more," Christian says.

As he presses his lips to mine, I know we'll be up all night, laughing, talking, and making love. I'll be dead for Ascot tomorrow.

And I won't regret any of it.

I gaze out at the spectators that fill the Ascot stands around the lush, green racetrack, a sea of amazing hats on ladies and morning suits on gentlemen. There's a spirit of fun in the air, of people drinking cocktails and laughing and discussing the fashions and races to come. I might have a wee bit of a headache, and I had hardly any sleep, but I'm wide-eyed and excited for experiencing everything Ascot has to offer.

"Worth all the running back and forth this morning?" Christian asks, putting a cocktail in my hand.

"Yes," I say, grinning happily at my gorgeous man, who is dressed in a morning suit and top hat and looking oh-so-British. "Worth every step."

Running is exactly what we did all morning. The royal family has a tight schedule on Ascot days. I've already changed twice. First, I wore a day dress for breakfast. Then I went back upstairs to put on my Ascot outfit for lunch. I feel like I've already had a full day, and it's only afternoon. Christian rode in a carriage with his brothers as part of the royal procession from the Great Park, a tradition since 1825.

Again, the weight of the history Christian carries hits me. He was born into this life, and whether he likes it or not, he must do these things. But when I saw the people lining the route, smiling and cheering for the procession, I understood the importance of these traditions. It's part of the fabric of this country, and while the monarchy has its detractors who think it should be eliminated, there are also many people who hold it dear in their hearts and believe in keeping these traditions alive.

So, while the royal family, along with exclusive guests, rode in the carriage procession, I joined Lady Felicity and Lord John in the SUVs carrying the rest of the royal guests to Ascot.

When we arrived, cameras began clicking, both the media's and the spectators'. I tried to act as normal as I could, talking and laughing with Isabella and Victoria. I was feeling wonderfully feminine and beautiful in my pink dress and fantastic hat, but I also felt awkward from the immense attention I was receiving.

Victoria was getting her own media buzz thanks to the outfit she chose for today: an '80s style, deep ruby-red satin, wide-legged jumpsuit, complete with cowl neck. She's wearing a statement black hat with a massive swirled bow on it. Nobody has to tell me Victoria is the fashion rebel of the Chadwick family, who will push the rules to the limit, stretching and bending them but not to the point of breaking them.

I take a sip of my pink cocktail—The Royal Blush, a glorious gin, rhubarb syrup, and lemonade blend—and glance around the royal box. Liz, who is engrossed in a conversation with her father, is dressed in all white, from her lace dress to her hat. Isabella is placing a bet, looking very chic in a crisp navy and white combo, with a navy hat with netting. I see Felicity and John talking with King Arthur, and Felicity is wearing a smart, icy-blue suit and matching hat. The Duchess of York is chatting with another guest, and she is dressed in peach, with a floral peach hat to match.

Hmm. I don't see Queen Antonia, not that it matters. After her royal blue comment to me before dinner last night, she hasn't said a word to me. Neither has the Dowager Queen, who is sipping a drink and talking to James.

"Let's study the racing form," Christian says, picking one up off the table behind us. "Who shall we bet on, love? Best odds or best name?"

"Best name, absolutely."

Christian doesn't lift his eyes from the form but smiles at my comment, which makes my heart dance.

"All right, best name it is," he says.

I lean into him, scanning the list of names for the first race.

I stop reading. I've found our horse.

"I see one that is perfect; do you see it?" I ask.

Christian stops reading and turns his attention toward me. "Wait no More?"

"Wait no More," I say, smiling at him.

"I'll go place our bet," he says.

"Before you place your bets," Queen Antonia's voice interrupts from behind, "I'd like to re-introduce you to someone, Christian."

We turn around to see Queen Antonia dressed in a white sheath dress, a fine millinery hat perched atop her glossy black hair, which, of course, is pulled back in her signature chignon.

Standing next to her is a young woman who appears to be the same age as Christian and me. She's a stunning brunette, wearing a blush-colored dress that accents her small waist and a high hat with swirly-type strips extending up from it.

"Christian, you remember Lady Penelope Winthrop-Armstrong, I'm sure," Queen Antonia says with a knowing tone in her voice. "Of course, first loves are always hard to forget, aren't they?"

What?

Christian told me he has never been in love before me. I was under the impression I'm the only woman he has said those words to. So, who is this? He said he had girlfriends before, but from the way Lady Penelope is staring at Christian, I know this relationship was more than casual.

So why didn't Christian tell me about her?

I glance at Christian, who has a stunned expression on his face.

"It's been two years," Lady Penelope says in a beautiful, posh-sounding accent. "While I'm sure many things have changed, some have not."

My stomach drops out. I know exactly what she means by this.

Her feelings for Christian are still there.

"Excuse me," Xander says, interrupting us. "May I borrow you for a moment, Clementine? I need your expert opinion on something."

The last thing I want is to leave this conversation, but I can't very well refuse the Prince of Wales in front of the queen, can I?

"Yes, of course," I say.

Xander offers me his arm, and I reluctantly take it. He leads me down to the first row of seats in the box, sitting me down first, and then taking the seat next to me. He casually picks up his binoculars and scans the crowd.

"Don't let Mum play with your head," he says, lowering

his voice. I realize he's not actively looking at anything but acting like we are engaged in something else.

"Who is that girl?" I ask, hurt that Christian might have lied about his past. "Christian never mentioned any first loves to me."

"Don't be daft. Curry Takeaway has only loved you. That's Mum's revisionist history. Penelope and Christian shared a mutual interest in old bones, God knows why, but he never loved her. I think he loved talking about dinosaur crap with her more than anything else."

Oh. I can see that.

"So ... they dated?"

Xander puts his binoculars down. He shoots me a look.

"Yes. Didn't you date when you were eighteen?" Xander asks pointedly.

I blink. "Well, yes."

"Do you long for that bloke over Curry Takeaway?"

I can't help but laugh.

"No. I prefer Curry Takeaway to all others."

Xander grins. "Then I think you know what's going on here. Mum is placing all her bets on Lady Penelope to woo my brother away from you. But here's what she doesn't know, or care to see: My brother is madly in love with you, Clementine. I've never seen him like this before. Christian is happy. He is finally coming out from behind the wall he's thrown up his whole life. At first, I was pissed for him when Father refused to let him join the army after Cambridge because I know how fantastic being in the army is, but now I don't think that's what he needs."

"No?"

Xander shakes his head. "He's starting to find himself now. I found my purpose in the service, but I think for Christian, it would be another place to hide. But he's not hiding now. In fact, I think he's damn ballsy to come out in public with you. I wouldn't do it, and I'm much more comfortable with the media than Christian is. But he's doing it for you because he sees you with him in the end, not Penelope. He loves you. And I think he's going to find his purpose with you by his side, Clementine."

He picks up his binoculars and goes back to looking at the track. I'm touched by how much Xander cares about Christian. I see so much of King Arthur in Xander, and despite his questionable reputation, I see potential for him to be a great king someday. Xander is aware of how people feel. He knows how Christian feels inside, and despite barely knowing me, he could see how I was feeling a few minutes ago by reading my face. That's a gift that will serve him well as a representative for the United Kingdom in the future.

"Xander?"

He puts the binoculars down and looks at me, his dark blue eyes fixed on mine.

"You are an exceptional man," I say softly. "Thank you for talking to me."

Xander blinks. I think he's not used to people calling him anything other than a philanderer or playboy prince. His face reflects genuine surprise at the compliment, and I don't think he knows what to do with it.

"I'm exceptional in the army and with ladies; those are my specialties," he says, giving me a charming smile. "Speaking of which," he says, handing me his binoculars, "check out the young lady with the tea service set on her hat. She's rather hot, but I don't know if I can do someone who has a pot, cups, and saucers on her head."

I burst out laughing. "You are making that up."

"Listen, I know you only have eyes for Curry Takeaway,

but you have noticed the rather ridiculous hats in play today, haven't you?"

I pick up the binoculars and follow Xander's directions to find the woman he's speaking of. She's a stunning blonde, and indeed, has an entire tea service replicated on the top of her head.

"Oh, wow, you weren't lying," I declare.

"Of course I wasn't."

"Well," I say helpfully, "she wouldn't wear the hat in bed, would she?"

"I could probably work around it if she did."

I look at him, and he's grinning wickedly at me.

Then we both burst out laughing.

"Do I even want to know?"

I smile as Christian takes the seat next to me, betting slips in hand.

"Of course you don't," Xander says, winking at me.

Christian sighs heavily and places his hand over mine. I gaze up at him and see his eyes are once again filled with regret.

"You have no idea," he says softly, "how sorry I am about that."

"About what?" I say easily. "I know you've had other girlfriends."

"Yeah, well, I wasn't expecting her to appear out of thin air during your introduction to Ascot. I'm sorry."

"Did you invite her without telling me?"

Christian furrows his brow. "Of course not."

"Then quit apologizing."

"This one's a keeper, Curry Takeaway," Xander chimes in. "Now if you'll excuse me, I think it's time for me to place my bets."

Xander gets up and excuses himself, and I turn back to Christian.

"He's right, you know," he says.

"About what?"

"You're a keeper. And I do intend to keep you. Forever."

Christian releases my hand and gives me the betting slip for our horse, Wait no More.

Wait no More is right.

We aren't waiting anymore to live our lives.

We are living now.

In public.

As a couple.

And no matter what is thrown our way, I know we'll handle it.

CHAPTER 27

FINDING PURPOSE

I'm everywhere.

I stare at my phone in shock as Google returns article after article on my appearance at Ascot today, with pictures of me smiling next to Christian, chatting with Victoria, and sitting with Xander in the royal box.

"What are you looking at?" Christian asks as we leave Windsor in his Audi, his security team following behind us in the Range Rover.

"It sounds egotistical to answer you truthfully, but I will. Myself."

"Don't believe all your press, Ace," Christian teases.

I laugh. "Oh, believe me, I won't, but I can't help but look at it. So far, the media seems to approve of my choice to wear a British designer for Ascot."

"Read me the headlines."

"Oh, God, it's like hearing yourself speak on video: cringeworthy."

"Go on."

I clear my throat. "*Fresh Air for the Royals! Clemmie Wows in Candy Floss Pink.*"

"I agree with that. Give me some more."

"Wait a second. What's candy floss?"

"You don't know what candy floss is?"

"No," I say, shaking my head.

"Spun sugar. You know, the candy that dissolves in your mouth?"

"Oh! Cotton candy!" I say. "That's what we call it in America."

"Cotton candy is a terrible name. UK one, USA zero. Now read me another one."

I chuckle. "I had no idea you were so passionate about what cotton candy is called."

"I'm full of secrets for you to unlock," he says dryly.

I grin and go back to skimming article headlines. "Here's one. *True Love? Prince Christian Invites His American Love to Ascot.*"

"Brilliant, so far they are factual for a change," Christian says, smiling as he drives.

Warmth rushes over me, and I read a few more for his entertainment. "*Betting on Love! Prince Christian Spends Ladies' Day With his Lady Love.* Oh, I like that one."

"Me, too."

"So far, very positive," I say, dropping my phone back into my bag.

"Clementine, remember they will turn on you. Not if, but when. My advice is to not read any of them, not that I'm telling you what to do. It's merely a suggestion, from someone who has been labeled a hoarder and will forever be called Curry Takeaway by his extremely annoying older brother."

My heart melts. Our mini argument last night has obviously stayed with him, so he's treading lightly.

"I know you're right. Xander will call you Curry Takeaway for the rest of your life."

He chuckles, and I reach over and play with the curls at the nape of his neck.

"Shall I make you spag bol tonight? For you and Jillian, if she's around?"

"That would be lovely," I say. "Jillian was so helpful yesterday; it would be a wonderful gesture to show her how much we appreciate her kindness."

"Brilliant. We'll stop and get the shopping before heading home."

Get the shopping. There are so many British terms I'm going to have to get used to.

"Good. I need to do that anyway, and I have to get a crapton of bacon for butties."

"You seem to be acclimatizing quite well."

"The bacon butty was almost as life-changing as falling in love with some bloke I met online," I tease.

"I'm relieved to hear I edged out the bacon butty," Christian quips.

I laugh. "Just barely. Better stay on your toes, Your Royal Highness."

He smiles, and I have no doubt his eyes are dancing behind those sexy aviator shades he has on.

"I intend to, Fiona," he says. "And I'll start by making you and Jillian a fabulous dinner tonight."

"Are you sure I can't help?" Jillian calls out to Christian in the kitchen.

"No, no, I'm good," Christian says as he stirs a pot on the stove. "You and Clementine enjoy your wine while I make the sauce."

Jillian turns back toward me and lifts an eyebrow. "I haven't lost my mind, right? The Prince of Wales is in the kitchen making me dinner?"

I grin as I ruffle Bear's head. "Nope. Christian does the shopping and the cooking. You should see the masterful way he whips through a grocery store. The man has purpose when he shops."

"I love doing the shopping," Christian says from the kitchen. "I did it for all my flatmates back at Cambridge."

"A prince who does his own shopping. I pay to have the shopping delivered because I hate that task so much. So if you don't propose to him by the time the dishes are cleared, I will," Jillian jokes.

I glance at Christian, who is blushing from Jillian's teasing.

"He's so cute when he gets embarrassed," I say, piling on. "Look at him blush."

"Stop," Christian says, turning a deeper pink hue as he throws some spaghetti in a pot of boiling water. "Or I'll start calling you Clemmie like the media does."

I groan. "Clemmie. Ugh."

Christian laughs. I swear his chuckle is my favorite sound in the entire world.

"You had tremendous press coverage today," Jillian says, pausing to take a sip of her wine. "All favorable, of course. Oh, and your dress? Sold out in minutes after it was tagged as the dress worn by *Captivating Clementine*. That designer should be sending you 'thank you' flowers tomorrow. You put her on the map today."

"Are you serious?" I ask. "I didn't get that far in my scrolling."

"She loves reading press about herself," Christian says.

"I do not, you liar. I was curious. This was my first introduction to the royal family, so this is different. I wanted to see how I went over."

"I told her they will love her at first but then look for a reason to kick her down," Christian says.

"Sounds like you are speaking from experience," Jillian says, tucking her feet up underneath her in her chair.

Christian pops some garlic bread into the oven. "Yes," he says simply. "I was criticized for hiding at Cambridge. Now that I've been forbidden from entering the military for a year, I'll be criticized for not doing my military service. You can't win."

"Well, not with them, but you can win with yourself and with your citizens with your support of causes," Jillian says.

"That's what I'm trying to sort out," Christian says, leaning against the countertop and staring at Jillian. "I want to find my purpose, my vision. On Monday, I'm filling in for Mum at a ballet school in Birmingham with a visit and meeting with school administration. She's a patron of the Birmingham Ballet, and it's important to support the arts, which is her cause, but I want to find *my* causes, where I can make a difference. There are so many great charities I can support, but I want to think of things that speak to me and Clementine."

"You don't have to decide them all this week," I say gently.

He rubs his hand over his jaw and lets out a sigh. "I know, but I don't want people to see me working only as a fill-in for the king and queen. I want them to see, if I must put off the military for a year, my time will be spent championing my own causes. I won't be sitting around living off the taxpayers' money, waiting for my time to go. I want to do good things."

"I don't have any doubt that you will," Jillian says firmly. "You are already thinking this through and taking it seriously. No matter what charity you choose, people will be interested. You've been a mystery to the world, and now you are finally letting us see who you are, starting with sharing Clementine with us."

A smile lights up his face, and my heart dances inside my chest.

"He loves paleontology," I say, watching Christian. "I think promoting science with children would be a great start, or animal conservation."

"Oh, yes," Jillian says, nodding in agreement.

"My family typically becomes patrons of loads of charities," Christian says, turning the flame under the pasta pot off and reaching for some mitts. He picks up the pot and dumps the water into the colander in the sink, getting a steam bath in the process.

He continues as he shakes the excess water from the spaghetti. "I think I want to be concentrated, though. Start with a few, eventually add more, like things I want to do with Xander and James, perhaps, and Clementine in the future, but still keep it limited so I can throw all my energy behind them, you know?"

"I think that's smart," I say, proud of how much thought he has put into his new role. "And the causes you support will be grateful for your efforts."

"I hope so," Christian says, opening the oven and removing the garlic bread. "Now ladies, if you will adjourn to the dining room, I'll bring dinner in."

Jillian shoots me a look. "You do need to propose to him if he breaks out dessert."

I laugh and take my seat, and Jillian sits down across from me. Bear follows us and drops his head in Jillian's lap.

"I think Bear has made himself a new friend," I say, smiling at her.

"Oh, he's just a big teddy bear," Jillian says, affectionately rubbing his head. "I took him for a walk this morning in Kensington Gardens, and it was lovely. You're good company, Mr. Bear."

"He's my big boy," I say. "I got him last year from a rescue group. The owner had to move and didn't want to take him. I couldn't imagine not taking him."

"I've loved all my animals; that's one of the things I missed after my last one passed. George was just diagnosed with his illness, and I knew I couldn't bring a new dog into the home," Jillian says matter-of-factly.

Christian enters the room and places a plate in front of Jillian and then me.

"This looks delicious," I say, excited to eat his spag bol again.

"It smells heavenly," Jillian adds. "Thank you, Christian."

"You're very welcome," Christian says, returning to the kitchen to retrieve his own wine glass and plate.

He comes back and takes a seat next to me.

"Before we start, I'd like to propose a toast," Jillian says, raising her glass. "To new friends and a home filled with conversation and laughter and two young people in love. Your presence has been a blessing to me."

Tears prick my eyes at Jillian's heartfelt words.

We clink our glasses together and take a drink.

"Jillian, if you don't mind me asking, what made you

participate in the roommate match program?" Christian asks as he picks up his fork. "I feel like Clementine and I are the lucky ones, to be matched with you. I'm curious as to how you became involved with it."

"The simple answer? I was tired of being lonely," Jillian says, pausing to take a bite of her pasta. Her eyes widen as she samples it. "Oh, this is fantastic. You actually can cook!"

Christian laughs. "I learned a few tricks from the chef at Buckingham Palace. So, it better be good."

"Well, he or she did you a great service. I can see why Clementine was craving this," Jillian says. Then she clears her throat. "Back to your question. When George was first diagnosed, our friends didn't know how to respond. A lot of them were uncomfortable. They couldn't handle it, especially when George began to show symptoms. He had problems following conversations. He was anxious doing social things he used to love, like dinner parties. Gradually, he reached the middle-stage, and he became delusional. He would constantly wring his hands and sleep during the day and be up all night."

"My God, Jillian, I'm so sorry," I say, a lump forming in my throat. I can't imagine watching the man you love disappear in front of your eyes and having no family and friends to turn to for support.

"I would do it all over again for the years we had together," Jillian says quietly. "But when all was said and done, I had lost many of my friends, either from them being uncomfortable with George, or from me not being able to leave him. I was his caregiver. I would occasionally hire someone to help if I needed to run errands or go to a doctor, but I lost myself in taking care of him. And when he passed, I felt like my world had gone dark. Not only did I lose George, but I lost my purpose. I was so alone.

"It took me a long time to get out of that depression, that black period of my life," Jillian continues. "My friends had moved on, and rightfully so. I had a very lonely existence. I had spent the end of George's life giving him round-the-clock care, and George was no longer George. After he passed, everything I held in came out, and I fell apart. I knew George would want me to find a life again, but I didn't know how. It seemed overwhelming."

I glance at Christian, who is intently listening to Jillian, his expressive eyes showing me something else is going on in his head. He's touched by her story, that I know, but he's also deep in thought.

Jillian continues. "Then one night I was watching the news on the telly, and they did a story on this program. I don't know why, but something compelled me to write down the website address. A few days later, I looked at it and thought, why not? It would be nice to have another voice in the house besides the ones on TV or from my iPhone. They asked if I was okay with an American, and I was thrilled. Someone completely different! I couldn't have hand-picked anyone better than Clementine."

"You're going to make me cry," I say, sniffling. "I feel the same way. I'm happy to have you as a part of my life here."

"We've become way too serious," Jillian says, shaking her head, but I notice her eyes are a bit watery. "We need more wine. Christian, will you be spending the night here?"

I stifle a giggle as Christian appears flustered by the question.

"Um, no, I will be going back home tonight," he says.

"Well, just so you know, I don't care if you sleep over.

Or stay over and choose not to sleep," Jillian adds with a devilish grin.

I don't think I've ever seen Christian look more embarrassed.

"Um, err … I …"

Jillian laughs. "If you will be staying over, I was going to pour you another glass of wine."

He smiles. "Well, there's nothing at home at Kensington Palace except for Lucy, and she's taken care of when I'm not there."

"Brilliant. Then you'll stay. I'll retrieve that bottle," Jillian says happily.

"That was so much fun. Jillian may be the coolest woman I've ever met," I say as I return to the bedroom after brushing my teeth, washing my face, and changing into one of Christian's Arsenal T-shirts, which I've claimed for myself.

Christian has stripped down to his boxer-briefs and has climbed into bed. He is typing something into his phone as he sits up against the headboard.

"She's such an inspirational woman. It's funny how we're both at a point of change in our lives. Jillian is moving forward to rebuild hers, and I'm moving forward to start mine."

Christian doesn't reply as he continues to read.

"Christian?" I ask, flipping back the duvet and climbing in next to him. "What are you reading?"

"Clem, I think I know my purpose," Christian says, shifting his attention to me. "It became clear to me as Jillian told her story tonight. I want to help caregivers.

Jillian carried all that weight on her own, not taking time for herself except to do errands. I want to do more, to provide relief for caregivers, to create places where they can go and connect with other people in their position. Not only support groups; I want to make something just for them. Perhaps fun outings like a tea or a football match. I was looking up organizations, and I'm going to have my secretary reach out next week and organize some meetings. With the monarchy behind these organizations, we can do something meaningful for people who truly need it."

"You are an exceptional man, Christian Chadwick," I say, love surging in my heart for him. "You are going to do remarkable things in your new role. You can impact lives for the better. What a gift you have to give to caregivers who truly need it."

"I want to do this," Christian says, his eyes lighting up. "I *need* to do this. I can't wait to get going on it."

I take his hand and draw it to my lips, kissing it softly. "Your work can change the lives of so many people. And I know, without a doubt, you'll do this brilliantly."

"I was so angry when father told me I couldn't go into the army," Christian says. "Furious. How could he let Xander do it and not me? How could he take that away from me when all I heard from Xander was how awesome it was to have a purpose and be treated like anyone else? But now I'm wondering if maybe that wasn't meant to be my path."

"What do you mean?"

"Maybe I'm meant to serve the country in this role," Christian says. "Maybe I'm meant to serve on boards and as a patron and do things to help groups that desperately need awareness and funding instead of in the army. As a young royal, I can bring publicity to any event I spotlight. Maybe this is my calling."

I snuggle in next to him, resting my head on his bare chest and feeling the warmth of his body against my cheek.

"I can see that," I say softly.

"Me, too," Christian says, dropping a kiss on the top of my head as he puts his arm around me, cradling me close to him.

I close my eyes as the long day washes over me. I'm ready to sleep with this man's arms wrapped around me.

Counting every blessing that he's mine.

CHAPTER 28

WORKING WOMAN

I pick up my black, Knomo brief tote—one of my graduation presents from Christian—and suck in a breath of air. I glance at my reflection in the full-length mirror in my room. I know I won't be giving tours for a while, but I also know I'll be doing a lot of walking, shadowing other tour guides. I've gone for functional chic—black, wide-legged trousers; a white, flowy blouse; and a black blazer, which I'll take off to be more casual in the home. I added a bit of myself with my shoes: a pair of pink, jacquard slipper-mules with a print inspired by vintage Japanese fabrics. I love them, and it gives a bit of personality to my outfit.

I'm ready, I tell myself.

Butterflies take off in my stomach as I head down the hall. There are no words to describe how thrilled I am to be able to report to Cheltham House for my first day of work.

As I step into the living room, Jillian is coming in with Bear. I smile as I see her dressed in chic yoga leggings, colorful Puma kicks, and a zip-up hoodie.

"Darling," she says, her voice serious, "there are hordes of photographers out there."

My stomach goes to ice.

It's finally happened. Christian has prepared me for this day.

The day the paparazzi started stalking where I lived.

"Well, at least the walk to the tube isn't far," I say, trying to reassure myself.

"Why don't I drive you?" Jillian offers as she unhooks the leash from Bear's collar.

I freeze. No, that's the last thing I want. I don't want Jillian protecting me from the press. I can't let any more people in my life protect or shield me from life.

I want to handle this myself.

"Thank you. I appreciate that, but I want to face them."

"Clementine, I know you have to face them, but this is your first day of work. Do you want to step into your new job frazzled by them? Because they'll do more than shoot pictures. They will scream awful things at you to try and get a reaction."

I nod, trying to ignore the sick feeling creeping into my body.

"I know."

Although I'm secretly hoping the goodwill from Ascot will keep them nice for today, I'm being #delusional.

I bend down and stroke Bear's head. "You have a wonderful day being spoiled by Ms. Jillian," I say, stroking his head.

"Oh, no, he spoils me with kisses," Jillian says, smiling at me.

"I'm happy he has you during the day," I say. "Bear is such a love; he deserves all of that back."

"So does his mum," Jillian says.

"I think I'm well taken care of in that department."

"Are you sure I can't drive you?" Jillian asks again, a look of concern flickering across her face.

"No, I've got this," I say, forcing my voice to sound confident when inside I'm terrified. "Okay, I'm off. I'll be home sometime after five."

"My turn for dinner tonight," Jillian says. "I decided to subscribe to one of those cooking box services, so I will no doubt make you something fantastic to eat. Or we will order a pizza. Either way, we win."

I laugh and open the door. "We do," I say, over my shoulder.

I shut the door behind me to a chorus of shouting.

I bite my lip and walk up to the gate, and as soon as I swing it open, I'm blinded by the flash of cameras and video lights.

"Oh!" I gasp aloud, as I can't even see now.

"Clever Clemmie, over here!" a man shouts as they close in.

"This way!"

"Can we get a smile, Clementine?"

"Are you going to marry the prince?"

"Are you a publicity stunt, Cunning Clementine?"

I try to take a step forward, but I can't. They've closed in on me, and it's impossible to move. Panic fills me. How will I make it to the tube station? Will they get on the tube with me?

As the cameras click away, I realize I don't have my game face on.

I force it into a bright smile and try to walk.

But they are suffocating me.

"Please excuse me. I must get to work," I say, trying to keep the shake out of my voice.

I'm jostled from behind, hard.

I stumble forward but get no apology from the photog shooting me.

A photographer runs around in front of me. "The American trying to hook a prince? Do you fancy yourself being a duchess someday?"

"Is this to rehabilitate Prince Christian's recluse image?"

All the air is sucked out of my lungs. I can't breathe. I feel a panic attack coming on. The media takes advantage, circling around me and taking bites like great white sharks on a feeding frenzy.

And they won't let go until I'm dead.

"Darling, sorry I'm late, just had to find where I left the keys," Jillian says, springing up the stairs. She cuts through the crowd with precision and puts her arm around my shoulders, guiding me forward. Her Jaguar is a few steps away, and she gets me to the car in one piece while photographers surround the car, determined to get my picture.

She turns on the car and keeps her eyes straight ahead.

"Smile. Smile like you are the happiest woman in the world to be pursued by these wankers."

I re-arrange my face as she instructs.

"I want to cry."

"Of course you do. They are vultures. But I was never going to let you walk down the street alone. Times are different now due to social media."

Jillian lays on her horn and begins driving forward.

"I'm sorry. I don't want you to have to protect me," I say, my voice breaking.

"Clementine. I'm your friend. Friends do things for one another. If I was in the same situation, I know you would help me."

As we move forward, the photographers race for their cars, wanting to pursue us.

I want to throw up.

"You are being thrown into the fire now, love," Jillian says softly. "But you will find a way to handle it. That's the funny thing about life. Sometimes we are tested in ways we never imagined, but we find a way to trod on."

I know she's talking about George, which puts my experience in perspective. It's going to be hideous. I'll want to cry and be upset, and I'll probably never be completely used to it, but compared to what Jillian went through with George? Or my surgery?

I can do this.

"Well, I hope they got a shot of my shoes because they are fabulous," I tease.

Jillian laughs heartily. "That's my girl. Now where am I going?"

I give her the address of the house, which is located near one of London's amazing parks.

"Oh, tomorrow we'll bring Bear. I can take him on a walk after I drop you off."

"Jillian," I say, my voice firm, "you do not have to be my chauffeur."

"Clementine, it's my pleasure. It gives me something to do. If you had a friend who needed a lift, you'd give her one, wouldn't you?"

"Well, yes, but—"

"No buts. Friends do things for friends. It doesn't mean you can't do it for yourself, but if it helps you out, let me, okay?"

I exhale. I still don't like this, but I know I can't deal with that crush every day on my way to the tube.

"For now," I say firmly.

"For now," Jillian says, grinning. "So with that said, what time should I pick you up?"

I give up. "Five, please."

Jillian navigates her way through London, and soon she pulls up in front of Cheltham House.

"I'll be here in this spot to pick you up this evening."

"Thank you," I say.

I slip out the door, and a few of the moped photographers are stopping to shoot me. I keep my smile plastered on my face but wonder if Felicity and John will want this circus around their estate. I wouldn't blame them for releasing me, although that idea breaks my heart.

I go to the gate and gaze up at the stunning neoclassical home, which is more beautiful in person than the website can ever portray. My thoughts shift to the treasures locked inside.

I get to work here, I think in absolute amazement, and I ignore the shouts of the paparazzi behind me. *I will spend every day surrounded by antiques, and I'll get to share this passion with every guest who walks in the door.*

With that thought tucked in my head, I mentally prepare for my first day at work.

I think I need to pinch myself.

I'm sitting in the part of the house that has been set aside for the offices, and I'm pouring over detailed floor plans of the estate that Felicity gave me. She told me my first week was going to be pure immersion, and my antique-loving heart has never been so excited. Okay, perhaps the feeling is equal to Sandringham and Windsor Castle, but I actually work here, so that gives Cheltham House the edge.

I started off this morning with Eric Bradley, one of the tour guides. He gave me a private tour first, showing me the staterooms that the public can access: the Great Room, the Library, the Dining Room, the Gallery Hall, the Rose Bedroom, Lady Wilimina's room—she was the third Countess of Westwick—and the Peacock Bedroom.

It was a glorious feast for my eyes. The Peacock room is named after the silk fabrics of the bedding, done in the shades of peacock feathers, and the rich, vibrant, blue taffeta curtains on the eighteenth-century canopy bed. There were exquisite tapestry chairs embroidered with a rose pattern in the Rose Bedroom, and portraits of previous earls and countesses in the Gallery Hall. The tour includes actual Thomas Chippendale furniture and a library with books dating back to the sixteenth century.

Of course, my favorite room was the State Dining Room. I wanted to spend hours in there alone, picking up and examining every piece of china and cutlery on display on the Chippendale dining room table. I wanted to sit in one of the chairs and study the portraits hung around the room, learning the identities of the families that lived here for years before. Painted in robin's egg blue, and with incredible, white crown molding, it has a gentle feel to it. I took pictures as I went along, unable to believe I was seeing an entire table set with Coalport porcelain plates in the chinoiserie style.

As I went on my tour this morning with Eric, I realized how much I must learn. He's going to be a hard act to follow. He's an incredibly gifted storyteller and knew exactly how to pace the tour and keep it moving while still taking the time to reveal the stories that connect the home to the visitors.

The tour ended in the gardens, where I met Clive

Lawler, the head gardener, and his grandson, Roman, who works alongside him. Everything is in bloom, and once again, I relished the beautiful English flowers in all their glory.

After I took the tour, Felicity took me into the archive room where more treasures are hidden away, either to be switched out as the seasons change or to be added when a new stateroom is opened to the public. She's collecting pieces now for a drawing room. I squealed inside with glee when I got to put on gloves and hold the Meissen tea service collection she wants to place in there, one from the 1800s and painted with people. It's enough to make me want to try tea again.

The house has a café, so I was able to grab lunch with Felicity while overlooking the gardens. As I ate my salad, I blurted out that the grounds would be a fantastic place for community yoga. Felicity's eyes lit up. She loved the idea. I was speaking off the top of my head, but I can tell Felicity is eager to have a younger person's ideas for bringing more people to the stately home.

Of course, that included paparazzi, but Felicity shrugged that off, filing it under "free publicity."

I can't wait to tell Christian all about my day. I want to hear how his day in Birmingham went, too. I haven't pulled out my phone, other than to take pictures, as I don't believe spending the day looking up pictures of Christian at his engagement makes for a good first impression.

Felicity comes back into the office, smiling brightly.

"I think you can go home now," she says. "You've been thrown a lot of information today. I'm sure your head is about to explode."

I shake my head. "No, no, I love this more than you

could ever know. I held a Meissen teacup today. That alone made me giddy."

"I completely get you," Felicity says, adding a conspiratorial tone to her voice. "Because I get giddy holding them, too."

We both laugh.

"Tomorrow, we'll go over more of the house stories. Listen to Eric, but I want you to find your own way of telling the details when you do your tours. I'm also planning to go to an auction on Thursday to look for more things for the drawing room, and I'd love for you to come with me."

Oh! It's all I can do not to leap out of my chair and hug her.

"I would love that."

"All right, go on, get your things and go have a nice evening."

"Thank you, and you enjoy your evening, too."

I gather up my notes and planner and tuck them inside my bag. If I know Jillian, she probably arrived fifteen minutes early and is shooting dirty looks at the paparazzi who are no doubt waiting for me.

I begin walking through the corridors, past more Chippendale benches and oil portraits, and retrieve my phone from my bag. I want to send Christian a quick text, as well as answer my group message on WhatsApp with Bryn and Chelsea.

My screen is filled with notifications, including missed calls from Christian and Mom and texts from Paisley, Mom, Bryn, Chelsea, and Christian.

Ah, must be from today's press escapades. I wince. Mom is going to freak if she sees video of that photographer jostling me. I have a feeling her phone calls and texts are about that, and I'll have to reiterate how all birds get bumped in flight now and again.

Then it hits me.

Christian will be livid about this.

Oh, no, in the shock of the morning, I didn't think how he would react. He will be upset, I'm sure. I'll be honest and tell him it was jarring, but Jillian made sure I got to work okay. I can handle this, even if I'll grudgingly have to accept a ride to work to do it.

The first message I tap open is from Paisley, a string of charged obscenities and rage against *Dishing Weekly* and a question if I am okay.

I open the garden side exit door, which is for employees. Foreboding fills me. Paisley is furious. I know a camera jostle wouldn't make her fly into a rage.

I don't want to look to see what has her so upset.

Christian has told me not to do it.

But I need to know.

I nervously bring up *Dishing Weekly* with my Google app, and, with horror, I see I'm the lead story on their website.

It's a photo of me walking down the sidewalk with Jillian, but they've drawn an arrow pointing to the paralysis on the side of my face. The headline screams:

BRAVE CLEMMIE BATTLED BRAIN TUMOR!

After life-saving surgery as a teen leaves the right side of her face in paralysis, she finds happiness at last with the Golden Prince.

My stomach lurches. Oh, my God. Oh, my God. I gasp for air, but I can't get anything in. *Dishing Weekly* somehow got a hold of my medical past and has shared my private pain with the world. I feel violated. That is something I wanted to share with only certain people. My right to decide who hears my story has been ripped away from me. The one thing I wanted from my new life here with Christian was to be a normal girl.

Now everyone will see me as the girl who had a tumor. They think I need a prince to rescue me when the last thing I want is for anyone to save me or protect me or think I need to be kept on a shelf so I can't break.

All of that is lost.

I'll never get it back.

And with that thought, I burst into tears.

CHAPTER 29

IT'S HARDER THAN I THOUGHT

Heavy sobs rack my body, and I drop my bag to the ground. I put my hands over my face, wondering how I can get myself together enough to walk to the car, to face the paparazzi, who now know about my medical past and will scream questions about it repeatedly in my face, forever trapping me in that box.

"Clementine?"

I turn toward the sound of someone running down the path toward me. Through my tears, I see Roman, the young gardener I met this morning.

"Clementine," Roman asks, stopping next to me, "what's wrong? Are you okay?"

I shake my head no. I can't speak, so I hand him my phone, which still has the awful article pulled up.

He quickly wipes his hands on his jeans, which are dirty from working in the shrubbery all afternoon. Roman takes my phone, and his eyes widen as he reads the article.

"I-It's true," I say, my voice wobbling. "B-but I d-didn't want everyone to kn-kn-know!"

"Of course not," Roman says, handing me back my phone. "They are vultures, those bastards."

"They're out there," I say, jerking my hand across my face. "I don't want to go out to the car. I can't face this now."

As I say the words, I feel weak. I should be all, *screw you, I don't care, I'm not letting you make me run* and walk out with my head held high. I'm proud of the fact that I went through the surgery and came out okay. I'm a survivor.

But I don't feel that way. Instead, I feel exposed. Vulnerable. Terrified.

And I hate myself for feeling this way.

"You don't have to," Roman says, his hazel eyes locking on mine. "Look, I know you don't know me, but I've known the earl and countess since I was a kid. They trust me. I have my motorbike out back. With a helmet on, nobody will know it's you. I can get you home, and those idiots will have no idea."

Roman is giving me a safe escape.

"Yes," I nod. "Please."

Roman nods. "Let me put a few things away and wash up. I'll be back."

"I don't know how I'll ever repay you," I say.

"It's okay, I'll invoice you tomorrow," he says, flashing me a brilliant smile.

I watch as he dashes back down the walk, toward the gardens. I sink down on the steps and look down at my phone. I see another message from Christian has dropped in, so I decide to start there:

Your voicemail is full. Please talk to me, Clem. I'm so sorry about all of this. Dishing Weekly will pay. Those bastards are not getting away with this. I will see to it.

Oh, no. Christian is already going to use his power to

strike back, and I don't want him to. The world will think I need him to save me. No, oh hell no, I can't let this happen!

I type back, my hands trembling:

Do not do anything until I speak to you. The paparazzi are here. Roman, the gardener, has a motorcycle, and he's going to sneak me out.

I hit send, and then my phone rings.

Before I can even say hello, Christian begins speaking.

"Darling, I'm sorry," he says, his voice shaking. "This is my fault, all my fault, and I hate myself for doing this to you. I don't know how you can forgive me."

"What?" I ask, confused.

"If you weren't sucked into my world, you would be living a normal life!" he yells, losing control. "If I would have stayed away, you'd have your privacy and a life and not be splashed across a freaking tabloid! I never dreamt they'd find out about the tumor. I'm such an idiot. I did this to you. Now it's going to be worse. I never should have let you in. You deserve better than this, and as someone who loves you, I should give that to you, don't you see that?"

My heart turns to ice. Oh, God. No. Is Christian going to shove me away to protect me?

"You are not doing this to me," I say through my tears. "And you're not going to keep talking crazy to me. I need you now. But I don't need this talk of what I deserve. I know what I need and deserve, and you don't make that decision for me. I do."

"I'm sorry," Christian says. "I need to see you. I won't be okay until I see you. Can Roman bring you to Kensington Palace?"

"Yes. I'll be there soon."

"I love you," Christian says.

I swallow hard. "I love you more."

I hang up with him and dial Jillian, who immediately picks up.

"Hello?"

"I know what the tabloid has done," I say through tears.

"They can stick their rag up their arse," Jillian says bluntly.

"I wish I didn't care."

"That would require you to not to be a human being, Clementine, and your heart is allowed to hurt right now."

I force down a sob. "I feel so vulnerable."

"Of course you do!" Jillian says. "Your privacy was violated in the most degrading way. But you know what? You will move past this. I promise you life is full of things that weaken you, drop you to your knees, cause horrific pain, but we get up, we move on, and we heal. We find our joys and hold on to them. That is what you will do."

As she finishes speaking, the sun overhead breaks through the clouds, shining down on me. The warmth of the English sun on my face tells me Jillian's words are true. Right now, I'm in the storm, but the sun will come out again.

"I believe you."

"You should. I'm old, and God knows that should be good for some tidbits of useful information here or there."

I manage a small smile, but she speaks again before I can respond.

"The paparazzi are hanging around the perimeter here," Jillian says.

"I know. Listen, a gardener here has a motorcycle. He's going to sneak me out the back and get me to Kensington Palace."

"Brilliant," Jillian says approvingly. "Text me as you are about to leave. I'll hang out here longer to confuse them."

"I owe you," I say, crying.

"You owe me nothing. In fact, I've been more alive this past week than I have been in two years. You are a gift, even if you come with paparazzi. Besides, outsmarting them has become one of my newest pursuits. I am going to take an evasive driving class. It's going to be fantastic."

"*What?*"

"If we have to deal with the paparazzi, I'm going to do it effectively. I'm going to learn all kinds of evasive driving skills so we can outwit those little bastards.'

Oh, my God. Jillian—seventy-year-old Jillian—is going to learn to drive like a badass because of me?

"You don't have to do that. It sounds extreme," I say.

"Bollocks. It's amazing!"

Roman comes up the sidewalk, and I rise.

"My ride is here," I say. "Leave in about ten minutes."

"All right. And Clementine?"

"Yes?"

"No matter what, you have love, and that will see you through."

Then she hangs up the phone.

I stare down at the phone in my hand, her words echoing in my head.

I know Jillian is right.

We will get through this.

But that doesn't mean it's going to be easy.

After checking in at the security gate, Roman guides his motorcycle through the private walls of Kensington Palace. When I first came here last week, it wasn't what I expected. There are the big apartments, of course—the famous buildings you see on TV—but a lot of the younger royals are moving in here and making a new, urban community. Upon graduation from Cambridge, Christian was given Ivy Cottage, a small, three-bedroom cottage with a white picket fence. He could have lived at Buckingham Palace, but Christian wanted a small place of his own. Liz is renovating Wren Cottage, which is next door, and Xander has Nottingham Cottage around the corner.

I had no idea these little cottages existed, and I love the fact that the family community here not only includes the modern royals, as I think of Christian's brothers and cousins, but Princess Helene in the large Apartment 1A. She's the sister-in-law of the dowager queen, and apparently, she loves gossip and dirty jokes and fights all the time with her sister-in-law, which Christian told me often leads to some rather interesting family dinners at the holidays. Xander adores her, and she has often told him the dowager queen and current queen consort need to "get over it" and "get with it" about modernizing.

I've decided I like Princess Helene, even though I haven't met her yet.

As the motorcycle zooms closer, I see Liz is standing outside her cottage, talking on her phone, animatedly waving her hands about. She turns when she sees the motorcycle and watches as Roman pulls to a stop in front of Christian's cottage.

Roman cuts the engine, and I take off my helmet and hand it to Roman, who has taken his off as well. Christian opens the door, and I see the agony on his face, the worry, the guilt over what has happened to me. He hurries down the path to the gate, pushing it open, and before I can take a step, he's enveloped me in his strong arms. I swallow back tears as I hear his heart pounding rapidly against my ear.

One hand spans across my back, the other cradles the back of my head, and I breathe him in, finding comfort in his clean scent, the feel of his skin, and the strength of his arms.

He steps back, putting his hands tightly on my shoulders.

"Are you okay?" he whispers.

"I am now."

Christian nods. Then he turns to Roman, who has been waiting next to his bike, as Liz hurries down the walk toward us.

"I'm Christian," he says, extending his hand to Roman. "I can't thank you enough for getting Clementine away from those bastards."

Roman bows to Christian. "It was my pleasure, Your Royal Highness." Then he extends his hand. "Roman Lawler. I work at Cheltham House."

"No, Christian. Please."

"All right, Christian," Roman concedes.

"Oh, my God," Liz says, hurrying forward and hugging me. "Are you okay? Those bloody vultures! We are all furious, Clem. They've gone too far. And we *will* answer."

I step back from her, knowing that is a conversation I need to have with Christian.

"Thank you," I say, nodding at her. "I appreciate you being here for me."

"These aren't the old days," Liz says, her light blue eyes flashing angrily. "I refuse to sit back and keep my mouth shut when someone's medical history is plundered for entertainment. That is your business and yours alone. I will be making a statement tomorrow, joined with Isabella and Victoria, that we stand with you and are appalled by the lack of human decency shown by *Dishing Weekly*."

Oh, no. No, no, no!

"No, that's not necessary."

"Oh, it is," Liz says, her voice growing angrier. "I have a voice. I'm going to be a working royal now that I've graduated, and I will not sit in my princess pose and keep a 'stiff upper lip' on this one. I'm a modern woman, who is appalled by this invasion of privacy, and I will express my thoughts and be heard."

I see the fire in her eyes.

I think it might be harder to get Liz to back off than Christian.

"Your Royal Highness, I think you're right," Roman says quietly.

Liz turns to Roman. "I'm sorry?"

Roman shakes his head. "I'm sorry, I shouldn't have spoken."

"No, no, I want to hear what you have to say," Liz says. "I'm Liz."

Roman bows again. "Roman, Your Royal Highness."

She extends her hand to him, and he shakes it. I notice Roman is the one to let go first.

She quickly clears her throat. "Thank you. I know a lot of people want me to appear at luncheons and make speeches and wear ball gowns. They don't want to hear from angry Liz."

Roman moves back over to his bike and straddles it. He pauses for a moment, holding his helmet in his hands, his hazel eyes locked on hers as a lock of his thick, mahogany brown hair is blown across his forehead from a sudden summer breeze.

"With all due respect, ma'am, I think angry Liz is the one who can make a difference," Roman says, reaching up and raking a hand through his hair to push it back in place.

Liz's eyes widen. Roman straps on his helmet, turns on

the engine, and zooms off, ready to go back to his own world outside of these protective gates.

Christian puts his arm around my shoulders as Liz watches Roman ride off.

"Let's go inside," Christian says to me.

Liz turns back around, and I notice her ivory cheeks are flushed.

"I'm going to be home tonight. Please call me later so we can coordinate our messages with your father's," Liz says.

King Arthur is involved? Good lord, getting this situation under control is going to be much harder than I thought.

But I have to do it, before statements are released and this blows up and, oh crap, becomes a worldwide circus about me needing an entire royal family to defend me.

No, I think, fear consuming me as I see my freedom beginning to slip away. *I can't have that happen.*

I have to put a stop to it.

Right now.

CHAPTER 30

ALL COUPLES FIGHT

As soon as we're inside the cottage, I drop my bag on the floor. Christian cups my face in his large hands.

"I'm sorry," he says, his voice choking up. "I should have predicted this. I keep letting you down. First I threw you into the spotlight on your first visit here, now this. I wish to God they were writing about me instead of you. I wish I could take this back. Please forgive me for dragging you into this world. I promise you this ends now. I've drafted a release to go out to the press, and I want your thoughts on it–"

"No!" I cry, removing his hands from my face. "That's the last thing I want! Don't do that!"

An incredulous expression passes over his face. "What? Why? What they did was over the line, Clementine."

"I don't care!" I yell back, beginning to pace in the living room as a trapped feeling consumes me. "This is my life. *Mine.* I won't have you or King Arthur or Liz go around issuing statements like I'm fragile and need the royal family to shield me from a few bad articles like a child. I don't want to be protected. I won't allow it."

"What? You think I'm treating you like a child?" Christian asks, his deep voice reverberating with shock.

"I don't need you or your family to fight my battles for me," I say, my voice growing sharp. There's a hysteria rising within me, one I know isn't fair to Christian, but as the waves build, I feel incapable of getting to the shore while I'm adrift in this emotional storm.

"We," Christian says slowly, "have dealt with this our entire lives. You haven't. What the press did today is unacceptable, and I'm in a position to try to stop it. Why are you opposed to this?"

"I don't want to be seen as the poor girl who needs the Golden Prince to ride in and rescue her, that's why," I say, my voice shaking with anger.

Christian's eyes flash. I know that comment has hurt him, and I wish I could take it back, but I can't.

"I'm sorry that me being in a position to help you is such a terrible thing. Along with being a prince, that is."

I let out a sob. "It's not that."

"That's exactly what it is. But you know what, Clementine? This isn't about me and my family issuing statements setting boundaries for you as one of us, which you practically are now. This is about your fear of everyone seeing you as your parents do. You're putting their vision on me, and I resent that. Not once have I seen you as a girl who had a brain tumor. Not once. Yet you stand here and rail against me like I have. It's not fair, and I'm not going to take it."

Then, to my shock, Christian storms over to the front door, opens it, and slams it shut behind him, leaving me alone.

The second he does, I know I was wrong. Yes, I'm having a horrible time with this, and while the idea of him issuing a statement on my behalf makes me uncomfortable, it's something they do to protect their privacy. This is not unique to me. The House of Chadwick has to set limits and make sure the press is accountable. This is normal for them. It doesn't mean I'm fragile.

It doesn't mean that the entire world will view me as if I am, either.

I drop down on the sofa and burst into tears. Is my childhood bound to mess up what I have with Christian? Am I really going to shove the one person away who truly sees me as the woman I am?

My phone begins ringing inside my bag. I slowly move over to it and see it's my mom. I draw a breath of air and answer it.

"Hello?"

"Oh, my God, you finally answered!" Mom cries, her voice shaking. "I've been absolutely sick about you since I saw what those awful tabloids are writing. Why isn't Christian handling this? Why don't you have security? Your father and I are about to fly over there and—"

"You will do no such thing," I warn, my voice firm. "I don't need you to come over here and play babysitter."

"Clementine! You were jostled. What if you fell? What if you hit your head?"

"I don't have a damn tumor! Would you stop acting like I do? Just stop it!"

Mom is stunned into silence, and I roll on.

"I'm not sick. If I fell down and hit my head, I'd deal with it like anyone else. Christian does want to help me, and so does King Arthur, and they'll be making a very sharp statement on my behalf tomorrow. I'm living my life over here, and it will be different because of the publicity, but this is my choice to make, not yours."

"I hope," Mom says, her voice tearful, "that you aren't caught up in the romance of being with a prince, because there is a steep price to pay for that, one you are only becoming aware of now. It's not all palaces and fairy tales, and you need to take your rose-colored glasses off and see that. These tabloids will dig up more people like Brandy Gordon to tell stories about you. The press will follow you the entire time you're dating Christian. Most of your days will be like this—hunted. They won't always treat you like they did at Ascot. So you need to get your head around this and think clearly."

Brandy Gordon. She's the one who sold me out? She was one of the mean girls in high school who loved to be the center of attention.

I bet she called the Dishing Weekly hotline, I muse, *just to see her name in print. Ugh.*

"This doesn't only impact you," Mom continues, interrupting my thoughts. "We have photographers parked outside the driveway, and they followed Paisley to work this morning. Your romance with a prince isn't just about you, Clementine."

Nausea rolls over my stomach. I never thought of the press stalking my family.

Once again, I'm reminded that Christian is right. I do need his help. My family never asked for this, and while I want to be independent, there are some things I can't do on my own.

Like get the press to leave my family alone.

"I'm sorry," I say, my voice thick. "I'll have Christian request for your privacy, and for Paisley and Evan's, to be respected."

"I'm more worried about you. We can handle this. You don't need this stress, sweetheart."

I can read between the lines: I don't need this stress because that might cause some weird reaction in me and somehow lead to me getting sick again.

I'm so frustrated I could scream. At my parents for treating me this way, for creating this mental gridlock that has now caused a problem with Christian. At myself for getting too much inside my head and not letting the man I love support me through this paparazzi minefield like anybody else would.

"I need to go," I say.

"I'm not done talking about this, Clementine," Mom says.

"Mom, I love you, and we'll talk more later, but I need to go. I'm going to be fine, and the world will go on and forget I had a tumor," I say.

If only you could, too, my heart whispers.

I hang up and put my phone on Christian's coffee table. I go to the window and part the curtains. The street is quiet, and silent tears fall down my face as I think of my outburst. All I want is for him to come home. I want to tell him I'm sorry, and that he was right, and I love him for wanting to protect me. I do need the help of the monarchy if I'm to lead anything close to a normal life.

My phone rings again.

This time, it's Paisley.

"Hello?" I answer.

"Oh, my God, are you okay?" Paisley asks, her voice steeped in concern.

"I was a complete asshole to Christian," I admit, heat filling my face as I proceed to tell her what I said to him.

"He knows you are upset, Clem," Paisley says, being the

voice of reason. "Christian is giving you time to calm down, and then you can talk this out."

"If he forgives me."

"Now you're being overly dramatic. All couples fight."

"I hate that we did."

"Only emotional drama-seekers love fighting. Nobody else does."

"I'm sorry the press is stalking you."

Paisley snorts. "You can claim you don't know me if pictures show up of me dragging the trash down to the curb in my milk and cookies fleece pajama bottoms with my *I don't do mornings* T-shirt on."

I finally laugh. I can always count on my sister to make me smile.

"I'll always be proud of you," I say. "I love you."

"I love you, too," Paisley says.

We talk for a bit, with me reassuring her that I'll get past this and her telling me damn right I will, before I hang up and set the phone back down. It feels like an eternity before Christian comes back, but finally, through the curtains, I get a glimpse of him coming down the sidewalk. I watch as he unhooks the gate and slowly moves toward the house.

Anxiousness fills me as I wait for him to step through the door. Will he still be mad at me? Will he want me to leave? Will he listen to what I have to say? We've never really had a huge fight, so I don't know how he handles being mad at me.

The door opens, and Christian steps inside. My heart is pounding against my ribs as I rise from the sofa. I'm about to speak, but Christian does first.

"I love you," he says simply. "I love you with everything I am, and I'm sorry I walked out when you needed me."

"I was awful to you," I say, wiping my eyes with the sleeve of my blouse. Geez, I really need to buy pocket tissues; this is getting ridiculous. "And I understand why you needed to clear your head. I love you more," I whisper. "More than you could ever know."

Christian moves over to me and draws me back into his arms. I breathe a sigh of relief as his arms span around my back, and I feel nothing but love and warmth from his embrace.

"I'm sorry," he murmurs, kissing the top of my head.

"Me, too," I murmur into the fine fabric of his dress shirt.

Christian steps back from me and takes my hand in his. He leads me back over to the sofa, where we sink down together. His arm is immediately around me, drawing me close to his body, and I close my eyes. We sit in silence for a few moments before Christian speaks.

"I will never try to stifle your spirit or your freedom," he says as he begins to play with my hair. "I love those things about you."

"I know," I admit, embarrassed for my outburst.

"But I won't stand by and let the press get away with violating you when I do have the ability to take action. I have resources you don't. And if the shoe were on the other foot, if you could do something to help me, I know you would because that's what love is. It's helping each other when you can, supporting each other. Helping you live your best life. That's all I want, considering the difficult circumstances I've dragged you into."

I push myself up so I can look at him. "You didn't drag me anywhere. I chose to be here, to be in this life. I won't lie to you, though. Seeing that picture—seeing my face drawn on and the headlines screaming to the world I had a tumor —hurts. It hurts more than I can say."

Tears fill Christian's light-blue eyes. "I know what your medical privacy means to you, and I'm gutted that has been taken away. Because of me."

I sniffle back fresh tears. "I don't want people to feel sorry for me."

Christian sweeps the tears away with his fingertips. "Nobody who gets to know you will feel that way. All they will see is the smart, ambitious, capable, funny woman that I do. If anything, they will see you as someone to be admired."

As I see myself through Christian's lens, a calmness takes over.

"Maybe," I say aloud as if hardly daring to believe it, "not everyone will see me as fragile like my parents do."

"Paisley doesn't see you that way anymore," Christian says. "She used to. But seeing you as an adult, she's changed her perception."

A switch goes off in me. He's right. She isn't hovering over me in an over-protective way. She sees me as an adult, as her peer.

Normal.

"I'm not the only one who has gone through this," I say, thinking aloud. "Either living with a disease or having recovered from one. When I had those tests last winter, I prayed that if I were spared, I'd somehow do good for people. I'd use my gifts to make a difference. I just didn't know how. But now I do. I want to help people who are facing their lives post-surgery or post-diagnosis. I want to offer support and share my story. This is what I'm meant to do, and if it took this horrible day to see it, that's okay. It's part of my story."

Christian's eyes search mine. "I love you so much, and I love that you've found your cause."

I nod. "I'm okay with a statement being released. You're right. Boundaries need to be set."

"Good. My communications secretary here at Kensington Palace is going to release what I wrote tomorrow. Would you like to read it?"

I exhale. "Yes."

Christian retrieves his phone, swipes a few things, and hands it to me. I begin to read:

As Prince Christian begins his new role in public life on behalf of the monarchy and for the people, he understands there will always be an interest in what he does. He will strive to inform the public of his work with organisations and charities through his relationship with the working media.

While Prince Christian does realise this interest extends to his private life as well, he is deeply concerned with the amount of attention focused on his girlfriend, Ms. Clementine Jones. Her medical privacy was violated, something that is unacceptable to Prince Christian. While she might be in the public eye, she has a right to privacy as any other citizen does. Her medical history, something deeply personal, was displayed for the world to read without her consent in a painful way that was disrespectful, hurtful, and humiliating. This sets a dangerous precedent, as the lines of decency and respect for her rights have been shoved aside. She has a right to privacy. She has a right to walk down the street without being jostled by photographers. Her family has a right to be able to leave their homes without being accosted by the press.

The prince hopes the media will reflect upon these words and give Ms. Jones the respect and privacy she deserves, the same as anyone else, as she creates her new life in London and with Prince Christian.

I grow emotional as I read his heartfelt plea on my behalf. I swallow hard and hand him back his phone.

"Thank you," I whisper, choking up. "Thank you for loving me like this, and for being such an honorable and good man. I'm lucky to have you."

"No. Thank you, for being here and for putting up with this. No man is luckier than I am."

I place my hand against his cheek. "There is no place I'd rather be."

Christian lowers his lips to mine, kissing me gently.

"I will always be here to help you navigate this life," Christian says, his light-blue eyes shining with everything that is in his heart. "Please don't hesitate to share your concerns or ask for my assistance, not just about royal things but all problems. We're in this together, but I can only be an active participant if you let me, sweetheart. We need to communicate openly and honestly to be a team."

"I promise. From now on, you'll know everything I'm thinking, and together, we'll take on this life."

As Christian kisses me again, I vow I will keep this promise. Whenever I face a problem, I will share it with Christian. It's not a sign of weakness to accept help but rather a sign of maturity.

We're in this together, I think, repeating Christian's words. *No matter what comes our way, we'll tackle it together. We're a team.*

And we always will be.

CHAPTER 31

TEA AT FIVE O'CLOCK

TGIF.

I exit Cheltham House on a beautiful summer evening in July. I stop for a moment and gaze out over the lush green lawn and vibrant summer flowers that make up the terraced garden, the sunlight shining brightly and bathing it in a beautiful glow. Coming from Phoenix, I still can't get over the lushness of England, even in the city.

Then it hits me.

I've been in London for exactly one month.

I take a moment to reflect on what a milestone this is. After my medical past was revealed in *Dishing Weekly,* I received a groundswell of support from the public regarding the media going too far. I started receiving letters from people who have not only dealt with brain tumors but other illnesses that they wanted to keep private from even the closest of friends. It opened my eyes to how many people struggle with the emotional weight of illnesses, whether past or present, and I knew I had found my purpose. While I cannot take on any cause in a royal capacity, I have decided to volunteer for patient support groups for brain tumor survivors.

To my shock, Queen Antonia—who hasn't spoken to me since that day at Ascot—said in a release she was "deeply touched" by my story and has now become a supporter of research to help children with brain tumors. Jillian called bollocks on that. She declared it a PR stunt, and I agree. Christian said he hoped his mother was truly moved in some way and that this would eventually lead to me being accepted by her.

As much as he knows the truth about her, she's still his mother. While he's not in denial like James, I saw a glimmer of a young man hoping to see his mother was changing for the good, and I refuse to take that hope away from him. I don't know how it will play out, but Christian was pleased she was going to do something that showed support for me, so I refused to put any negativity on it, choosing instead to be grateful for what it was.

Christian has flourished in his new role. He's gone all in on his support for caregivers and is now a patron for the non-profit group Care 4 Caregivers, a support network. He's going to speak on their behalf, chair fundraisers, and create awareness.

He's taking his message global, too, and is now on a tour of Australia and New Zealand and will visit caregiver organizations there as part of his trip. He's also going to see some wildlife refuges, too, and I think that will springboard his next charitable cause.

While Christian has been gone, I started giving tours at Cheltham House on my own. People started asking for me by name, not because of my skills but because they want a snap of Prince Christian's girlfriend. The press has mocked me for being a tour guide, and worse, mocked Christian for dating one, but I don't read the articles anymore. *Dishing Weekly* taught me a valuable lesson: that unless I want to feel like crap about myself, I don't need that garbage in my headspace.

Good vibes only, please, I think with a grin.

At the estate, we're going to start yoga classes outdoors. And to tie-in to Christian's cause, Felicity is going to host a tea in the State Dining Room for members from Care 4 Caregivers as a treat. Jillian doesn't know it yet, but Christian and I made sure she's on the guest list for that one.

I spy Roman pruning along the pergola in the rose garden. Since I'm not having dinner with Liz until later—she and I have become good friends since all that crap went down a few weeks ago—I decide to see if I can get Roman to come around to a new idea I have. I walk down the steps to the path where Roman is, and a warm smile spreads across his face as he notices my approach. A sun hat covers his hair, and I can't see his eyes behind his dark sunglasses. A gray T-shirt stained with sweat and khaki work pants make up his uniform, along with gardening boots. Roman stops and tucks a tool into a work belt that is slung around his hips.

"Fancy some more flowers for your house?" Roman teases.

I smile. "While I love you for always giving me enough for a weekly arrangement, no," I say. "I have an idea to run by you."

He takes a moment to remove his sunglasses, and his hazel eyes regard me with curiosity. "Okay. Go ahead."

"You know how we are testing yoga as part of a program to build our relations within the community and bring new visitors to Cheltham House? Well, I have another idea. What about Master Gardener classes? We could have different kinds, like teaching people how to grow and care for roses, prepare for fall, or plant bulbs. We could even have kids' classes and get them involved in nature. I think there are a lot of opportunities here, and we can teach the history of the garden at the same time."

Roman appears thoughtful. "I think Grandfather would enjoy that," he says slowly. "He can't do much physically anymore, but he has an incredible knowledge base. I think he'd love it, actually."

"What about you teaching?" I ask, curious to see if he would.

Roman throws his hand up. "Oh, God, no. I'm great with plants. With people, not so much. Grandfather is a much better option, believe me."

"I think you are pretty good with people, Roman."

"I'd rather be knee-deep in dirt than at a party," Roman says, winking at me.

"Well, I love Clive," I say, referring to his grandfather, "so I'll happily have him teach, but I think you underestimate yourself."

"No, I know myself," Roman corrects.

"Okay, no more talk of that," I say. "Will you ask Clive? If he's okay with the idea, I'll go to Felicity with it."

"Sure, no problem," Roman says. He reaches up and picks at a dead bloom on the vine. Then he clears his throat. "So, how is Liz?"

Ooh! He hasn't asked me about Liz since the day he met her. I'm intrigued by this change in conversation.

"She's good," I say. "I'm having dinner with her tonight, as a matter of fact. She's keeping me company while Christian is out of town." Then I decide to do something completely off the cuff. "Would you care to join us?"

Roman blinks. I can tell my invitation has caught him off guard.

"No, thank you. I have plans," he says, putting his sunglasses back on. "Besides, the private club restaurant scene Liz fancies isn't my world."

"Hmm, that's too bad. Because Liz and I are going to grab pizza and pints in Notting Hill. Her idea, by the way. But have a good weekend. I'll see you Monday."

I don't need to see behind his sunglasses to know his eyes now reflect surprise. I plant that seed and walk away, wondering if something could grow between Liz and Roman. She's asked about him several times, including last week when I was her guest at Wimbledon.

I head back up the walk, as I know Jillian is waiting for me. She started her evasive driving course and said it's been the biggest thrill of her life. As I walk, my phone rings inside my bag. I reach inside and pluck it out, glancing down at the ID. I don't recognize the number, so I wait for it to go to voicemail. The caller leaves a message, and I replay it.

As soon as I hear the voice, I stop walking:

"Clementine, this is Queen Antonia. Please call me at once."

Oh, my God. Why is she calling me? Has something happened to Christian? That would be the only reason she would ever call me, right? In a panic, I call her back. She picks up on the second ring.

"Hello, Clementine. Thank you for returning my phone call so promptly. I have a matter I'd like to discuss with you, and time is of the utmost importance."

I freeze at the sound of her clipped, formal tone, but I'm relieved nothing has happened to Christian.

"Good evening, Your Royal Highness," I say, somehow remembering to speak amidst my profound shock.

"I would like to have you come to the palace tomorrow for tea at five o'clock," Queen Antonia says, getting straight to the point. "I believe we have some pressing issues to converse about. I also anticipate you will keep this date between us, unless you feel you need Christian's approval and protection to accept a tea invitation from me."

My heart roars in my ears. If we were playing that old game Battleship, she would have scored a direct hit on me with that line.

She is implying if I tell Christian about this tea, there will be ramifications to pay.

I'll look weak, unable to stand up for myself, and she'll use that to her advantage.

It's a real life *Real Housewives*.

"I'll be there," I say. "And I can keep it private."

"Don't be late. I hate tardiness, among other things."

Then she hangs up.

I stare down at the phone in my hand. I have a feeling we've each made a move in our game of Battleship.

And I pray that I'm not sunk by the time the teapot is emptied.

I'm brimming with anxiety as I follow Queen Antonia's lady-in-waiting to her sitting room at a quarter to five. Her Majesty sent a blacked-out Range Rover to retrieve me and bring me to Buckingham Palace. Then I was escorted to a private elevator, and now a woman named Lena is leading me into the room where I'll take tea with the queen.

Or the lion's den.

Probably the latter.

"Her Royal Highness will be in at five," Lena informs me.

"Thank you," I say, sinking down onto one of the pale cream sofas. The room, which is on the first floor, overlooks the gardens, where there is more color than in this entire space. The whole room is cream, from the sofas to the carpeting, with the only pops of color being gray and navy in the pillows and curtains.

The room is like her wardrobe, I think. *Very defined. Rigid. No room for something outside the lines.*

Like me.

I smooth my hands over the hem of my dress and move my legs into the princess slant, angled, knees together. I chose a V-neck, banded dress, color-blocked with a bright cobalt blue top and black bottom. I slipped on a pair of navy pumps as another nod to color, and to break the taboo of no black and navy together. I did acquiesce and put on a pair of sheer pantyhose, even though it's July and hot and it's a private tea between the Queen and me.

I continue to trace the hem of my skirt, which hits right below the knee, wondering what her agenda is today. When I talked to Christian last night, it killed me to keep this tea a secret from him. But when he talked about how his mother had called him to say he was doing an admirable job on the tour, and after hearing his genuine surprise at the compliment, I knew I couldn't tell him. What if this tea is a disaster, and I have to shatter the few illusions that remain of her? He'd tell Xander, and he'd be furious.

And James is the most vulnerable of all because he doesn't know he was born as a PR stunt. He genuinely believes in his mother, and it would destroy him to know the truth. If she's awful to me today, it will create more hurt for him than anyone else.

Maybe I'm overdramatizing. Perhaps tea will be pleasant. Queen Antonia will recognize that I'm not a fleeting romance, and we'll embark on building a friendship.

Ha-ha. I almost laugh out loud at that idea, which is about as likely to happen as I am to suddenly crave fish and beg Christian to take me out for fried cod and chips upon his return.

The door opens, and Queen Antonia strides into the room, wearing a cream-colored sheath and pumps. If it weren't for her jet-black hair and olive coloring, she'd blend into the walls.

I stand up to greet her, and I dip into a curtsy. "Thank you for inviting me today, Your Royal Highness."

Queen Antonia stares at me, her eyes moving over my outfit, her face remaining expressionless.

"Are you aware that your shoes are navy instead of black?" she asks coolly.

So much for a tea to set the foundation for friendship.

"Yes, I am. I planned it that way," I say.

Servers come in with a trolley, smoothly heading to the coffee table and setting up the elaborate preparation for tea.

Queen Antonia stares at me. "I don't like mismatched outfits. The public expects more from us, Clementine. Please, have a seat."

I grit my teeth and sit down, reminding myself this is for Christian. I must make an inroad with her on some level, and if it means matching my damn shoes to my dress, I'll do it.

Queen Antonia sits on the sofa across from me, going into the same princess pose that I'm using.

Which is super uncomfortable.

Especially with stupid pantyhose on.

"I assume you like tea," Queen Antonia says, breaking through my thoughts. "It's an important tradition in the House of Chadwick. Not that you'd know that, of course."

She might as well put an asterisk next to my name and a footnote: the House of Chadwick, which said inappropriate American shall never be a part of.

I hate tea.

It's right up there with fish as far as I'm concerned.

But I'll be damned if Her Majesty will ever know that.

"Yes, that would be lovely," I say, watching as Queen Antonia lifts a silver teapot that is sitting over a small burner.

I watch in fascination as she pours some water into a teapot, swirls it around, and then pours the water into another bowl, which a nearby server immediately dispenses of. Then I watch as she measures tea leaves into the pot and sets it aside to steep.

No words are said. The only sound in the room is the ticking of a clock on her mantle.

I clear my throat. "Thank you for inviting me to tea," I say, extending an olive branch. "I've never had a formal tea before."

Queen Antonia lets a wisp of a sigh escape her immaculate red lips. "Of course not."

Tick.

Tick.

I think I'm going to have an anxiety attack. I need something to do, something to talk about.

"These cakes look lovely," I say, staring at a glossy ganache creation.

Queen Antonia stares at me. "I always offer cake to my visitors. I myself won't indulge in the calories."

Visitors. That's what I am to her. Not a guest. Not soon-to-be family.

Boy, her hate for me is practically radiating throughout the room, it's that hot and intense.

She reaches for the teapot and pours me a strained cup.

"Thank you," I say, and I fight the urge to wrinkle my nose at the horrible scent.

"How do you take it?" Queen Antonia asks, picking up a tiny sandwich off the elaborate tray of buttery scones, cookies, and immaculately cut finger sandwiches.

"I can handle tartness," I say, throwing my own shot across the bow. "So, with lemon," I continue, selecting a slice of lemon with silver tongs. But instead of getting it to my saucer, I drop it in the middle of my teacup, sending a splash of the dark brew across the white tablecloth and leaving a puddle.

Dammit!

Heat flames my face as a young man swoops out of nowhere, cleaning up the mess while Queen Antonia raises her over-tweezed eyebrow at me.

"I'm so sorry, ma'am," I sputter, wishing I could dive under the table and eat all the scones in misery.

She doesn't say a word as another page brings a new cup, and Queen Antonia pours again.

"Please, have a finger sandwich," Queen Antonia urges. "They're salmon, perfect for those of us trying to watch our weight."

What? Is she implying I need to lose weight? Okay, I'll never be a size four, but I'm rather happy with my body and how I look.

I want to cut a huge wedge of that gorgeous chocolate

cake to spite her, but instead, I reach for a fish sandwich and shove down the icky feeling growing in my stomach from looking at it.

I decide to forgo the acid in my new cup of tea and make myself take a sip. Gag, gag, gag! Ugh, why do the British people have to love this so much?

I quickly set it down and try to steel myself to take a bite of the salmon sandwich, which is taunting me next.

"I think I shall get right to the point, Clementine," Queen Antonia says, giving me a long, dramatic pause while she takes a sip of her tea. "Christian is my shining star. He's bright. He's handsome. He has an air of mystery, which is exactly what the monarchy must maintain to survive. We *can't* be like everyone else. Being a royal means having mystique and an air of glamour. It sets us apart from others. Christian needs someone who adds her own allure and sophistication to the role. I'm sorry to say that is not you, Clementine. You are not what the House of Chadwick needs to cement our legacy and make sure it continues to grow."

Her words sicken me, not for myself, but for the son, who despite all her shit, loves her as his mother.

"Christian is your son, not a star," I say, keeping my voice even. "I would hope that your love for him as a human being, as your child, would be your priority as his mother, as it is with King Arthur."

Boom! Her face finally cracks.

Direct hit.

"I don't need to spell out my love for my son to you," she says, collecting her face into her Queen Antonia signature look of emotionless balance again. "You are getting favorable press now, as people love a good victim story, but you don't have the elegance or sophistication to be a part of our family. Christian has all the potential in the world if he chooses the right wife. Do you want to be responsible for changing the face of the monarchy?"

My skin prickles with anger. A hot flush climbs up my neck.

"I'm not right because people connect with me? Find me to be a breath of fresh air? Because I'm an American? Because I hold a normal job? Or wear prints? I fail to see how this would bring down the House of Chadwick."

"*Ordinary* is not what we want," Queen Antonia continues. "The public thinks they want us to be ordinary, but they don't. Why do they turn out to see us walk to Christmas service at Sandringham? Trooping the Colour? Taking carriages to Ascot? They love us for being different, for carrying on the traditions that this country holds close to its heart. They don't turn out for ordinary, Clementine. They turn out for magic, which you have none of."

I sit still for a moment. I hold my head high and, after a moment, speak very deliberately.

"I am the woman who loves your son. I might not be what you envisioned for Christian, and I might not be in the mold of the current House of Chadwick, but I'm a good person. I'm a hard worker, and I'm capable of doing great things when given a chance. Christian has a vision for his future, to help the causes that are close to his heart and not select ones that make for a perfect photo op."

Her eyes flicker angrily, and I know I went too far with that last comment, but I can't help myself.

I take my linen napkin and place it over my uneaten sandwich.

"I will be leaving now, and I will pretend, for the sake of your son, this conversation never happened."

Queen Antonia doesn't move. I think she's used to people being afraid of her rather than walking out in a fury.

"Clementine, think carefully. This is your last chance to make a graceful exit from our lives."

I stare at her, feeling nothing but pity for the woman who wants this life, this monarchy, more than she wants her husband or her incredible boys.

"I will do no such thing. I love Christian. We are planning a future together, and I only hope you choose to be a part of it."

"Oh, you can very well plan for one. But sometimes the best-laid plans go to waste, don't they?"

My blood goes cold.

Queen Antonia has issued me a warning.

I turn and exit her sitting room and head toward the private elevator. I'm shaking violently as I punch the button. I wrap my arms around myself, trying to control my physical reaction to her words.

I know she will do everything in her power to get me out of Christian's life.

But I also know we are strong enough to survive it.

I only pray that Christian will be able to recover when the truth about his mother, that she is a horrible narcissist who only cares about herself, is revealed. It's one thing to have thoughts of it, like he does now, but it's another thing to discover all the awful details and realize the truth is worse than you ever dreamed.

The day will come; I can feel it in my gut.

And when it does, I only hope it won't send Christian retreating back from the world like he used to do.

CHAPTER 32

A BIT OF A MESS UP

I can't shake the bad feeling that is swirling through me this Friday night.

I stare back at my reflection in the bathroom mirror at Ivy Cottage. King Arthur and Queen Antonia have invited Christian and me to dinner to celebrate Christian's well-received trip to Australia and New Zealand, which he returned from on Monday. James will join us, along with Prince Henry and Arabella, but Xander is back with the army, so he will be missing. The Dowager Queen will also be in attendance, along with her nemesis, Princess Helene. Isabella and Victoria are on holiday in New York, so Liz is the only cousin in attendance tonight.

I've decided to play Queen Antonia's game and send a message with my outfit for the evening. I found a floor-length, ivory satin gown with a boatneck and capped sleeves. There's nothing wrong with this dress. It's pretty and demure and fits the bill for a dinner at Buckingham Palace.

But it's not me.

Which is exactly the point. I want to prove to Queen Antonia that if she wants me to blend in on royal occasions, I can. I don't want to, but I will do it to make Christian's life easier, even if he doesn't know it. This is nothing more than a uniform that Queen Antonia expects me to wear.

Guilt surges through me. Christian knows nothing of my tea with Queen Antonia, and I swear I will take this secret to my grave to protect him and his brothers. They know enough. I refuse to pile on further hurt and disappointment by revealing what she said over cups of tea.

I step back into the bedroom, where I find Christian standing in front of a mirror, tying his tie. I sneak up from behind and slide my arms around his waist, pressing my cheek to the back of his dress shirt.

"I shouldn't do this, I'll get makeup on your shirt, but it feels too good," I murmur into his strong back.

He chuckles, and the sound reverberates sexily against my cheek.

"A bit of a mess up is always good in my book," Christian declares. "It keeps life real. And a trace of you on my shirt? What's more real and sexy than that?"

He turns around, but as soon as he sees my dress, his brow furrows.

"What?" I ask, knowing damn well what his look is for.

"This dress doesn't look like you," he says quietly. Christian's tone isn't accusatory but flat.

Which is almost worse.

"I want to have a few pieces that are appropriate for BP occasions," I say, referring to Buckingham Palace. "Don't worry, all my prints and colors are safely in my closet back at my flat."

Christian puts his hands on my shoulders, his blue eyes growing intense as he stares down at me.

"But you don't have to do this," Christian pleads. "You know how I feel about you changing to please her."

"I do, but showing your mother I can dress in her realm is important."

"I don't care what she thinks or what she says," Christian says, his voice taking on an irritated edge. "You need to do you."

"I'm still me. It's just a dress. Please remember that."

"What if it's not?"

Now I'm getting edgy. "Do you trust me?"

"What does that have to do with anything?"

"Do you?"

"You know I do. I trust you more than I've trusted anyone in my life."

"Then trust me when I say this is a dress and nothing more."

I still can't figure out Christian's issue with clothing and why he thinks it's significant. Someday I'll bring it up with him to try and get to the root of this irrational fear, but now is not the time to have that conversation.

"I do trust you," Christian repeats, dropping a kiss on my mouth. "I love you."

"I love you, too," I say. "Now come on, let's go."

We head over to Buckingham Palace in Christian's Audi with his security detail following behind. It's a quick ten-minute drive, and soon we are whisked through the gates and led inside. My sick feeling grows stronger as I remember the last time I was here.

We head up in the elevator to the private apartments. Christian leads me to King Arthur's sitting room, which is the opposite of Queen Antonia's. It has a country English vibe, with pictures of horses and dogs and tartan plaid sofas

—plump, oversized ones that look perfect for sinking into and having a long conversation.

The family is standing around having cocktails, and as soon as we enter, Princess Helene makes her way over to me.

"I've been dying to meet you," Princess Helene declares, her eyes twinkling. "I'm Helene. I like a dirty joke and a dirty martini, and if you have any dirty men hanging around to enjoy them with, all the better."

Then she winks at me.

Despite my state of anxiety, I burst out laughing.

"That is the best introduction I've ever heard. I'm Clementine. I like hot chocolate, I'm terrible at anagrams, and I love this golden-haired man right here."

I glance at Christian, who smiles at me.

"Would you like a gin and tonic, sweetheart?" he asks.

"Yes, thank you."

"I'll be right back," he says.

I watch as he cuts across the room to the bar, where he's greeted by King Arthur. I see genuine happiness on King Arthur's face as he talks to Christian, which warms my heart. Christian does have a tremendous father who loves him as he deserves to be loved—for being Christian, his son.

"Christian has grown up since the last time I saw him," Princess Helene says, interrupting my thoughts.

I turn toward her, intrigued. "How so?"

"This past Christmas, at Sandringham," Princess Helene says, pausing to take a sip of her martini, "he loathed being out in public. The walk to the church was always painful for him. Christian hated being watched. He hated having to talk to people. I think those moments reminded him of the unavoidable road that was to come. Cambridge would end, and since my nephew threw down the gauntlet and said no military service yet, there would be nowhere to hide. Christian knew this is what his life would be, and it terrified him. The poor boy was lost."

She takes another drink and continues. "Then Easter rolls around—you know us old folks, we only get to see the younger generation at forced gatherings—he was smiling, talking, and not so much inside his head as he used to be. Christian told me all about this girl he had met. He said you had energy and passion and overcame a lot to be where you are now. He showed me pictures of you doing T-rex arms together and ones of you making faces at him on the punt on the River Cam. Christian seemed excited to start the next part of his life, with you, something I've never seen before. Christian said you helped him realize he could use his position for things that mattered to him, and he was ready to take that on. In that conversation, I knew you had turned my great nephew from a boy into a man."

"Christian did all that on his own," I say proudly. "I only helped him see it."

"That is what a good partner will do: help the other grow and become a better person. And you are the woman who reached him, my dear."

Christian reappears and hands me a gin and tonic.

"What are you two talking about over here? You look like you are up to no good," Christian teases.

"I was telling Clementine she must sit with me at dinner," Princess Helene says. "It's nice to have someone outside the company business come through these boring, gilded doors."

"Aunt Helene, I'm offended you think I'm boring," Liz says, walking up and giving her great aunt a kiss on the cheek.

"You're not boring, but you are never here. I'm stuck with this lot, and they are dreadfully dull. Not a good sex joke between all of them strung together. Well, unless Xander is here. Now that boy has good dirty jokes and then some."

I need to introduce Princess Helene to Jillian, I think, grinning. *They would get on famously.*

"Well, I will be around a lot more now," Liz says. "I'm officially done with university and am a working royal."

I've asked Liz why she is choosing this path when, unlike Christian, she can go off and pursue a career of her choosing. Liz is passionate about education and children's programs, and she feels she has more power to make change by working as a royal than by entering the field. She is called to continuing the legacy of the monarchy, and I admire her for that.

"Well, for that, I'm glad," Princess Helene says, patting her cheek. "God, was that an old lady move or what?"

"I'll forgive you for it if you promise to never do it again," Liz teases.

James comes up and affectionately puts his arm around my shoulders. "So, we haven't scared you off yet?" he teases.

I laugh. "Nope, you are stuck with me."

I see Queen Antonia, who is talking with Arabella and Prince Henry, and her cold eyes are locked on me.

"It's more like you are stuck with us," James jokes.

"Isn't that the truth?" Christian asks.

Another royal household employee—this time a steward, I believe, as I'm trying to memorize stripes on uniforms—approaches King Arthur, who nods in response. The steward retreats and King Arthur clears his throat.

"Let's make our way to the dining room," King Arthur says.

Dinner will be served in the Chinese Dining Room. I've seen pictures online of its elaborate flower-shaped chinoiserie chandelier, and I can't wait to see it in person.

Christian's hand finds the small of my back as we enter, and I try to hold back a gasp when I see the history before me. There are two chinoiserie panels adorning the walls—commissioned by George the Fourth—porcelain vases, and a Kylin clock on the mantle. I need to ask Christian if I can come back and study everything with the palace curator. It's still hard believe that Queen Victoria herself sat in this room.

Queen Victoria.

Even after a month of living in this world, I can't wrap my head around it.

The table is once again set to perfection, with candelabras and floral arrangements. Christian guides me to a seat in the middle because, since it's a family dinner, we can sit wherever we like. Christian pulls out my chair for me and another for Princess Helene on my left.

King Arthur sits at one end of the table, and Queen Antonia sits at the other end. Next to her is the Dowager Queen, who is never far from her side at any occasion. Servers approach the table with champagne, and King Arthur speaks as the bubbly is poured.

"I'd like to thank you all for coming tonight to celebrate Christian's first solo trip abroad," King Arthur says, smiling at his son. "You have grown tremendously in the last few months, and I couldn't be prouder of all the ways you are engaging in your new role."

Christian blushes. "It's my duty, Father. I realize now how important it is not only to do it but to be genuine in my efforts. That clarity came from the woman here by my side," he says, shifting his attention to me.

"I can see that," King Arthur says, his gaze regarding me with genuine affection.

"A toast," Queen Antonia says, picking up her champagne flute. "To Christian and the future of the monarchy. With you, my son, it looks very bright indeed."

We all clink glasses and take a sip.

"I've always loved New Zealand," Prince Henry says. "Such a beautiful spot in the world."

"I'm surprised you didn't say Sydney," Arabella says flatly.

Prince Henry shoots her a look. "Why would I, *darling?*"

What is even happening here? I feel like we've been dropped into the middle of a private conversation. I glance at Liz, whose face is flushed with embarrassment. She quickly stares down at the table, looking like she wishes she could be anywhere but here.

As if the staff senses the tension, they begin appearing with the first course. A plate is placed in front of me, and I nearly weep with relief that it's not a fish course but a mushroom tart. I glance at Christian's plate, which has a white fish in a sauce. Princess Helene has fish, too, so obviously Christian alerted the chefs that I don't eat fish.

I love him.

"I take it you don't like fish," James says, picking up his fork.

"No, I don't," I admit.

"She doesn't care for tea, either," Christian offers, outing me. Then he places his hand on my knee and gives it an affectionate squeeze.

"What? You don't like tea?" Princess Helene asks.

I laugh. "I know, yet they still approved my work visa," I joke.

"Interesting," Queen Antonia says from her end of the table. "Because when we had tea two weeks ago, you not only had tea but proclaimed you took it with lemon. You also selected a salmon finger sandwich, which my lady-in-waiting can attest to. So, is your dislike a sudden development, Clementine?"

Oh, my God.

My stomach drops out.

Queen Antonia has openly declared war.

My heart is roaring in my ears. I can't speak. I know my entire world is about to be blown apart, and I can't stop it.

The table falls silent, and all eyes are on me.

"What?" Christian asks, his eyes questioning me. "What is she talking about, Clem?"

"Oh, she didn't tell you? I invited her for tea while you were in Australia," Queen Antonia says, pausing to savor a bite of her fish. "I'm surprised she kept that a secret from you, along with her love of tea."

"Clementine wouldn't lie to me," Christian says, his voice taking on an angry edge. "But you would."

"Christian," I plead.

"Antonia, stop," King Arthur demands, his voice like ice.

"I'm sick and tired of all these damn games this family plays. I will not stand for you trying to manipulate me," Christian snaps.

"I'm not the one manipulating you, my precious son," Queen Antonia says. "Your so-called love is. She did come to tea, and she pretended to enjoy it while doing everything else she could to appease me. Look at her dress tonight; she thinks she can be one of us."

"You told me to keep the tea a secret," I shout across the table, losing my temper.

A collective gasp goes up.

Christian removes his hand from my knee, his eyes now desperate for me to say something different. "You … it's true?"

I want to die when I see the look of anguish on his face.

"She asked me to keep it a secret," I say, my voice breaking.

Christian is reeling. I move to touch his hand under the table, but he jerks it away.

"I did no such thing," Queen Antonia lies. "Clementine made the decision to lie to you, Christian, not me, just like she made the decision to pretend to like tea, just like she made the decision to dress like me tonight. Apparently, she does want to be a part of this monarchy, even if it means deceiving you, or changing to please us."

King Arthur smashes his fist on the table, sending the plates and cutlery rattling.

"You will stop this instant," he bellows at Queen Antonia. "I have had more than enough of your underhanded games, and it shall cease now."

"Why should she stop?" the Dowager Queen pipes up. "Clementine lied to Christian."

"Oh, sod off, you old bag," Princess Helene snaps. "Everyone here knows Queen Antonia is jealous of Clementine. She's young, beautiful, and adored for being a genuine breath of fresh air."

"How dare you speak to me like that!" the Dowager Queen cries at her sister-in-law, looking aghast.

"I am not jealous of *her*," Queen Antonia cries, her composure breaking.

"Look at the way we are acting. This is ridiculous," James says.

"It's embarrassing!" Liz says, pushing her plate away in disgust. "I am so sorry, Clementine. We all are."

"I will not apologize to a woman who lied to my son," Queen Antonia declares icily.

"Christian," I say, putting my hand on his arm. "Please, this isn't the whole story. We need to talk."

He jerks his arm away and stands up. Christian tosses the napkin angrily on top of his plate and storms out without saying a word.

I leap up from my seat, running behind him. "Christian, wait!"

Christian is walking in long, angry strides down the corridor. I'm trying to run in heels and this damn column dress, and I can't keep up. He's going to be out of my sight soon if I don't stop him, so I yell out the truth.

"I didn't tell you to protect you!" I cry.

Christian whips around. "*What?*"

I run until I'm standing in front of him.

"I didn't tell you because it would hurt you," I say, gasping for breath. "Your mother said awful things to me, Christian. She threatened me. I didn't want you to hear that about your mother, so I kept our tea a secret, but not to deceive you. I wanted to protect you."

"Protect me?" Christian roars. "How dare you decide what I get to know based on what you feel I need to be shielded from. You, of all people. You, the one who screams you're being stifled if I try to do any damn thing to help you!"

Anger rises within me. "That's different."

"How? How is it different, Clementine?"

"I have been suffocated my entire life by people wanting to protect me," I snap, my voice shaking.

"Not every single person who wants to protect you or help you is trying to suffocate you! You are so scarred by what your family did you can't see the difference!"

He's made a direct hit on my battleship. I feel like I'm sinking now.

"How ironic, when I protect you, it's telling the truth via a statement," Christian continues. "When you protect me, you *lie.*"

"I didn't tell you, because your mother told me to leave you," I cry. "She said I wasn't good enough for you. I didn't have the mystique and elegance the role demands, and I would ruin the monarchy. So, I sat there, and yes, I accepted tea and a salmon sandwich and wore hose because I was trying to make an inroad with her, which I was very, very, wrong about. She didn't invite me there to get to know me. She invited me to tea to make me go away."

"You've changed," Christian says, taking a step back from me as if he's revolted.

"Did you hear what I said? Your mother wanted me gone, Christian!"

"You pretended to be something you weren't," Christian says as if that's more of a problem than what his mother did.

"You are focusing on the wrong thing," I say angrily. "Your mother tried to get me to leave you."

"I heard you!" Christian roars. "My mother is an awful person who doesn't love me. I hear you loud and clear."

I wince. "I'm not—"

"I expect that from her, what she pulled," Christian continues. "But I didn't expect you to lie to me, to go over there and be something that you are not."

"Don't you see I am me?" I cry, exasperated. "I was

trying to be proper. I'm the same damn person, and a cup of tea won't change that."

"Bollocks! Everything starts to change. You started lying. You're going to be lost to them. It's already happening!" He begins to pace, tearing at his hair as if he wishes he could pull it out.

"No! I love you. I put up with your mother ripping me to shreds because of you. I know you love her. She's your mother. Do you think I wanted to tell you all these things? Do you think I wanted this to get back to Xander? To James?" I cry, thinking of how fragile James is in particular. "It would devastate you. She asked me to keep the meeting private, and I did."

He pauses. I know I've reached him with those words, but within a second the angry expression returns.

"So, the woman who is scarred by her parents protecting her without her consent turns around and does it to the man she says she loves?"

"That's not fair," I say, my voice trembling.

"It the same thing, except you won't acknowledge it."

He's scored another hit, but I can't process that now, not when everything is spiraling out of control.

"I did what your mother asked because I didn't want to hurt you."

"Your parents never wanted to hurt you either."

His words feel like a slap. I want to fall to the floor, but I refuse to do so in front of him.

"Your biggest fear was losing me to them," I say, the tears I've desperately tried to hold back brimming over. "But you didn't lose me to them. If I wear a damn dress for a Buckingham Palace occasion, I'm not lost to them. It's dressing for business, no different than you putting on polo gear for a match. Why is clothing so significant to you? Why?"

"Because my mother was different once!" Christian yells, his voice echoing down the halls as his truth finally comes out.

"What?"

Christian shuts down. Just as he's on the verge of revealing what his past was, he slams the door shut.

"It doesn't matter. You are standing before me dressed like my mum," Christian snaps angrily. "You drank tea. You ate salmon. You lied. Congratulations, you *are* one of them now."

I feel my heart snap in half, one side anguished, the other side furious.

The fury inside of me takes control.

"I do think congratulations are in order," I say, tears dripping down my face. "I was invited to a function, and I dressed accordingly. It's no different than you putting on a suit for a luncheon, Christian. But for some reason, your brain refuses to believe I'm doing these things to assimilate for a role. I'm still the same person. The woman who loves you made a mistake trying to protect you."

Christian blinks. I know that got to him, and I continue.

"The tragedy tonight is that I never became one of them, Christian. I'm still me, but by doing your math tonight, you finally got the answer you've been so desperate to find. Congratulations are in order, but for you. You finally found a way to shove me into your self-fulfilling prophecy. But there's one twist: You lost me because of *you,* not because of them."

And then I stride past him to the elevator, angrily punching the down button.

"Clementine, don't go," Christian yells after me.

The doors open. Christian is running to catch me. I leap inside and jam the button for the doors to close. Christian tries to stick his hand in, but he's not fast enough.

The last thing I see is his eyes, the eyes of the man I love, filled with tears, as the doors shut.

In that moment, I know I've made a huge mistake by walking away.

We can never come back from this.

And with that thought, I burst into heavy sobs and cry like I will never stop.

CHAPTER 33

THE MARBLE HALL

I make it as far as the Marble Hall before I can't go any farther. I collapse onto a settee, sobbing uncontrollably. How are we over? Did that actually happen? Did I walk away from Christian in a fit of anger?

Yes, you did, my heart whispers to me. *You made your choice.*

And it wasn't to fight for Christian.

I try to catch my breath, but I'm crying so hard I can't. I half expect palace security to escort me out and tell me Christian wishes for me to never return, but they are probably going to wait until I get over the hysterical stage before daring to approach me. A woman walks by, dressed as a maid, and keeps her eyes straight ahead as if she's trained out of discretion to not see me falling apart.

I start sorting through our fight, the accusations we threw back and forth at each other. I close my eyes as I see the devastated look in Christian's eyes when he realized I had lied to him. I hurt him trying to protect him and oh, the irony, it's the one thing I've argued with him about before. Now I see exactly what he meant.

Sometimes you do want to protect the people you love, I think, wiping the tears from my face with my fingertips. *Christian was never trying to suffocate me when he tried to protect me. He was doing something I needed out of love. Accepting his help didn't make me weak, nor did it change my freedom.*

I was so terrified of losing my new life I couldn't see that having someone help you when you need it is okay.

The sobs start to subside as I continue to sort through our fight, picking up the pieces and examining the wreckage of my shattered heart.

My fear was having my normal taken away. I thought Christian would somehow become like my parents and fear for my every step, my every wince and every pain, and I would become fragile in his eyes. That, I couldn't bear. I projected those fears onto him, but he's the one person who has never viewed me in that way.

It dawns on me that Christian's fear was similar. He was terrified of his normal with me being ripped away from him. By wearing this dress and pretending to like tea, he thought I was beginning to change on him, and I would assimilate to the monarchy and no longer be the woman he had fallen in love with.

We were both terrified of losing the normal we had found with each other, I think.

I still don't understand what drove his fear. It will forever remain a mystery to me because I chose to walk out. I chose to end things in a fit of upset instead of taking a step back to calm down and to let Christian calm down. He didn't want me to leave, and by the time I realized what I was doing, it was too late.

My lower lip quivers, and a single tear rolls off my face,

dropping onto the pink damask of the settee. I silently apologize to Queen Victoria for crying on her furniture, for breaking the heart of her great-great-great-I-don't-know-how-far-back-great-grandson.

I wonder if she and Albert fought in these same halls. Their love story seems like a grand one. I was writing my own wonderful fairy tale with Christian, not because he was a prince who lives in a palace, or because he's part of one of the most incredible legacies the world has ever known.

It was a fairy tale because he was *Christian Chadwick* to me.

I fell in love with him before I knew who he was. I loved him after I knew who he was. I loved him for his beautiful heart, his incredible mind, and the way he saw the world. He's coming into his own now, and he's going to do amazing things in this life.

With someone else by his side.

My world goes black with that thought. The idea of never seeing him again, except to say goodbye, is more than I can bear. I can't imagine him not being a part of my life. I can't imagine never seeing him again, except on TV or online. I can't imagine not hearing his voice or his ideas or that chuckle when he's amused. I can't imagine never feeling his touch or kiss ever again.

I begin to shake. Fresh tears fall.

There will always be a place in my heart for him.

Always.

I know I need to go. I don't belong here. Yet I know as soon as I walk out these gilded doors, I'll never return.

I'll never again be a part of Christian's life.

I close my eyes. I don't know how long I've been here, but it feels like an eternity.

I have to leave now, I will myself. *I have to find a way to leave*

Christian behind.

I slowly rise from the settee, staring at the walk ahead. I'm about to take a step toward the Grand Staircase when I see Christian turn the corner, freezing in his tracks the second he spots me.

Oh, God. I want to run to him and beg him to forgive me and make our world whole again.

Christian runs toward me, and he blurs in my vision.

"Don't go," he calls out with urgency. "Please, God, please, Clementine, don't leave, not yet. Not until you hear what I have to say."

Christian stops in front of me, his eyes rimmed with red as if he's been crying.

"I want to talk to you, too," I say, my voice breaking.

Christian takes my hand in his and leads me back to the pink settee. He sits me down and drops to his knee in front of me, clasping my hands in his.

"I love you," he says, his voice thick with unshed tears. "I know you might not forgive me for what happened up there, and I don't blame you if you didn't, but I can't let you leave here not hearing what is in my heart."

Christian takes one hand to wipe my tears away.

"I love you, Christian, and I'm so sorry for what happened," I say, somehow forcing the words out. "Please forgive me for lying. It was wrong, even if I thought it was for the right reason."

"I wanted to come after you the second those doors closed," he says, his eyes searching mine. "Before you left, I knew I couldn't let you go. But I had to get myself together before I came to find you. I had to sort out my thoughts. If you weren't still here, in the Marble Hall, I would have found you."

"I was afraid I had destroyed what we had," I admit.

"As soon as I left, I regretted it. I want to work through our problems, Christian, not run from them. I swear I'll never do that again."

"What we have," Christian says, his voice firm, "can't be destroyed. I believe this now more than ever. We had an awful row, but the first thing we did was think of each other and how we wanted to fix it, reconcile, and be stronger for it. That is another way this love is different. It's strong. It's forever."

"Forever," I repeat.

Christian draws a breath of air before speaking.

"There's something you don't know," he says softly, his fingertips stroking my cheekbone. "My mum, she used to be different."

He reaches into his coat pocket and retrieves his phone. Christian swipes something and turns the screen toward me. With shock, I see a young Antonia from thirty years ago. She had long, jet black hair that tumbled past her shoulders and a natural smile that lit up her face. There are pictures of her watching a young King Arthur play polo, where she's in jeans. Another where she's going out to a nightclub in a short skirt. She looks young and carefree and happy in all of them.

"Mum used to be like that," Christian says, his voice so quiet I can barely hear him. "When she met Father, that is who she was. She was happy. All of that changed after Father proposed."

"What happened?" I ask, stunned by the pictures I'm looking at. It's like two completely different lives.

"The monarchy," Christian says. "Once they became engaged, Father said everything changed."

I gasp. "Arthur told you that?"

Christian shakes his head. "No. A fight erupted during

dinner when I was a child, not unlike the one that just happened. Father was yelling that she was not the same woman he fell in love with. She was consumed with privilege and power and keeping up her image. Mum yelled back that he had no idea what was expected of her in her role and she felt a responsibility to the monarchy. For the first time in her life, she was respected, and that was everything to her. In the end, she chose to be Arthur's queen, not his wife."

"Oh, my God," I whisper, as now I see everything clearly. "You saw my tiny changes as the beginning of the end."

Christian shifts his gaze away from me, staring down at the pink damask I'm sitting on, and he swallows hard. Finally, he lifts his gaze to meet mine, and I see nothing but heartbreak in his eyes.

"Yes," he admits. "It pains me to admit that, but my childhood reared up and made you sipping a damn cup of tea a sign when it was nothing more than that—a cup of tea."

"I promise you, with everything that I am, that I am not going to change," I say. "I might sip a tea here or there if it's expected, or wear a hat if protocol calls for it, but at the end of the day, I'm the woman who is going to put on your Arsenal T-shirt and ripped up jeans and ask if we can take our dogs for a walk. I'm that woman now. I will be that woman if I become your wife, too."

"After watching what my mother did—that's not you. It will never be you. I was so terrified of losing you, I couldn't think straight. You are the most important thing in the world to me. I love you, and I promise I have my head on right about that now."

"I was wrong to lie to you," I say, my face growing hot

in shame. "You were right. I should have told you everything and let you process it. I'm sorry. Please forgive me for that, Christian."

"I do," he whispers, "as long as you forgive me."

"I do. And after protecting you, I understand that sometimes you are going to protect me because you love me, not because you want to stifle me. You'll never treat me as fragile. You never have. That's my childhood messing me up."

A smile tugs at the corner of his mouth. "So we're both messed up."

I smile back. "Completely. But we know how we're messed up, so we can work on it. Together."

"I'm going to marry you someday," Christian says, cradling my face in his strong hands. "But first, I have to ask you something. You witnessed that dysfunction upstairs firsthand. It's your last chance to back out, Ace. Speak now, or you are forever locked into the House of Chadwick."

Happiness fills my heart. "Not a chance. I love you, Christian. As wheels off as your family is, that doesn't change what I want. And that is you. All of you, for the rest of my life."

"I love you," Christian whispers.

"I love you more," I whisper back.

As his lips find mine, I know this is my forever. What started as an Instagram exchange between two strangers ended up as a love story with a promise of a future at Buckingham Palace. Our love is one of friendship, of passion, of respect. We'll work together for our causes, in our own way, for things we value and believe in.

We're a team, and we always will be.

I smile against his lips as I kiss him back.

Somehow, I think Queen Victoria would approve.

EPILOGUE

PHOTOCALL

The following December

I close my eyes as the makeup artist sprays my face with a setting mist.

"This will give you a dewy look," Hannah says as the mist settles on my skin.

"Does it have a calming effect?" I ask, half-joking.

"That is what a cup of tea would do," Princess Helene says knowingly. "But so would an extra dirty martini, and that's what I'd choose if I were you."

I open my eyes as laughter echoes in the dressing room in Princess Helene's apartment at Kensington Palace. I'm surrounded by all the women in my life this first week of December: all of Christian's princess cousins, Jillian, Felicity, Emma, Bryn, Chelsea, my mom, and Paisley.

"An extra dirty martini would leave me a mess for the TV interview," I say.

"I love the dress you've chosen," Liz says, beaming at me. "It's so you."

"And perfect for your engagement photocall," Jillian adds, winking at me.

I glance down at my bare left hand. I've been engaged since November, but we've kept it a secret until we were ready to announce it.

Which is today.

Happiness radiates through every inch of me. Today is the day we step forward and tell the world that we are getting married.

We've grown so much this past year. Christian has flourished in his new role as a champion for caregivers, science education for children, and wildlife conservation. He has banded with his brothers and cousins to create a foundation for their causes, called the House of Chadwick Charities. Christian and Liz have taken the lead as the two working royals, and they have put a new shine on the monarchy. They are the next generation of royals, ones who are working hard to do good for others. Christian used to hate his public position, but now that he's made it his, and understands how much he means to people, he relishes going to events and doing walkabouts to bring attention to causes that need his help.

I have quietly resigned my position at Cheltham House, which had to be done. I was so sad to leave my work, but I also know I have a new career ahead of me. I will join Christian and Liz and be an active working royal. One of my causes will be historical preservation and education, along with illness survivor support groups, and I'm excited that I will have my own work along with championing Christian's causes.

Additionally, all of my social media accounts have been wiped, so that was the first tip-off to the media that an engagement was coming. The tabloids have been running with stories for months, either guessing we were engaged or a proposal was imminent. One even ran with the story of "Prince Christian's Secret Proposal!" which was so wrong we died laughing when we read it.

Queen Antonia still hates me, and of course, sent her regrets that she couldn't be here this morning to send her "regards." The Dowager Queen also is absent and has taken to her bed with a severe chest cold. Princess Helene snorted at that and called bollocks, which made her new best friend Jillian nearly spit out her champagne.

King Arthur is over the moon for us, and says we are the beginning of a whole new future for the monarchy. Xander and James already told me I was like the sister they never had, and they were thrilled when we told them we were engaged. Xander will be the best man for his Curry Takeaway, and James will stand beside him. Paisley is my matron of honor, and I've asked Liz to stand with her, as she has become my best friend in London, and I couldn't have navigated these royal waters alone.

"I think we'll leave you for a few minutes before Christian comes," my mom says, affectionately squeezing my shoulder. "I love you, and I'm so happy for both of you."

She places a loving kiss on my head, and happy tears fill my eyes. Mom and Dad have completely come around on Christian after they came to visit us here in London last August. And it wasn't having dinner with King Arthur at Balmoral in Scotland that sealed the deal, but Christian himself. He had all of us over at his cottage, grilled steaks for dinner, and had us all take a walk with Bear and Lucy around the private grounds. I know these actions proved to my parents he was simply a man who loves their daughter. Everything changed after that, and my parents trusted our love and what we were building together.

I've also learned how to set boundaries, too. Whenever my mom goes into one of her obsessing-about-my-health modes, I shut it down. I've also set the same boundaries with Queen Antonia and the Dowager Queen. If anything snide is said to me, I end the conversation. There's no fighting. No argument. I simply draw the line and move on.

As my family and friends hug me goodbye, saying they'll see me at Buckingham Palace for a luncheon as soon as our TV interview is done, I'm finally left alone. I take a look at myself in the large mirror. I'm radiant. I'm confident.

And I'm madly in love with the man I'm going to spend forever with.

I'm wearing a red wrap dress today, no pantyhose. In fact, I only wear pantyhose if I'm attending a service in a church with Christian. My hair is down and loose, lightly curled by the hairstylist, and I have a beautiful matte red lip that matches my ruby dress. I see my coat draped across the sofa, one that is a black and red plaid, adding the pattern to my outfit that "Captivating Clemmie" has become known for. The designer is the same one I selected for Ascot—Emilia Wentworth-Hay—and we've become good friends, too. In fact, nobody except the inner circle knows she is already sketching bridal gowns for a spring wedding.

There's a knock at the door, and my heart skips a beat, knowing that it's Christian.

"Come in," I call out.

Christian opens the door, and oh, swoon, looks absolutely sexy as hell in his black suit and red tie.

I rise to greet him, and his eyes quickly appraise me.

"You have never looked more beautiful," he says softly. "How did I get so lucky, Ace?"

"You stumbled on the right Instagram account," I tease.

He chuckles, and my spine tingles in response.

Christian takes my hands in his. "Are you ready to share that story?"

I grin. I love that it was Christian's idea to tell the truth about our Instagram love story. The boy who hid away from everyone has now become a man who wants to share his life with the world—and admit that while royals aren't supposed to have social media accounts, he did—like the young, modern man he is.

"Yes," I nod. Then I laugh. "Xander better brace himself for women around the globe trying to figure out if he's on social media—and how to land in his inbox."

"That's his problem," Christian says, smiling. "Now, there's one important detail we have to take care of before we face the press in the sunken garden."

Christian reaches into his pocket and drops down on one knee before me. My heart melts as he takes my hand in his.

"I asked you this question after we spent Thanksgiving with your family in Arizona," Christian says. "When we were on top of Camelback Mountain, I asked you if you'd marry me. I'm asking one more time, just to make sure, Ace. *Aime lyly murrow?*"

I burst out laughing as this is the only anagram I have no problem sorting out.

"Yes, yes, I will still marry you," I say, grinning.

Christian beams as he opens the box and reveals the huge, five-carat ruby encrusted in diamonds. The ruby belonged to Princess Helene, who eagerly gave it to Christian for my ring. King Arthur provided the diamonds that surround the ruby from the royal collection, which melted my heart. It's truly a ring from the older royals who love us and believe in the way we are going to define our own roles in the monarchy.

He slides the ring on to my finger, and joy fills my heart. I now can wear my ring all the time, which I have been dying to do since he first gave it to me a few weeks ago.

Christian rises and slides his arms around me. "Let's go share our love story with the world."

Love for this man fills my heart. "I love you, *Your Royal Highness.*"

Christian's blue eyes sparkle back at me. "I love you more."

I put my hand in his as we walk out of Kensington Palace, ready to share our love with the press waiting in the gardens.

Our story is not a conventional one. We both had to resolve issues from our childhood pasts to become the people we are now. Together, we found ourselves. Our purpose. Love.

Our own version of normal.

I can't imagine any other love story I'd want to star in.

THE END

Wondering if anything happened between Liz and Roman? Look for their story in the second book of The Modern Royals Series, *The Princess Pose.*

CONNECT WITH AVEN

Website
www.avenellis.com

Facebook
https://www.facebook.com/AvenEllis1/

Kate, Skates and Coffee Cakes-The Aven Ellis Reader Group
https://www.facebook.com/groups/597292903766592/

Twitter
@avenellis

ALSO BY AVEN ELLIS

If you enjoyed this book, you might enjoy my other romantic comedies:

Connectivity

Surviving The Rachel

Chronicles of a Lincoln Park Fashionista

Green Tea Latte To Go

Waiting For Prince Harry (Dallas Demons #1)

The Definition of Icing (Dallas Demons #2)

Breakout (Dallas Demons #3)

On Thin Ice (Dallas Demons #4)

Playing Defense (Dallas Demons #5)

The Aubrey Rules (Chicago on Ice #1)

Trivial Pursuits (Chicago on Ice #2)

Save the Date (Chicago on Ice #3)

Hold the Lift (Rinkside in the Rockies Novella)

Sugar and Ice (Rinkside in the Rockies #1)

Reality Blurred (Rinkside in the Rockies #2)

Squeeze Play (Washington DC Soaring Eagles #1)